**"You drive me mad, little thief," he whispered, and
gave in to the constant, terrible temptation.**

203-488-8702

He kissed her.

He was prepared to be shoved away, but instead her lips
parted beneath his. It might be an aberration. She might remember in seconds that she hated him.

But in the meantime, he'd take what she offered.

His tongue slid into her mouth, the scent of honeysuckle
heady in his nostrils. When she spoke her tongue held only
bitterness and bile, but when she kissed she tasted of honey
and wine.

Sweet.

Unattainable.

He slanted his mouth over hers, changing the angle, holding her close, so close. She stood on tiptoe and pressed
against him and he rejoiced.

"Hoyt's writing is almost too good to be true."
—Lisa Kleypas, *New York Times* bestselling author

"There's an enchantment to Hoyt's stories that makes you believe in the magic of love."
—*RT Book Reviews*

PRAISE FOR ELIZABETH HOYT'S MAIDEN LANE SERIES

Duke of Desire

"4½ stars! Top Pick! Far darker than many of Hoyt's romances, *Duke of Desire* is emotionally powerful, and readers will be transfixed by this poignant tale of revenge and redemption." **—*RT Book Reviews***

Duke of Pleasure

"4½ stars! Top Pick! Hoyt...[is] a powerful storyteller whose novels have a depth of emotion and originality that lifts the genre to new heights. Always unique, wonderfully romantic and highly sensual, Hoyt's stories take readers' breath away."
—*RT Book Reviews*

"Hoyt once again successfully deploys her irresistible literary triumvirate of marvelously engaging characters, boldly sensual love scenes, and elegant writing brightened with just the right dash of dry wit."
—*Booklist*

"So many ingredients make this story phenomenal. First and foremost, the chemistry between our hero and heroine. It drives the narrative and we can't get enough of their interactions."

—HeroesandHeartbreakers.com

Duke of Sin

"4½ stars! Top Pick! Hoyt delivers a unique read on many levels: a love story, a tale of redemption, and a plot teeming with emotional depth that takes readers' breaths away. Kudos to a master storyteller!"

—RT Book Reviews

"A darkly humorous and lushly sensual historical romance.... Hoyt truly outdoes herself in *Duke of Sin*."

—HeroesandHeartbreakers.com

"Hoyt has created two dynamic characters.... [The book] includes a delicious collection of hot and steamy scenes. A wonderful balance of comedy and pathos, Hoyt's latest is a deeply satisfying read."

—BookPage

Sweetest Scoundrel

"While I've long been a fan of the Maiden Lane series, I think this is my favorite."

—FictionVixen.com

"4½ stars! Maiden Lane and its inhabitants have long captivated readers, and the latest series installment is just as enchanting as fans could desire.... It is a story that takes your breath away and leaves you uplifted. Hoyt does it again!"   **—RT Book Reviews**

Dearest Rogue

"[This] superbly executed historical romance is proof positive that this RITA Award–nominated author continues to write with undiminished force and flair. When it comes to incorporating a generous measure of dangerous intrigue and lush sensuality into a truly swoonworthy love story, Hoyt is unrivaled."

—Booklist (starred review)

"4½ stars! Hoyt takes an unlikely pair of characters and, through the magic of her storytelling, turns them into the perfect couple....A read to remember."

—RT Book Reviews

"Sexy, sweet, and emotionally satisfying....*Dearest Rogue* is everything the reader of a Regency historical wants; it's funny, fast-paced and has plenty of historical flavor and a romance that develops as naturally as a flower opening in the sun. Fans of the Maiden Lane series will cheer for this couple."

—BookPage

Darling Beast

"Hoyt's exquisitely nuanced characters, vividly detailed setting, and seemingly effortless and elegant writing provide the splendid material from which she fashions yet another ravishingly romantic love story."

—Booklist (starred review)

"4½ stars! Top Pick! *Darling Beast* is wondrous, magical, and joyous—a read to remember."
—**RT Book Reviews**

"A lovely book that I very much enjoyed reading. I love the Maiden Lane series and can't wait until the next book comes out!"
—**BookBinge.com**

Duke of Midnight

"Top Pick! A sensual tale of forbidden love....Plenty of action and intriguing mystery make this a page-turner."
—**BookPage**

"Richly drawn characters fill the pages of this emotionally charged mix of mystery and romance."
—**Publishers Weekly**

"4½ stars! Top Pick! There is enchantment in the Maiden Lane series, not just the fairy tales Hoyt infuses into the memorable romances, but the wonder of love combined with passion, unique plotlines, and unforgettable characters."
—**RT Book Reviews**

"I *loved* it. I loved Artemis. I loved Max, and I loved their story. I have enjoyed every Elizabeth Hoyt book I have read (and I have read most of them)."
—**All About Romance (LikesBooks.com)**

Lord of Darkness

"*Lord of Darkness* illuminates Hoyt's boundless imagination....
Readers will adore this story."
—RT Book Reviews

"Hoyt's writing is imbued with great depth of emotion....
Heartbreaking.... An edgy tension-filled plot."
—Publishers Weekly

"*Lord of Darkness* is classic Elizabeth Hoyt, meaning it's
unique, engaging, and leaves readers on the edge of their
seats.... An incredible addition to the fantastic Maiden Lane
series. I Joyfully Recommend Godric and Megs's tale, for
it's an amazing, well-crafted story with an intriguing plot
and a lovely, touching romance.... Simply enchanting!"
—JoyfullyReviewed.com

"I adore the Maiden Lane series, and this fifth book is a very
welcome addition to the series.... [It's] sexy and sweet all
at the same time.... This can be read as a stand-alone, but
I adore each book in this series and encourage you to start
from the beginning."
—USA Today's Happy Ever After blog

"Beautifully written.... A truly fine piece of storytelling and
a novel that deserves to be read and enjoyed."
—TheBookBinge.com

Thief of Shadows

"An expert blend of scintillating romance and mystery.... The romance between the beautiful and quick-witted Isabel and the masked champion of the downtrodden propels this novel to the top of its genre."

—*Publishers Weekly* **(starred review)**

"Amazing sex scenes.... A very intriguing hero.... This one did not disappoint."

—*USA Today*

"Innovative, emotional, sensual.... Hoyt's beautiful blending of the essential elements of a fairy tale into a stunning love story enhances this delicious 'keeper.'"

—*RT Book Reviews*

"All of Hoyt's signature literary ingredients—wickedly clever dialogue, superbly nuanced characters, danger, and scorching sexual chemistry—click neatly into place to create a breathtakingly romantic love story."

—*Booklist*

"When [they] finally come together, desire and long-denied sensuality explode upon the page."

—*Library Journal*

"With heart and heat rolled into one, *Thief of Shadows* is a definite must-read for historical romance fans! Hoyt really has outdone herself...yet again."

—**UndertheCoversBookblog.blogspot.com**

"A balanced mixture of action, adventure, and mystery and a beautifully crafted romance.... The perfect historical romance."

—HeroesandHeartbreakers.com

Scandalous Desires

"Historical romance at its best.... Series fans will be enthralled, while new readers will find this emotionally charged installment stands very well alone."

—*Publishers Weekly* (starred review)

"4½ stars! This is the Maiden Lane story readers have been waiting for. Hoyt delivers her hallmark fairy tale within a romance and takes readers into the depths of the heart and soul of her characters. Pure magic flows from her pen, lifting readers' spirits with joy."   **—*RT Book Reviews***

"With its lush sensuality, lusciously wrought prose, and luxuriously dark plot, *Scandalous Desires*, the latest exquisitely crafted addition to Hoyt's Georgian-set Maiden Lane series, is a romance to treasure."

—*Booklist* (starred review)

"Ms. Hoyt writes some of the best love scenes out there. They are passionate, sexy, and blazing hot.... I simply adore Ms. Hoyt's books for her sensuous prose, multifaceted characters, and intense, well-developed story lines. And she delivers every single time. It's no wonder all of her books are on my keeper shelves. Do yourself a favor and pick up *Scandalous Desires*."

—TheRomanceDish.com

"*Scandalous Desires* is the best book Elizabeth Hoyt has written so far, with endearing characters and an all-encompassing romance you'll want to hold close and never let go. If there's one must-read book, especially for historical romance fans, it's *Scandalous Desires*."

—FallenAngelReviews.com

Notorious Pleasures

"Emotionally stunning.... The sinfully sensual chemistry Hoyt creates between her shrewd, acid-tongued heroine and her scandalous, sexy hero is pure romance."

—*Booklist*

Wicked Intentions

"4½ stars! Top Pick! A magnificently rendered story that not only enchants but enthralls."

—*RT Book Reviews*

NOT THE DUKE'S DARLING

ELIZABETH HOYT

NOT THE DUKE'S DARLING

FOREVER
New York Boston

Copyright © 2018 by Nancy M. Finney
Preview of *When a Rogue Meets His Match* copyright © 2018 by Nancy M. Finney
Patience for Christmas copyright © 2016 by Grace Burrowes. *Patience for Christmas* was originally published as part of a compilation entitled *The Virtues of Christmas* in 2016 by Grace Burrowes Publishing.
Cover design and illustration by Elizabeth Turner Stokes
Cover copyright © 2018 by Hachette Book Group, Inc.

Forever
Hachette Book Group
1290 Avenue of the Americas, New York, NY 10104
forever-romance.com
twitter.com/foreverromance

First Edition: December 2018

Forever is an imprint of Grand Central Publishing. The Forever name and logo are trademarks of Hachette Book Group, Inc.

The publisher is not responsible for websites (or their content) that are not owned by the publisher.

The Hachette Speakers Bureau provides a wide range of authors for speaking events. To find out more, go to www.hachettespeakersbureau.com or call (866) 376-6591.

ISBN: 978-1-5387-6352-0 (mass market), 978-1-5387-6353-7 (ebook)

Printed in the United States of America

OPM

10 9 8 7 6 5 4 3 2 1

For every woman who works day in and day out, who takes care of family and friends and community, who sometimes despairs late at night but then gets up in the morning and does it all again anyway.

You are strong and brave and beautiful and this book is for you.

ACKNOWLEDGMENTS

Thank you as always to my fantabulous editor, Amy Pierpont, to my wonderful beta reader, Susannah Taylor, and to my writer helper dogs who faithfully sit by me as I write: Rue, Darla, and Ellie, aka Miss Puppy Pie.

And very special thanks to my Facebook friend Paola, who named Tess the dog!

CHAPTER ONE

Now this is how it all began.
Long, long ago there lived a powerful prince who
had but one child, a daughter.
She was beautiful, haughty, and spoiled, and her
name was Rowan....
— From *The Grey Court Changeling*

MAY 1760
LONDON, ENGLAND

Had someone asked Freya Stewart de Moray at the age of twelve what she expected to be doing fifteen years later, she would've listed three things.

One, writing a pamphlet on the greater intelligence of females compared to males—especially males who were *brothers*.

Two, indulging in as much raspberry trifle as she pleased.

And three, breeding spaniels so that she might have an endless supply of puppies to play with.

She'd been *very* fond of puppies at twelve.

But that was before the Greycourt tragedy, which had torn her family apart and nearly killed her eldest brother, Ran.

Everything had changed after the tragedy.

Which was possibly why Freya's twelve-year-old self

could never have predicted what she was *actually* doing at seven and twenty: working as an agent of the ancient secret society of Wise Women.

Freya hurried along the London street toward Wapping Old Stairs. At the last cross street she'd realized that they were being followed. She glanced at her charges. Betsy was a nursemaid only just turned twenty. The girl was red faced and panting, her mouse-brown hair coming down around her damp cheeks, her eyes wide with terror. In the nursemaid's arms was Alexander Bertrand, the seventh Earl of Brightwater.

Age one and a half.

Fortunately His Minute Lordship was asleep in Betsy's arms, round cheeks pink and tiny rosebud mouth pursed.

Behind them were two disreputable men who looked very much as if they were stalking Freya and her charges.

Freya racked her brain, trying to think of a plan of escape. The day was sunny. Seagulls screamed above the Wapping streets. She and Betsy walked parallel to the Thames, only blocks away, and the fetid smell of the river was strong in the air.

She estimated that it was less than a quarter mile to Wapping Old Stairs. The street was busy at this time of day. Carts rattled by, filled with foreign goods brought through the Port of London. Smartly dressed merchants and ship captains bumped shoulders with staggering sailors already in their cups. Working-class women made sure to avoid the sailors, while women who worked the streets made sure to accost them.

Freya chanced another look behind.

They were still there.

The two men might simply be traveling in their direction. Or they might have been sent by Gerald Bertrand,

Alexander's paternal uncle, with orders to bring back the baby earl. If they took him, she wouldn't have a second chance to rescue the toddler.

Or, of course, they might be Dunkelders.

Freya's pulse picked up at that last thought. The Wise Women had long been hunted by Dunkelders—nasty, superstitious fanatics who knew about the Wise Women and believed they were witches who should be burned.

If the followers were either Dunkelders or Bertrand's men, she had to do something soon, or they'd never make it to the stairs.

"What is it?" Betsy asked breathlessly. "Why do you keep looking back?"

"We're being followed," Freya told her as a huge black carriage came around the corner, moving toward them at a snail's pace due to the crowded street.

Betsy moaned and hitched His Lordship higher in her arms.

The carriage door bore an ornate gold crest Freya didn't recognize. Not that it really mattered. They needed safety and a place to hide from the men. Whoever the aristocrat in the carriage was, Freya was certain she could stall him for a minute or two.

That was all they needed.

She seized Betsy's arm. "Run!"

Freya darted behind the carriage, pulling Betsy along with her. There was a shout from the men following them, and the carriage shuddered to a stop.

On the far side of the carriage she dragged Betsy to the door, wrenched it open, and shoved both nursemaid and baby inside. Freya leaped in, slamming the carriage door behind her.

She landed on hands and knees and looked up.

Betsy was sitting on the floor of the carriage, cowering away from a large yellow dog, who appeared to be regarding the maid with surprise. Miraculously, Alexander, the tiniest earl in all the land, hadn't woken.

The gentleman beside the dog stirred. "I *beg* your pardon?"

At least that was what he *said*. What he quite obviously *meant* was, "What the bloody *hell*?"

Freya tore her gaze from the dog and looked up into cerulean eyes framed by thick black eyelashes. Lounging on the squabs, his legs stretched clear to the opposite seat, was Christopher Renshaw, the Duke of Harlowe.

The man who had helped destroy her brother Ran.

Freya's breath seized, her eyes dropped, and she saw something else.

The bastard was wearing Ran's signet ring.

Her gaze snapped back to his, and she waited for him to shout her name. For her true identity to be revealed after five long years of hiding in London.

Instead his expression changed not at all as he said, "Who are you?"

He didn't recognize her.

He and Julian Greycourt had been Ran's best friends. He had seen her every week of her life until the Greycourt tragedy. She'd once vowed to *marry* the swine. Of course she'd been *twelve* and that was before he'd nearly gotten Ran killed, but even so.

He didn't recognize her.

What a complete and utter *ass*.

Freya straightened her bonnet and glared up at the duke. "*You* are not Lady Philippa."

The duke's eyebrows snapped down. "I—"

"What," Freya said with rather enjoyable ire, "are you doing in Lady Philippa's carriage?"

Said carriage lurched and began moving as Alexander woke with a whimper.

Outside a man cursed.

Freya made sure to keep her head below the level of the open window.

Someone pounded on the carriage door.

Harlowe looked from Freya to Betsy and the baby and then back to Freya again.

Holding her gaze, he stood.

Freya stilled.

Betsy and the baby sobbed.

Harlowe leaned over Freya and glanced out the window before shutting it and drawing the curtain. He resumed his seat, a muscle twitching in his jaw as his right hand dropped to the dog's head. "I don't know what trouble you might be in or why those brutes are after you."

Freya opened her mouth, desperately thinking of a story.

The duke held up his hand. "*Nor* do I care. I'll take you to Westminster. After that you're on your own."

Harlowe was offering to *help* them, two strangers? That didn't make sense from the man who had so coldheartedly abandoned Ran.

But she had no time to ponder his vagary.

"Thank you," Freya said, the words like acid etching hatred on her tongue. "But that won't be necessary." She looked at Betsy. "I'm going to jump out when next the coach slows. I want you to wait to the count of twenty and then follow."

"What of the child?" the duke interrupted imperiously. "Surely you don't wish to endanger the both of them by ordering her to jump from a moving carriage?"

"Then stop the coach for her," Freya replied sweetly.

For a second they locked gazes. His face was wrathful.

Obviously he wasn't used to being given orders by anyone—
a woman least of all.

Too bad.

Freya leaned close to Betsy and murmured in her ear,
"Remember to head for Wapping Old Stairs and to look for
the woman wearing a black cloak with a gray hood."

"But what of you?" Betsy whispered frantically.

Freya straightened and gave the girl an encouraging smile.
"I'll find you, never fear."

"Oh, miss—"

Freya shook her head firmly, bussed the baby earl on his
adorably fat cheek, and winked at the duke. "A pleasure,
Your Grace."

Then she leaped from the carriage.

She stumbled when her boots hit the cobblestones, and
for a ghastly second she thought she might go under the
carriage wheels.

But she recovered.

Just as she heard a shout from behind her.

Freya hitched up her skirts in both hands and *ran*. She
ducked down a road, heading to the river.

Behind her came the clatter of pursuit.

She turned into a narrow alley and skidded to a stop. At
the other end was the second man.

Freya spun.

The first man was behind her, closing fast.

She darted into an arched opening to her right, coming
out almost at once into a small courtyard enclosed on all
sides by the surrounding buildings. The stink of the public
privy was near overwhelming. She could see, straight ahead,
the back of a tavern.

A man opened the door to the tavern and threw slops to
the side.

Freya ran up the steps, pushed past him, and rushed into a steaming kitchen. Two maidservants looked up in astonishment as she ran through. The man at the back door belatedly swore behind her.

She found herself in a dark passage. There was a common room ahead and stairs to her right. She could try to hide in one of the rooms above, but that was a dead end. If they chased her up there, she'd be cornered.

Freya ran through the common room, where, except for a single lewd suggestion, no one paid her any mind. She came out of the front of the tavern onto the wharves. She could see the Thames beyond, the water sparkling in the sun prettily. Of course that was deceiving: the privy she'd just run past would empty directly into the river.

Freya turned to the left, heading east with the river on her right hand. She walked rapidly, for she'd gotten a stitch in her side from running. Her pursuers hadn't emerged from the tavern. Perhaps she'd lost them.

Perhaps they'd caught Betsy and the baby.

Dear God, no.

A figure emerged from the alley just ahead. Freya started before she recognized Betsy. Relief nearly made her stumble.

The nursemaid was wild eyed. "Oh, thank the Lord I found you, miss. If Mr. Bertrand's men catch me I don't know what he'd do."

"Then we shan't let that happen," Freya replied stoutly. She glanced at the earl and found him grinning at her around a fat finger stuck in his mouth. She pressed her lips together. "No, I won't let *either* of you fall back into his hands."

Behind them came a shout.

They'd been found.

"Hurry," Freya urged, breaking into a jog. She could see the alley that led to Wapping Old Stairs just ahead.

Betsy was praying under her breath.

They weren't going to make it. The stairs were too far, the men behind them too close.

"Give me the baby," Freya said.

"Ma'am?" Betsy looked terrified, but she did as Freya ordered.

Freya wrapped her arms around Alexander's little body. He started to cry, his open mouth wet against her neck. "Run for the stairs!"

Unencumbered by Lord Brightwater, Betsy flew.

The earl was wailing in Freya's ears as she ran, his body shaking, his little face bright red with distress. If they caught her, she'd be unable to fight them off with the baby in her arms. She'd lose Alexander. His uncle would hide him away behind walls and guards and the laws made by men and she'd never get him back.

Up ahead a figure emerged from the mouth of the alley leading to the stairs. She was short and slight and wearing a black cloak with a gray hood.

She raised her arms, a pistol in each fist.

Freya dove for the ground, landing hard on her shoulder so the baby wouldn't be hurt.

The blasts were simultaneous and so loud Lord Brightwater stopped crying, his mouth open, his eyes wide as he gasped.

He blinked up at her, tears in his big brown eyes.

Freya kissed him and then checked behind them.

One man was on the ground, swearing. The other had turned tail and run.

When Freya looked back, the Crow was striding to her. "You're late." She held out her hand to help Freya up.

"Thank you," Freya muttered, taking the hand.

Together they hurried to the stairs.

Betsy was there, sobbing in the arms of an elegantly dressed woman with a beauty patch on her upper lip.

"Alexander!" The woman turned to them.

The Earl of Brightwater started struggling in Freya's arms. "Mama."

Freya handed the baby to his mother.

"Oh, my precious darling." The widowed Countess of Brightwater hugged her only child close, pressing her cheek to his. She looked up at Freya, her eyes shining. "Thank you. You cannot know how much this means to me. I thought I'd never see Alexander again."

The countess's fears had nearly come true: her brother-in-law, Mr. Bertrand, had barred her from her son so that he could control both the countess and the estate left to his tiny nephew.

Freya nodded, but before she could draw breath to reply, the Crow said, "Best we leave immediately, my lady. We don't know if there's other men behind."

Lady Brightwater nodded and turned to descend the stairs with Betsy. Freya could see a wherry waiting below.

"She and her servants have passage on a ship to the Colonies," the Crow murmured. "They'll be out of her brother-in-law's influence there."

"Good," Freya replied softly. "A child should never be raised without a loving mother if it can be helped."

The Crow cocked her head at Freya, but said only, "Be in the mews at midnight tonight. I have word."

She turned and swiftly ran down the stairs.

Freya inhaled. Her part of the matter was finished. She watched as the little party got in the wherry and the wherryman pushed off from the steps. Betsy raised a hand in farewell.

Freya waved back. She'd probably never see Betsy, the adorable earl, or his mother again, but at least she'd know they were safe.

And that was everything.

* * *

Christopher Renshaw, the Duke of Harlowe, stared out the window of his carriage later that day as he traveled toward the West End of London.

His morning had been like any other since he'd returned to England—tedious—until a spitting wildcat had hurled herself into his carriage. He found himself entirely unable to stop thinking of her. She'd been like a splash of cold water to the face: shocking, but also refreshing. And like a splash of water she'd woken him up for the first time in months.

Perhaps years.

The woman had glared up at him from the floor of his carriage with beautiful green-gold eyes and challenged him, indifferent to the disadvantage of her position, literally at his feet.

It had been dumbfounding.

Intriguing.

In the two years since he'd rather implausibly gained the dukedom, he'd almost grown used to the awe, fawning, and frank greed his rank prompted in others. Few if any regarded him as a living, breathing man anymore.

And none treated him dismissively.

Except the wildcat.

She'd worn a plain brown dress and one of those ubiquitous white caps with a ruffle around her equally plain face, hiding both the color and style of her hair. She might've been a tavern keeper's wife or a fishmonger, and had she not opened her mouth, he would've assumed her accent to be common. Instead he'd detected both education and a hint of Scotland.

And then there'd been that venomous glare, as if she knew him somehow and had cause to loathe him.

Tess leaned against his thigh as the carriage swayed around a corner.

Christopher absently dropped his hand to her head, rubbing the soft points of her ears between his fingers. "Perhaps she's mad."

Tess whined and placed her paw on his knee.

A corner of his mouth lifted. "In any case, no doubt that will be the last we see of her."

He sighed and once again glanced out the carriage window. They were past Covent Gardens and nearly to Jackman's Club. After a morning spent in Wapping warehouses, overseeing a new venture in shipping, followed by a tiresome afternoon in the city center, consulting with men of business, Christopher had a strong urge for coffee and an hour or so reading the newspapers in quiet.

And, as always, alone.

For years he'd been exiled from these shores. Had lived in a country with foreign sights and smells and people. And he had thought all that time—thirteen *years*—that when he returned to England, his birthplace, everything would be different.

That he would be *home*.

Except when he returned it was to a title too grand. To parents dead and friendships destroyed and turned to dust. To enormous manors that echoed with his solitary footsteps when he walked through them.

England was no longer home. All that he could've built and loved there had been lost as he spent his youth in India. It was too late to find a home now.

He did not belong anywhere.

* * *

Five minutes later Christopher entered Jackman's with Tess. The livery-clad footman at the door blinked at the dog padding by Christopher's side, but was far too well trained to make any objection.

Being a duke did have *some* advantages.

Jackman's was fashionable but not *too* fashionable, and frequented by gentlemen who had lived in India and abroad. The selection of newspapers was one of the best in the city and the main reason he'd become a member.

He found a chair near the fire, had a footman open the window behind him, and was soon immersed in the news, a coffeepot on a small table at his elbow. Tess lay nearly under the table. He'd ordered a plate of muffins with his coffee, and every now and again he dropped a torn-off piece to Tess, who snapped it up.

Christopher was frowning over an account of the battle with the French at Wandiwash in southeast India when someone sat in the chair across from him.

Tess growled.

Christopher tensed. *No one* bothered him at Jackman's.

He raised his head and saw that idiot Thomas Plimpton looking nervously at Tess.

Christopher snorted. He'd been back in England for nearly two years now and hadn't seen Plimpton in four, but unless a miracle had occurred, the man was still the worst sort of coward. Plimpton had startled blue eyes, a round face, and a mouth that always seemed to be half-opened. Oddly these features somehow combined to make the man handsome—at least in ladies' eyes.

Christopher stared at him.

"Ah...," Plimpton said, sounding nervous, "might I have a word, Renshaw?"

"Harlowe," Christopher drawled.

"I...beg your pardon?"

"I am," Christopher said slowly and precisely, "the Duke of Harlowe."

"Oh." Plimpton swallowed visibly. "Y-yes, of course. Erm...Your Grace. Might I have a word?"

"No." Christopher turned his attention back to the newspaper.

He heard a rustling and glanced up.

Plimpton had a piece of paper in his hand. "I'm in need of funds."

Christopher didn't reply. Frankly, he saw no point in encouraging the man's impertinence. Plimpton knew well enough that Christopher despised him—and *why*.

But Plimpton must've found a shred of bravery somewhere. He lifted his chin. "I need ten thousand pounds. I'd like you to give it to me."

Christopher slowly arched an eyebrow.

Plimpton gulped. "A-and if you don't I shall make public *this*."

He shoved the piece of paper at Christopher.

Christopher took it and opened what was obviously a letter. The messy handwriting inside was instantly recognizable and brought a small pang to his heart. *Sophy.*

His wife had been dead four years, but that didn't end Christopher's vow to honor and protect her.

He balled up the letter and flung it into the fire.

The paper immediately caught, flaming brightly before dying almost instantly. Gray ash crumpled into the grate.

"That's not the only one I have," Plimpton said predictably.

Christopher waited.

Plimpton still had his chin up, a gallant, defiant look in his eyes. No doubt the man fancied himself some sort of chivalrous knight. He'd certainly cast himself in the role of hero in India. "I have many more letters, hidden in a safe place. A place you won't be able to find. A-and if something happens to me, I've left instructions to publish them."

Did the idiot think he'd *murder* him? Christopher merely looked at the man, but Tess growled again, the sound low and threatening.

Plimpton's eyes widened, darting to the dog and back up to Christopher's face. "In a fortnight your brother-in-law, Baron Lovejoy, will hold a house-party. I've been invited and no doubt you have as well. Bring the money there and in exchange I'll give you the letters."

Christopher inhaled and for a moment debated his next action. He despised social events, and a house party by its very premise was a confined affair without respite from fellow guests. He *could* refuse and do something nasty to Plimpton instead, but really in the end paying for the damned letters was the easiest and least complicated course.

"*All* the letters." Christopher made it a statement.

"Y-yes, all the—"

Christopher stood and walked away while Plimpton was still stuttering out his reply, Tess trotting by his side. Better to leave rather than do something he might regret later.

He'd failed Sophy once. He wasn't about to fail her again.

CHAPTER TWO

Rowan had hair the color of flames, skin as white as clouds, and eyes as green as the moss that grew on the riverbanks.
She had three cousins who were her constant companions. They were named Bluebell, Redrose, and Marigold. Rowan was fond of Bluebell and Redrose, but Marigold she loathed.
Why has never been told....
—From *The Grey Court Changeling*

Late that evening Freya selected a strand of floss silk and threaded her embroidery needle.

"Whatever are you embroidering, Miss Stewart?" the eldest of the Holland girls, Arabella, asked, leaning over Freya's arm. They shared a settee together in the sitting room of Holland House.

Freya had been Lady Holland's companion ever since she'd come to London five years ago to be the Wise Women's Macha. From the beginning she'd used her middle name, Stewart—a Scottish name to explain her Scottish accent. The Dunkelders knew that women of the de Moray family had been Wise Women for generations, so it was imperative that no one know she was the daughter of the Duke of Ayr.

"It's a merlin," Freya replied now, placing a bright scarlet stitch below the raptor.

"What's it doing?"

"Tearing the heart out of a sparrow," Freya said serenely.

"Oh." Arabella looked a little pale. "It's quite realistic."

"It is, isn't it?" Freya said. She smiled down at her violent artwork before glancing at the mantel clock. It was just after ten, which meant she had another two hours before her meeting with the Crow.

Freya's job as Macha was to gather information, gossip, and news for the Wise Women, the majority of whom lived at their estate near Dornoch in the far north of Scotland. It was the Wise Women like her and the Crow—the ones who lived outside the compound—who were fighting a war against the Dunkelders. A war for survival.

A war for women in Britain to live freely.

"What did you do on your day off, Miss Stewart?" Lady Holland asked absently. She sat in the armchair to Freya's left and was frowning at her own embroidery, which appeared to be tangled.

"Not anything very exciting, my lady," Freya replied. She set down her hoop, reached for Lady Holland's, and started teasing apart the tangled silks.

"Oh, thank you," Lady Holland said with what sounded like relief. Freya's employer was a short lady with an unfashionably rounded bosom and a practical, decisive personality, but embroidery defeated her. "And how was your outing with Mr. Trentworth, Regina?"

"He has a new pair of bays and they were simply gorgeous," Regina said from the chair across from Freya. "Perfectly matched and so high spirited. I begged him to give the team their heads and race about Hyde Park, but he refused."

"I should think so," Lady Holland said, but smiled fondly. "I'm pleased that he's a young gentleman of sense."

"*And* he has a classical profile." Regina looked dreamy for a moment before straightening. "Mama! Mr. Trentworth said today that he's thinking of calling on Papa."

"*Did* he?" Lady Holland's head came up like that of a greyhound sighting a rabbit. "I shall have to tell your father."

Regina frowned worriedly. "What do you think he'll say to Mr. Trentworth?"

"Don't be silly," Lady Holland replied. "Mr. Trentworth is of an indisputably good family and has quite a nice income. If he hadn't your father would've sent him packing long before now. He'll give his blessing to your beau, never fear."

Regina squealed and Arabella hugged her, but Freya noticed that Lady Holland's gaze lingered on Arabella. She had a small line between her brows.

"May Arabella and I retire for the night, Mama?" Regina asked, clearly eager to gossip with her sister.

Lady Holland waved her assent and the girls hurried from the room.

Freya handed back the embroidery hoop. There was a silence as Lady Holland frowned down at it.

She cleared her throat, choosing her words carefully. "You disapprove of the match, my lady?" She couldn't think why her employer would—Lady Holland had already enumerated Mr. Trentworth's assets, and she'd always seemed fond of the young gentleman. Freya thought that if Regina *must* marry, he was well suited to her.

"Not at all." But Lady Holland sounded disturbed.

Freya glanced sideways at her. "Then...?"

"I would prefer that Arabella be settled first." Many mothers wouldn't particularly care in which order their daughters married, but Lady Holland fretted about Arabella.

"Ah." Freya bent her head to her own embroidery and reminded herself that the ways of the Wise Women were *not* the ways of London society ladies—though they *really ought to be.*

Neither Regina nor Arabella was a great beauty, but both had their mother's wheat-colored hair and creamy complexion. Regina was the prettier and more vivacious of the two. Arabella had her father's long face and nose, and his serious manner. She had a dry wit and could speak intelligently on philosophy, literature, and history—none of which were attributes that seemed to attract London aristocrats.

As far as Freya could see, the average London gentleman looked for wealth, a noble lineage, and comeliness.

Things that lay *outside* a woman rather than within her.

Even dog breeders knew to value intelligence in their animals. Really, it was rather surprising that the English aristocracy hadn't descended into drooling idiocy.

"If only she had a chance for quiet conversation with an eligible gentleman," Lady Holland murmured absently. "It's a pity the London season is ending."

"Yes, my lady." Freya hesitated, then said, "Perhaps a country house party?"

"For Arabella, you mean?" Lady Holland narrowed her eyes and then shook her head. "You're aware Lord Holland dislikes large gatherings. I don't think I can make him change his mind on the matter, particularly since he considers the country house his retreat."

Freya nodded thoughtfully. "Then perhaps one of the invitations we've already received."

"Perhaps. We'll look them over in the morning." Lady Holland stifled a yawn. "I'm for bed now, though. Are you coming up?"

"Not yet." Freya indicated her embroidery. "I'd like to finish this bit here."

Lady Holland shook her head as she rose. "I don't know how you do it, Miss Stewart. I should be quite blind if I embroidered as well as you."

Freya permitted herself a small smile. "One must have an interest to occupy one's time."

They said their good nights, and then Freya was alone in the sitting room.

She waited, diligently working on the merlin and his meal, and her thoughts turned to the Duke of Harlowe and how she would get the ring back. He'd seemed so certain of his power as he'd sat above her in the carriage, so *arrogant*. She gritted her teeth. That a man such as he should be able to swan about London while Ran had been all but destroyed by the Greycourt tragedy . . .

She shook her head. No use thinking of Ran and what he was like now. Better to find a way to bring down the prideful duke. Harlowe had inherited a fabulously wealthy dukedom through sheer *luck*. Society had been rife with gossip two years ago when the old duke died and Harlowe—a very distant relative—had returned from India. But in all the time since, she'd never seen him at any London social events. Was he shunning society? If so, it might be difficult to run across him again without rousing suspicion. Perhaps if she bribed a servant—

The clock on the mantel struck midnight with a tinkling chime, pulling her from her thoughts.

Freya put her embroidery away in a basket and went into the outer hall.

Everything was quiet.

She crept to the back of the house without a candle—

she'd lived here for five years, after all. She slipped out of the door that led to the back garden.

The moon had risen and the garden was cast in black and white, the scent of roses in the air. She took the path straight back to the mews, gravel crunching beneath her slippers. It was chill this late at night and she regretted not fetching a shawl from her room.

The back gate had been oiled and opened smoothly beneath her hand. She made sure to push a rock against the gate to keep it from closing behind her.

It wouldn't do for prim Miss Stewart to become locked out of the garden after midnight.

Freya stood looking up and down the mews for a minute. She'd just decided to walk toward the road when the Crow emerged from the shadows.

"Lady Freya."

Freya stilled. "You shouldn't call me that."

The Crow drew back her hood. An earring glinted in the mass of her thick black hair. "I'm sorry."

By rights, as the daughter—and sister—of a duke, Freya should've been at the pinnacle of power. Should've been able to move among the most influential of London's elite to do the work of the Macha. But the Greycourt scandal had destroyed all that. The de Moray name had sunk into the mud, the ducal fortunes beggared. Not long after the scandal, Papa had died from the shock, and then she and her sisters, Caitriona and Elspeth, had gone to live with their aunt Hilda in Dornoch.

It was because of Aunt Hilda that Freya was the Macha. She'd vowed to the old woman to preserve the teachings and the ways of the Wise Women.

That thought brought her back to the present. The Crow's sharp eyes watched her, black and impossible to read.

Freya frowned at her. "What have you to tell me?"

"You are recalled by the Hags."

"What?" Freya couldn't hide her shock. The Hags—three appointed women—were the ruling body of the Wise Women. "Why would the Hags recall me? Are they displeased with my service as the Macha? Do they wish to replace me?"

"Not at all." The Crow pressed her lips together as if she wished to say more but dared not.

"Then why? It's imperative that I be in London right now. You know that there's talk of a new Witch Act before Parliament. What has changed?"

"We have a new Cailleach," the Crow said carefully, naming one of the positions within the Hags. "She feels that 'twere better if the Wise Women *all* withdrew to Dornoch."

Freya stared. "You jest."

The Crow shook her head. "Nay, my lady."

"Retire and do what?" Freya demanded. "Forget about all the women who need our help? Pretend we don't have a sacred duty to right the wrongs of a man-led society? Hide like cowering mice in a nest until the Dunkelders finally discover and burn us all?"

The Crow shrugged, watching her.

Freya's upper lip curled and she hissed, "If the new Witch Act passes we'll be hunted by *everyone*, not just the Dunkelders. There will be tribunals and burnings again. The Wise Women will not survive another great witch hunt."

"*I* know that," the Crow murmured, "but I am not the Cailleach."

"And the other two Hags are growing old," Freya said bitterly. The Hags ruled equally together, but of course if one was a particularly strong personality she could persuade the others to her cause.

The Crow nodded. "I heard the eldest has taken to her bed. They say she hasn't long and her successor is of a like mind with the Cailleach."

"What of the Nemain?" Freya asked. The assassin of the Wise Women was used only in the direst of circumstances. "Is she recalled as well?"

"Yes."

"And you?"

"I will follow you and the Nemain to Dornoch after my work is done," the Crow said.

Freya squeezed her eyes shut. *Think.* She'd known there was a movement within the Wise Women to retire entirely from the world of men. She'd just not known how strong it was. If they retreated to Scotland and the Witch Act passed, she truly believed that the Wise Women would be destroyed.

And with them a millennium of knowledge, tradition, and dedication. *Aunt Hilda's* knowledge, tradition, and dedication.

She could not let that happen.

Freya opened her eyes to find the Crow waiting patiently, her black gaze fixed on Freya's face. "Give me a month. Tell the Hags that I'll return to Dornoch in four weeks. That I cannot leave before then without arousing suspicion."

The Crow's brows rose. "What can you do in a month?"

"Listen to me," Freya said. "Lord Elliot Randolph spearheads the Witch Act in Parliament. I've searched these many months for his weakness. He has none that I can find—save possibly one."

The Crow cocked her head in question.

"His wife," Freya said. "Lady Randolph suddenly died last year and was buried at his country estate in Lancashire before her family in London was even notified of her death. It seems to me that Lord Randolph might have had a reason to prevent his wife's family from seeing the body. If I can find evidence that he had a hand in her death, then we can stop *him*—and with him the new Witch's Act before it's ever brought to Parliament."

The Crow shook her head. "It's the end of the London season. All the English aristocrats will be deserting the city for their country estates."

"Yes, they will. Everyone including Lord Randolph."

"Then how—?"

"Lady Holland has an invitation to a house party at Lord and Lady Lovejoy's estate." She met the Crow's eyes. "In Lancashire. They're neighbors. The estates adjoin."

Understanding dawned in the Crow's face. "You plan to attend the house party."

Freya grinned fiercely. "Give me a month. I'll investigate Lady Randolph's death—and find evidence to destroy Lord Randolph."

* * *

Two weeks later Freya winced as the carriage jolted over a rut in the Lancashire road. She sat facing backward with Regina on one side and Selby, Lady Holland's middle-aged lady's maid, on the other. Arabella and Lady Holland were across from them.

They'd been traveling for a week, and everyone was heartily sick of dusty roads, inns with dubiously clean linens, and the constant rattling of the carriage.

"We *must* be nearly there," Regina said, staring hopefully out the carriage window. "If we drive much further we'll be in *Scotland*."

"Perhaps that's why Miss Stewart was so keen that you accept Lady Lovejoy's invitation in particular amongst all the others we received," Arabella murmured, darting a small smile at Freya.

"Not at all," Freya replied loftily. "For one thing, Lovejoy House isn't anywhere *near* Scotland proper."

Both Arabella and Regina stifled giggles at that— Scotland and all things Scottish had become something of a jest between them and Freya over the years. Freya felt a sudden pang. She'd lived with the Holland sisters for five *years*. Had watched them grow from gawky young girls into elegant ladies.

It wouldn't be easy leaving them or Lady Holland in two weeks.

Freya squared her shoulders. Two weeks to find out what had happened to Lady Randolph.

Two weeks in which to prevent disaster to the Wise Women.

"Why did you choose Lady Lovejoy's house party, Mama?" Regina asked, interrupting her thoughts. "I thought you were set on Bath this summer?"

"There'll be more than enough time for Bath later in the summer, my darlings," Lady Holland replied. "Lady Lovejoy is a particular friend of mine. She assures me that Lord Lovejoy has an extensive stable, and the countryside is wild and romantic around Lovejoy House." She nodded at Freya. "And finally, our dear Miss Stewart was in favor of the idea."

"Not to mention Mr. Aloysius Lovejoy will be attending with his friends," Regina murmured.

Arabella blushed rather splotchily.

Freya hid a smile. The younger Mr. Lovejoy had the most beautiful golden hair she'd ever seen, but beyond that he seemed a kind man. Arabella would need a sensitive gentleman to match her quiet intelligence. It was the prospect of several eligible bachelors that had been the deciding factor for Lady Holland in attending the Lovejoy house party in particular.

"We've arrived, my lady." Selby nodded to the carriage window, and all of them leaned forward to look.

The carriage had stopped to let a gatekeeper pull back the massive iron gates. The man touched his hat as the carriage turned in to a gravel drive.

Lovejoy House stood surrounded by a tended lawn, the better to be admired. The house itself was a red stone building that looked at least several centuries old. It rose arrogantly certain of its place in the cosmos, and for a moment Freya had a longing for her own ancestral home. Ayr Castle was older and bigger than Lovejoy House, a stately gray monolith that no doubt looked arrogant to strangers as well.

But not to her. To her it had been home.

"Oh, someone's come just before us," Arabella said, bringing Freya's attention back to the present.

A black coach with a familiar crest stood before the doors, the coachman still in the box.

Freya schooled her features even as her heart began to thud in her ears. If the master of that coach was who she thought it was, she should be afraid. Worried that her identity would be revealed and her mission imperiled.

Instead she felt herself readying for battle. Her muscles tightening, her senses quickening. Oh, this was a divine gift indeed. She'd not expected *him* here, would never have guessed he would attend. And yet she could see the booted foot emerge from the carriage, the flash of lace at the masculine wrist. She inhaled leather and mud and the scent of her own body warming.

She felt alive.

Oh, let it be him.

She wanted that ring. She wanted to make him *pay*.

"Perhaps it's Mr. Lovejoy," Regina said, darting an impish look at Arabella.

"*That*'s not Mr. Lovejoy," her sister replied. "He's far too broad in the shoulders *and* too tall."

The man stood beside the carriage, large and commanding as others scurried around him.

"Do you recognize the crest?" Regina whispered as their carriage drew to a stop.

Lady Holland pursed her lips in thought. "No, but whoever he is, he's wealthy. That carriage is new."

Freya's heart felt as if it had climbed into her throat.

The footman set the step, and then there was the flurry of gathering items and exiting the carriage.

Freya made herself wait. She was the last to leave, ducking her head to clear the carriage doorway.

A male hand appeared before her, wearing Ran's signet ring. The fingers long, the nails square, and the palm broad and strong.

She inhaled to steady herself and placed her hand in his, stepping down.

"I don't believe we've been properly introduced," the Duke of Harlowe rumbled over her head.

She looked up...into cerulean eyes watching her with complete attention. His gleaming chestnut hair was pulled neatly back from his forehead, and he wore a nut-brown suit that made his eyes nearly glow.

Not that she was particularly noticing. "Are you sure, Your Grace?" Oh, this was playing with fire.

His eyes narrowed. How often did anyone question him? "I certainly thought I was."

"Have you met our chaperone, Miss Stewart, Your Grace?" Regina asked with innocent curiosity.

He cocked his eyebrow at Freya, murmuring too low for Regina to hear, "Have I, Miss Stewart?"

"I believe we met at the Earl of Sandys's ball," Freya replied, pulling a story from thin air. "I'm afraid I was so clumsy as to bump into His Grace."

"I seem to remember you falling at my feet," Harlowe said, a too-attractive smile playing about his lips. "I do hope you've recovered from the incident?"

"Entirely."

She lowered her gaze and imagined disemboweling him. Vividly.

He nodded in dismissal and turned to Lady Holland. "May I?" he asked, offering his arm.

Lady Holland blushed. "Your Grace is so—"

The yellow dog bounded up and shoved her nose into Freya's skirts.

Regina stifled a shriek—she'd never liked dogs, having been bitten as a child.

Lady Holland said sharply, "Whose dog is that?"

"Mine." The duke snapped his fingers. "Tess, come here."

Tess ignored him, sniffing with great interest all about Freya's hem. She remembered now that there'd been a friendly cat at their last stop.

Freya glanced up and said blandly, "I don't believe Tess knows that you're a duke, Your Grace."

He sighed. "No, she most certainly doesn't."

Freya's lips twitched before she regained control of them. She held out her hand to the dog—it wasn't Tess's fault that she had such a vile man for a master.

The dog snuffled wetly against her fingers and then looked up, letting her jaw hang open in a friendly canine

smile as her tail gently waved. Her ears were upright trian-
gles, her eyes and nose black against the dust yellow of her
fur, and her head reached nearly to Freya's hip. She didn't
seem like an aristocratic dog, but then Freya wasn't sure
she'd ever seen a dog exactly like Tess before.

"She's quite harmless," Harlowe said, glancing at Regina.
"Would you care to meet her?"

Regina visibly hesitated, her hands clutched to her chest.

Tess turned and trotted to her master.

"V-very well," Regina said.

"Come. Give me your hand," Harlowe said, and it was
amazing how gentle he sounded when Freya *knew* what he
was capable of.

Regina held out her trembling hand. The duke took it and
bent with her hand in his to let Tess sniff them both. "That's
my girl, Tess. Softly now. What do you think of Miss Holland, then? Will you be friends?"

Freya swallowed. His voice was deep and rumbling as he
spoke to the dog, and the sound made her belly tremble.

The *cad*. Freya tried to look away but found herself
strangely loath to do so.

A smile bloomed on Regina's face when she petted Tess's
head. "Her ears are so soft." She glanced shyly at Harlowe.
"Thank you, Your Grace."

He bowed gravely, but a corner of his wide mouth
quirked. "My pleasure, Miss Holland."

"Your Grace! I'm so pleased you could come." Daniel
Lovejoy, Baron Lovejoy stood on the steps of his house. He
was a man of forty-some years with gray powdered hair.
"And Lady Holland. A pleasure as always, ma'am."

That seemed to be the signal to go inside the house, Freya
trailing behind, all but forgotten.

Just the way she liked it.

* * *

Two hours later Christopher descended the grand staircase of Lovejoy House to the main floor, Tess padding by his side. He'd had a hot bath and changed his clothes and finally felt rested after a week of travel in a confined carriage. He hoped to find Plimpton and settle this matter as soon as possible. It made his skin itch to know the bastard still had Sophy's letters. The letters were a last chore—a mess he needed to mop up so he could set Sophy's memory in order.

They came to a larger hallway, and he could hear male voices nearby.

Christopher pushed open a sky-blue door and entered a room with dark paneling and several groupings of chairs—evidently his brother-in-law's study. Three gentlemen seated by the fireplace turned to him.

Tess huffed, raising her head alertly.

Absently Christopher dropped his hand to her head.

"Ah, there you are, Harlowe," Lovejoy said, sounding jovial.

The man was nearly two decades older than his sister had been, and yet the resemblance was marked. Fifteen years ago, when Christopher had married Sophy, he remembered thinking that at a distance Lovejoy and Sophy might've been twins, both with round, moonlike faces and impossibly blond hair. Lovejoy powdered his now, so it was difficult to tell if it was still that nearly white color.

Lovejoy stared at Tess as Christopher crossed to him. "Erm…perhaps the dog would be more comfortable in the stables?"

"No," Christopher said, "she wouldn't. Thank you for inviting me."

Lovejoy went a delicate pink, though his next words were obsequious. "Entirely my pleasure, Your Grace. May I present my son, Aloysius Lovejoy?"

The younger man sprang to his feet. He had the Lovejoy white-blond hair, worn in a tail and with fussy curls across his forehead and at his temples. If Christopher didn't know that the color ran in the family, he would swear it was a wig.

"Your Grace." Aloysius bowed. "It's a pleasure to meet you at last. At least, I know I met you when I was but ten at your wedding to Aunt Sophy, but it *has* been fifteen years. Shall I call you Uncle?"

Christopher eyed the man, wondering if Aloysius was mocking him. The younger Lovejoy looked entirely serious. The man was only eight years younger than Christopher, though Christopher felt much older than Aloysius.

In any case, the request was quite inappropriate.

"I think not."

Aloysius's eyebrows flew up, but he didn't seem particularly put out.

The third man in the room snorted. "Shot down at once. That'll teach you, Al."

"And this"—Lovejoy indicated the man—"is Aloysius's friend Leander Ashley, Earl Rookewoode."

The earl was thirty-odd and handsome, with sardonic eyes beneath a white wig. Rookewoode bowed elegantly and with a bit of a flourish. "It's quite an honor to meet you, Your Grace. I fear you're not much seen in society. You've become almost a legend."

"Have I?" Christopher murmured dismissively. The truth was that he avoided balls and soirees. The press of bodies made him ill at ease, brought a choking feeling of pressure to his throat, and filled him with the urge to escape to untainted air.

On the whole, he'd rather drink poison than attend a crowded event.

Rookewoode narrowed his eyes at Christopher's tone, though his grin was quick and charming.

"May I present Christopher Renshaw, the Duke of Harlowe," Lovejoy hastily continued. "My late sister's husband, of course." He glanced at Christopher. "We were about to join the rest of the party in the small salon."

Christopher nodded and fell into step beside Lovejoy, Tess loping by his side.

"Have all your guests arrived?" Where the hell was Plimpton?

"Not as yet, Your Grace," Lovejoy said. "I know Lady Lovejoy will be ecstatic that you've deigned to attend our little party. We've hardly seen you since you returned from India."

The last was said with a stiff little smile.

Christopher supposed he was meant to feel guilty.

"My business affairs have kept me busy," he replied with complete honesty.

"I'm sure, I'm sure," Lovejoy murmured. "Ah, here we are."

They'd arrived at a sitting room painted a deep shade of crimson. At one end a fire roared, making the place stuffy and overheated.

The room felt too small.

He took a slow breath, letting his hand fall to Tess's head.

Christopher scanned the seated crowd, not realizing he was looking for someone until his gaze snagged on Miss Stewart. Even from across the room her eyes seemed to blaze at him, though her prim face was carefully composed.

What was she up to? She seemed perfectly respectable—even boring—in this setting, yet only a fortnight before he'd seen her fleeing two hulking men and leaping recklessly into his carriage. With a baby no less.

He set his questions aside and brought his attention back to the present. There were other people in the room and Lovejoy was introducing each.

He'd already met Lady Caroline Holland and her daughters. Regina was sitting with her mother. Across from them were Arabella and Miss Stewart, who apparently had no Christian name—at least none that he'd been given.

At right angles to the Hollands, Lady Lovejoy shared a settee with Malcolm Stanhope, Viscount Stanhope. The man looked to be under the age of thirty, but he held himself as rigidly as a cantankerous old man.

Lovejoy finished the introductions and Lady Lovejoy turned to Christopher. "Will you take a dish of tea, Your Grace?"

Christopher indicated he would and selected a chair closest to the French doors. They were shut, but they looked as if they led onto a terrace. The prospect of escape was at least near.

Tess crawled under his chair to lie down. Unlike her husband, Lady Lovejoy didn't bat an eyelash at her guest's bringing a dog to a country house party. Either she was more liberal than Lovejoy or—more likely—she'd let Christopher do just about anything because of his title.

People usually did. The moment they realized he was a duke they scraped and bowed and stuttered, as if he pissed gold.

As if he were set apart, alone and immune to human contact.

That is, *most* people treated him that way.

There were exceptions.

At the thought he felt his pulse pick up. He turned his head and caught Miss Stewart staring at him with loathing in her lovely green-gold eyes.

CHAPTER THREE

One day Rowan and her companions rode deep into the forest until at last they came to a clearing. To one side stood a grotto, beautiful, green, and silent. The horses shied away.
"They say that Fairyland lies in there," Marigold whispered, and Redrose and Bluebell looked frightened.
But Rowan said, "Bah! A wifes' tale. Let us explore inside and prove the tale wrong."…
—From The Grey Court Changeling

He'd been a skinny boy with a man's full height at eighteen, but not his weight. He'd looked like a medieval king, his face long, sensitive, and ascetic. And his eyes had been blue, luminous, and beautiful—at least that was how Freya remembered Christopher Renshaw.

She sipped her tea and contemplated the Duke of Harlowe. He was fully formed now, big and solid, his shoulders wide, his calves muscular in his fine stockings as he stretched his legs before him in his chair. His face had filled out into craggy cheekbones and a strong jaw. He was no longer a dreamy poet.

No, now he more closely resembled a warrior king—hardened and merciless. A man who could betray his friend without thought.

A man who *still* didn't recognize her.

Well, why should he? she thought rather irritably. When Harlowe had last seen her she'd been a skinny girl in the schoolroom. The younger sister of his great friend Ranulf. Someone he'd had no reason to notice. A child while he'd been a young man and a student at Oxford with Julian Greycourt and Ran.

Freya pressed her lips together to stop them trembling at the memory. They'd been so bright, the three of them, shining like young gods. She'd thought them invincible, and now...

Now Ran was crippled because of Julian and Harlowe.

"Does your head ache?" Arabella asked softly beside her.

"No, not at all." Freya caught herself frowning. She forced a smile and turned to the elder Holland sister. "Have you recovered from the carriage ride this morning?"

"I'm glad to have a bit of a rest from bouncing up and down," the younger woman replied with feeling.

"What do you think of Lady Lovejoy's guests?"

"You mean the gentlemen?" Arabella asked with a wry twist to her lips.

Freya winced. "I *was* trying to be more subtle than that."

"I don't know that there's any point." The younger woman sounded bitter.

Freya glanced at her quickly.

Arabella gave her a half-hearted smile. "I know Mama wishes me wed before Regina, and with Mr. Trentworth ready to propose..."

She shrugged.

Freya tightened her mouth and silently patted Arabella's hand, which felt like no comfort at all. Ladies of Arabella's rank sometimes didn't wed, but the vast majority did, and Freya knew that Lord Holland expected his daughters to not only wed but wed *well*.

Freya silently gave thanks that she was a Wise Woman. If she wished to, she could certainly marry and have a family, but it wasn't an imperative. In fact, were she to wed she might be *less* welcome at the estate in Dornoch. The Wise Women were very careful about which men they let into their sanctuary.

Freya said, "If you truly dislike everyone you meet here, I have no doubt that your mother will give you time to find another suitor."

"Yes." Arabella scanned the gentlemen in the room with an oddly dispassionate eye. "But I've had three years to find a husband. She and Father cannot wait on me forever."

"You sound quite grim."

Arabella turned and gave her a small curl of the lips. "I'm planning a campaign to find a husband, Miss Stewart. Such things should be done most gravely."

Freya took a sip of tea, trying to cover her own unease. So many things could go wrong in a marriage, and once the vows were said there was no returning to what freedom there was in maidenhood.

A grave business indeed.

Freya cleared her throat, attempting a lighter note. "Lord Stanhope is quite beautiful, don't you think?"

Arabella sent her an appalled glance.

Freya tried to look innocent.

"You're awful," Arabella whispered. "Lord Stanhope looks like he swallowed a toad. And quite recently."

Freya repressed a smile. "Perhaps he's shy."

Arabella widened her eyes disbelievingly.

"Well, he *might* be." Freya shrugged. "I've noticed that

sometimes gentlemen who present a forbidding exterior are simply timid."

"*Timid*." Arabella raised a single eyebrow. "Then the duke must be a rabbit. He was kind to introduce Regina to darling Tess, but I would never have guessed him to be so gentlemanly from simply his appearance. He looks as if he might bite one's head off if his tea wasn't to his satisfaction."

Freya glanced at Harlowe before she could stop herself.

He was seated with Lord Lovejoy. Tess was under his chair, watching the assembly alertly, her head on her crossed paws. Harlowe listened with a frown on his face to something their host was saying. As she watched, he glanced at the fire and then the door and shifted in his chair, almost as if he wished to leave the room.

She shook her head at her own ridiculousness. Harlowe was hardly the sort of man to be *shy* in a gathering. No, Arabella was right.

He did appear rather intimidating.

"I should avoid him were I you," Freya found herself saying.

"What do you mean?" Arabella asked. "I've always thought that when a man has the devotion of a dog it shows his true character, and Tess quite obviously loves the duke."

The thought of Arabella setting her cap at Harlowe made Freya feel irritable. She glanced back at the girl.

Arabella's brows were knit.

Freya shook her head. "Dogs are such loving animals, and really it takes little to win them over. Food and companionship, mostly. I don't think the duke is very nice." Arabella looked so young in a pretty pale-pink gown. "At least, not nice enough for *you*."

"You're quite cynical on occasion, Miss Stewart," Arabella said. "Sometimes I wonder if a gentleman hurt you in the past. If there was a beau who spurned you and broke your heart."

"Alas, nothing so romantic," Freya said dryly. "What do you think of the younger Mr. Lovejoy? You've met him before, I believe."

Arabella gave her a disconcertingly considering stare. "You always turn the conversation away from yourself. Really, I hardly know anything about your past."

"There's not much to know," Freya said lightly, meeting her gaze.

"Hmm." Arabella sighed and glanced again at the gentlemen. "As to your question, yes, I danced with Mr. Lovejoy at a ball last winter. Once. He danced with Regina twice."

Freya ignored the last. "Mr. Lovejoy seems quite nice."

"Mama would prefer a titled gentleman."

"Of course," Freya replied, refraining from rolling her eyes. *Naturally* the lineage of the prospective groom was more important than whether or not the bride actually liked him. "But Mr. Lovejoy will inherit a barony someday— and quite a wealthy one at that. I think, in the end, Lady Holland wishes above all that you be happy."

"I know she does, but I also know Papa would like me to marry someone of rank." Arabella raised her eyes, meeting Freya's gaze frankly. "I want to make them both proud of me, but I'm not as vivacious as Regina. I don't know if I *can* attract a titled gentleman."

"You can," Freya said, taking her hand. Arabella's vulnerability made her heart want to break. "I *know* you can if you set your mind to it. You are kind and intelligent and very witty when you wish to be. We simply need to find the right gentleman to appreciate you."

Arabella looked uncertain, and Freya pressed her lips together. She didn't want to see Arabella hurt.

"Arabella," Lady Holland called. "Lady Lovejoy has the most intriguing embroidery patterns. Come see."

Lady Lovejoy had joined Lady Holland on a settee.

"Of course, Mama," Arabella said obediently, rising to cross and sit with her mother and their hostess.

The fact was that Freya *wasn't* certain the girl could make a suitable match. Titled gentlemen had their pick of aristocratic ladies. What she wished she could tell Arabella was that there was no need to worry. That there was plenty of time for Arabella to find a gentleman who was kind and who loved her for herself.

But the awful reality was that Arabella was expected to marry. To make familial ties for her father and to breed the next generation of aristocrats. The girl really had no choice.

Freya might, on the surface, work as a companion and chaperone—quite near the bottom of aristocratic society—but in reality she had more freedom than any duchess.

Because she was a Wise Woman.

And now she had only a fortnight to save the Wise Women.

She had to find something to hold over Lord Randolph.

Freya sipped from her teacup and scanned the room. Her gaze almost immediately clashed with the duke's.

He was staring at her, his sky-blue eyes narrowed in what looked like consideration.

The sudden surge of hatred for him caught her off guard. Made her chest so tight it was hard to breathe. Had Harlowe forgotten not only her but Ran as well? It was a thorn in her breast, the knowledge that he was living his life freely and without remorse while her brother Lachlan toiled over the remaining de Moray lands.

While Ran hid himself away from the world.

Across from her, Arabella laughed at something.

Freya glanced over. The girl was smiling at the pattern book Lady Lovejoy was showing her and Lady Holland. If only Arabella could be so relaxed when conversing with a gentleman. Unfortunately she became stiff when—

"Miss Stewart," a deep voice said next to her.

Freya fancied that she could feel the reverberations to her bones. "Your Grace."

She turned to find that Harlowe had seated himself in a chair pulled up beside the settee she perched on. He was at a perfectly proper distance. No one could look askance at the fact that he'd sat down beside her. But the point that he was *talking* to her might cause comment. She was the hired companion and chaperone. She wasn't supposed to be noticed at all.

She didn't *want* to be noticed.

And he was well aware of it. There was a gleam in his startlingly blue eyes as he murmured, "I find myself curious, Miss Stewart. I don't think you are what you seem to be."

"Are any of us?"

He shrugged. "Perhaps not."

She smiled, aware that it was closer to a grimace. "What dire secrets do *you* hide, Your Grace?"

"How do you know I hide any?"

"Intuition?" She tilted her head, studying him, and picked her words carefully. If she mentioned Greycourt, the game would be given away directly. All the same she was tempted to do it. Instead she settled on something more vague. "You're a gentleman past thirty, widowed, but in the two years since you gained your title you've not bothered remarrying."

"I wasn't aware that lack of a wife is a suspect state," he drawled.

"It is for a gentleman who holds such a lofty title. Shouldn't you be searching for a young, nubile maiden? One you can tie to your side and who will bear for you your heirs? Duty to the dukedom surely demands it."

His lips curved cynically. "Are you acting as a pander for the Misses Holland?"

"No." Her reply was curt. No, this man wasn't for Regina or Arabella. He was a powerful man—a *dangerous* man. The woman who married him would have to be not only strong but stubborn, able to hold her ground. Not that she would wish marriage to him on *any* woman, of course. "I would not recommend you to a young girl."

"Should I be offended?" His eyes were so blue it was hard to look away.

"Yes." She lifted her chin. "You are not good enough for them."

He was very still, and only the tightening of his jaw gave away his ire before he said caustically, "And am I good enough for *you*, Miss Stewart?"

"I am a companion, Your Grace. You know well enough that you are not for me." This was too close to flirtation. She could not be distracted by cerulean eyes, blunt conversation, and her own heightened awareness of him. She turned her hand over in her lap, exposing the vulnerable palm. "Tell me. What are your thoughts on revenge?"

Silence.

She glanced up.

He was watching her as if she were a cannon poorly primed. "What an odd question."

"Is it?" she asked carelessly. "I beg your pardon. I shall

return to proper subjects of conversation. The weather is quite pleasant, don't you think?"

He snorted and said seriously, "I think revenge destroys the soul, Miss Stewart."

She felt an odd thrill. He'd accepted her conversational gambit. "I disagree. If I am wronged, shouldn't I seek revenge for it?" She leaned a little toward him, wondering how much further she could push him. When he reached his limit, would he walk away—or turn on her? "What would you do, Your Grace, if you were vilely used, terribly hurt, had everything you held dear taken from you?"

"I would be more careful in the future," he said slowly, but without hesitation, as if he'd actually mused on the topic before. "And I would try to live my life as honorably as I could."

For the first time it occurred to her that perhaps he *had* been wronged at some point. After all, it was fifteen years since she'd last seen him. Wouldn't it be ironic if the sinner was himself sinned against?

"What a paragon of restraint you are, Your Grace," she said, sweetly mocking. "You would simply let your tormentor free? Wish him a long and happy life?"

"No, naturally not." He sighed impatiently. "I am only human. I would want to bring him to justice. But justice is not always possible—or for the greater good. Surely you realize this."

"I realize that to give up the drive for revenge—or justice, as you put it—is to relinquish a part of oneself," she said far too passionately. "To succumb to the mundanity of life instead of reaching for the most valiant part of ourselves."

"You think revenge *valiant*." He glanced away from her as if he couldn't bear to see her face. "And after you have revenged yourself, what then, Miss Stewart?"

She didn't want him to turn from her. "Then I will have *peace*."

His expression when he looked at her was sardonic. "Madam. Have you ever sought peace in your life?"

She couldn't help the wry twist of her mouth. "Truthfully, no."

He nodded as if unsurprised. "I thought not. So tell me, who is this man you wish to revenge yourself upon? Was it one of the men chasing you through the streets of east London a fortnight ago?"

Good Lord, had anyone heard him?

She caught her breath at her own idiocy. She wasn't a shallow girl, to have her head turned by a pair of pretty eyes. This was her *enemy*. "Do keep your voice down, if you please."

"Why?" He lounged back, watching her with the dispassionate interest of a tomcat playing with a crippled mouse. "Are you hiding something?"

She widened her eyes. "*Obviously.*"

"What?"

"Why do you think you have any right to ask?" Talking to this man was far too seductive. She was perilously close to giving everything away. Freya took a sip of tea to cover her disquiet.

"Possibly because I *didn't* throw you and your companions from my carriage," he replied mildly.

"I am forever in your debt," she snapped.

He paused, his eyes narrowing. "I could simply ask your employer."

"You *could*," she replied, a tight smile firmly in place, "but by doing so you admit that you are unable to handle me by yourself. And then I should know you for a coward."

He stilled, and she knew she'd found the line.

Found it and crossed it.

"Most people in your position, Miss Stewart," he said very quietly, "would be careful *not* to offend me."

* * *

Christopher stared at Miss Stewart, aware that he couldn't remember when he'd last been this angry. Come to that, he hadn't felt *any* emotion so deeply in a long time.

She wasn't cowed by his ire. Quite the opposite—those green-gold eyes were glittering with almost feverish excitement as she replied, "Your pardon. If you want careful argument, then you must seek it elsewhere."

"I certainly would be a coward if I left the field to you," he said softly. "And I assure you, madam, that I am not."

Her smile this time was quick and *real*, revealing a dimple on one cheek. He caught his breath at the sight. This, *this* was what he'd been missing without even realizing it: genuine conversation. Genuine *feeling*.

In the next second her smile was gone, almost as if she were ashamed of the lapse. "I'll have to take your word for it, Your Grace."

Another insult. They seemed to spill off her tongue. What was it about this awful woman that held him so? Her appearance didn't match her personality at all. On the outside she was dowdy and forgettable, her clothes prim and drab. The cap on her head particularly irritated him—it hid most of her brownish hair and distracted from the rest of her.

"You wear the most ghastly cap," he said.

One never spoke to a lady in this manner. A gentleman always used polite little lies, glossing over anything that might distress a lady.

He remembered once when he'd tried to talk with Sophy about a maid who was stealing. His wife had been so upset over even the *thought* of reprimanding the maid that she'd taken to bed for the rest of the day. He'd dealt with dismissing the maid himself. Sophy hadn't seemed to notice beyond commenting on the new maid's lazy eye.

It had been better all around to live a polite fiction with his wife. A sort of make-believe life in which the truth was never mentioned. In which he always cared for her and her worries, and she existed in a childish state of dependence.

Never an equal adult.

Never a real partner.

Miss Stewart's acid retorts were refreshing.

Her eyes had widened in something like outrage—certainly not shock. *Is she shocked by anything?* "How rude to say so, Your Grace."

He tutted. "A miss, I'm afraid. Have you grown weary, darling?"

Her upper lip curled, baring her teeth, and for a moment he thought she might hit him. He inhaled, strangely anticipatory. Would she throw aside her thin disguise and reveal herself to the sedate sitting room as the warrior she was?

To his disappointment she controlled herself and in the next second was looking at him *almost* serenely. "I can't think that you're an expert in ladies' millinery fashions. At least not *respectable* ladies' fashions."

He wanted to laugh at her restraint. "Are you attempting to imply I'm a roué, madam?"

She pursed her lips, drawing his attention to her mouth. Undoubtedly she was trying to look proper and disapproving, but she was rather betrayed by her own mouth. She might have the personality of a harpy, but her lips were voluptuously lush. Wide and plump and curved. Naturally tinted pink. Her smile would be glorious. And if she were to use that mouth for other, more erotic tasks…

No, those weren't the lips of a prude.

And they were parting now. "I don't know what you mean."

"Oh my dear," he said gently. "Have you lost your nerve? Surely you can do better than that feeble riposte. Perhaps you can imply that I have the pox. Or simply stand up and call me a ravisher of women." He watched her outraged eyes, enchanted. She had the loveliest dark lashes. "You must admit that if nothing else it would enliven the party."

If he hadn't been staring at her he might've missed it: a slight twitch of those luscious lips. The sight sent a thrill through him. He wanted to make her smile again—that full-fledged smile that brought out her dimple.

"I'll do no such thing," Miss Stewart bit out.

"Pity. I don't see how you'll make me face my sins otherwise."

"Perhaps you need to face your sins on your own."

"Oh, I already have." He smiled humorlessly as he met her eyes. "I assure you."

Her eyes narrowed in what looked like grudging curiosity. "What do you mean?"

"Do you think I'd tell you my weaknesses?" he asked softly. "You, my adversary?"

"I'm not your…" She caught herself before she could say it, blinked, and lifted her chin.

A point to him.

"You are." He smiled. "You've taken pains to impress your antagonism upon me."

"Have I?"

He gazed at her thoughtfully. "I'm not sure how I've offended you."

"*Aren't* you?" Her voice was mocking.

His jaw clenched and he said abruptly, "I'm not, you know. A ravisher of women."

"I suppose I should simply believe you?" she inquired politely. "Because if you *were* a libertine that is *exactly* what you'd say, you realize."

"I don't recollect ever being so insulted," he said slowly, "by man or woman. Are you trying to goad me into revealing to the party what you were doing in Wapping?"

She made an abrupt movement, then stilled. Her eyes when she looked at him burned. "You have no idea what I was doing in Wapping."

"No, but I do know you don't want me speaking about it," he mused. "Otherwise I think you would've told me to go to the Devil. I don't suppose you'll tell me?"

"Tell you my secrets?" She arched her brows. "You, my adversary?"

For a moment he savored her repartee—the bright satisfaction in her eyes, the way she leaned a little forward as if waiting for him to bat back a tennis ball.

He let his lips quirk. "No, you're right. That would be most unwise. For both of us, I think."

He should stand and leave her. Go speak to another member of the party.

And yet he found something compelling about her, this seemingly ordinary woman.

Or perhaps he simply found her frank animosity refreshing.

He was about to say something else, see if he could make that dimple appear again, but there were footsteps and voices from in the hallway.

Christopher straightened, his attention entirely on the door. Had Plimpton arrived?

Two ladies entered the salon, and Christopher felt a shock of recognition that went straight to his core.

The nearest, a tall, striking woman with black hair, glanced up. For a second her gaze flickered to Miss Stewart, and then it was on him.

She walked toward them, her hands outstretched as her handsome gray eyes widened. "Christopher, darling, it's been an age since we've seen you. How are you?"

* * *

The problem with having grown up with a person was that they never forgot that once upon a time one had been a girl.

No matter how old one might be now.

Messalina Greycourt watched as Christopher Renshaw rose from his seat beside Freya. "*Messy?*"

Her eldest brother, Julian, had christened her with the ghastly nickname when she'd been five and he a very superior eleven. Sadly the name had stuck...at least until the events of her twelfth summer, when they'd lost their sister, Aurelia—and with her Julian's playfulness.

"Not even Julian calls me that anymore," she replied. "Do you remember my sister, Lucretia?"

Christopher turned to Lucretia. "Of course, though I would never have known you."

Lucretia curtsied. "I'm so glad. It would be rather lowering if I still looked the same as I did in leading strings."

That provoked what looked like a reluctant smile from Christopher.

Messalina glanced from Christopher to Freya de Moray. The two had been deep in discussion when she and her sister had entered the sitting room, and she had a multitude of questions.

The foremost among them: had Freya told Christopher why she was working as a companion? Messalina had been curious about that for *years*.

Messalina looked away from Freya and nodded at Christopher. "We knew that you'd returned to England, but we never saw you. I think Julian even invited you to tea, didn't he?"

Christopher simply shrugged. His smile was already gone.

Were he and Julian no longer speaking? If so, she'd not been aware of the rift. Although of course Christopher had been in India for all those years. And Julian was damnably closemouthed.

Messalina cleared her throat. "Do you mind if I call you by your Christian name? I'm afraid habits made in childhood are hard to shake."

She glanced at Freya and saw her former friend staring at her, a haunted look on her face. Freya turned her head before rising and quietly moving away.

Messalina couldn't help the pang of hurt. *Damn Freya de Moray.*

"Not at all," Christopher replied, bringing her attention back to him. "I can hardly stand on ceremony when you once saw me after a night of *very* unwise drinking."

She recalled her smile. "You *did* have trouble holding your liquor at sixteen."

His expression was melancholy, but then it was Ranulf de Moray who'd been his illicit drinking partner that night.

"I'd heard you'd come into the title," Messalina said to change the subject. "It was the talk of the ton for almost the entire season."

She'd heard, too, that he'd lost his wife, Lord Lovejoy's sister. What had been her name? Becky or Molly or Lizzy—

some sort of diminutive at any rate. She wondered suddenly if there was anyone to call him by his given name now. Both his parents were dead, he had no brothers or sisters, and as far as she knew he hadn't remarried.

"Yes, I inherited quite unexpectedly," he said dryly. "The last duke was a second cousin, and suffered the tragedy of his own sons and grandson leaving this world before him. My cousin was ninety when he died and appeared to have placed far too much trust in a none-too-honest man of business. The title came with two years' worth of work."

"Your Grace?"

They both turned at Lord Lovejoy's interruption.

Their host was looking apologetic. "I've word that dinner is ready. Perhaps you'd care to lead us in?"

Of course. Christopher was the ranking aristocrat.

He bowed to Messalina and strode to their hostess, offering Lady Lovejoy his arm. Lord Rookewoode, escorting Lady Holland, followed them. The rest of the company trailed behind.

Lucretia murmured beside Messalina, "Will you ask Lady Lovejoy for help tonight?"

Messalina shook her head. "Tomorrow, I think."

"Mm." Lucretia hummed. "He *is* very handsome, isn't he?"

Messalina blinked at the non sequitur. "Christopher?" She'd never thought of him in that way.

"No, not him. It's strange, I didn't recognize the duke at all."

"Well, you were only what, seven when we last saw him?"

"Eight," Lucretia said with the exactitude for age found only in the youngest members of families, "and in any case, no, that's not who I meant. I was referring to the earl." She nodded at Lord Rookewoode's back. "There's something about him that just draws a lady's eye. Though I suppose the duke is quite nice to look at as well."

"Hussy," Messalina murmured.

"I noticed that Freya is still ignoring you," Lucretia whispered.

"Is she?" Messalina replied with feigned disinterest as they came to the dining room.

They had to part to find their seats before Lucretia could call her out. Naturally they weren't seated together. Jane Lovejoy had done her best to seat them lady-gentleman-lady, and Messalina found herself between Viscount Stanhope and Mr. Lovejoy. Directly across from her was the earl, flanked on either side by Lucretia and Arabella Holland. And down at the bottom of the table was *Lady* Freya de Moray.

Messalina dipped her spoon into a lovely eel soup and considered Freya. It was rather ironic, really. As the daughter and sister of dukes she was in actuality the highest-ranking lady at the table.

Something that no one knew besides Messalina, Lucretia, and Freya herself.

And Christopher. *Had* he recognized Freya? Messalina was beginning to wonder. She glanced at him speculatively. Would Freya have told him who she was if he hadn't recognized her?

Considering how matters stood between Christopher and the de Moray family, Freya might've kept her identity to herself.

It was a possibility at least that Christopher didn't know who Freya was. Freya was no longer the skinny, tangled-haired wild lass of their youth. Now she was sedate, her adult curves confined and stifled by boring brown gowns, her red hair hidden and tamed. No doubt she fooled the vast majority of people she met, mostly by simply being over-looked.

Messalina humphed under her breath.

Freya de Moray had *never* been sedate in their youth, and she very much doubted the other woman had changed so very much in fifteen years. She didn't know why Freya was presenting herself as such a staid and boring person, but that was almost certainly *not* who Freya truly was.

And she could not ask Freya why she was essentially in disguise because, simply put, they did not speak to each other.

Messalina had first seen Freya in London society four years ago. It had been at an afternoon musicale, a quartet of string instruments or perhaps a harpsichord player, she couldn't remember now. There had been seating on either side of the entertainment, and only a few minutes in, Messalina had found herself staring across the way into the eyes of Freya de Moray.

Her best friend from childhood.

It had been a strange experience. She'd had no doubt it was Freya, even though they hadn't seen each other in years. She knew those green eyes, the shape of her chin, and the slight slope of her nose.

Freya had stared back without expression. Without recognition.

Without emotion.

As if they'd never hidden from Freya's governess or begged cakes from Cook or lain together in a dark bed, whispering their deepest secrets to each other.

As if they hadn't loved each other better than sisters.

Damn Freya.

She hadn't been the one to lose an older sister that night. Bright, sparkling Aurelia, dead at only sixteen.

That long-ago night Messalina had woken to her mother weeping, Julian's silent, white face, Lucretia confused and crying, and Aurelia's twin, Quintus, vomiting again and again until the whites of his eyes were flooded red with burst blood vessels.

No, Freya hadn't any cause to snub her. If anyone should be snubbing someone, it was Messalina. It had been Freya's brother Ran who had murdered Aurelia.

Messalina reached for her wineglass and in doing so caught Lucretia's eye. Her younger sister raised a pointed eyebrow.

Messalina nodded and inhaled to calm herself. She wasn't here to brood on Freya, their awful past, and what exactly she was doing working as a companion under an assumed name now. Messalina was here to flirt, laugh, and, most importantly, find out what had happened to a very dear friend.

Eleanor Randolph.

Lord Randolph had buried poor Eleanor without ceremony or even notice. Messalina hadn't even found out that Eleanor was dead until weeks afterward. The least she owed her friend was to find out how she had died.

Thus recalled to her mission, Messalina turned to her right and smiled at Viscount Stanhope. "I hope your travels were pleasant?"

The viscount swallowed before speaking in a marked Scottish accent. "I would not say pleasant precisely. The inns I was told to stop at were not at all as was expected. Loud and licentious behavior in the first, and in the second bed linens stinking quite terribly of mildew. I had something to say to both innkeepers, I can assure you."

"Oh, indeed?" Messalina couldn't keep her lips from twitching. Lord Stanhope sounded as if he spent quite a bit of his time complaining to innkeepers and the like. It was a pity really. He was quite a nice-looking gentleman, with wide beautiful eyes and a Roman profile—if only he didn't have a moue of distaste on his face.

"I was very happy to arrive, I can tell you that," the viscount said. "Although I think that Lady Lovejoy needs a firmer hand with her servants. There was *dust* on the picture frame in my room. Do you think I should inform her?"

"Well…" Messalina darted a glance at Jane Lovejoy. Darling Jane had eyes too small for her round face and a nose too big, making her rather plain. That hadn't stopped her from becoming a popular London hostess. She was known for her salons and balls, quite packed with the cream of society. Though she was nearly two decades older than Messalina, they'd struck up a fast friendship on first meeting. "Perhaps not tonight. Our hostess no doubt has much to do."

"Hm." Lord Stanhope's brows drew together. "I don't see what. Surely she simply needs to make conversation."

Messalina kept her smile intact with difficulty. Obviously the viscount had never planned a house party.

Fortunately she was saved from having to reply when Regina Holland said something to the viscount.

Messalina turned toward her other table mate and her eye snagged on Freya. Her former friend was staring rather intensely up the table. Messalina picked up her wineglass and took a sip to cover following Freya's line of sight. She was watching Christopher.

Interesting.

Freya had had quite a tendre for Christopher fifteen years ago, but back then she'd been in the schoolroom. Surely Freya hadn't started something with him now?

Messalina felt a pang of hurt. How could Freya forgive Christopher—who had been there that night with Julian and Ran—and not Messalina?

They'd only been children.

Back then they'd told each other everything.

Back then they'd been innocents.

CHAPTER FOUR

The princess and her three friends dismounted and entered the grotto.
Moss grew up the sides and water dripped slowly, but the cave was quite shallow.
"That's a disappointment," Rowan said, and the girls returned to the entrance.
Rowan was beside Marigold, and she noticed the strangest thing. Instead of ducking her head shyly as she'd always done, Marigold stared at her boldly and grinned....
—From *The Grey Court Changeling*

At a little past one in the morning, Freya crept from her bedroom into the narrow hallway outside. As a companion, she'd been given a small bedroom at the very end of the hall, apart from the house party guests.

Her single candle cast a wavering light on the pink-painted walls as she briskly walked to the area of the house where the guests' bedrooms were.

Where the Duke of Harlowe was.

The rest of the house party was abed early, having spent but a short time in the sitting room after dinner. Freya had watched Messalina all evening in case the other woman should suddenly reveal Freya's identity. They'd never discussed the matter—never, in fact, talked at all, even on that afternoon when they'd first seen each other in London at a musicale—but for whatever reason, Messalina had always kept Freya's secret. Sometimes late at night or when she was very tired Freya wondered if Messalina kept her secret out of love for her.

But in the cold light of day Freya knew that couldn't be the case. How could Messalina still love her when all the world thought Ran had killed Aurelia?

She sighed. This was an old sorrow—one she couldn't let distract her.

Tonight all her thoughts should be on revenge.

The corridor met another hall and Freya turned. She'd paid a maid earlier in the evening to tell her which room the duke was sleeping in. The maid had been surprisingly forthcoming without undue curiosity about *why* Freya needed the information. The maid also hadn't asked questions when Freya had given her a small satchel of powder to stir into the brandy decanter in Harlowe's room.

Uncurious servants in need of ready cash were rather a boon in her line of work.

On her right was a painting of dead birds on a table—not very well done—and after that was a portrait of a piebald horse with its groom. Freya nodded in satisfaction. Her informant had said the duke's room was the one next to the piebald horse.

Freya laid her hand on the doorknob and carefully turned it without making a sound.

Well. A sound a *human* could hear.

It wasn't until she saw the eyes at hip height reflecting back her candlelight that she remembered Tess.

Freya froze…or she started to in any case. A large, masculine hand seized her arm and dragged her into the bedroom.

She gasped as the door was closed behind her and she was shoved up against it.

Her candle was plucked from her hand.

Harlowe set the candle on a table by the door. He propped his hand on the wall and leaned over her, smiling a very untrustworthy smile. "Had I known you were coming to visit me tonight, Miss Stewart, I would've called for a tray of bonbons."

Freya glanced at the decanter of brandy, sitting on a table next to his bed.

It was full.

Blast. Why hadn't he drunk a glass before bed like every other gentleman she knew? For that matter, why ask for a brandy decanter in the room at all if one wasn't going to *drink the brandy* in it?

What a maddeningly capricious creature he was.

And that was *not* excitement rising in her breast at the realization that he was awake and ready to spar.

She put both hands on his chest and pushed.

Nothing happened.

"Let me go," she snarled at him.

"Oh dear, I *am* sorry," he said with patently false concern. "You must've mistaken the room. Were you looking for Lord Rookewoode? Or was it Lord Stanhope?"

Her nostrils flared with rage. "I—"

"No." His smile disappeared and what remained on his face was an expression that made her shiver involuntarily. "Whatever lie you were about to tell me, darling, *don't.*"

For a moment he simply stared at her and she stared back, her breaths coming faster and faster.

Tess sat down and whined under her breath.

"Now," the Duke of Harlowe said, "why are you in my rooms?"

She raised her eyebrows and said in a voice made steady only through great will, "You've already guessed, Your Grace. I find I'm overcome by a sudden tendre for you."

His mouth twisted into something ugly and for a second—just a *hair* of a second—she thought he might strike her.

Then he straightened. "Tell me, Miss Stewart, do you loathe all men or am I special?"

"Oh," she whispered, and this time she couldn't still the waver of pure hatred in her voice, "you're *very* special."

His brows drew together. They stood only inches apart. Every time he inhaled, his chest nearly touched her unbound breasts beneath her chemise and wrap. They were so close, she could almost hear his heartbeat.

They might've been lovers.

Or enemies about to kill each other.

"Do I know you?" he murmured. "Have I caused you harm in some way?"

She couldn't afford to have him recognize her.

She should apologize. Allow him to believe whatever he wished so long as he let her go and she *left*.

That was the smart thing to do.

The *responsible* thing.

Rings, memories, and revenge shouldn't matter at all.

She reached up and placed her palm gently—so gently!—against his hard cheek, feeling his bristles, and widened her eyes. "If you can't remember, I'm sure it's nothing to worry about."

His eyes began to narrow, but she rose on tiptoe, wrapped her hand around his fingers, and jerked him toward her in a single movement.

She ground her mouth against his.

His lips tasted of betrayal and wine. Night and childhood memory.

Love and loss.

The emotion he aroused in her was so profound she *almost* lost herself in the embrace.

She opened her mouth, licking across his bottom lip until his own tongue came out to tangle with hers.

Then she bit him.

"*Fuck!*" He stepped back, blood beading on his mouth, his face twisted in confusion and outrage. "You're insane."

The dog was on her feet, whining in distress.

"No. I'm not." Freya opened the door. She glanced over her shoulder at him. "Oh, and you might want to avoid the brandy."

Freya closed the door and all but ran down the corridor, her breath coming in shaky gasps. When she reached her own room she shut the door behind her and pushed a chair under the doorknob.

She sat on the side of her bed, trying to calm her heart.

Perhaps she *was* insane.

For five years she'd been nothing but dull and circumspect, polite and utterly forgettable. She'd served the Wise Women well as the Macha. Every step she took, every word she spoke, was considered carefully so she would not be revealed. She had a mission that was *vitally* important to the continued existence of the Wise Women.

And yet in less than twelve hours she'd thrown all that away.

Freya opened her hand. Nestled in her palm was Ran's ring. She'd wrested it from Harlowe's finger when she'd bitten him.

She held it up, studying the worn gold of the band. It was a signet ring with a carved onyx meant to be used to seal wax. The intaglio was of a bird of prey. The bird, worn about the edges, might've been a falcon or even a hawk, but Freya knew that it was a merlin.

The de Moray family symbol.

Merlins were the smallest of the falcons. Swift and ruthless, merlins caught other, smaller birds on the wing before landing and devouring their prey.

This ring had been worn by generations of de Moray men, including her own papa before he'd given it to Ranulf on his eighteenth birthday.

Freya closed the ring in her fist again. No doubt Harlowe would soon realize his ring was gone.

Too bad.

He might be a duke now, but she was a de Moray woman, small, swift, and above all *ruthless*.

* * *

It was barely light the next morning when Freya slipped out the back door of Lovejoy House. A misty fog lingered just above the wet grass, swirling around her skirts as she walked across the lawn. Last night she'd let herself be distracted by rage and revenge and that damnable *kiss*.

She touched Ran's ring, strung on an old silver chain about her neck, then tucked it under her fichu. Memories and regret and whatever that *feeling* was that Harlowe provoked in her. Today she had to put aside all of that. She was a Wise Woman, and she had a mission to complete.

To that end she was headed to Randolph lands. Lady Randolph had been buried on unconsecrated ground within the estate—an odd choice—and Freya wanted to see the grave.

The lawn ended abruptly at the edge of an overgrown wood. Freya paused, eyeing the trail that led into the dim interior. It reminded her a bit of the sorts of woods that had featured prominently in her nursemaid's fairy tales: dark, forbidding, and wild. Nothing good had ever happened in those fairy-tale woods.

She glanced behind her.

The sun had fully risen, shining brightly on the dewed lawn and a formal garden surrounded by a tall hedge. It seemed a bit odd that the woods so close to the house should be untended.

Still. She had only a few hours before the rest of the party rose.

She stepped into the woods.

There was a trail, thank goodness, though it looked little used. Around her the wood was oddly quiet for daybreak. Where were the singing birds? She hastened her step—and not entirely because she was worried about the time.

Five minutes later she saw sunlight and stepped into a clearing. To one side was a small stone structure, and for a moment her hopes rose, though she couldn't have crossed into Randolph land yet. Then she saw that the building wasn't a mausoleum. She hesitated, staring at it, but she would run out of time if she didn't keep going, so she crossed the clearing and continued through the woods.

It was another fifteen minutes before the woods began to thin. Freya emerged onto a small hill overlooking what must be the Randolph estate. She could see a manor, probably half the size of Lovejoy House, but still grand. There were stables behind the house and a garden that looked in need of tending.

She followed the path toward the manor, wondering where Lady Randolph might be buried. Perhaps on the other side of the house? She could see a drive disappearing into trees. It must lead to the same road that passed by Lovejoy House.

A thorn pricked at her calf and she bent to pull it from her skirts.

Someone cleared their throat.

Freya straightened to see a man walking toward her with a musket over his shoulder.

She might've been afraid had he not been positively ancient.

"You there," the man wheezed as he came closer, "what're ye doin' on Randolph land?"

"I beg your pardon," she replied with her most disarming smile. "I had no idea I was trespassing." Freya gestured to the wood behind her. "I'm a guest at Lovejoy House."

"Are ye, then?" The old man paused, hawked quite disgustingly, and spit to the side of the path. "Beggin' yer pardon then, miss. Have to be vigilant-like, as it's my job as gamekeeper. Right early for a stroll, though, isn't it?"

"Oh, it is," Freya assured him earnestly. "But I do so like to take a brisk walk at sunrise. I believe it's good for the constitution."

"Argh," the man replied, rather enigmatically.

"I understand that Lord Elliot Randolph lives here," Freya said.

"Aye, so he does, though m'lord's not here now."

"Really? I'm afraid I've not had the honor of an introduction to Lord Randolph, but I *did* converse with his wife once or twice," Freya lied outrageously. She'd seen Lady Randolph at a few social events, but she'd never spoken to her. "I thought it such a pity..." She paused delicately.

The old man snapped up the bait. "Oh aye, 'tis a tragedy one so pretty should die young." He shifted, placing the butt of his musket on the ground and leaning on it. "Course she weren't quite right at the end." He eyed her expectantly.

Freya hastened to prompt him. "Oh?"

"Aye," he replied with the relish of a good gossip. "Shoutin' and carrying on and the like as if she were bedeviled. Heard it from the head footman himself. *And* His Lordship not one to like a fuss. Why 'tis said she was quite mad, the poor lassie. Went running through the stable yard near naked. Wearing just her shift she were, her hair all about her shoulders. They say up there"—he tilted his head to the manor—"that she caught an ague after that. Died the next night, she did."

"My goodness," Freya murmured, placing her hand to her chest and hoping she wasn't overacting. "How shocking! I suppose Lord Randolph must've consulted with all the best doctors about his ill wife?"

"Nay." The gamekeeper shook his head. "Wasn't time, was there? Caught ague, was abed with fever, and dead the next day."

"What a tragedy for Lord Randolph. He must be devastated."

"Well, aye," the man said, but he sounded doubtful. "The rich do things different, I understand. He left directly after she were buried." He nodded in the general direction of the house. "She's right there, across the garden."

Freya feigned surprise. "Lady Randolph was buried here?"

"She were." The old man leaned closer. "Afore sundown on the same day she died. They say her body were putrid. Rotted as if it were weeks old rather than a day." He nodded and straightened. "Most like because of her brain sickness."

Freya wasn't sure how madness would make a corpse decay faster, but she wasn't about to argue. "My!"

"Would you like to see?" The groundskeeper beamed, and at first Freya had the horrible thought that he was talking about Lady Randolph's *remains*.

Then her common sense reasserted itself. "Oh yes, I'd like to visit her grave and pay my respects."

The old man turned without further ado and led her down the shallow slope and to the house.

Randolph House might not be as large as Lovejoy House, but there was something forbidding about it nonetheless. Perhaps it was the dark reddish brown of the stones used to build it, the color of dried blood. Or maybe it was the small, narrow windows. There could be little light let inside the house, Freya thought. It would be a dark, gloomy place.

They rounded the corner of the building, stepping through a sadly overgrown cobblestoned yard. No one stirred. The house in fact seemed empty.

"Are there any staff at the house now?" she called softly to the gamekeeper.

He shrugged but didn't turn. "The housekeeper, Mrs. Sprattle, the butler—what is her father, old man Deacon— and a maid or two."

Behind his back Freya raised her eyebrows. Most manors had dozens of servants working, even when the master wasn't in residence. Lord Randolph must be a parsimonious sort of man.

In the back of the manor was what had once been a formal garden but was now rather sad and messy. To the side was a small stone. Had Freya not been expecting the grave she would've entirely overlooked it.

They walked to it and paused, silently regarding the simple gravestone. Under a crude bas-relief of a skull were the words:

HERE LIETH THE BODY OF
ELEANOR RANDOLPH
WHO LEFT THIS WORLD APRIL 2, 1759
MAY GOD GRANT HER FORGIVENESS

"Forgiveness for what?" Freya whispered.

"Her earthly sins?" The gamekeeper shook his head and spit—fortunately not on the grave. "Mayhap she did something in her madness that needs forgiving."

"Such as?"

"Don't know," the man said, suddenly looking cagey. "But she's a restless spirit, she is. Sometimes at dusk, just when the nightjars come out, I've heard a wailing."

He made a gesture against his side and Freya glanced down.

His fingers were crossed—an ancient sign in this part of the world. To ward off evil and the devil.

And witches.

* * *

Christopher woke gasping.

The room was black and he could feel the press of hot, sweating bodies. The stink of urine and wet earth. The sound of panting and moans.

Then Tess stuck her cold nose in his ear and reality came rushing back.

Christopher sagged back against the damp sheets, feeling the sweat chilling on his arms and neck. He reached up and stroked Tess's warm head.

He ought to order her off the bed, but he hadn't the heart. She must've known he was having another nightmare and crawled up beside him to show her concern.

She whined as if to agree.

"It's all right," he said to her, his voice cracking. He cleared his throat. "I'm all right."

Tess huffed and nosed his cheek.

Obviously he hadn't convinced her. Perhaps because his fingers were *trembling*.

God. This was unacceptable. It'd been four years now. He'd returned to England, he'd become a duke, he held power and wealth in the palm of his hand.

And at night he shook.

He grimaced and looked at the window. There was a sliver of light peeking from behind the drawn curtains, so it must be morning. Early yet, but he wouldn't be able to fall back asleep again.

He never could.

Christopher sat up and Tess jumped off the bed, making it quake. She stood looking hopefully at him.

"Very well," he muttered to her, and stood.

She watched him intently as he shaved with cold water and dressed hastily. Gardiner, his valet, would be most disapproving when he found out his master had readied himself on his own.

At the moment Christopher didn't give a damn. He slapped his thigh and strode out the door, Tess eagerly trotting beside him.

The house was still quiet, except for a few housemaids tiptoeing around with ash buckets. They would be sweeping the grates and lighting fires. A footman showed him the way to a door at the side of the house, and then Tess and he were outside in the brisk morning air.

Lovejoy House was surrounded by carefully tended lawns, but Christopher could see a wood beyond and he started toward it.

As he walked he thought about last night. About Miss Stewart—and that kiss. Her lips had been soft and giving—until she'd bitten his mouth bloody and stolen his ring. How could such a sour woman kiss so sweetly—even when pretending attraction?

He scoffed to himself. He was a fool to be taken in by her

for even so much as a minute. She'd made it clear enough that she had no interest in him as a man and in fact loathed him. She'd only been after his ring.

The thought made him melancholy.

Miss Stewart—what *was* her given name?—had twisted the ring off his finger sometime during their kiss. He'd been so angered by the goddamned *bite* that he hadn't noticed for a crucial few minutes that his ring was gone.

Which had been enough time for her to disappear.

Was she some sort of thief disguised as a companion? Was that why the bullies in Wapping had been chasing her— because she'd stolen something from them? But he discarded the thought as soon as it came. A thief with any intelligence would hide the theft. Miss Stewart had made no attempt to.

It was almost as if she were *goading* him.

He grimaced as he entered the wood with Tess running ahead.

In his rage he'd nearly chased Miss Stewart down last night.

He inhaled and kicked a rock in the path. Something about her prodded him to the very edge of his control as no one—no *woman*—had ever done before. Her hostility, the excitement of their clashes, his curiosity about what she was doing, *something*, made him feel as if he were waking from a long, drugged sleep. Opening his eyes wide to the light of her pure *passion*.

Thankfully his reason had ruled last night. No point in causing an uproar in the wee hours.

Besides. He didn't know which room was hers.

He snorted now at his own stupidity. That ring—*Ran's* ring—was important.

Tess came running up, her tongue hanging half out of her

jaws, panting happily. He absently fondled her ears and she went racing off again.

Julian had given him the ring on that night at Greycourt. It must've fallen off Ran's hand as he was beaten. Julian had bent down and picked up the ring after the Duke of Windemere's toughs had dragged Ran away, after the duke had sauntered off, and after Christopher had realized—far too late—what a terrible mistake he'd made. Ran could never have killed Aurelia. Christopher had known that then as he knew it now, but he'd been paralyzed by the sudden violence and the urgent way that Julian had told him not to interfere.

There had been fear in Julian's eyes that night.

No, someone else must have murdered poor Aurelia—perhaps a stranger or a servant. That was the best conclusion, for if it hadn't been a stranger or servant that terrible night, then a person far closer to Aurelia had snatched away her life. Perhaps Julian.

Perhaps the Duke of Windemere himself.

Christopher shook his head and remembered the way Julian had looked at Ran's ring that night. His face had been both sad and determined. Then he'd drawn back his arm as if to throw the ring. Christopher had caught his hand and Julian had looked at him and then given him the ring.

Ran's ring.

Christopher had meant to give it back to Ran. But he'd been immediately caught up in his arranged marriage and shipped off to India still bewildered, and by then he'd grown used to the ring on his finger.

Like a criminal's brand.

The beating was so long ago now, but at the same time it was forever near. That night—that *damnable* night—had changed him forever.

Had changed them all.

The ring was a reminder of that. Of how utterly he'd once failed as a friend and a gentleman, and how he had to spend the rest of his life making sure he never did so again.

He had to get his ring back from the harpy. He could simply inform Miss Stewart's employer of her theft. Her rooms would be searched and the ring found, and no doubt she'd be let go without reference.

Somehow that method seemed unsporting. Miss Stewart was brave, if nothing else. Quite possibly mad, but brave.

No, the matter was a personal one between the two of them, and he'd handle it the same way: *personally*.

Tess barked and continued barking in that joyful way dogs had to signal they'd found something *important*. She was out of sight beyond a turn in the path, and Christopher quickened his step. Just in case she'd done something silly such as cornered a badger.

He rounded the bend and saw that what Tess had found was a bit bigger than a badger. She was circling an ancient building, like a stone house for Lilliputians, squat and immovable. *Strange.* It was standing here all alone in a clearing.

But as he approached, Christopher discovered stones half-hidden in the leaves under his feet. He scuffed aside the leaves and could see that the buried stones were the remains of walls. Something had once stood beside the little structure—a house, perhaps? He reached Tess and followed her around the building. There were no windows, and the doorway was only to his shoulder. Christopher peered at the padlocked door and saw that over it was a crude carving of a waterspout.

Of course. This must be a well house, built over a well both for safety's sake and to keep the water untainted.

He glanced at the ruined walls he'd uncovered. The little building appeared to have survived the house it had belonged to.

Christopher shook his head and whistled for Tess. She raised her head from where she was sniffing the foundation, but she wasn't looking his way. She was focused on something farther in the woods.

Suddenly Tess was off, dashing ahead on the trail.

Christopher swore under his breath. If she was on the scent of a rabbit he might lose her in the trees.

"Tess!" He loped after her. "Tess!"

A single bark came from ahead of him, and then he rounded a bend in the trail and saw the dog's quarry.

His idiot dog was standing by Miss Stewart's side, tongue lolling happily, as the woman ruffled Tess's ears.

Miss Stewart glanced up and saw him. "Good morning, Your Grace."

She seemed perfectly composed, as if the events of last night had never happened.

As if he hadn't tasted her mouth. As if she hadn't taken his lip between her teeth.

As if she hadn't stolen his ring.

"Miss Stewart." He wondered if her heart beat as savagely as his beneath the layers of wool and linen. "I believe you have something of mine."

"*Do* I?" she answered carelessly, and he wanted to either laugh or strangle her.

"You know you do," he said, advancing on her. "I don't want to bring your unconventional activities to the attention of your employer, but don't think I won't."

That got her attention. Her head went back and she stared at him with loathing and defiance in her eyes, which, oddly, made his cock twitch.

Before she could reply, though, Tess barked once, staring behind him.

Christopher turned, hiding his irritation at the interruption.

Messalina Greycourt was approaching along the path. "Christopher! I had no idea anyone else was about this morning."

Her gaze went beyond him, and a strange expression crossed her face.

He glanced at Miss Stewart, but she was merely standing there, her hand on Tess's head and her face blank.

When he looked back at Messalina, her expression was calm.

Did she think he was having an assignation with Miss Stewart? Surely not. They weren't even standing near each other.

"And...Miss Stewart, is it not?" Messalina asked.

"It is," the chaperone replied, almost with significance.

What the hell? He whistled to Tess and both ladies jumped.

Tess trotted over.

He fondled her ears before saying to Messalina, "I'm thinking Tess will be wanting her breakfast. Will you walk back with us?"

"Yes," Messalina said, a smile suddenly lighting her face. "I will."

They tramped back side by side with Tess running ahead, but Christopher was aware at every moment of Miss Stewart, trailing behind like a malevolent cloud. It was strange. Messalina had grown into one of the loveliest ladies that Christopher had ever met. Her conversation was amusing and he knew her to be intelligent. She was, in fact, a beguiling lady.

But it was the silent termagant behind him who made him want to shove her up against a tree and taste her mouth.

It made no sense, and he found his mood turning black. Why should he be so viscerally attracted to a woman who couldn't stand him?

And why did she refuse to soften to him?

By the time they made it back to Lovejoy House the sun was well into the sky and Christopher was using all his determination not to turn and confront Miss Stewart again—even with Messalina as witness. He glanced up as they turned the corner of the house and saw a rather old-fashioned carriage enter the drive in front.

"Oh, who do you suppose that is?" Messalina asked. "It seems a strange time to arrive to a house party, doesn't it?"

A man in a rumpled bottle-green suit descended. He turned, and Christopher couldn't stop his upper lip from curling. For a moment all thought of Miss Stewart fled his mind.

Thomas Plimpton had finally arrived.

CHAPTER FIVE

*Marigold was strangely changed. She was no
longer shy, but stood tall and looked others in the
eye, a secretive smile about her lips.
Rowan began to think that Marigold was no longer
the same girl.
That she wasn't Marigold but something else.
But the strangest thing of all was that no one else
seemed to notice....*
—From *The Grey Court Changeling*

"I do hope you all won't consider it *too* rustical, but I thought we'd take a stroll into Newbridge today," Lady Lovejoy announced at breakfast an hour later. "There's a rather lovely Norman church and today is market day. Nothing like London, of course, but quite quaint."

Freya spread a slice of bread with fresh butter—sweet and lovely—and wondered if she might gather more rumors about Lady Randolph in Newbridge.

"Oh, let's!" Regina exclaimed, leaning forward eagerly and imperiling her teacup.

"A country market can be so interesting sometimes," Lucretia Greycourt observed. "I once was offered what I was assured was a potion to arouse lust in gentlemen by a wrinkled old woman with quite a staggering amount of moles on her chin. The kind that sprout hairs. I do believe she thought herself a witch."

Lord Lovejoy cleared his throat portentously. "One oughtn't discount the evil of witches in this part of England."

Freya found herself glancing at Harlowe and caught him staring back, a smoldering intensity in his eyes.

She swiftly averted her gaze, realizing as she did so that she was holding her breath. He'd threatened to expose her. At the time she'd felt only rage, but now cold fear made her back prickle. She hadn't completed her mission.

She needed more time.

"*Real* witches?" Messalina asked with polite skepticism. "The sort who dance about fires naked at midnight?"

Young Mr. Lovejoy chuckled, but he sounded a tad nervous.

Lady Holland frowned—probably at the mention of nude cavorting.

But Lord Lovejoy was quite grave. "Nearly every year a woman is brought before me as the local magistrate and charged with witchcraft."

The Earl of Rookewoode arched a black eyebrow. It made a stark contrast to his snowy wig. He wore an elegantly cut dark-blue suit today and looked exceedingly handsome and urbane. "But Parliament has made witch-hunting no longer legal."

"Oh, indeed, my lord," Lord Lovejoy replied. "But these are provincial people who adhere to the old ways. They care not for London's laws."

"London's laws will soon change," Lord Stanhope said importantly. "A new Witch Act is to be put before Parliament in the autumn, making witch-hunting once again both legal *and* encouraged."

There was a short silence as everyone at the table digested that.

Freya's hands were clenched in her lap, where no one could see them. She only hoped her expression didn't give away her unease at this discussion.

"And thus we descend back into the superstitious Dark Ages," Rookewoode drawled.

The viscount pursed his lips together as if cutting off a nasty reply.

Lord Lovejoy looked troubled. "Hunting witches is no step back in these parts. Not when nearly everyone believes in them."

The earl's lips twitched as if he were amused by the discussion, but he asked gravely, "What do you do when you're presented with a supposed witch, if you don't mind me asking?"

"Naturally I have to dismiss the cases, but that doesn't keep the people from believing most sincerely in witchcraft," Lord Lovejoy replied. "You have to understand that these people blame witches for sickened sheep, blighted crops, and miscarriages. Even if I can't convict them, often the accused witch's house is burned or they meet with some other misadventure." He shrugged. "It's a sort of rough justice, I suppose."

"But surely these women are innocent, my lord?" Messalina objected, looking quite appalled.

"One shouldn't discount the strength of the devil or his subjects," Lord Stanhope muttered. "No doubt these people have reasons for chasing away these ungodly women."

Freya glared at him from under her eyelashes. What a horrible man. She'd met his sort before, and though she should be wary of him, what she truly felt was indignant anger.

The door opened and a pleasant-faced gentleman entered.

"Ah," Lord Lovejoy exclaimed. "Our newest guest. May I present Mr. Thomas Plimpton?"

Mr. Plimpton smiled and bowed and then took a seat next to Arabella, saying something to her as he sat that made her blush.

Once again Freya glanced at Harlowe without conscious thought. This time, though, she was not the center of his attention. Now he was staring malevolently at Mr. Plimpton.

Freya took a sip of tea. Whatever had the rather nondescript Mr. Plimpton done to offend the duke? She was almost piqued that his attention was divided.

"We had just made plans to visit Newbridge today," Lady Lovejoy said after an awkward pause. "Would you care to join us, Mr. Plimpton? We have a lovely Norman church and other country sights."

"Of course," that gentleman replied.

Which was how, half an hour later, they all set off to the little town nearby.

Freya walked behind Arabella and Lucretia Greycourt. The two girls hadn't met until the day before, but had somehow already found a close bond.

She was aware of Messalina in quiet conversation with Lady Lovejoy, slightly ahead and to the side. Messalina wore an elegant walking dress, the rose-pink overskirts pulled back and bunched in deceptively casual disarray in the back. Her yellow underskirt was revealed, scattered with tiny knots of embroidered roses.

It was a beautiful dress, although with her olive complexion and black hair Freya privately thought Messalina would do better in richer colors. But yes, she was beautiful.

She could admit that.

Her childhood friend had grown into a strikingly handsome lady only a little taller than Freya.

In another life they might be walking arm in arm down this country road.

"I hadn't taken you for a thief," Harlowe growled in her ear, and Freya was hard-pressed not to jump.

She took a deep breath, trying to slow the wild beat of her heart. Stupid to have lost track of where he was in their little party. "I'm not a thief."

He waved his hand in front of her nose, and it took her a moment to realize it was the hand he'd worn Ran's ring on.

She could feel heat enter her cheeks, which only made her defensive. There was no reason for her to feel guilty. "I'm *not*."

"Then you won't mind returning to me *my* ring." He faced forward, his aristocratic profile cold and heartless.

"It's not *your* ring," she replied, her voice calm. They trailed the rest of the house party, but she didn't want to draw anyone's attention.

Harlowe stalked along beside her, a dark cloud on an otherwise beautiful day. The sun was out, not too hot, not too cold, and with a gentle breeze. The hedges along the road were full of wild roses, exuberantly in bloom, and the sky was blue and wide.

She'd grown up in the country. In the Scottish Lowlands just across the border. She and Messalina had loved to walk or ride through the Scottish hills, and for a moment longing filled her breast—whether for Scotland or the innocent days of her childhood she wasn't entirely certain.

Beside her, Harlowe cleared his throat. "I can lend you money if you're in need of it."

Her brows rose. "I don't need your money."

"Don't you?" He glanced at her quickly. "Then why steal my ring?"

"I don't intend to *sell* it," she snapped.

"You are the most irritating woman," he said softly, his expression not changing at all. "Admit you need my help and I'll give it to you."

"Even if I *did* need your help," she replied through gritted teeth, "I would never ask you for it."

"*Darling*," he rumbled, his deep purr raising the hairs on the back of her neck. "Don't press—"

He was interrupted by his dog bursting from beneath a hedge and running straight into his legs.

Freya couldn't help it; she laughed.

"Get down, Tess," Harlowe muttered, but his hands were gentle as he scrubbed her ears.

The dog shook herself happily, then shoved her nose into Freya's skirts.

"Tess," Harlowe growled.

"She's all right," Freya murmured. She might dislike the master, but she had nothing against the dog.

She scratched Tess beneath the chin.

Tess wagged her tail.

"She's dirty," Harlowe said gruffly.

"Dogs like being dirty," Freya replied, scratching Tess's ears now.

Harlowe looked at her oddly.

Tess's ears perked, and then she wheeled and went running off into the shrubbery again.

"What sort of dog is she?" Freya asked impulsively, wiping her hands on a handkerchief. The dog *had* been rather muddy.

"Indian."

Freya's brows rose. "You brought her all the way back from India?"

He shrugged. "She's my dog. I couldn't leave her there."

She stared at him. Of *course* he could've left Tess across the sea when he'd returned home to England. Gentlemen did it all the time. "Is she a special sort of dog? An Indian dog of aristocratic breed?"

He turned his head and grinned at her, two dimples incised into his cheeks.

Freya blinked, feeling as if she'd been hit in the chest. Harlowe was absolutely devastating when he smiled.

But he didn't seem to notice her reaction. "She's a street dog, quite common in India. Her dam whelped in the fort three years ago. Tess was the sole survivor of the puppies. She was only two months old when her mother disappeared—too young to survive on her own—so I brought her into the house and a year later to England."

She stared at him. "Didn't your wife object? Many ladies prefer small lapdogs to larger animals, let alone a stray dog."

A muscle in his jaw flexed. "Sophy died a year before Tess was born."

"Oh." It was obviously a topic he didn't want to talk about. His voice held sadness when he said his wife's name.

Which shouldn't bother her at all.

Up ahead someone laughed loudly. Mr. Plimpton had angled himself between Arabella and Lucretia.

Harlowe cursed beneath his breath.

Freya threw him a startled glance. "I collect you don't like Mr. Plimpton."

"He shouldn't be allowed near ladies," the duke replied, not bothering to lower his voice. "You should warn Lady Holland."

Freya's brows drew together. Arabella was well dowered and Freya had no doubt that Lucretia, as the niece of a duke, was as well.

In fact both girls were heiresses and thus prime pluckings for a fortune hunter.

"Why do you say that?" Freya asked worriedly. "What do you know of him?"

He shook his head. "He once dallied with the heart of a lady I knew."

Freya frowned. "I've never heard anything against him. Why isn't this common knowledge if what you say is true?"

"You needn't take my word for it, madam." He glanced at her, his eyes no longer friendly. "I'm losing patience. Give me back my ring by midnight tonight or I'll tell Lady Holland how I *first* met you."

And with that he lengthened his stride, drawing ahead of her.

Freya stared after him, angry, frightened, and a bit disappointed that he so obviously didn't care to walk with her anymore.

Silly.

The last thing she wanted was to become further involved with His Grace the Duke of Harlowe. He was her *enemy*. And now she must find a way to put him off *without* giving him Ran's ring.

Messalina happened to look over her shoulder at that moment and caught Freya's eye. She smiled tentatively.

Freya glanced away and felt a shard of pain through her breast.

It was so tiring. So useless and fraught, and it would never end, would it?

What had happened at Greycourt fifteen years ago would reverberate forever in their lives.

The thought was a weight on her shoulders. If only she could put it down. Forget.

But there was no forgetting, was there?

Aurelia was murdered.

Ranulf maimed.

And Papa dead from a broken heart.

The world could not go back from that one point in their history.

Freya inhaled and straightened, looking up. Messalina was no longer glancing back, and she saw that they were at the outskirts of the town.

There were wagons on the road, laden with goods to be sold at the market, and a boy driving a half dozen geese in the same direction.

Their little group moved off the road and onto a walking path, and in the shuffle Freya found herself beside Lady Holland.

Freya leaned close. "I've heard that Mr. Plimpton is not a suitable gentleman."

Lady Holland's dark eyebrows shot up at the news. "Good gracious. I can't believe Lady Lovejoy would invite the man if she knew of such a thing."

"Perhaps she doesn't, my lady."

Lady Holland frowned at Mr. Plimpton's back. He was whispering something to Lucretia now. "She dashed well *should*. Drat. That reduces the eligible gentlemen to only four."

Freya murmured, "I'm not sure Lord Stanhope is..."

Lady Holland waved a hand. "I know. I know. The man's a toad. I shouldn't count him and that makes only *three* now and with the Misses Greycourt in attendance hardly a level playing field for my Arabella."

"Arabella has much to recommend her," Freya said.

"Not least her dowry," the older woman murmured. "Oh, don't look at me like that, Miss Stewart. I love my daughter, but I'm also a practical mother. Arabella doesn't shine in company—particularly vivacious company." She shot another look at the trio ahead of them. Mr. Plimpton was laughing at something Lucretia had said while Arabella looked on with a faint smile. "I want her *happy* and with a gentleman who will care for her."

Freya cleared her throat delicately. "Have you thought what you will do if we cannot find a gentleman good enough for her?"

"I can't let myself do that, Miss Stewart," Lady Holland said. "A lady of Arabella's rank without a husband lives but a half life—at least I'm sure that's what Lord Holland would say."

"She'd have to live with Regina eventually, wouldn't she?"

"Quite. And that, I'm afraid, is a recipe for discord."

Freya frowned. There was another option for Arabella, of course. Freya could offer her sanctuary with the Wise Women in Dornoch. Arabella could learn their ways, perhaps find a calling in silversmithing, weaving, beekeeping, or any of the many other traditional Wise Women occupations. She could even find something entirely unique to do— all were welcome as long as they contributed to the community. But in exchange Arabella would have to give up her present life. Live in faraway Scotland and never, ever tell her family or friends about the Wise Women.

Lady Holland looked up as they entered the crowded town square. "Oh, here we are at last."

Ahead of them, Arabella and Lucretia had stopped by a woman selling hot buns while Mr. Plimpton had moved on to charming Messalina and Lady Lovejoy. The man was a menace, and Freya felt grudgingly thankful to Harlowe for warning her. She knew that Lady Holland would have a quiet word not only with her own daughters, but also with Messalina and Lucretia tonight.

"Would you like one?" Arabella smiled, indicating the currant buns, as Freya came abreast of them.

"Thank you," Freya replied. She met Lucretia's curious gaze and looked away. Lucretia had been only eight when the Greycourt tragedy happened—a mischievous girl who had often tagged along with Freya and Messalina, determined not to miss any excitement. They'd sometimes hid from little Lucretia in that cruel way older children had, but there had been other days when Freya had spent whole afternoons teaching Lucretia to look for birds' nests in the heather.

The stab of melancholy? longing? *regret?* was sudden and overwhelming.

Freya turned to survey the market.

On one side of the square was an inn with a painted sign proclaiming it the Swan. In the center of the square was an ancient fountain. And on the other side was the Norman church. Stalls and carts were crowded all the way around the fountain, the owners bawling their wares. Here was a woman selling onions and leeks, there a man with a string of fresh sausages, and farther on a man sharpening knives, his foot furiously working his grindstone. People crowded the little town square, no doubt come from several miles around.

Someone must have information about Lady Randolph here.

Freya trailed behind Arabella and Lucretia, eyeing the various stalls. She decided on an elderly woman hawking vegetables, berries, and small bunches of flowers.

"Fine strawberries I have," the woman cried as Freya stopped before her.

Freya smiled as she looked at the berries, temptingly displayed. "You must be the strawberry woman my friend Lady Randolph told me about. She spoke highly of you."

The old woman's toothless smile faltered before she rallied. "Aye, I have the sweetest strawberries of any in a day's ride."

Freya glanced up, meeting her eyes. "That's exactly what Lady Randolph said. But I'm thinking of buying one of your posies today."

The woman had been eyeing her nervously but perked up at the prospect of a sale. "Pick the one you like, mistress, only a halfpenny a bunch."

"Well, then I'll have three," Freya replied, opening her purse. She held out a shilling. "Someone told me that my friend died of a strange disease. Do you know aught of it, mother?"

The old woman eyed her hand for a second. Then with a quick look right and left she snatched the shilling. "Weren't disease what killed her, my lady."

"Witchcraft, then?" Freya murmured to test her.

The old woman surprised her with a derisive snort. "No, nor witchcraft, either. 'Twas the sins of a man that laid her low. And now you must move away, mistress." She tilted her head in the direction of the stall next to hers. A young man was openly staring at them. "This talk is dangerous."

Freya nodded and took her posies, sticking one in the top of her fichu where the ends crossed over her chest. Then she wandered away from the old woman's stall, handing the other two posies to a couple of small girls who giggled at the gift.

Sins of a man. Had Lady Randolph taken a lover before she died? If so, it would give Lord Randolph one of the oldest reasons for murder.

She glanced at the crowd, looking for the best person to approach next, and glimpsed Arabella's bright gold hair. She was standing next to Lord Rookewoode, her face tilted up, her expression painfully open. The earl was handing her some sort of pastry from the stall in front of them, his smile framed by devilish dimples.

The man was dangerous.

Freya bit her lip. No doubt Lady Holland would be pleased if that resulted in a match.

Freya was less certain.

She turned away and saw Harlowe, standing at the edge of the market crowd, his hand on Tess's head. He was looking around the marketplace as well, and even from across the square Freya thought he looked tense.

How strange.

She started in his direction and then heard a particular cry.

"Ribbons and trim! Pretty ribbons and trim I have!"

She glanced at the crier.

It was a woman dressed in a ragged black cloak with a gray hood. She stood beside a cart drawn by an enormous dog, a shaggy gray-and-white lurcher. The cart was filled with her wares. The woman looked up, and Freya recognized the Crow.

What was she doing here? Freya had had no notice of a meeting.

She strolled over.

"Will ye have a pretty blue ribbon, mistress?" the Crow called loudly, her black eyes glinting. "I have sky blue and sea blue and robin's-egg blue."

Freya peered in the cart. She fingered one of the ribbons tied loosely to a pole. "Have you green? A nice grass green?"

The woman met Freya's eyes. "O' course."

She bent over her cart to rummage in a box and Freya leaned closer, taking care that her expression remain the same when the Crow whispered, "I've news that someone at the house party is a Dunkelder."

"Who?" Freya murmured as she held up a ribbon, squinting at it.

"I don't know," the Crow said, and then louder, "Only two a penny, mistress. An' if you buy four I'll give you the fifth free."

"Does the Dunkelder know who I am?" Freya asked, ducking her head as her breath came faster.

The Crow murmured, "I don't think so. But should he find that you're a de Moray he'll know all." Her black eyes flicked up. "And this is Dunkelder territory. There'll be others. Walk softly."

Freya stared blindly at the colorful ribbons in her hand.

"Lady Macha," the Crow whispered. "I cannot stay here. I've other business to see to. You're on your own."

Freya met the other woman's worried gaze. "I'll be fine."

She fumbled for a coin from her purse and took the ribbons.

"Be careful," the other woman warned as Freya turned to go. "If the Dunkelder finds out who you are, he'll kill you."

* * *

Christopher watched as the members of the house party scattered about the town market. He followed, winding through the crowd, keeping an eye on Plimpton and trying to ignore the press of all the bodies around him. Plimpton was ushering Lady Lovejoy about as if he had not a care in the world, damn him.

Someone jostled his elbow.

Christopher turned, his upper lip lifted in a snarl, and the youth who had run into him stepped back. "Beg your pardon, m'lord."

The boy hurried off.

Christopher closed his eyes and took a deep breath, smelling the stink of too many bodies, feeling the pounding of a headache start.

When he opened them again, he saw Miss Stewart across the square staring at him. *Damn her.*

He turned away, shame making his neck hot. Why must it be she to see his weakness?

Tess whimpered and pressed against his leg.

He dropped his hand to her head, letting her soft fur calm him. This was England. The crowd wasn't pressed together here. There was no danger of suffocation. And he shouldn't care one whit what the bloody little thief thought of him.

Still. Coming along on this outing hadn't been a good plan.

He blew out his breath and searched for Plimpton. Lady Lovejoy was walking ahead, arm in arm with Messalina now, while Plimpton had fallen behind as he peered at a stall selling penknives.

Christopher pushed his way through the crowd to get to Plimpton.

"Do you have them?" he asked when he reached the other man's side.

Plimpton started as if a gun had gone off beside him.

He turned, wincing delicately as if Christopher had made a particularly egregious faux pas. "I think we need privacy for this discussion, don't you, Your Grace?"

"I think I want this done with as soon as possible," Christopher retorted. "When we return to the house, for example."

He saw Plimpton swallow. Evidently the man hadn't expected Christopher to demand the letters immediately.

"Erm...b-but that won't do."

"Why not? Do you have the letters or don't you?" Christopher's upper lip curled.

Plimpton's gaze slid away. "A-as a matter of fact, I shan't have them until another few days, when the post delivers them to me."

"What game are you playing?" Christopher snarled quietly.

"No game!" Plimpton licked his lips nervously. "Truly! I thought it safest to travel separately from the letters, that's all. I'll have them very soon and then I'll send you a note to meet."

It sounded like a load of balderdash, but then Plimpton had never struck Christopher as very bright. Perhaps he *had* chosen such a convoluted way to bring the letters to Lovejoy House.

"Take care you don't forget," Christopher said through gritted teeth. "Else I'll take matters into my own hands."

"Is that a threat?" Plimpton's face had gone white. "Are you *threatening* me?"

He leaned forward and flicked a nonexistent speck off Plimpton's coat front, murmuring, "If I've left you in any doubt, I do apologize."

Christopher pivoted to make his way through the mass of people and saw, not half a dozen feet away, Miss Stewart hastily turning away.

Had she overheard their conversation?

It was the last straw in a trying morning. He wasn't about to let Miss Stewart's curiosity mar Sophy's name.

He strode to Miss Stewart and pointedly offered his arm. "Will you walk with me?"

She opened her mouth, looking mulish.

He stretched his lips in a parody of a smile, all his teeth bared. "I won't *ask* again."

She snapped her mouth shut and placed her hand on his arm. "How boorish."

"Am I?" He guided her to the edge of the crowd, Tess close by his side. "Were you spying on me?"

"No!" She looked so indignant he considered believing her. Then her expression turned to one of speculation. "Were you and Mr. Plimpton discussing something you didn't want heard?"

"That's my own business." He felt his temples begin to throb. He needed a reprieve from this crowd. "As it happens I don't particularly enjoy self-righteous spinsters listening in on my private conversations."

A quick glance around showed that no one was paying attention to them. He steered her in the direction of the church, away from the marketplace stalls and the gathered people.

Miss Stewart huffed, saying rather breathlessly, "I don't particularly enjoy being accused of nefarious doings by a man so stupid he'd conduct private business in a crowd."

"What a little witch you are," he said absently—and felt her stiffen. He glanced down at her and saw that her green-gold eyes had widened in something that looked almost like fear. "What is it?"

"You threatened poor Mr. Plimpton," she said.

Christopher snorted and pulled open the door to the Norman church. Tess darted in with them. "He's only poor in pocket, I assure you."

Inside, the church was cool and dim, and it took a moment for his eyes to adjust from the bright sunshine outside. It was a pretty little church. The inverted U-shaped arch of the door was repeated in the arch between the nave and chancel, and both were decorated with a chevron pattern.

He glanced down at Miss Stewart and saw that her face

was upturned as she studied the windows. Less than an inch of her hairline peeked beneath her cap. Her hair might be dark blond or dusty brown—impossible to tell—and he had the wild urge to rip the cap from her head.

"Do you think they were smashed during the Reformation?" she mused.

The windows were all clear glass. If there had once been stained glass in the church it was all gone. "Probably. Or by Cromwell's Roundheads."

"Men do seem to enjoy smashing things—even beautiful things."

"Not all men, surely." He watched her with her prim little mouth, her sad eyes, and said gently, "Besides. Women can be just as destructive, I find."

He felt her stiffen and was glad. Here was a proper opponent to take his ire out on. She might be a virago, but she was also strong and strongly opinionated. He needn't fear that she would collapse into a weeping heap at the slightest comment.

She made a scoffing sound. "Do you really think so? When the destruction that men wield results in wars? Death and maiming?"

"You don't count women such as Helen of Troy?" he murmured, watching her. She couldn't speak this way with every man she met—otherwise she'd be without a job. What made her so confrontational with *him*?

"Helen of Troy is a myth," she said with scorn. "Butcher Cumberland isn't."

He raised his eyebrows. The Duke of Cumberland had been the English commander at the bloody slaughter of the Scots at Culloden only fourteen years before. "You're a Jacobite."

"No, of course not. They were idealistic fools fighting a

war they had no hope of winning." She blew out an impatient breath. "I just don't approve of wholesale butchery."

"And you hate men," he said slowly.

"Don't be silly." She walked away from him, up the little nave, her heels echoing on the flagstones. "I don't hate *every* man."

Him. She hated *him.*

He intended to find out why. He felt heat rising in his chest as the pain in his head returned full blast. "What have I ever done to you, madam?"

She threw a mocking glance over her shoulder. "You still don't know?"

Suddenly his patience was at an end.

He took two strides and grasped her arm, halting her. Swinging her around to face him. "No. I can only imagine that your brain is inflamed and you've dreamed up some injury. You've been waspish to me since the moment I laid eyes on you—despite the fact that I *helped* you."

"I didn't need your help."

"No? You and the lass and baby would've been fine against those bullies had I tossed you from my carriage?"

Her lip curled. "I can't think how an *animal* like you is allowed into polite society."

The heat, the weeping, the *stink* of sweaty bodies. Did she know somehow? How once he'd been reduced to the nearly subhuman?

He gritted his teeth. "Can't you?" He bent over her, breathing in the scent of honeysuckle, of *home*, enraged beyond what the circumstance required. "I'm a *duke*, while you, madam, are merely a thief."

"I'm not—"

"*Give me back my ring*," he growled. "I'll no longer wait for tonight. Give it to me now or I'll tell them all."

"Never," she hissed.

Something within him snapped. Perhaps it was the scent of honeysuckle, perhaps it was the way her soft lips curled in a sneer.

He took both her upper arms, drawing her so close he could feel the heat of her skin. "You *will* give me back that ring."

"If I were a man, I'd call you out," Miss Stewart said with complete earnestness. "I'd meet you with swords and gut you."

"What a bloodthirsty little thing you are," he drawled, knowing his indifference would provoke her the more. He was aware that his cock was half-hard. *This is madness.* "As if you could best me at swords—or any combat, armed or not. You've the inflated pride of a child in the nursery."

"I'm not a *child*." Her glare was full of scorn.

He let his gaze drop pointedly to her bosom, heaving beneath her fichu and a silly little bouquet of flowers. He cocked his head, slowly appraising her figure. "No, I suppose you're not."

For a moment he thought she might explode, like a dueling piece poorly primed.

Then she said, low and deadly, "Tomorrow morning. Five of the clock. Name the place."

He hauled her against his chest, so close he felt her breath brush his lips. "You want an assignation with me, madam?"

She ignored his double entendre. Her gaze was direct and fiery. "I want your blood."

"For God's sake." He sneered.

"If you can best me at swords, I'll give you the ring," she said softly, her voice shaking—though he knew it wasn't from fear. "If I win, you'll not ask for it again and you'll not tell *anyone* of what happened in London."

"Do you really think I'd take up a sword against a woman?"

"*Coward.*"

He let her go, stepping back so suddenly she staggered. He'd wanted to shake her—or fuck her, he wasn't entirely sure which.

For a moment they stood there, chests heaving, glaring at each other.

He should ignore her and her ridiculous goading. Should turn and simply walk away. But he was tired of her insults. She needed to be put in her place.

And he needed his ring.

"Very well. But when I win, you will hand over my ring without further ado." He pulled his lips back in a grin. "I accept your challenge, Miss Stewart."

Chapter Six

*Rowan made up her mind to return to the grotto in
the forest to see if there was something to explain the
change in Marigold.
But when she arrived it was exactly the same, green
and mysterious, echoing with the sound of dripping
water and apparently leading nowhere.
She turned away in disappointment and only then
saw a man standing watching her....*
—From *The Grey Court Changeling*

Late that night Messalina drew on her wrapper to answer a
tap at her bedroom door.

Jane Lovejoy, wearing a gold silk wrapper with butterfly
embroidery that Messalina was *not* at all envious of, slipped
into her room.

Messalina shut the door and turned to see Jane watching
her, arms akimbo. "Now what is so secret you couldn't tell
me on the walk to the village today? And why must we meet
in the dead of night to talk? You're quite lucky that Daniel
drank so much brandy after dinner—he's snoring like a fleet
of drunken sailors."

Messalina winced. "I do apologize—I hadn't considered
how you would explain your absence to Lord Lovejoy."

Jane let her militant stance slip. "Yes, well, as it happens
it doesn't matter, so please tell me what is so urgent."

"It's Eleanor Randolph," Messalina said. "I want to know what happened to her."

Jane frowned, slowly sinking into one of the chairs grouped by the fireplace. "What do you mean? Eleanor died last spring."

"Yes, I know," Messalina said, beginning to pace. "But the thing is, *how* did she die?"

"I think it was a fever—or at least some illness that took her suddenly." Jane watched as Messalina turned at the door and walked back across the room. "Why are you so interested now?"

"I'm not entirely sure." Messalina glanced quickly at Jane and away. "You know that Eleanor and I were friends? We met when we were eighteen and newly out, you see."

For two years she and Eleanor had giggled together and discussed gentlemen and their relative assets until Eleanor had inevitably married Randolph. *Inevitably* because Eleanor was kind and intelligent, the niece of an earl, and had a very nice dowry. Randolph was a big handsome man, a little older at five and thirty, but very powerful in the House of Lords.

Since Messalina was the niece of a *duke*, one might think she'd be married by now as well. But Messalina had been... picky.

She still was, in fact.

But that was neither here nor there.

Messalina drew a breath. "We used to send each other regular letters, Eleanor and I, but it had been several years since I'd actually seen her in London. She wrote that she liked the countryside and found London too wearying."

She stopped and looked at Jane's reaction.

Jane shrugged and shook her head.

Messalina grimaced. "I know! It doesn't seem like much,

but the thing you have to know about Eleanor was that she *loved* to dance. And to go to balls. And shop. When I thought about it, this sudden urge to rusticate seemed...odd."

"Well, people do change," Jane said practically. "When I first married Lord Lovejoy he was the most dreadful prig." She looked thoughtful. "Actually, he still is. But you wouldn't believe how much better he's become—or perhaps I'm more tolerant of his foibles—which is the point. One changes when one marries. In a good marriage, you no longer make decisions on your own—you do it as a partnership. If Lord Randolph liked rusticating, perhaps Eleanor found out how much she enjoyed the country as well—particularly once she had her own house to manage."

"Perhaps," Messalina said reluctantly. "But there's another thing." She dropped into the chair next to Jane's. "You mustn't tell anyone because I might be simply mad."

Jane nodded encouragingly.

Messalina took a deep breath. "In the last letter she wrote me, Eleanor said she was going to leave Lord Randolph."

Jane blinked. "Leave as in...?"

"Leave as in cause a huge scandal. She asked if she could seek refuge with me and I replied that of course she could, but I wasn't sure for how long. It's Uncle Augustus, you see. We might not live with him, Lucretia and I, but we're rather *beholden* to him." Messalina delicately chose each word to describe her relationship to the man she knew to be the devil. "If he took a dislike to Eleanor, or-or disapproved of her running away from her husband, he could make things very difficult for all concerned."

Which of course was a great understatement. Dear Uncle Augustus was capable of much worse than merely causing *difficulty*.

Fortunately Jane didn't seem to notice Messalina's

unease in regard to Uncle Augustus. She merely asked, "What did Eleanor reply?"

"She didn't," Messalina said. "She died a fortnight later."

"Oh, my dear," Jane said with awful gentleness, "I realize her death was a shock to you, but might your worry that her death was unnatural simply be, well, *guilt* that you weren't able to offer her permanent refuge?"

Messalina's eyes welled up all of a sudden, which was *most* annoying and really not at all helpful. Of course she'd considered that her disquiet over Eleanor's fate was merely her own guilty conscience. She'd even—*horribly*—thought it was possible that her own letter informing Eleanor that she had no place to run to permanently might've led her to take her own life.

"The thing is," she told Jane now, resuming her pacing, "I *did* think about that. I thought about it for months, and I eventually decided that it was all my imagination. That Eleanor was dead and I merely felt grief and guilt about her passing."

"Then why are you here?" Jane asked.

Messalina halted at the far end of the room and turned. "Last month I saw Elliot Randolph at a ball. I hadn't seen him since the news of Eleanor's death, so I went to him to offer my condolences." She inhaled, remembering that cold face, emotionless, inhuman—or nearly so. "He looked at me and *smiled*. I knew in that instant. I knew without doubt."

"Knew what?" Jane asked.

"Lord Randolph murdered Eleanor." She met Jane's wide eyes. "I have no evidence—he *said* nothing at all suspicious—but the look he gave me was...was...*monstrous*, Jane. He was gleeful, I could tell. What's more, I'm sure he let me know. He thinks that there's nothing I can do about her death. That Eleanor is dead and he's won."

"But even if your suspicion is true—and you must know it's very far-fetched, my dear—what can you do?" Jane asked, her brows knit. "It's been a year. Eleanor is *buried*."

"I know." Messalina came and knelt before her friend, grasping her hands. "I know it will be difficult, but I want to know what really happened to Eleanor. And I need your help to do it. I'm a stranger in these parts, but *you* aren't. People will talk to you as they might not to me. Will you help me find out if Eleanor was murdered by her husband?"

"Yes." Jane straightened her shoulders. "Yes, I will."

* * *

They'd decided on the well house clearing. Even as Christopher made his way through the gloomy woods to their rendezvous the next morning he knew that this was a mistake. There was no way that Miss Stewart—short, delicate, and *female*—could best him in a sword fight. The very fact that she thought she could was evidence that she was mad.

She was a woman ruled by her emotions—as all women were supposed to be. Many men thought women little more than children who must be guided and guarded.

Except that he didn't believe women were such base creatures. Certainly Miss Stewart wasn't. She seemed perfectly intelligent and not particularly emotional—except when it came to *him*.

Were he a simple man he might think her explosive anger merely a symptom of sexual attraction to a man she didn't like.

He wasn't a simple man, though.

He was a man who had lived among strangers in a strange land for nearly half his life. He'd long ago learned not to believe what was only on the surface.

The best he could hope for was that he'd beat her quickly and regain his ring. If he did so she'd merely hate him even more than she did already.

The worst possibility was that she'd somehow hurt herself during their so-called duel.

He was scowling over that thought when he walked around the last turn and saw her already waiting for him.

Tess took off galloping toward Miss Stewart as if the woman were the dog's long-lost friend.

Stupid animal.

She looked down at Tess and smiled.

A bright, beautiful, easy smile, and he was struck with jealousy.

For his own *dog*.

She glanced over the dog's head—she was fondling Tess's ears—and the smile disappeared at the sight of him.

He refused to be disappointed.

"Do you still mean to go through with this, madam?" he asked, unwrapping the swords he'd brought with him.

"Yes," she said without hesitation.

Of course. Christopher decided he would beat her as swiftly as possible so as not to prolong her humiliation.

Were she not so stubborn, he'd let her decline gracefully and find another way to retrieve his ring. But he knew her well enough by now to know she would not back down.

Therefore, best to get it over with.

He placed both swords over his forearm, the hilts toward her, so she could choose her weapon.

She stepped forward and examined them carefully before picking the slightly shorter one. The one a smaller, weaker swordsman—or woman—would be better able to handle.

That was his first hint.

She swept the sword through the air and then brought it before her and looked at him. "Ready?"

He nodded. "Call it."

"En garde!"

His second hint was when her sword nearly took his nose off.

Jesus.

He leaped back. Thrust his sword before him to block her next attack. He watched how she moved as he defended.

Perhaps Miss Stewart wasn't insane after all.

She fought like someone familiar with a sword.

She fought like a woman who might very well *best* him.

Her sword sang as it scraped along his. She disengaged before their swords could catch.

Pivoted.

Bared her teeth and went for his belly.

Christopher wheeled back, barely bringing his own sword up in time.

Her face was set and determined—too determined. She truly wanted to beat him.

Perhaps kill him.

Why?

He had no intention of wounding her. He'd meant to simply disarm her. Teach her a lesson about better reach and stronger muscle.

But agility and better *skill* also came into play—unfortunately.

He was a fool to ever have agreed to this.

She darted at him, her sword flashing, her eyes intent and furious.

He turned away a stab meant for his shoulder. Stepped into her next attack.

And was rewarded with a pink to his left arm.

"Bloody *hell!*"

She flashed him a triumphant grin.

He blinked.

There was something familiar in that grin.

She lunged for him.

Forcing him to dodge.

He circled her.

She whirled to follow, and her cap fell from her head.

"Stop this," he commanded.

"Not good enough?" she mocked, trying to impale him, the wildcat. "Perhaps you prefer to stand aside and let others do your gory work."

He stared, confused. *Aroused.* "*What?*"

Her gaze was almost feverish. Her hair coming down about her shoulders. "You're a coward who orders others to beat a man nearly to death."

She lunged again, past his guard, the tip of her sword at his throat. He felt the needle prick of pain.

She stood, panting, her hair wild about her shoulders. Her *red* hair—not dusty brown at all. Red, fiery curls, waving in the breeze as if they had a life of their own, and he saw her as if for the first time.

"Yield," she demanded, an avenging fury.

His world tipped upside down. "*Freya?*"

Her eyes widened.

He knocked her sword tip away from his throat. Caught her wrist and twisted.

She yelped and dropped her sword.

Her lips parted—most likely to curse him.

He didn't care anymore. He yanked her into his arms and kissed her.

She opened her mouth to him. Teeth clashing, lips snarling together. *Anything* but yielding.

Freya.

How could this be? That slim girl, running wild over hills so long ago, her flaming hair a banner. This woman, voluptuous and furious, her hair still a flaming banner.

He thrust his tongue into her mouth, confused and angry. How had this happened? Why was she here?

But those thoughts melted away as he explored her hot mouth, felt her hands clench in his hair, pulling him closer.

Freya.

Her passion was exhilarating. He wanted to strip this drab gown from her body. Find out how plush her breasts really were. If her sweet hips would cradle him.

He caught her glorious hair and held her, taunting her tongue. Licking at her teeth.

Drinking her—*Freya*—memory and reality.

He felt a change in her body, a stiffening of her shoulders as her hands left his hair, and he broke the kiss just in time. Her teeth clicked together on the bite she'd meant for his lip.

"Why are you here?" he rasped. He was still hard, despite her effort to bloody him more.

"Why shouldn't I be here, *Kester*?" she mocked.

No one had called him that in...

Fifteen years.

It had been a nickname—a shortening of Christopher—that Ran and Julian had given him. Kester had meant friendship, warmth, *Scotland*. A place where he could relax from the constant pressure to be correct that his father put on him.

Where he could be *himself* without apology.

He was almost brought to his knees by longing.

But he wouldn't let himself show weakness. "You know

what I'm asking. Why are you working as a chaperone? You're the daughter of a *duke*."

"And the sister of one," she growled, low. "Have you completely forgotten Ran?"

He inhaled, letting her go. "I could never forget Ran."

"No?" She bent for her sword where he'd dropped it at their feet.

He stepped on the blade.

She straightened, glaring. "He lost his *hand*, did you know that? Gangrene set into the wounds and they had to *amputate*."

"I..." He swallowed, remembering when he'd heard that ghastly fact. A stranger in a tavern had mentioned it. He'd had to walk outside to cast up his accounts. "I didn't know until I returned to England."

"He's crippled," she whispered as harshly as a shout. "It was his *right* hand. He can't draw, can't write. Can you imagine that? Ran unable to *draw*?"

He felt ill. Ran, tall, whip-thin Ran, laughing as he sketched comic faces. Frowning as he drew glorious trees and mountains. "Oh God."

He felt her blow against his chest, but didn't register the physical pain.

His soul was shattering.

"I wanted to punish you," she whispered. "You deserve it for what you did to him."

He closed his eyes. "*Freya*."

"He doesn't go out anymore," she hissed, tears glittering in her eyes. "Not for years and *years*. We used to try and corner him in his town house in Edinburgh. Try to draw him out, or simply *talk*. He refuses to converse with anyone. Lachlan spent a year, screaming at him, pleading with him, *begging*—"

She choked and he opened his eyes.

Freya was weeping, her green-gold eyes wide open even as the tears leaked out. Her face ruddy with her wrath.

"I'm sorry," he whispered.

She slapped him.

His head jerked back as his jaw began to burn. He pulled her into his arms even as she hit him open handed, pummeling him.

"I'm sorry. I'm sorry." He didn't know what else to say.

Knew at the same time that there was nothing he *could* say to make this right.

It would never be right again.

Ran was gone—*destroyed*—and it was his fault.

He waited, holding her, as she sobbed and struggled and gasped. Clutching at his chest when she gave up hitting him.

After a bit he sank to the cold, damp ground, still holding her. He stroked her hair, letting her weep on his chest, and continued to murmur his sorrow.

His regret.

At last she heaved a great breath and grew silent.

The sun was all the way up now, shining in the sky. Tess had come to lie beside them, her head on Christopher's knee. They'd have to return to the house soon or risk being found to be missing.

He took a breath. "Did Ran tell you what happened?"

She shook her head. "He was brought home by Julian's uncle the Duke of Windemere's men. They said he'd tried to elope with Aurelia but had murdered her instead in a fit of insanity—"

"But did he *tell* you?" he asked.

She frowned, a small crimping of her red lips. "He was too injured. He caught a fever almost at once."

He nodded. "Then please listen."

He felt her tense and prepared himself to hold her, but she did nothing.

She was listening.

He watched as Tess got up to dig at the foundation of the well house. "We were young. That is the most important thing. We were too young."

She scoffed, but didn't interrupt.

"Ran came to Julian and me and said he needed to marry Aurelia."

"Needed?"

He shook his head. "Apparently her uncle was against the union for some reason. Ran was determined to marry Aurelia before her uncle could make another match for her."

She hadn't known that—he could tell by the frown incised between her brows. "That's why he was going to elope."

"Yes." He carefully stroked her hair. The last time he'd seen Freya she'd been eleven or twelve. A sweet younger sister.

She was no longer sweet.

And he didn't feel at all brotherly now.

"Wasn't Julian upset?" she asked. "After all, Aurelia was his sister and only sixteen."

"No." Christopher considered. "He was irritated that Ran was so insistent that they elope right away, but I don't think he was angry. If anything he wanted to make Aurelia happy. You were young. Perhaps you don't remember how...*vital* she was. How charming. We all adored her."

"I remember," she said in a stiff little voice.

He hugged her closer. "Then you know that once Aurelia had made up her mind to elope with Ran nothing would've dissuaded her. No *one* would've stopped her. She was beautiful and spoiled and young."

She moved to look at him, and he saw that her eyes were swollen and red.

The sight struck a chord within him—an urge to protect and shelter, though she was the last woman to need protection. An urge to lay his mouth against hers again, though she would surely bite him if he did.

"How did she end up dead? *Murdered?*" she demanded.

Christopher shook his head. He could feel sweat running down his back. It might've been from the duel, but he thought it more likely was the memories.

The awful memories. "I don't know exactly."

Her lip curled. "How can you not *know*?"

He took a breath, aware that whatever he might say, it would never be enough for her. "You have to remember that we were all only eighteen. All of us beside Aurelia, but she was probably the most certain of us. We thought it was a lark. A grand adventure. We made plans to meet at Greycourt House, by the stables at midnight, and ride away, over the border to Scotland, so they could wed. But…"

She frowned. "What happened? What changed?"

"Aurelia," he said and swallowed. "Something happened to Aurelia and she was killed."

Freya sat up straight. "You don't *know* how she was murdered?"

"That's my mistake," he said, watching her. "I got there after Ran. There was shouting and I almost turned away, but I saw Ran being beaten in the courtyard and I went to him. Julian came forward and held me back. His face was so white it was near gray and he said, "Don't." Just that. *Don't.* He told me that Aurelia was dead. That her bloodied body was in the stables and that Ran had killed her."

"He *didn't*," Freya said fiercely. "Ran wouldn't kill anyone, let alone Aurelia. He *worshipped* her."

"I know," Christopher said, his heart leaden with old, old grief. "I knew that then. But in the night, with Julian telling me that Ran was a murderer, with the Duke of Windemere bellowing and his men beating Ran..."

She shook her head wearily. "Ran was your *friend*. How could you betray him so?"

"I was weak." He looked at her and told her his shame without any hope of sympathy. "I failed him that night. That's why I wore his ring: to remind me of my failure. To remind me to do what is *right* no matter the personal cost. To remind me to never retreat when I can and should take action to help another."

She pulled away and he let her, watching as she stood and shook out her skirts.

Freya looked at him, beautiful and stern. "Your regret can't restore Ran's severed hand. It won't give him the ability to draw again or to forget what happened. He's spent fifteen years entombed just as surely as if he'd died that night."

"Freya," he whispered, and bowed his head, feeling the weight of her censure.

But still she wasn't done. "I cannot forgive you."

Her footsteps were quiet as she left him.

CHAPTER SEVEN

*The man was tall and slender, with eyes as purple as
a wood violet. His thick hair stood up in tufts and
was as silvery gray as the ashes on a hearth.
He grinned a foxy grin. "Good fortune and well met,
Princess Rowan."
Rowan scowled. "Who are you and how do you know
who I am?"
"I am Ash," the fairy said—for of course he must be
a fairy. "And I know many things... including where
your friend is."...*
—From *The Grey Court Changeling*

Three nights later Freya sat at the side of the Lovejoy ballroom and watched Harlowe partner Arabella on the dance
floor. The Lovejoys had thrown a small ball for the evening
with rented musicians.

Harlowe and Arabella moved well together. The duke
wore a pewter-colored suit edged with silver embroidery.
Arabella had on a new frock—a pretty sky blue with white
lace accents. Her golden head was a striking contrast to
Harlowe's dark hair.

Arabella was smiling—a bit shyly, but perhaps the love-
lier because of that. Harlowe watched her indulgently.

They made a beautiful couple.

Freya grimaced and glanced away. The thought of

Harlowe with Arabella was a thorn in her side—and not simply because of the Greycourt tragedy.

He'd explained his part in the crippling of Ran. Indeed he had acknowledged his guilt.

He'd apologized.

She couldn't forgive him, but she could no longer see him as evil incarnate, either.

Freya sighed. Such a basic impression of Harlowe had been rather childish anyway—probably the result of her having formed her opinion at only twelve. In all the years since, she'd never had opportunity to amend her thoughts about him.

But now that she'd actually *met* him again—as an adult—she could see that he was obviously more than the monster she'd hated all these years.

He was arrogant, true, but he was also tender with Tess. He had offered her money when he'd thought her merely a companion. He was kind to the Holland girls.

He was a *man*, both good and bad and everything in between.

A man who made her very aware that she was a woman of blood and bone and *wants*.

Freya shook her head irritably, turning her thoughts to her mission. Sadly, she'd learned nothing new in the last several days. She'd attempted to talk to the Randolph housekeeper or another servant. But when Freya tramped over to Randolph House, she'd found to her puzzlement that no one would open the door, even though she'd seen smoke coming from the kitchen chimney.

The entire thing had been most frustrating.

And not at all helpful in keeping her mind off the duke.

She needed to think of another plan, but the last three days had been filled with games, jaunts about the countryside, and now a ball. Freya wasn't even certain when next she might be able to slip away from the party to investigate.

And then there was the Dunkelder. Which of the guests was a secret witch hunter? And had he discovered who *she* was?

She scanned the room, and her gaze couldn't help stopping on Lord Stanhope. He was frowning at the dancers as if he disapproved of their merriment. The viscount had a Scottish accent, and most Dunkelders were Scotsmen. If she had to guess she'd choose him as the hunter.

Which might be good—Lord Stanhope hadn't paid her any attention at all.

The dance came to an end and Freya watched as Harlowe bowed to Arabella. Harlowe hadn't attempted to talk to her since their duel. Hadn't even looked at her. She might as well be dead as far as he was concerned.

Which was *good*.

She'd accomplished what she'd set out to do with him: retrieved Ran's ring and bested him in the duel. There was no further reason to interact with the man. The fact that he was respecting her on the matter should make her *happy*.

"You look as if you swallowed a lemon," Regina said, and plopped rather gracelessly into the chair beside her. She was panting and pink cheeked from the dance, and she vigorously fanned herself. "Mr. Aloysius Lovejoy is quite a good dancer. Did you see? His father went a bit wide on that last turn and Mr. Lovejoy guided us away without missing a step." She cocked her head, appraising Mr. Lovejoy rather dispassionately. "We could certainly use more dancers like Mr. Lovejoy in London. I don't know how my toes survived last season."

Freya sent her a fond glance. She'd spent many a late night after a ball hearing about the clumsiness of society gentlemen. "Then we're lucky Mr. Trentworth is so graceful."

"Yes, he certainly is." Regina's face took on the dreamy look her beau's name usually inspired. "I do hope Arabella finds a gentleman just as good at dancing. Wouldn't it be horrible to spend the rest of one's life having to dance with a clumsy brother-in-law and never complain?"

"That would indeed be a purgatory," Freya said solemnly. "However, there may be other attributes we should look for in a gentleman for Arabella."

Regina blinked as if she'd never considered anything else but proficiency in dancing. "I suppose," she said doubtfully. "It *would* be rather awkward if one's husband couldn't read, for instance."

It was Freya's turn to blink. "Yes, that would be a problem. Erm...were any of your suitors illiterate?"

"Oh no, I don't think so," Regina replied carelessly. "Although I always rather worried about Georgie Langthrop. He used to laugh like a horse whinnying." She shuddered delicately. "Can you imagine *that* across the supper table every night?"

"No, I don't think I can," Freya replied absently.

She noticed that Harlowe had deposited Arabella with Lady Holland and Lady Lovejoy. The Earl of Rookewoode sauntered over and bowed elegantly to Arabella, before whispering something in her ear. Arabella turned bright pink and took his proffered arm. The earl must be her next dance partner.

Harlowe had gone to stand beside the door that led outside to the back terrace and lawn. Freya studied him. She'd noticed over the last couple of days that he often lingered by doors or windows. Perhaps he secretly wanted to escape the party?

What a whimsical thought.

As she watched he jerked his head to someone across the room.

Freya turned her head, following Harlowe's line of sight, and was just in time to see Mr. Plimpton give a small nod.

When she looked back at Harlowe, he was no longer there. *What was he doing?* It was none of her business. Neither Harlowe nor Mr. Plimpton was a woman in need of help. They were outside her purview.

Even so, she wanted to know.

She stood casually. "If you'll excuse me?"

"Of course," Regina murmured. The next dance was about to start, and she was smiling in the direction of Lord Stanhope. No doubt she'd promised the dance to the viscount.

Freya strolled toward the garden door, making sure not to move too swiftly or in a straight line. She was still yards away when Mr. Plimpton ducked out the door.

She remembered what she'd seen on the trip to the market. Harlowe in intense discussion with Mr. Plimpton, who had looked wary and nearly frightened. What had the duke said to the man to make him look that way? Harlowe had told her that Mr. Plimpton was a cad, but she had only the duke's word for it.

She reached the door and cautiously opened it, slipping outside.

The summer night was lovely. The sky was clear and lanterns had been placed around the terrace, casting a soft glow.

Mr. Plimpton wasn't on the terrace, and she peered into the darkness beyond just in time to see him dart between the tall hedges that surrounded the garden.

Freya picked up her skirts and followed, stepping in the grass rather than on the gravel path to avoid making noise. At the hedge she paused, peeking into the garden. She couldn't see either Harlowe or Mr. Plimpton. Bother. She'd just have to go in and hope she didn't run into them.

The garden was dark, but the moon was nearly full, out-lining a walkway and a fountain at the center. Shadows hid the paths just under the tall hedges, and Freya began walking down the one to her right.

She'd taken only half a dozen steps when she heard voices. Cautiously she crept closer on tiptoe.

"—Let Eleanor's maid go."

Freya frowned. That was neither Harlowe nor Mr. Plimp-ton, but Messalina. Perhaps Freya had gotten it all wrong. Perhaps Harlowe had come out here for an assignation with Messalina.

Strange how her chest hurt at the thought.

But when she peered around the corner of the path she saw that Messalina was talking to another woman.

"But that's entirely natural. If Lord Randolph—"

Both women turned at the sound of a man's voice near the center of the garden, and Freya saw that the person Messalina was talking to was Lady Lovejoy.

Why would they be speaking about Lord Randolph together?

"Someone's here," Lady Lovejoy whispered.

"Come," Messalina said, taking Lady Lovejoy's arm.

They turned toward where Freya lurked, and she hastily stepped off the path.

She stood still, the scent of roses lingering in the night air as Messalina and Lady Lovejoy hurried by.

Freya walked toward the center of the garden—toward the male voices—and as she neared they became clearer.

"—Damned if I'll give you even a shilling without them. I'm not a fool." That was Harlowe, his voice low and angry.

Freya shivered. He sounded menacing.

"But I'll have no insurance should I do that," Mr. Plimpton

replied, his voice nearly whining. "You can't think I'll leave myself so vulnerable."

"That's your problem," Harlowe returned, growling. "You started this. It's not my fault if you neglected to consider the result."

"Let me think," Mr. Plimpton pleaded. "I need to think."

"You *do* have them now, don't you?" Harlowe said, his voice relentless. "I saw a parcel arrive this afternoon for you."

"I . . . Yes. Yes."

"Then quit stalling. Tomorrow night you give them to me." There was a clear threat in Harlowe's voice that Mr. Plimpton would regret it if he did not do as the duke told him.

"But—"

Someone shouted at the house.

"They're looking for us," Mr. Plimpton said urgently.

"I doubt it," Harlowe replied, "but you'd better go in."

Freya heard Mr. Plimpton rush by, and then the garden was silent again.

Where was Harlowe? Had he returned to the house as well?

She thought over what she'd heard. It sounded very much as if Harlowe was being blackmailed by Mr. Plimpton—or at least extorted over some object. The realization gave her an odd feeling. She'd never have thought that Harlowe would let himself be blackmailed. He seemed too contained and arrogant. Too self-confident to care what anyone else in the world thought of him.

Freya shook her head and waited a moment more, but the night was still and quiet. Obviously he'd gone in.

She tiptoed toward the main path, the one leading out of the garden.

A dark shape ran at her, so fast and sudden she nearly screamed. Tess pressed her nose into Freya's skirts and then backed up a step, her tail furiously wagging.

Freya bent to pet her.

Heavy hands fell on her shoulders, and a deep voice breathed in her ear, "I don't remember you being such a sneak thief."

* * *

Freya stilled beneath his hands. Christopher inhaled the scent of honeysuckle in the night air and wondered if she wore it just to drive him insane.

Plimpton had already put him in a foul mood. Now to find Freya spying on him was too much.

She reviled him and withheld her forgiveness for his admitted sins and yet he *could not stop thinking of her*. The revelation of who she truly was—a link to his youth—had made him vulnerable somehow. Vulnerable to *her*. When he walked into a room he knew where she was without looking. She *glowed*, a fire, burning brightly, luring him closer, appearing to offer him peace.

Peace he would never have. She was not for him, she'd made that clear.

He turned her to face him. The moonlight cast her in shades of gray, almost otherworldly.

But she was a real woman, her arms warm beneath his hands, her eyes sparking irritation at him, her mouth twisting down.

"You drive me mad, little thief," he whispered, and gave in to the constant, terrible temptation.

He kissed her.

He was prepared to be shoved away, but instead her lips parted beneath his. It might be an aberration. She might remember in seconds that she hated him.

But in the meantime, he'd take what she offered.

His tongue slid into her mouth, the scent of honeysuckle heady in his nostrils. When she spoke her tongue held only bitterness and bile, but when she kissed she tasted of honey and rare wine.

Sweet.

Unattainable.

He slanted his mouth over hers, changing the angle, holding her close, so close. She stood on tiptoe and pressed against him and he rejoiced.

Eager. Wanton. Open.

Oh God, if only.

He'd lived so long alone, wandering a foreign desert of solitude, barren of friendship or comfort.

Her breasts were heavy against him and he wanted to tear that ugly cap from her head, let down her glorious hair, and bury his face in it.

She was memory. Family. Love.

She was home.

He groaned aloud and murmured, "*Freya.*"

She pulled away immediately, breaking their embrace and the spell.

He opened his hands and let her go.

She took a step back, looking grave and remote now. "Don't call me that."

He stared at her, trying to read her expression. "Why not?"

"You know why," she said, her voice cold. "No one knows my name here."

He raised his eyebrows, a flash of irritation making his voice sharp. "Not even Messalina?"

She frowned and glanced away. "Of course Messalina knows me. But we haven't spoken since that night at Greycourt."

He cocked his head, confused. "Then how—"

"I just *know*," she said, quite obscurely. She must've seen the skepticism in his face because she sighed heavily and expanded. "It's in the way she looks at me. She knows who I am and she knows that I don't wish others to know."

How Freya could tell all that from a simple look was beyond him, but women did seem to communicate in a nearly fey way at times.

Her words reminded him of something else that had been bothering him since he'd discovered who she truly was. "What are you hiding, F—"

The sound she made was nearly a growl.

He caught himself and said precisely, "Miss Stewart. Why do you not talk to Messalina?"

She closed her eyes as if in pain. "You know why. You know what her brother, Julian, did."

"Her *brother*, not she." Christopher frowned, wishing he could see her better. "You cannot blame Messalina for what happened. She was a *child*, the same as you. Julian, me, the Duke of Windemere, even Ran himself, *we* are to blame for the tragedy."

She opened her eyes and stared at him sadly. "That might be, but nevertheless the lines were drawn between our families, and we found ourselves on opposite sides."

"But you don't have to be on opposite sides." She started to protest, but he pulled her close. "No, listen. Hurl invectives and abuse at me—or never speak to me again—but do not take your anger and pain out on Messalina. She is just as innocent as you."

"You do not order me," she hissed, as dangerous as any cornered wildcat.

"I know I don't," he whispered, running his hands soothingly over her arms. "But I can plead her case to you."

She was breathing hard, her breasts pressing into his

chest. She yanked away her arms and he forced himself to open his hands.

To let her go.

She stepped back, staring at him, her eyes made black by the moonlight.

Then turned and walked swiftly back to the house.

He didn't follow.

Christopher threw back his head and gazed sightlessly at the stars. Why did she bother him so? Perhaps it was because after he'd grown inured to the prospect of spending the rest of his life alone, an alien in his own land, she'd reminded him of all he'd lost.

Family.

Friendship.

Home.

He shook his head. Freya might smell of Scotland, her red hair might remind him of a girl, long ago, running over heathered hills, but she was *not* that girl anymore.

What he thought he saw in her was an illusion.

And he was just as much alone tonight as he had been last month. Or last year. Or a decade ago.

Or, for that matter, as alone as he would be decades hence.

He'd sinned and he was an outcast.

Now and forever.

Tess nudged his hand and he looked down.

She was sitting, her head cocked to the side, gazing up at him. All the canine love in the world was in her eyes.

He smiled and caressed her head, then snapped his fingers for her to follow as he walked toward the house.

But as he did so, he couldn't help but notice that the taste of wine and honey lingered on his lips.

* * *

Freya stood by a table holding the ugliest mock china vase she'd ever seen. The ballroom was stuffy—heated with a roaring fire and dancing bodies. The hired musicians were playing, and couples bobbed on the floor in a line. No one had noticed when she'd slipped back into the room. Her dress was straight, her hair neat.

She might never have kissed Kester Renshaw. Never have felt her blood rise in his arms.

Except for the way she had to control her breath, the dampness between her breasts, the thud of her heart.

She watched the dancers and wondered why she hadn't shoved him away. She *despised* the man and yet she'd yielded to his embrace almost at once.

And she'd do it again if he kissed her.

She glanced down and saw that her hand was trembling. What was *wrong* with her?

The doors to the garden opened and Harlowe strolled back inside, Tess trailing behind.

She hastily looked away.

Messalina was laughing at something Lord Rookewoode was whispering in her ear as they danced. Arabella was smiling at her mother as they stood at the far side of the room with Lady Lovejoy, but her gaze was fixed on Messalina and the earl. Mr. Lovejoy danced with Regina while Lucretia did her duty with Lord Lovejoy.

Suddenly Freya felt weary. It had been years since she'd seen her family. Since she'd wandered the Scottish hills. Since someone looked at her and *knew* her.

Truly knew her.

The music came to an end and the dancers bowed and curtsied to each other. The Earl of Rookewoode murmured something and Messalina's peal of laughter rang out over the ballroom.

When Freya had overheard Messalina in the garden, she had been talking about an Eleanor with Lady Lovejoy. Lady Randolph's Christian name was Eleanor.

Could Messalina possibly know something about Lady Randolph's death?

Freya felt her lips twist. She'd been estranged from Messalina for *years*, had thought that Messalina would naturally take her brother Julian's side in the matter. That Messalina was and always would be her enemy.

But what if Harlowe was right?

What if Freya had it all wrong and Messalina was just as much a bystander as she? To snub the other woman because of her family seemed all of a sudden childish and foolish.

And yet, having gone all these years without talking to Messalina, how was she to break her silence now?

Lady Holland looked up and gestured to Freya.

She nodded and made her way across the room. "My lady?"

"I'd like to show Lady Lovejoy that rather unusual embroidery design you've been working on, Miss Stewart," Lady Holland said. "Would you mind fetching it for me?"

"Not at all, my lady." Freya smiled politely and turned to the door. She was glad, truth be told, to have a respite from the stifling ballroom.

She stepped into the corridor, sighing with relief at the cooler air.

She hurried upstairs to her room, found her embroidery bag right away, and returned downstairs. She had just passed the library and was almost to the ballroom when the door to a retiring room opened and Messalina stepped into the hallway directly in front of her.

Freya stopped.

Messalina stared at her with wide gray eyes.

Freya inhaled and made to step around her.

"Freya." Messalina's voice sounded loud in the hallway.

Freya moved without thinking, placing her fingers on Messalina's mouth. "Hush! Don't call me that."

Had there been anyone in the library? She glanced behind them, listening for any voices, any movement.

All she heard were the distant sounds of the ball.

Messalina pried Freya's fingers away from her mouth, an irritated look in her eyes. "Miss *Stewart*, then, though I find it ridiculous that you've decided to hide under a false name."

Freya's eyes widened. "I…" She winced. Only minutes before she'd been thinking of Messalina and how she might reestablish contact. Here was an opportunity handed her on a platter, but she didn't know what exactly to say.

How did one ask to be friends again after fifteen years?

She looked at Messalina, patiently waiting for her reply, the hopeful light in her eyes nearly hidden, and blurted, "Oh bother. I need to talk to you."

"Really?" Messalina asked, looking delighted, and then continued without waiting for Freya's answer. "Good. I thought you'd never come to this point."

Freya could feel heat rise in her cheeks. "But not here."

"Tonight, then," Messalina said.

Freya was already shaking her head. "Lady Holland will want to discuss the ball in her rooms later."

"Then tomorrow night," Messalina said.

Voices came from the direction of the ballroom.

Freya darted a quick glance behind them. Someone was coming.

She blurted without giving herself time to think. "Yes. Tomorrow night."

She turned, but Messalina grabbed her arm. "*Where?*"

"Your rooms," Freya whispered hoarsely, pulling her arm from Messalina's grip. "I'll come to your rooms."

Freya flashed a grin at her and turned and hurried away, her heart suddenly singing.

* * *

It was nearly six of the clock the next afternoon when Christopher rode into the courtyard at Lovejoy House feeling irritable that he had to wait until later tonight to settle with Plimpton.

Christopher had spent the afternoon with the gentlemen of the house party touring the countryside on horseback. Normally he would've enjoyed the ride, but today it had been a rather boring exercise. At least Tess had delighted in the jaunt. She was sniffing alertly about the stable now as if she hadn't spent the day running.

He dismounted, handing the reins of his horse to a stable lad. He had to consciously refrain from running up the steps and into the house. Plimpton had begged off the ride this morning by pleading a headache—he'd hinted at too much drink the night before. But Christopher had been suspicious the entire day that the man was simply avoiding him.

Christopher had to suffer through nearly a half hour more of social niceties until he could escape. He turned to the house, calling for Tess, but she'd found something in the stables—most likely a rat—and was pretending deafness.

He shook his head and left her to her sport.

Once he was done with Plimpton he could leave this damned house party.

Leave Freya and all she represented.

He paused at the top of the stairs, closing his eyes and

tipping back his head to inhale. He'd been reconciled to his life. Reconciled to being alone and without a family. Reconciled to never feeling completely at ease.

And then Freya had burst into his life, set fire to his apathy, and burned everything he thought he knew down around him.

He *wanted*. Home. Family. Familiarity.

Freya.

That was the most ridiculous thing of all: he wanted her as a woman. She spit hatred at him with soft lips and at the same time gazed at him with those green-gold eyes as if he meant something. As if she might want him.

As if he might win her and find respite.

And it was all illusion.

A man could go mad longing for a woman just out of the reach of his fingertips. That was why he needed to leave this bloody house.

Christopher shook himself and strode to his room.

He found Gardiner, his valet, waiting for him there with a hot bath and a change of clothes.

Christopher scrubbed himself vigorously, splashing the water and dunking his head. It was a relief to rid himself of the sweat and dust.

He dried himself and Gardiner helped him into a fresh shirt and suit and then Christopher waved him off.

The hell with waiting, he needed to confront Plimpton now.

The man had put him off too long. The thought made him angry enough that when he turned the corner into the main corridor he was scowling.

A boy was lingering in the passage, and at Christopher's advance his expression changed from uncertain to cowed.

Still he got up the courage to call out. "Your Grace?"

Christopher paused. "Yes?"

The boy gulped. "You're the Duke o' Harlowe?"

"Yes." Christopher looked at the boy impatiently.

"For you, Your Grace." The boy thrust out a simply folded piece of paper, sealed with a blob of wax.

Christopher took the letter, and the minute he did, the boy hurried away.

Christopher raised his eyebrows and then tore the note open.

I have what you want. Meet me in the well house at seven of the clock with the money.

He turned it over, but the back of the page was blank. Of course there could be no doubt as to who had sent the note.

As he wondered what time it might be, a clock nearby started tolling and Christopher swore under his breath.

It was already seven of the clock.

He swiftly took to the stairs. Plimpton might want his money, but Christopher had no intention of giving it over until he had the letters—*all* the letters—in hand.

He strode to the side door and went out, making for the wood at the edge of the lawn.

Inside the trees it was dark and silent. The place had an odd feel to it, as if time had stopped or did not matter here. He realized suddenly that he'd forgotten Tess in the stables. *Damn it.* Still. She should be fine there for an hour or two—the grooms all knew who she was.

Behind him something rustled.

He turned, expecting Tess to come bounding up.

But nothing moved.

Christopher turned back to the path, grimly intent. If

Plimpton thought to enact some sort of ambush he was going to be very sorry indeed.

Another ten minutes' walk and the path wound around a large tree and then revealed the little well house.

The door was standing open.

"Plimpton?" Christopher paused, eyes narrowed, but didn't hear a reply.

Was the man playing hide-and-seek?

"Plimpton!" His shout was swallowed by the trees.

Ducking his head, Christopher stepped into the well house.

God, it was small. And dark.

He shuddered all over like a horse and immediately had to fight the impulse to back out again.

Plimpton wasn't here. He could see that right away. Perhaps he'd wait in the clearing outside.

Behind him, someone stumbled into the chamber.

He whirled.

A woman with a man's neckcloth wound around her eyes crashed into him. Instinctively he caught her and snatched the neckcloth off.

He had only a moment to glimpse Freya staring up at him with wide eyes.

And then the door slammed shut.

CHAPTER EIGHT

"What do you mean?" Rowan cried.
"The King of the Fairies has stolen the lady
Marigold away to the Grey Lands," said Ash, "and
left a changeling elf in her stead."
"But how can she return?" Rowan asked.
Ash laughed. "She cannot. A mortal would have to
journey to the Grey Lands and ask the Fairy King to
let her go, but that's dangerous and quite
impossible besides."
"But you could *take me there, I think," Rowan said....*
—From *The Grey Court Changeling*

Freya froze as the well house was plunged into darkness, compounding her disorientation from the cloth that had been over her eyes.

There was a shout. She was shoved aside, and then there was a frantic pounding at the door.

Growling and pounding at the door.

She found herself ducking, her hands over her head as if she were afraid the next blow would land on her. The racket was terrific, making it hard to *think*.

Harlowe had caught her when she'd been pushed into the well house. She'd seen his face when he pulled the cloth from her head. The banging and growling—that must be *Harlowe*. He sounded like a wild beast driven out of his mind, bigger and stronger than she, and *dangerous*.

Her instinct was to cringe away.

What had happened to him? Was he hurt or somehow out of his mind? But he'd seemed perfectly fine—if angry—in that brief glimpse she'd had of his face.

Before they'd been shut in darkness.

Surely...?

She shook herself. It hardly mattered *why* he was like this. She had to stop him somehow.

She held out her hands blindly and walked toward the sound of chaos.

Her fingertips touched a broad shoulder, shaking as he slammed himself against the door. Dear God, he was going to do himself violence using his body as a battering ram.

"Harlowe." She felt over his shoulder to his arm, tugging. "*Harlowe!*"

He didn't seem to hear her. It was as if he were in a strange thoughtless state.

As if he'd been driven instantly and completely insane.

She fought down animal fear and reversed the progress of her hands, feeling up his arm to his face.

It was slippery with sweat, and a pang of sympathy went through her. Whatever this was, it was seizing him hard. She would've had to be soulless not to respond to such agony.

She curved her palms over his cheeks, embracing his face with her hands. "Harlowe. *Please*, Harlowe."

She pushed at him, and at first she thought she could not move him. He was too big, too strong. But she was relentless, ducking under his arms and wriggling in between him and the door at the risk of being accidentally hit by his fists. His big body jerked and heaved as if he were in spasm, but she would not be shaken off. She wrapped her arms around him, pulling him as close as she could to herself.

The blows stopped.

In the sudden silence his heaving breath was loud.

She hugged him, feeling the heat radiating off him.

His panting slowed as he calmed a little.

Until he inhaled shakily.

"I need...," he rasped. "I need to get out."

His voice sounded as if he'd drunk lye.

"Yes," she said, trying to keep her voice calm. Soothing. "Yes, we need to get out. But I don't think pounding at the door will open it."

His strong hands gripped her shoulders.

She could feel them trembling.

"No," he said, his voice uneven. "No, you're right."

"Why don't we sit for a bit?"

He took her suggestion quite literally, sinking suddenly to the floor and pulling her down with him. He kept his arms around her as if her presence—the *feel* of her—were the only thing keeping him sane. He maneuvered until his back was against the door, his knees bent, and she sat sideways between his legs.

Was his fit over?

She tried peering into his face, but it was too dark to see his expression clearly. "Are you better now?"

"Talk to me. Distract me from..." He stopped and coughed before continuing. "Why did you follow me?"

"Curiosity," she said. "I saw you leaving the house by yourself and wanted to know where you were going. Who you were meeting. I saw you open the well house door, and then someone grabbed me from behind." Freya swallowed, remembering her fear and surprised anger. "I couldn't shout before they slapped a hand over my mouth and wound the neckcloth over my eyes. I was pushed in and the door slammed behind me."

"You didn't see your attacker?" His voice was sharper.

"No." She shook her head, frustrated. "But it must have been a man. He was taller than me and stronger."

"How did you know I was meeting anyone?" His voice was absent sounding and she somehow knew that he was only partially paying attention to their conversation.

The majority of his mind was concerned with beating back whatever ailed him. It was strange to witness such a capable, arrogant man be brought low. His big body surrounded her as if to shelter her, but she could still feel tremors rack him every now and again.

She kept her own voice carefully level. "I wasn't sure you were meeting anyone. But Mr. Plimpton didn't go out riding with the rest of the gentlemen, and I know that there's some sort of business going on between you two."

He grunted something close to a laugh. "You're too curious. You always were. I remember you and Messalina spying on Julian, Ran, and me when we were boys home from school."

The mention of Julian and Ran together sent a streak of anger through Freya, but she controlled it. Her anger and sorrow wouldn't help now. And besides, as he'd reminded her more than once, that was in the past.

So she replied lightly, "You three seemed to always be doing something more interesting than we." She twisted a little, trying to look up into his face, though she knew it was useless. "Why did you come into the well house?"

"You were right—I was meeting someone." He snorted. "I received a note from Plimpton telling me to meet him here—or at least I thought it was from Plimpton. The note wasn't signed."

"Why were you meeting him?"

He sighed and lifted his hand to her cap, picking at the ties under her chin. "Plimpton's blackmailing me. Or trying to. If I die in here, then he will have lost what money he thought to extort from me."

"That won't happen," she said. "Someone will realize we're missing and come looking. Quite soon, I should think. I'm sure Lady Holland has already missed me."

She said it confidently enough, but she wasn't sure of any such thing. She'd retired to her room earlier, pleading a headache so that she could think alone in peace. No one had seen her leave the house. She was supposed to meet with Messalina in her rooms tonight. Perhaps Messalina would raise an alarm when Freya didn't appear. Or she simply might assume that Freya had reneged on their agreement to meet. After all, Freya had been stubbornly refusing to talk to Messalina for years.

If Messalina disregarded her absence, Freya wouldn't be missed until the morning.

But Harlowe—the most important member of the house party—surely there would be a hue and cry looking for the *duke*.

She hoped so at any rate.

She glanced at the tiny square window to one side of the door. It couldn't be much past seven of the clock, for there *was* a little light still. But they were in a woods. Sunlight didn't hit the window directly.

And night would be falling soon.

Right now she had to keep Harlowe's mind away from that realization. She had the feeling that complete darkness would only compound his problem. "What was Mr. Plimpton blackmailing you over?"

"Letters." His chest heaved against her side. He didn't

seem to realize the intimate position they sat in. Or possibly he knew and didn't care.

She'd move away if she were certain that he'd retain his composure.

At least that was what she told herself.

Harlowe coughed. "Plimpton has letters from Sophy. Ones that I don't want publicized."

Her brows shot up. What sort of letters? And what did they say?

She knew that his wife had died in India. Had there been some mystery involving her death? Could he have hurt his wife?

What did she really know about Harlowe?

He'd let Ran be beaten when they were both only eighteen.

He'd helped her in Wapping when they were strangers.

He loved his dog.

He was a terrible swordsman—well, at least against her.

And when he kissed her, his lips were both angry and desperate.

She sighed silently. She might not know *intellectually*, but her heart knew without question: he was not the type of man to hurt any woman, least of all his *wife*.

Mr. Plimpton she wasn't so sure about. Blackmailers were a cowardly breed—and, when cornered, apt to do something stupid. She'd already overheard Harlowe threatening Mr. Plimpton. Had the man decided that the Duke of Harlowe was too big a bite to swallow?

Were they meant to *die* in here?

"How did these letters come into his possession?" she asked to distract both herself and Harlowe.

He grunted, and for a moment she thought he wouldn't answer.

His breath began to come faster.

"Harlowe?" She took one of his hands and squeezed it between her own. How could such a strong man be brought so low by...*nothing*? Shadows and a confined space? "How did Mr. Plimpton get Sophy's letters?"

"She wrote them to him," he got out with an explosive breath. "They were...She...He seduced her."

For a moment Freya was honestly shocked. Why would a woman betray a man like Harlowe, so big, so *male*? And for a little weasel such as Mr. Plimpton?

She blurted, "Why would she do that?"

He barked a laugh. "I would've thought you'd sympathize with her—you seem to hate me enough."

She glanced up at him, trying to see his face in the muddy light. "Perhaps not quite enough for that."

"Thank you," he said so quietly she almost didn't hear. Then he sighed. "As to your question of why, I can only answer that it was India. Bloody India. It was hot and strange and Sophy hated it and our exile from the start."

"I'm sorry," she said helplessly. "That must've been..." *Horrible.* Stuck in a foreign land with an unhappy wife. "Hard to endure."

"That's one way to put it. We were much too young to wed. Sophy was..." His voice trailed away and then started again. "We didn't suit. Even had we been at home it wouldn't have gone well, but in India..."

She cleared her throat. "You hated it, too?"

"No," he immediately replied. "*Hate* is too strong a word. There were wonderful sights. Wonderful food and experiences. Wonderful *people*. But it wasn't home. I love England."

"Why did your father send you there, then?"

"The scandal." He shifted, rearranging her so that she

rested more comfortably, with her back against his chest. He gave no indication that he wanted to release her. His legs were to either side of her, and his left arm was wrapped loosely about her waist. She still held his right. "You may not have been aware of it because you were a child, but that night at Greycourt became a terrible scandal. The news that Ran, the heir to the Dukedom of Ayr, had tried to elope with Aurelia Greycourt was in London within days. People said that Ran murdered her, as you know. Julian and I were known to be somehow involved, and the gossip made us out to be wastrels bent on violence. My mother took to her bed and my father shouted at me until he lost his voice. They were both afraid that we would be ostracized from society."

"But you're a *duke*—"

"I wasn't back then," he said. "You must remember that. Nor was my father a duke. I inherited from a distant cousin. I didn't even have the *prospect* of inheriting back then."

Freya blinked. She'd never considered what had happened to Harlowe and Julian after that night.

She hadn't really cared.

But now...

"Were Julian and his family disgraced as well? Was Messalina?"

"Julian was disgraced, yes, but..." He shrugged, the movement lifting her bodily up and down. "Not as much as me and my family, I think. I suspect that the Duke of Windemere had a hand in turning the worst of the gossip away from his family. In any case, I haven't seen Julian since that night."

She jerked upright, turning to him. The sun must be setting, for what little light there had been was fading fast. His face was shadowed. "Whyever not?"

"I was ashamed by what we'd done." He pulled gently on her arm, making her relax against him again, arranging her to his satisfaction. "I don't know how Julian felt, but he never attempted to contact me while I was in India. We'd let Ran be beaten." He breathed in shakily. "It seemed as if everything from before that night—our friendship, our youth, our *life*—was gone."

"But when you returned to England?"

"I did receive an invitation from him to tea, I believe. I thought by then that it was best that we not see each other again. He doesn't move much in society—you must have noticed that," he replied. "I didn't call on him, and our paths haven't crossed."

"So you're estranged?" she asked wonderingly. All this time she'd pictured Julian and Harlowe cozy together. Laughing as Ran suffered. But that was an image that had formed when she was twelve. They had all changed in the ensuing fifteen years.

And obviously she'd been wrong about some things.

Perhaps many things.

"Julian never wrote me while I was in India," Harlowe said. "And I never wrote him. In my case it was shame. I don't know what it was in his."

Something else occurred to her. "I don't understand. You married *before* you left for India?"

"Yes."

"I didn't know you'd been courting." Once upon a time the knowledge would've crushed her. "Your marriage must've been rushed."

The laugh Harlowe gave was more cough. "Rushed? The entire thing was arranged. There was a piece of land that her father wanted—land that my father held title to. In exchange for this land her parents were willing to overlook my scandal. I met Sophy twice before we married, both times in a room full of people. I think Father was of the opinion that only marriage, exile, and work could restore our name."

She inhaled on the word *exile*. He'd used it before, but at the time she'd thought he meant he'd exiled *himself*. "You mean your father wouldn't let you come back to England?"

She felt him shrug. "I don't know. I never tried. Didn't want to try. What was there for me in England? Scandal and a father who'd made it plain that I'd lost his favor forever. No, I determined to stay in India."

"Despite Sophy's hatred of it?" she asked slowly.

He sighed. "I would've sent Sophy home eventually. She wasn't meant to be so far away from her family. But at first I hadn't the money, and by the time I did, Plimpton had ensnared her. And then..."

He stopped. Simply stopped speaking.

She waited in the darkness, but nothing came from him.

Finally she stirred. "And then what?"

"And then she died," he said, so quietly she almost didn't catch the words.

"How did she die?" she asked carefully.

She heard the shuddering inhalation he took before speaking. "I was in service to the East India Company. We were in Calcutta," he said, and she thought that there was something she should remember about that place. "At Fort William. Everyone in the company lived in the fort—it wasn't safe for us outside its walls. Sophy loathed it. She spent days at a time in her room."

Sophy seemed to have been a very delicate sort of lady. "Go on."

"In the summer of '56 the Nawab of Bengal took a dislike to the activities of the East India Company. Well..." He shrugged his shoulders again. "It was the fort itself that was the last straw. We found out later that he'd expressly told the people in charge not to expand the fort. Naturally they went and did it anyway, arrogant fools." He laughed without humor. "Can you imagine it? If foreigners who didn't even speak our language came and built a great whacking fort outside St James's Palace? If George himself came out and said, "Stop that at once," and instead of listening they built it even higher? We wouldn't stand for it, good Englishmen that we are. But put us in another land with the prospect of piles of gold to be made and suddenly we're in the right no matter what. Sometimes . . ." He stopped.

"What?"

He heaved a sigh. "It's just that sometimes I wonder if they did it a-purpose—flagrantly ignored the nawab's orders until he started a war. It ended in the East India Company's favor, after all. The old nawab was defeated, and now they pull the strings of a puppet nawab."

She smoothed one hand over his chest, feeling the silk of his waistcoat. That sounded positively evil. She hated to think that Englishmen might do something so calculating. "What happened that summer?"

"The nawab's army besieged us, of course," Harlowe said, his voice hoarse and weary. "The entire army against a small garrison. We were lucky not to be killed outright. The commander of our forces—what forces there were—when he saw it was a lost cause, ordered most of the soldiers to flee."

"But why?" Freya asked in horror. She couldn't imagine such a thing—English soldiers abandoning their station. Abandoning *families*. Harlowe had said that Sophy was there as well, and if she was, there must have been other women, and most probably *children*.

"Because," he replied, reclaiming her attention, "he knew

that the soldiers would be slaughtered if they stayed. In that, at least, I think he was right."

"What did you do?" she whispered.

"Surrendered," he said. "I and the rest of the remaining men and soldiers surrendered. Most had sent their families away, so it *was* mainly men. But some hadn't or couldn't. Sophy was scared out of her mind. She refused to go until I finally put her in a carriage myself a day before the siege began. But somehow she bribed the coachman. She returned just before the fort's gates were closed and after that..."

"I'm sorry," she said helplessly, unable to think of what else to say in the face of such catastrophe. "You must have done as well as you could."

"I tried," he replied, but his breathing was growing labored again.

"What happened when the fort was surrendered?" she asked.

And then, too late and horribly, she remembered what she'd heard about Calcutta.

Dear God, surely...

"We were put in the fort's own jail cell," he said, his voice emotionless as his chest heaved beneath her. "There were nearly seventy of us."

She heard him swallow and she wanted to tell him to stop, that she didn't need to know.

That she already knew.

But she'd *asked* him. To silence him now seemed a betrayal—as if she couldn't bear the weight of knowing what had happened to him.

She wasn't that weak.

"Tell me," she whispered.

"The soldiers of the fort called it the Black Hole. It was the prison cell for the fort, meant for one or two men. I'd

NOT THE DUKE'S DARLING · 139

never seen the inside, never really thought about it. The Black Hole had a dirt floor, stone walls, one door, and one small window." He inhaled before saying quietly, awfully, "And it was the size of this well house."

Freya stopped breathing. Nearly seventy people in a space this big? How had they all fit in? She couldn't see in the dark, but she had in her mind's eye the size of the little well house. The interior space was perhaps fifteen feet by a little longer—maybe sixteen or seventeen feet. That was...

She simply couldn't imagine.

"Harlowe," she whispered, laying her head against his chest, hearing his heartbeat and glad for the sound. "How did you survive?"

"I don't know," he murmured. "Many didn't. They put us in toward evening. There was space only to stand. And then night fell. It was hot—so damned hot—and we had no water. One of the men near the window implored the guard outside for a cup of water and, when a cup couldn't be found, handed out a hat for the water to be poured in. But so many grabbed for the hat when it returned that all the water was lost before any tasted it."

She squeezed her eyes shut. "I remember now, reading an account of it."

He sighed. "I've read the accounts as well. They're written by agents of the East India Company. They blame the Calcuttans in an attempt to justify their own actions."

She lay, listening to his heartbeat for a minute before she gathered the courage to ask, "What happened to Sophy?"

"I failed her," he said. "I failed her and she died."

* * *

He felt as if he were suffocating.

Christopher closed his eyes and tried to calm his breathing, but the dark and the walls were pressing in on him.

He shook his head and concentrated on the terrible tale he was relating to Freya. "People started to panic in that small, hot prison, almost at once, but it got worse and worse as the night wore on. Men shoved other men. Some wept in fear or horror. Some fell and were trampled. Sophy was against a wall. I'd tried to get her to the window, but no one would move to let us by." He winced at the memory. The heat and the smell of packed, frightened bodies.

Because that was all they became in that hole: bodies. Sweating. Weeping. Pissing. Shitting. Just bodies, all the soul and mind that God had given them gone.

But he didn't tell that to Freya. Some things should never be said aloud.

"I tried to guard her—to protect her with my body. I stood against her, facing outward, bracing myself as they pushed and pushed. She wept behind me. She was so frightened. Until the pressure of the bodies in front of me pushed me back against her." He opened his eyes, remembering the weight against his chest. "Until she stopped weeping and made no sound."

"Oh, Kester," said the woman in his arms.

Freya was soft and small, but her spirit was made of iron.

He plucked off her cap, running his fingers through the hair beneath. He couldn't see it, but he knew she burned with fire.

He bent his head and laid his cheek against hers, inhaling honeysuckle, the scent of his boyhood. If he closed his eyes perhaps he could pretend he was in the rolling hills of Scotland, the wind in his hair.

Pretending hadn't worked in Calcutta.

It didn't work now.

He drew in a breath and continued, "I couldn't move until dawn. Until they opened the doors finally. Out of all who had gone into that hell, only three and twenty lived to see the sun rise. We were surrounded by corpses. And when I turned I found Sophy dead. Suffocated by the bodies. Suffocated by *me*."

"No, no, no." She shook her head against him, her voice urgent. "It wasn't you who killed her."

Her fierce defense of him warmed him somehow.

Still he replied, "If not me, then who?"

"I don't know," she replied. "I don't think it was anyone's fault—not even the people who panicked. They didn't want to be there. They didn't *want* to lose their sense. The whole thing was awful, but you said yourself that you meant to protect Sophy."

She was so certain, but how could she be? He'd let her brother be maimed, had been gone for years. Perhaps he'd grown into a monster, a murderer of women.

He shook his head now. "I don't understand you."

"What don't you understand?" she asked, sliding her fingers through his. For some reason the feel of her small hand in his steadied him.

"Why do you believe me?" he asked helplessly. "You don't know me—not anymore. And what you *do* know you hate."

She was silent for a moment, her fingers drifting over the palm of his hand, tracing the base of his thumb, delving between his fingers, encircling his wrist with both her hands.

Finally she said, "The first time I saw you again after all those years, you offered help. Even though we'd invaded your carriage. Even though you didn't recognize me. Even though you had no idea what I was doing with a maid and a baby. You saw us, you saw the men chasing us, and you made the decision to help. In my experience that is not usual."

He felt her fingers drifting over the back of his hand, delicate and light, like the brush of muslin. "What *were* you doing?"

She huffed, perhaps in laughter. "I was helping the widow of an earl take her only child from her villainous brother-in-law."

He opened his mouth to chide her for bamming him, and then closed it because he had the sudden overwhelming feeling that she *wasn't*. "Freya?"

"Yes?"

"What have you been doing while I was in India?"

"That," she said, "is a bit of a tale."

CHAPTER NINE

*"I?" Ash's purple eyes widened. "Now why should I
help you, Princess? The King of the Fairies is a
powerful being, and 'twould be most foolish of me to
cross him."*

*Rowan lifted her chin. "I'll give you a purse of
gold coins."*

"What use have I for such?"

"The ring upon my hand?"

*"No." He stepped closer—so close that Rowan
realized no heat came from his body—and smiled
into her eyes. "Again. What can you give me for
my trouble?"...*

—From *The Grey Court Changeling*

The sun must have set, because the well house was so dark
Freya couldn't see her hand in front of her face. "I suppose
everyone is at supper by now."

"Yes." Harlowe wasn't frantic anymore, but she could
feel his body tense around her.

"In the normal way of things I wouldn't miss my supper,
I think. But when it's been taken away I suddenly feel ravenous." She sighed. "And thirsty."

"Sit up," he commanded. She scooted forward and heard
the sounds of him getting to his feet. "We *are* in a well
house."

"Do you think it still has drinkable water?" she asked, simply to give him her voice in the darkness.

"Maybe." She could hear his shoes scrape on the stone floor, and then there was a rattle. "Here it is." More rattling. He must be drawing a bucket up. "Damn. It's dry."

Her heart sank. "That's a pity." Would they die of thirst? How long did it take to die of thirst? She had no idea.

His shoes scraped on the stones again, and she called, "I'm over here."

And then his hand touched her head. He lowered himself to the floor, sitting beside her but close enough to bump shoulders with her.

She was surprised to find that she rather missed his arms about her.

"Are you going to tell me what happened to you after that night at Greycourt?" His voice seemed somehow warm in the darkness.

She realized suddenly that if she *had* to be locked in a well house she was glad that it was *he* with her. Her brows drew together. When had her attitude toward him changed? When had he gone from an enemy to something very close to a friend?

"Freya?"

His voice brought her back to the well house and his question.

She sighed. "Ran was ill after the beating. You know that. They'd crushed his right hand and infection set in. That led to fever. He was very badly off." She stared into the darkness, remembering days of fear and tiptoeing around Ayr Castle. Hearing the servants weep and low voices behind closed doors. The important stride of the doctors as they came and went.

"I'm sorry," he said.

Only a week ago she would've scoffed at his apology. Would've railed against him and replied with the cruelest words she could muster.

But that was a week ago. "I know," she said quietly, and felt his shoulder relax a fraction. She inhaled. "A day after the doctors had to amputate Ran's hand, Papa died."

She heard him swallow. "I hadn't realized the old duke died so soon after the beating."

"I think"—she inhaled shakily—"that Papa died of a broken heart. Ran hadn't yet woken fully from the beating, and the doctors weren't sure he would survive. Mama died when Elspeth was born, of course. That left Lachlan as the next eldest of us children. It was he that the men of business and the vicar consulted. He was fifteen, and if Ran had died he would've inherited the dukedom."

"But Ran didn't die." He was tapping one foot against the floor. It must be torture to be locked in such a small, dark space after what he'd endured in Calcutta.

"No. He survived, though it was months before he rose from that bed. He limps still when he's tired."

"So he became a duke at eighteen," Harlowe said gruffly. "Damn me. I wouldn't wish that on anyone."

Freya turned toward him, though of course she couldn't see him. He sounded weary. Resigned. He did not sound as if his own dukedom had brought him any joy.

She cleared her throat. "Ran was the Duke of Ayr, yes, but he was also in disgrace. He became a recluse. Lachlan continued to manage the estates and the dukedom. He still does."

"And you and your sisters?"

"We needed someone to take care of us. Elspeth was only six—she hardly remembers before the tragedy. Caitriona was ten and I twelve. My father's sister, Aunt Hilda, came for us." Freya's lips curled. "We'd never met her before. She was a tall, thin woman with burn scars on her face and she came stomping into Ayr Castle. I think she thoroughly scandalized the butler and housekeeper. We girls really should've been scared of her—she was a daunting woman—but I think we were just so grateful to have someone to take charge that we clung on to her. Aunt Hilda lived in the north of Scotland, and she took us to live with her."

"She left Ran and Lachlan behind?"

She couldn't tell if he was disapproving or simply curious. "Yes. Ran was still not well, and Lachlan needed to see to the dukedom. Aunt Hilda was the daughter and sister of dukes. She understood duty and why the dukedom had to be maintained. I think she would've lived with us at Ayr Castle but for the burn scars that disfigured her face. She didn't like people staring."

The tap of his foot was rhythmic in the darkness. "You grew up there? In the north of Scotland?"

"Yes." She tilted back her head, remembering a house full of women. "It was actually quite lovely. There were hills to roam around in, beautiful streams, winter nights by a roaring fire. Aunt Hilda was our tutor, and she had friends who would stay with us to teach us things she couldn't."

"Fencing?"

She laughed. "Yes, fencing. Aunt Hilda thought it a wonderful exercise, and since it was only we three girls, there was no one about to disapprove. Not that she would've cared for anyone else's opinion."

"She sounds like a tartar."

Was he smiling? She wished she could see. "She could be. Aunt Hilda had very definite ideas. She believed in rising early. Porridge for breakfast and plain mutton or fish for supper—not any fancy *English* dishes, as she called them. She thought children should exercise every day. That we should know how to shoot and fish. We learned Latin, French, and Greek and all the names of the Roman emperors. And every week we read a philosophical book or tract and debated it amongst ourselves on Sunday."

"Impressive," he said. "You had a better education than many men—certainly a better education than I did."

She turned to him in the dark. "But you were at Oxford."

"Only for a year." His voice was wry. "Your aunt Hilda sounds as if she was a strong-willed lady. I think I would've liked to have met her. Is she . . . ?"

"She's dead." Freya cleared her throat. It had been nearly a decade and the sharp edges of her grief had worn down, but it was still there. Would always be there. "When I was eighteen. She had been in a fire—that was what caused the scars she was so self-conscious about. But the fire and smoke also hurt her lungs. Every winter she would cough terribly. One winter the cough took her."

"I'm sorry," he said.

There was a pause and she shivered. With the sun down, the temperature had dropped. If they were here all night it was going to be very uncomfortable soon.

Next to her, Harlowe inhaled. "Is that when you got a position as a companion?"

"No." She wrapped her arms about herself, trying to keep warm. "I came to London when I was two and twenty."

"Then why—"

She shivered again, rather violently.

"Damn it, you're cold." He moved, something rustled, and then she felt his coat drop on her shoulders. "There. Better?"

She should protest, but honestly she was so grateful for his coat she didn't bother. It was much too large for her, of course, but that meant she could tuck her hands in the sleeves. "Yes. Thank you."

"Come here now," he said, his voice husky and close in the dark. He pulled her into his arms, holding her close. The heat of his body was lovely.

She groaned in appreciation.

He bent his head so that his voice was right in her ear as he said slowly, "I don't understand why you took work."

She couldn't tell him about the Wise Women, so she gave him a partial truth. "After Papa died, Lachlan found that the dukedom was in debt. My grandfather invested heavily in the Darien scheme to found a Scottish colony in Panama. When it failed, most of the Ayr fortune was lost."

"I never knew that," Harlowe murmured.

"I think Papa made sure it wasn't common knowledge," she replied dryly. "Lachlan has said that from the records he's seen, Papa spent his lifetime trying to regain our moneys with various ventures. When he died, his creditors called in his debts, and because of the scandal, because they thought Ran a murderer, no one would extend further credit."

"And that's why you needed to find work," he said, his breath fanning the back of her neck.

She didn't reply. Because of course it *wasn't*. She'd come to London to be the Macha. The de Moray funds had been depressed, but not enough that she had to work.

She'd lied and prevaricated many times in the last five years and never felt a bit of guilt. Now, though, she was uneasy. She wished very much that she could tell Harlowe the truth.

Which was foolish. It was unsafe to tell *anyone* that she was a Wise Woman.

But she had an urge to trust Harlowe, when days before

she'd called him enemy. Was it just the intimacy of the darkness and cold?

Or was there another reason she felt, deep in her chest, that she could trust him?

"And when I first saw you in Wapping?" he interrupted her thoughts. "How did you come to be rescuing a baby?"

She cleared her throat. "Aunt Hilda always said it was the duty of every lady to offer assistance when she saw those in need of help. The girl was a maid and the baby was the Earl of Brightwater. His father is dead and his father's brother had imprisoned the child, keeping him from his mother. He hoped in this way to control the earldom and its assets. The countess asked for my help, so I helped her."

"By kidnapping a child." His tone was careful.

"Yes."

His chuckle in her ear was unexpected. "You really are a firebrand."

"Am I?"

"You know you are."

His admiring tone brought a glow to her heart. She'd never before met a man outside her family who considered a woman's willingness to act on her own decisions a *good* thing.

She could feel the press of his body against her back. Now that she was no longer thinking of how to keep him calm or how to explain her position in London, other things crept into her consciousness.

The strength of his arms keeping her warm. The rising and falling of his broad chest.

The scent of his male musk enveloping her.

He was a compelling man, and he made her feel very...
female.

"Shall we lie down?" she whispered.

For a moment he made no movement.

Then he pulled her to lie on the ground next to him.

She turned to face him, and he let her use his arm as a pillow.

They lay face-to-face in the darkness. She could feel his breath on her lips. She leaned a little forward and touched her mouth to his.

When they had embraced before it had been like dueling—hard, swift, and angry. Not really a kiss at all.

This was different.

She hadn't kissed many men in her life. And none had ever let her control the embrace. But Harlowe lay still as she brushed her lips against his.

She pulled back a little, waiting.

But he did nothing.

She opened her mouth and kissed him again, tasting his lips with her tongue. She found that her limbs were trembling. How could that be? From such a simple touch—one little kiss?

She curled her fingers into the back of his neck, feeling his hair brushing against her hand and the strong muscles of his shoulders.

His lips parted under hers and she licked into his mouth, angling her head. Wanting more.

His tongue brushed hers. Teasing. Tangling.

For a moment she forgot everything: who she was, who he was, where they were. All she could do was *feel*. A rising heat. A promise of all her binds unraveling.

It was that very loss of self—of *control*—that finally made her pull back, her lips parting from his reluctantly.

"I..." Her voice broke and she had to clear her throat. "I'm sorry. I didn't mean to offer something I won't give."

"No." His voice was rough. "It's I who should apologize."

"Why?" She asked part irritated, part frustrated. "I was the one who kissed you."

He chuckled quietly. "So you did. But I am a gentleman. Such things are always the responsibility of the gentleman."

Freya wished then that she *could* tell him what she was. Lay at his feet a history of women making decisions for themselves in Britain that had begun before Julius Caesar.

Instead she contented herself with saying, "I am an adult. I take responsibility for my own actions—good or bad. If I wanted to bed you, it would be *my* decision, not yours."

He was silent for a second. "But you don't want to bed me."

She *did* want him. She wanted to taste his mouth, taste his *skin*.

She shivered at the thought.

"I *want* to," she whispered, telling him the truth because she wasn't a coward. "But I don't think it... wise."

"Why not?"

She wished she could see his expression. "I think I'm afraid I won't know how to stop."

"Must you stop?" he asked, his voice a gentle murmur in the dark.

She closed her eyes as if she could block out the temptation in his voice that way.

"Yes, I think so." Whatever had happened between them in the last hours, he had still hurt Ran. Even if she could forgive him, that fact would always be between them. "I'm sorry."

Freya started to push away from him—it seemed less than honorable to take his heat while rejecting him.

But he pulled her back. "I'm not a ravening beast. Stay. For my sake, if not your own. I find comfort holding you."

That at least she could allow. She relaxed inch by inch, muscle by muscle, into his warmth.

* * *

By eleven of the clock the next morning it was obvious that something had happened to Freya and Christopher.

Messalina had waited and waited the night before for Freya to come to her rooms as arranged. When she'd finally gone to bed at well past midnight, she'd tried to convince herself that she'd never expected Freya to keep her word. That her childhood friend had long disappeared into the stranger who looked at her so coldly.

Still, even with that lie, she'd been hurt.

Now she watched as Lord Lovejoy argued with Lord Rookewoode.

"Perhaps he left suddenly," their host said, looking rather frantic.

"Without leaving a note?" The earl arched a skeptical eyebrow. "More to the point—without his *valet*?"

"The man said he was new to the duke's employment," Lord Lovejoy said distractedly. "When Harlowe didn't retire to his own bed last night the valet obviously thought that he—" Lord Lovejoy cut himself off hastily with a sheepish glance around the room.

The guests were all gathered in the sitting room. Regina sobbed on Arabella's shoulder while Lady Holland looked simultaneously irate and worried.

Lord Lovejoy loudly cleared his throat. "Harrumph! That is—"

Lord Rookewoode sighed. "Obviously the valet was wrong. Had Harlowe been about what his man suspected, he would've turned up long before now."

"Oh, but—"

"My lord," the earl said softly but with a definite note of command in his voice, "I think we must start a search party."

"I agree," young Mr. Lovejoy said, and *that* only set off another round of masculine dithering.

"Could they have eloped?" Lucretia murmured.

Messalina turned to frown at her younger sister.

Lucretia had taken the opportunity of everyone's mixed distraction and hysteria to settle into the chair next to Messalina with a plate of tiny cakes.

"Where did you get those?" Messalina demanded.

Lucretia's eyes widened innocently. "The cook gave them to me. I was famished. Breakfast was interrupted, if you remember. I only got a piece of toast before Lady Holland started accusing the duke of kidnapping and ravishing her companion."

Messalina grabbed for the plate, but Lucretia had been her sister for over three and twenty years. She moved the plate to her other side without blinking.

Messalina huffed.

"Well?" Lucretia asked.

"Well what?" Messalina muttered. She'd gone back to watching the byplay.

Lucretia sighed as if long put upon. "Do you think they ran off on purpose?"

"No," Messalina said, and rose.

"Where are you going?" Lucretia hissed, following her still clutching the plate.

"Outside," Messalina said.

"Why?"

"Because they've already searched the house."

"Oh, that *does* make sense," Lucretia replied, mouth full of cake.

She trailed behind, but Messalina had other matters on her mind. She might not be friends with Freya anymore, but Messalina *knew* her.

Freya would never have done something as silly as run away with Christopher. Even if she had been lovesick over him when they'd been children.

Which meant either that Christopher had kidnapped her forcefully—unlikely, unless he'd changed *quite* a lot since they'd all been children together—or something else had happened to them both.

Messalina quickened her step.

Possibly something very bad.

"Not so fast," Lucretia called from behind her.

Messalina ignored her, striding into the stable yard. She caught movement at the corner of the stables. A flash of something black and sinister.

Her step faltered.

But no, there was nothing there now.

And besides, *he* couldn't be here.

She went to the stables with the thought that she could request a horse. Riding would be preferable to—and quicker than—tromping over the estate. But no one seemed to be around as she entered the cool darkness of the stables.

She wandered farther into the building, murmuring to the horses as she passed occupied stalls. Wherever were the grooms?

"Hi there!" Lucretia suddenly said from behind her, and Messalina spun.

A gnarled groom was standing with a pitchfork, blinking at them.

"Where is everyone?" Messalina asked impatiently just as she heard a muffled whine from behind the man. "What have you there?"

"Jus' a cur," the groom said nervously. "Nothing to be worried over, my lady. Shall I ready two horses for you?"

But Lucretia had already slipped behind the man and was making for a low door with a latch on it.

"Oi!" the groom called.

Messalina moved past him and was just in time to see as Lucretia pulled open the door.

Inside was Christopher's dog. The animal had a scarf tightly tied around her muzzle and had been tethered to a pillar.

"Isn't that Tess?" Lucretia said indistinctly. She was still chewing on a cake.

Messalina arched an eyebrow at her. "How do you know her name?"

Lucretia shrugged. "I like dogs."

Messalina rolled her eyes and rounded on the groom. "What is the meaning of this? Why have you tied up the duke's dog?"

"Had a note, didn't I?" the man said, looking wary. "Wrapped around a guinea. Said to put her there and muzzle her. Not my fault if dukes got odd orders."

Messalina shook her head, dismissing the man.

She went to the lunging, whining dog. "There, there, darling. We'll get this muzzle off you right away."

The dog wriggled and whimpered, obviously overjoyed to be found.

Messalina had to pry the scarf off with her fingers, worried that she'd hurt Tess, it was tied on that tightly.

But the dog proceeded to lick her hand when the scarf finally came off, so all appeared to be forgiven.

She moved on to the knot in the rope around Tess's neck, contemplating who might've ordered this. She very much doubted that the note had been from Christopher. Not only did the man bring Tess everywhere with him, he had the habit of sneaking food to her as well. Quite obviously they adored one another.

Lucretia watched her struggle with the knot for a moment and then wandered off.

Messalina glanced at the groom. "Fetch some water in a bowl, please."

He stumped away.

Lucretia returned with a huge knife just as the groom set down the bowl of water.

"Where did you get that?" Messalina huffed at her sister.

Lucretia shrugged vaguely. "It was sitting around."

The groom had taken the opportunity to disappear.

"Hm." Messalina looked back at Tess, now sitting alertly, water dripping from her muzzle. "If I hold her head, can you cut off the rope without hurting her?"

Lucretia cocked her head. "I think so."

The minute Tess was let loose, she ran out of the stables.

"Dash it," Messalina said, "now we've lost her."

But then Tess came galloping back into the stables and barked at them.

"I believe she wants us to follow her," Lucretia stated, as if this were something Messalina hadn't already realized.

Messalina sent her a jaded look. "What are you still doing with that knife?"

Lucretia swished the knife through the air as if it were a very short sword. "I like it."

Tess barked again, as if to remind them of more important matters.

"Fine," Messalina said to the dog, and they set out.

Tess bypassed the house altogether and then led them past the garden. When she entered the small wood nearby, Messalina began to feel uneasy.

"It's just as well you kept the knife," she muttered to her sister.

"Do you think so?" Lucretia brightened. "Perhaps they've been captured by highwaymen."

Messalina looked at her out of the corner of her eye. "*Highwaymen?*"

Lucretia shrugged. "More likely than pirates, you must admit."

"Humph."

Ten minutes later Messalina began to wonder if Tess simply enjoyed running through the woods. But then the path they were on turned and an odd, small stone house came into view.

Tess barked at the door.

"Hello?" came a voice from within.

Something relaxed in Messalina, and she realized suddenly that she'd been bracing herself all this time for tragedy. "Is that you, Freya?"

"Oh yes," Freya's voice sounded weak from relief. "Messalina?"

"Yes, it's I." Messalina pressed her palms to the door as if she could get closer to Freya inside. "Are you by yourself? Only Christopher is missing, too."

"We're both here," Christopher shouted. "Can you open the door?"

Lucretia looked at the door at the same time as Messalina. There was a huge rusting padlock affixed to the door.

Someone had locked them in.

"I don't think so," Messalina replied slowly. Who could have done this? "We'll have to go for help."

She turned to Lucretia, but at that moment Lord Stanhope stepped from the woods. Behind him was Lord Lovejoy, Aloysius Lovejoy, and Lord Rookewoode.

"What are you doing?" Lord Stanhope asked disapprovingly as Tess circled the newcomers.

The earl shot him an irritated look. "Obviously the same thing *we're* doing—searching for the duke and the companion."

"Open the door, Rookewoode," Christopher shouted from inside the house.

The earl's eyebrows rose. "And you ladies have found them. Well done."

There followed a few minutes of debate before Aloysius Lovejoy volunteered to go get an ax and some sturdy footmen.

The little group waited in uneasy silence before Viscount Stanhope said, "I can't think who would play such a vicious joke on Miss Stewart and His Grace."

"You think this a prank?" Lord Lovejoy asked. "If the dog hadn't led the Misses Greycourt here, the outcome might have been dreadful."

In fact they might've died. "Who do you think did it?" Messalina asked.

"A poacher or the like," Lord Stanhope said with disapproval. "A ruffian of the lower classes."

"He'd have to have done his poaching whilst equipped with a padlock," Lord Rookewoode said mildly. He straightened from where he'd been examining the lock and the door and frowned. "Seems dashed unlikely. Do you have many poachers here?"

"We do," Lord Lovejoy replied.

Lord Rookewoode shrugged. "Perhaps a poacher, then." He still looked doubtful, though.

Lucretia idly whacked at the bushes with her knife.

Lord Stanhope stared at her with pursed lips, disapproval fairly radiating off him.

Messalina turned to Lord Lovejoy. "How did you know to come here?"

"Aloysius remembered the well house."

"You didn't?"

"No." He paused, glancing at Lucretia, who was still destroying the vegetation. "Perhaps you should take your sister back to the house."

Lord Stanhope nodded. "All this must've been terribly wearying for a young lady."

Messalina tilted her head, still smiling with effort. Was the viscount implying that she was no longer young at seven and twenty? Of course there were many who considered a lady on the shelf if she wasn't married by five and twenty. But they didn't usually tell her so to her face. "I think we'll stay."

"How did you think to come here?" Lord Stanhope inquired suspiciously.

"We had a guide." Messalina pointed to Tess, who had sat down by the door, patiently waiting for her master to emerge from the well house.

The arrival of the rescue party was announced by voices and tromping feet. Mr. Lovejoy emerged on the path, followed by two imposing footmen.

Lord Rookewoode greeted his friend with a muted, "Huzzah!"

Mr. Lovejoy grinned and bowed while Lord Stanhope sniffed at their drollery.

The footmen consulted with the gentlemen on the best way to break the padlock, and then a ginger-haired fellow stepped up to the door and took a mighty swing with his ax.

The padlock broke with a loud clang.

Immediately the door swung open to reveal a disheveled Freya and a pale but composed Christopher.

He gestured for Freya to exit the well house before him.

She stepped into the clearing and straightened, turning to Messalina. "Thank God you found us."

"We didn't do it," Lucretia said cheerfully. "It was Tess."

They all turned to where Christopher was on one knee over Tess, ruffling the delighted dog's ears.

Beside Messalina, Freya gasped softly.

Christopher looked up sharply and then followed her gaze.

Messalina did also, peering into the well house. There, high on the wall opposite the door, was a carving, illuminated by the light shining in.

"Is that a *W*?" asked Lord Rookewoode, sounding intrigued.

"Oh no," Lucretia said, shaking her head. She'd come to stand on Messalina's other side. "It's two *V*'s crossed together. Virgo Virginum."

Everyone turned to stare at her, including Messalina.

"The Virgin Mary." Lucretia blinked. "It's a sign to drive out witches."

"Witches?" Lord Lovejoy exclaimed.

While at the same time Mr. Lovejoy cried, "What rot!"

"Rot indeed," Lord Rookewoode mused. He'd entered the small building to peer closer at the letters. "But this is freshly carved." He turned and smirked at Lord Lovejoy, his face oddly highlighted in the dark well house. "Perhaps someone nearby has cause to fear witches."

* * *

A witch's mark.

Freya brooded over the matter on the trek back to the house. Was the mark a coincidence? Surely not. The Crow had warned her about a Dunkelder in attendance at the party. And now to find a witch's mark?

No. No coincidence.

Usually a witch's mark was simply a sort of good luck charm, meant to ward away any evil—or evil persons—from a building. This witch's mark, however, felt like a warning. Had the Dunkelder discovered who she was? Had he followed her as she followed Harlowe, then snatched her and locked them both up in the well house?

Except the mark was *already* carved in the well house when they were locked in. And why involve a *duke* if the Dunkelder was only after her?

Damn it. Nothing made sense.

"Are you all right?" Messalina asked her.

"Yes." Freya cleared her throat because that had sounded curt and she didn't want to offend Messalina. "I'm sorry I missed our meeting last night."

"I think, under the circumstances, that I can forgive you." Messalina's tone was very dry.

Freya felt her mouth quirk. "Shall we try again tonight?"

"Yes, please." Messalina sent her a grateful glance.

Freya felt a near-giddy burst of warmth in her breast as she smiled back. "Your room?"

Messalina nodded, and for several minutes they walked companionably in silence before she said, "You must've been frightened to be locked in all night. How did it happen?"

Freya shrugged and, because she was tired and really couldn't think of anything else, told the truth. "I was following Harlowe when I was grabbed and a neckcloth tied about my eyes. I was pushed into the well house. Then someone slammed the door closed behind us."

Messalina raised both brows. "Did you have an assignation there with Christopher?"

"Erm, no." Freya supposed she should feel insulted, but she was just weary. "He told me later that he'd received a note to meet Mr. Plimpton in the well house. I saw him leave the house and..." Actually, now that she thought of it, it was rather hard to explain. She ended rather lamely, "I just...followed him."

"Ah," Messalina said, sounding doubtful.

Freya had a sudden urge to blurt out the whole complicated matter to Messalina. Years and years she'd been alone, living under a false name. And although the Hollands were quite kind as employers, she couldn't ever confide in them. Couldn't really talk to anyone.

Once, she would've told Messalina *everything*.

She wanted that closeness back with all her heart.

Freya glanced at the other woman out of the corner of her eye and said softly, "Thank you for looking for us."

Messalina shrugged. "We—Lucretia and I—didn't know what we were about. We simply followed Tess. I'm afraid she's the real heroine."

Freya glanced at the dog trotting along beside Harlowe, her head lifted adoringly to him. "I wonder why she didn't come find Harlowe last night? Was she locked in the house?"

"No," Messalina said slowly. "She was tied up in the stables. The groom who was guarding her says he received a letter from Christopher, but that seems unlikely, doesn't it?"

"Yes," Freya said, watching Harlowe's back. She remembered the horrible story he'd told her the night before. Tess was always with him, wasn't she? Almost like a talisman against the memories. "I don't think he'd tie up Tess by herself. He's very fond of her."

"I can tell. She did not like being apart from him."

"No." Freya smiled at how at ease Harlowe looked now that he was with the dog.

Messalina lowered her voice, "Do you know who did this?"

Freya darted a quick look at her, thinking of the Dunkelder and who might want Harlowe scared away. "I might have an idea."

"Who?"

Freya shook her head. "I think it better we discuss this tonight. Alone."

The other woman raised her brows. "Very well."

Lovejoy House finally came into view. Freya could see Lady Holland waiting by the garden with Regina and Arabella.

When Freya reached her, the older woman said nothing, but surprised Freya by folding her in her arms. "I was so worried for you, Miss Stewart."

"Oh, Miss Stewart!" Regina exclaimed, and hugged her as well.

Arabella smiled shyly, taking her hands. "Thank God you are well."

Freya nodded to them both, but she couldn't help but notice that Lady Holland's worried face hadn't yet relaxed. In fact, her employer nodded significantly to someone over Freya's head.

But when she turned, she couldn't tell who had been the recipient of that silent communication.

The ladies ushered Freya indoors and up to her room, where she finally—thank goodness!—relieved her overextended bladder. A warm bath had been ordered, and she gratefully stripped off her clothes and bathed. Then she dressed, taking pains to make herself neat and assume once again the role of boring companion.

She winced.

After their discovery this morning she might never be entirely unnoticed again. Well, that couldn't be changed, and perhaps it didn't matter anymore. She was due to return to Dornoch in a little over a week.

Her heart sped as she realized how little time she had.

She gave herself a last inspection in the mirror on the dressing table and decided she could no longer avoid the rest of the party.

Taking a deep breath, she descended the stairs and found the salon, where it seemed the entire house party had gathered to discuss the morning's events. Naturally everyone stopped talking and turned to stare at her when she entered.

Harlowe had been in discussion with Lady Holland. He looked up, meeting her eyes gravely. He, too, had refreshed himself. Tess was by his side, and he looked every inch the duke in a severe black suit and snowy neckcloth that made his blue eyes blaze.

For some reason the sight of him sent a tremor down her frame. For the first time in five years she rather wished she were wearing something fit for her true station instead of a dowdy companion's dress.

Silly! she chided herself. She was a Wise Woman, and her mission was far more important than silk dresses.

Freya lifted her chin and crossed the room, ignoring all the other gazes on her, aware only that Harlowe watched her the entire time.

He stood and bowed as she neared, taking her hand in his.

She would *not* let her fingers tremble at a simple touch.

"Miss Stewart," he greeted her. "If you don't mind, I would like a private word with you."

Freya frowned. They'd spent the night together—mostly talking, true, but still. What did he need to say now—and so formally?

But she nodded and followed him into a small sitting room across the hall.

"Please," he said, indicating a chair.

She raised her eyebrows but sat.

"I think you must know why I've asked to speak to you," he began, his blue eyes intent and serious.

She interrupted, her nerves frayed after the morning and after having run the gauntlet in the salon. "Actually, I don't."

He stopped and stared at her.

Then he crossed to her and gravely went down on one knee before her. "Freya de Moray, would you do me the honor of becoming my wife?"

CHAPTER TEN

*'Tis well known that to make a bargain with a fairy is
a perilous thing, but Rowan had no other choice if
she wanted to speak to the Fairy King.
She took a silver dagger hanging at her waist and
cut off a lock of her own fiery hair. "Will you take
this in payment?"
"Oh yes," Ash said. "Now close your eyes, take my
hand, and kiss me."
Rowan did as he said and pressed her lips against his
chilly mouth....*
—From *The Grey Court Changeling*

Despite having been married once before, Christopher had never proposed. That was because his last engagement had been a fait accompli by the time he was informed of it. The entire thing had been arranged by his father and Sophy's mother. Even her brother hadn't heard until he was called home from London to attend the hasty wedding.

So Christopher had never before contemplated how best to propose to a woman. Though if he had, he would've acknowledged that a hasty, forced-by-circumstances proposal probably wasn't the ideal option—especially for a woman such as Freya.

After all, she'd not only challenged him to a duel, she'd *won*.

Still, even knowing she wouldn't be happy about his proposal, he wasn't entirely prepared for outright refusal.

"Are you insane?" Her green-gold eyes blazed at him as fiercely as if he'd suggested running nude through the sitting room.

He blinked, nonplussed. "I—"

"*No*," Freya said calmly, if a bit lethally, "I won't marry you, Kester."

He tried to rein in his irritation. Did *everything* have to be difficult with this woman?

"We spent the night together, Freya," he said through gritted teeth. "Even if nothing truly happened, the tale will get out. If you don't marry me, people will talk about you. I don't want that."

"You're concerned that people will *talk* about me?" she replied mockingly. "Don't you think they might talk if a *duke* marries a penniless *companion*?"

"Don't be ridiculous," he snapped. "Wonder at a formally disgraced lady marrying a duke is not at all the same as speculation that I seduced and abandoned you."

"This sounds very much as if you're worried over your own name," she drawled. "You needn't fret. Most couldn't care less about a poor companion."

Try though he did, he felt his own ire rise. "Damn it, Freya. You *aren't* a companion. When you marry me you can resume your true name and your place in society."

Her eyes went wide, and for a fraction of a second he thought his logic had prevailed.

Then her upper lip lifted, revealing perfect white teeth that bit out, "You presume to know what I want. Has it never occurred to you that I'm perfectly happy as I am? That I don't *want* to take back my name and position?"

"No," he growled back, "because that's *ridiculous*. You're

the daughter of a duke. Why the hell would you want to continue serving those inferior to you in rank?"

"You don't know me, Christopher Renshaw."

"Don't I?" For some reason those words made his irritation boil over into anger. He braced his hands on the arms of the chair she sat in and leaned into her, staring into those gorgeous eyes. "I know your family and where you grew up, Freya de Moray. I know that your tongue is sharp enough to cut to ribbons any man so foolish as to cross you. I know you hide a tender side under your thorny exterior, because you spent all night in my arms just to calm me. And, Freya, I know what you taste like when I kiss you."

He suited action to word by leaning forward and catching her lips in a brief, hard kiss.

She didn't protest, but she didn't actively return his passion.

Which should've been a warning to him.

When he pulled away, she was lounging back in the chair, as cool and unmoved as a queen about to pronounce sentence upon some filthy peasant.

"You think *embracing* me is the same thing as knowing me?" she whispered. "What of my wishes, my fears, my *dreams*? You don't know anything true about me, Harlowe. That's proved by the very fact that you think I'd want to marry you because of *social mores*."

And now she'd regressed to calling him by his title. How could he desire such a contrary woman?

Because she challenged him. Because when her anger rose so did her passion. Because he'd caught a sweet light in her eyes more than once when she gazed at him.

Because beneath all those sharp thorns lay an intelligent, warm woman. He inhaled, trying to calm himself. "I don't want to marry you only because of society—"

"Would you have proposed had we not been locked in the well house?" she interrupted sweetly.

"You know damned well I wouldn't have!"

She raised haughty brows. "Then I think this discussion over."

He took a deep breath, trying to reclaim reason. He *had* to protect her. "Freya, I've compromised you."

"I won't marry merely because you feel guilty." She stood, making him rise as well and give her room. "Frankly, your guilt is not my problem."

He closed his eyes. He hadn't slept last night, not really, and had spent most of the hours in a state of high tension because of the dark and the cramped little house.

He was exhausted.

Christopher opened his eyes and looked at her. "I failed your brother. I failed Sophy. I will not fail *you*."

Her lips were trembling now. She was no doubt as tired and irritable as he. "Not marrying me isn't *failing* me. If it makes you feel better, I very much doubt that even Lady Holland truly expects you to marry me."

He took a step forward, standing close enough that he could smell the faint traces of her honeysuckle perfume, and said desperately, "I am not proposing for Lady Holland or anyone else. I want you as my wife because of who you *are*."

She cocked her head. "And who do you think I am?"

"Lady Freya de Moray," he replied, quietly, but with heat, for his patience was wearing thin. "The daughter and sister of the Duke of Ayr. A lady of considerable heritage. A lady who deserves to be married when she is compromised. I want what is best for you."

Her sweet mouth flattened almost as if she were hurt. "If you wanted what was best for me, you would not insult me by proposing for society's sake."

"I am proposing because it's what's *right*," he said helplessly. Their conversation was unraveling in his hands and he had no idea how to put it back together again. He didn't know the *words* to convince her. "I'm proposing because if I did not, I would no longer be an honorable gentleman. Can't you see that?"

Her eyes went wide, and for a fraction of a second he thought he saw tears in her eyes.

Then she turned away, hiding her face. "Perhaps," she said as she swept from the room, "you should worry less about your honor and more about my feelings."

* * *

That night Freya took a deep breath before tapping softly on Messalina's door.

Messalina immediately opened it and beckoned her inside.

Freya walked in and turned, feeling nervous.

The strange thing was that Messalina seemed nervous as well, her smile tentative as she gestured to a chair and a settee by the small fireplace. "Will you sit?"

Freya lowered herself to one of the chairs. Messalina was wearing a lovely jade silk wrapper embroidered with cranes. Her hair was in a single smooth braid. Freya felt a pang as she remembered all the times when as children they were allowed to sleep at each other's home. Messalina had always had glossy, straight black hair—hair easily tamed into a smooth braid for sleeping, unlike Freya's own wild curly hair.

Freya inhaled and looked at her dearest childhood friend. "I think I need to begin by apologizing to you."

"What?" She appeared to have caught Messalina by

surprise. Her eyes widened as she sat on the very edge of her chair. "*Why?*"

"For the way I've treated you for the last fifteen years. I'm sorry." Freya gripped her hands together. "I think when it happened, I was in shock. We feared that Ran might die, you see, and then with Papa's death..."

"I understand," Messalina interjected. "Truly I do. You don't have to go on."

"But I think I do," Freya said softly. "I need to tell you that I'm sorry—so very sorry—that Aurelia died. I've never believed that Ran killed her, but that doesn't stop me from mourning her. I need to tell you all this so that there won't be any more lies or hurt or confusion between the two of us."

Messalina half smiled. "Can we really do away with all hurt between us?"

Freya answered her smile with her own. "We can *try*, I think. I can look at you and understand that none of this was your fault—any more than it was my fault. We both suffered. We both lost family members. But when I should've gone to you for comfort I turned away instead. I thought that you must have taken the side of your brother and uncle. That you were my enemy now."

Messalina sighed. "I've never been your enemy—even if I still love my brother Julian."

"And I'm not your enemy, even if I still love Ran," Freya said softly. "I'm sorry for being scared. For *assuming* instead of talking to you."

Messalina blinked rapidly, her eyes shining. "Well, I think I can forgive you if you promise to talk to me in the future."

"Yes," Freya said, her voice wobbling. "*Yes*, I can do that."

Freya didn't know how she came to be standing, but Messalina had her arms wrapped around her neck and they were hugging as if they were still girls, their hair down, running over the Scottish hills, and it was *good*, so very good to know that Messalina was her friend again.

Freya felt tears sliding down her cheeks, which was simply silly. She didn't know when she'd last been so happy.

When Messalina finally let her go, she drew Freya down to sit on the settee close beside her. "Oh, I've missed you so! What has your life been like? Why are you acting as a paid companion, and why the name Miss Stewart? I confess I've been dying to ask for the last four years."

Freya looked at her and opened her mouth to tell her the usual lies, but instead what came out was, "I'm a Wise Woman."

It was such a relief to say it *aloud* that she grinned.

Though, of course, her statement led to an explanation that took nearly an hour.

"Good Lord," Messalina said after Freya finally ran out of words. She was lounging on the settee. She'd produced a bottle of wine sometime in the last half hour and was now sipping from a tiny, delicate wineglass. "I had heard the rumors, of course. One can hardly grow up on the border and not hear whispers about Wise Women, but for them to be *true*." She shook her head. "And you say that's why you were locked in the well house? Because of a Dunkelder in our midst?"

"It must be," Freya said, swallowing a mouthful of wine. "I think it was a warning to me."

"Who do you suppose it is?" Messalina mused. "Have you a guest in mind? I'd point to Lord Rookewoode myself. That man is far too handsome for his own good."

Freya laughed. It was so nice to be able to discuss this with someone else. To discuss it with *Messalina*. "I've wondered about Lord Stanhope—he seems so dour and disapproving. But Lord Lovejoy actually talked about witches and *he* at least is from the area."

"Of course it could be Christopher," Messalina said innocently.

Freya shot her a baleful look.

"No, I suppose not." Messalina grinned. "Whatever is going on between the two of you?"

"Nothing," Freya said, attempting to sound innocent.

Messalina arched a disbelieving eyebrow.

Freya wrinkled her nose. She'd never been able to pretend with Messalina. "He proposed."

"No!"

"Yes." Freya shrugged and sipped her wine to cover her sudden pang of sadness.

"And I take it you refused." Messalina seemed thoughtful.

"Why do you say that?" Freya hedged.

It was Messalina's turn for the look. "One, because you're as stubborn as a mule. Two, because Christopher would've announced the engagement at dinner had you accepted, and instead he spent the meal glaring at his peas, poor man."

"I see you've already taken his side," Freya grumbled.

"Not at all." Messalina waved her wineglass rather recklessly. "I merely feel sorry for him because he should've known that asking for your hand out of a sense of duty was guaranteed to make you decline—even if you truly were interested in him."

Freya felt heat mount her cheeks. "Who says I'm interested in Harlowe?"

"I do because of the way you stare at him when you think no one is looking," Messalina said slyly. "When I first arrived, your stares were nearly all angry. Lately they've revealed an entirely different emotion."

"I don't know what you mean," Freya said, though her face felt as if it were burning now. Was it true? Was she betraying herself every time she glanced at Harlowe? Because she knew that Messalina was right in one respect: she no longer hated him.

And if he'd asked her to marry him without the threat of scandal hanging over her head? Well, she wouldn't have accepted him, of course.

But she might've told him so in less harsh terms.

Freya cleared her throat. "We've rather gotten off the subject of the Dunkelder and my mission for the Wise Women."

"Mission?" Messalina cocked her head inquisitively. "What mission is that?"

Freya bit her lip, but she'd already told Messalina everything else. "When Parliament reconvenes in the autumn, some members intend to propose an act making witch-hunting not just legal again, but encouraged." Her mouth twisted. "The Witch Act that Lord Stanhope mentioned the other day at breakfast. It's meant as a morality measure—eradicating the ungodly from Britain. That sort of thing. In the past, though, the Dunkelders have made no distinction between witches and Wise Women. They believe we *are* witches—evil worshippers of the devil. Obviously, I can't let that act be passed."

Messalina sat up a little straighter. "How do you intend to stop it?"

Freya leaned forward. "The man spearheading the act is Lord Elliot Randolph. If I can find something to hold over the man, I'm hoping I can prevent him from proposing the act." She sat back. "I think Lord Randolph killed his wife, and I want to prove it."

Messalina's eyes grew wide. "*Eleanor* Randolph?"

"Yes?" Freya said warily.

Messalina jumped up and went to her dressing table to rummage in a box holding her toiletries. "*Ah.* Here it is." She turned and thrust a letter into Freya's hands. "Read it."

Freya bent to the letter, rapidly scanning the page and then reading it again more slowly. The letter was from Eleanor Randolph, stating that she wished to leave Lord Randolph.

She stared at Messalina. "When did you receive this?"

"Only weeks before Eleanor died."

Freya folded the letter, thinking. "I walked to the estate the first day here and talked to the gamekeeper. He said that Eleanor had run into the stable yard at night wearing only her chemise. Of course everyone thought she was mad...but what if she *wasn't*?"

Messalina nodded, looking fierce. "She could've been trying to escape from Lord Randolph." Her face fell. "But how can we prove it?"

"Someone in the house must've known," Freya said. She wasn't *quite* as confident as she hoped her voice sounded, but she had to think there was *some* possibility of revealing Lord Randolph as a murderer. "I tried talking to the housekeeper, but no one would answer the door there."

Messalina was frowning. "We tried to find Eleanor's lady's maid, but she was dismissed before Eleanor died."

Freya blinked. "We?"

"Jane and I," Messalina said. "She's a good friend and very practical. Enlisting her help was the first thing I did when I came."

"Do you know where the lady's maid went when she was dismissed?" Freya asked. "Perhaps she returned to London."

Messalina shook her head. "She was a local girl—she shouldn't have gone far."

"But if she knows anything, she's probably too frightened to speak out." Freya worried her lip for a moment, thinking. "What we need is someone from the area, someone she might *trust*, to look for her and approach her." She glanced at Messalina. "Are any of Lady Lovejoy's servants locals?"

"I'll ask her." Messalina looked at Freya. "Then we are investigating Eleanor's death together?"

Freya nodded. "*Together.*"

Messalina's face lit with a broad smile. "Oh, good."

* * *

Christopher woke the next morning with the realization that he'd slept peacefully through the night.

Without any nightmares.

Strange. He'd thought that after the night in the well house his night fears—his aversion to the dark and small spaces—would worsen. He'd fully expected a restless, nightmare-filled sleep.

Instead he was more refreshed than he had been in years.

He very much doubted that he was entirely cured of his affliction, but he was certainly glad that it hadn't worsened. Was this because Freya had been with him in the well house? Because she distracted him with conversation and her very presence?

If so, he owed her a debt of gratitude.

Tess nosed his hand.

He turned and saw her sitting patiently by the side of his bed.

Well, not so patiently—she backed up and barked, once and sharply, when she saw that he was awake.

"Did you want something?" he inquired politely.

Tess spun in a circle, then bowed to him.

"Oh, all right."

He rose and quickly dressed, then led the way out of the room and down the stairs, Tess padding behind.

They stepped out of the house and into the gentle morning sunshine. Tess ran ahead as they headed for the garden.

Christopher had had quite enough of the woods the day before.

He pondered Freya as he strolled behind Tess's loping form. He wanted her as his wife—and not merely because marrying her was the honorable thing to do. He wanted to spend his life arguing with her, watching her lips twitch when she baited him, feeling the thrill go through his chest when he provoked her laugh.

She wasn't an easy woman, but she made him feel alive. More, she made him want to *live*.

And she saw him as a *man*—not a son, employer, husband, rich relative, or duke. He was Kester to her.

Plain and simple.

He longed for that—to be a human again. To be intimate with another person again.

To be intimate with *Freya*.

Which meant he needed to somehow learn Freya—both who she was as a woman and what she wanted in order to agree to become his wife.

But first he needed to confront Plimpton and be done with that matter, because he'd never met with the man the night before. Somehow Plimpton had made sure to avoid him.

No more.

Christopher whistled for Tess and turned toward the house.

* * *

Late that morning the entire house party set out on horse-back for a picnic alfresco.

The horse Freya was given to ride to the picnic was so old she could practically hear its bones creaking. She'd tried to nudge the mare into a trot, but the poor thing kept lapsing back into a steady walk. She trailed the rest of the party by quite a bit.

Which suited her just fine. She'd finally had to break the news to Lady Holland just this morning that she hadn't accepted Harlowe.

Lady Holland had shaken her head, looking as if she had too many things to say all at once.

Thankfully, Lady Lovejoy had chosen that moment to an-nounce the picnic, and Freya had made a hasty escape to change into her riding costume.

Now Freya sighed and watched Arabella riding ahead of her. Arabella was beside young Mr. Lovejoy, who wasn't a very good horseman but made up for it by not taking himself terribly seriously.

Lady Holland was on the other side of Mr. Lovejoy and smiling benignly. Freya concurred—really that would be a good match. Not as good as with a titled gentleman, of course, but Mr. Lovejoy was *nice*, especially when it came to Arabella. He didn't seem the sort to ride roughshod over his wife's opinions. He was a good listener, and Freya had the feeling he would truly respect Arabella.

When one came right down to it, *nice* was a very good thing in a gentleman.

The thought made Freya's gaze slide to Harlowe, who was riding a bit ahead of the three in front of her. He *wasn't* nice. He was stubbornly certain that he knew what was best for her—and, more, that he would *save* her even if she didn't want saving.

She *ought* to be well done with the man.

On the other hand, she herself was not a nice woman. Freya's lips quirked at the thought. She enjoyed arguing with Harlowe. Enjoyed knowing she could say exactly what she thought and he wouldn't pull his conversational punches with her.

Enjoyed kissing Harlowe.

Perhaps...even if she had no wish to marry the man, perhaps she could kiss and argue with him some more.

Maybe even do more than kissing.

She was so busy thinking on the matter that she nearly missed the party's turning off the track to stop at a pretty clearing.

The servants had been sent ahead to lay out their "rustic" picnic: colorful cloths and cushions were artfully placed on the ground in groups, and the footmen were busy setting out the food and wine.

"Oh, how lovely!" Lady Holland exclaimed as a groom helped her dismount.

It was rather enchanting, Freya had to admit.

She guided her mare to the side and dismounted by herself, careful of her old riding habit's skirts. She was handing her reins to a groom when she was hailed.

"Miss Stewart," Regina called. "Come dine with us."

Freya turned. Regina had already chosen a pile of cushions and was sitting with Messalina, who gave Freya a small nod.

Early that morning Messalina and Lady Lovejoy had introduced her to James, a young redheaded footman from the area. Freya had already explained that she'd been friends with Lady Randolph and, like Messalina, wanted to discover what had happened to Eleanor. Lady Lovejoy had assured her that James had been in her employ for several years—

starting as a bootblack in the kitchens—and was to be trusted. Freya had liked James's levelheaded demeanor. She'd given him careful instructions on what she wanted— to locate and question Lady Randolph's lady's maid—and the man had simply nodded and said it might take him several days.

He seemed competent, if a man of few words.

"This wine is quite good," Regina was saying as Freya neared. "What a wonderful idea of Lady Lovejoy's, to plan this picnic. Don't you think so, Miss Greycourt?"

"Yes, indeed," Messalina replied as Freya took a seat. "But please call me Messalina."

"Oh, and you should call me Regina," the other replied with a happy little bounce. "I feel as if we'll be great friends."

"I think so, too," Messalina said. She turned to Freya with a devilish gleam in her gray eyes. It was the same look she used to wear when she was about to dare Freya to do something quite stupid with her. Such as swim in the loch wearing only their chemises. In *November*. "And you, Miss Stewart? Surely you have a Christian name as well?"

Regina giggled. "Do you know, Miss Stewart has been with us since I was sixteen, and yet I don't think I've ever heard her Christian name."

"Of course I have a Christian name," Freya said, widening her eyes innocently. Messalina really ought to realize that she couldn't catch Freya out.

"And?" Messalina prompted, her lips twitching.

"Aethelreda," Freya replied with a perfectly benign smile.

Regina paused with her wineglass halfway to her lips, her eyes wide. "Truly?"

Messalina coughed. "What an . . . *interesting* name."

"I think so."

When they'd been girls there had been a painting at Greycourt of an old, rather irritable-looking lady. No one seemed to know who she was—the best guess was that she'd been a relative of someone who married into the family. But Messalina and Freya had been fascinated—and a little frightened—by her wrinkled visage. They'd named her Aethelreda, which had been the most hilarious name they could think up.

Actually, Freya still found the name rather funny.

Apparently Messalina did, too—she was quite obviously trying not to laugh.

Freya wanted to grin, but really that wouldn't do.

She was still a companion, after all, and it would be very hard at this late date at the party to explain that she'd been childhood friends with Messalina.

"Why is Mama glaring at you?" Regina asked, looking over Freya's shoulder.

Freya winced. "I'm afraid I've been quite the coward and have been avoiding Her Ladyship."

"Why?" asked Messalina.

"Because I declined His Grace's proposal."

"*What?*" Regina exclaimed, much too loudly.

"Oh my goodness, Aethelreda," Messalina murmured, and Freya thought she was enjoying Freya's embarrassment far too much.

"He was only offering because of the well house," Freya muttered.

"Really?" Messalina turned to look at Harlowe. "And I suppose that's why he's staring at you now?"

"Is he?" Regina said, craning her neck.

"If you'll excuse me," Freya said with what remaining dignity she had. "I believe I should talk to Lady Holland."

She rose before either Regina or Messalina could protest.

She'd walked only a half dozen steps, though, when a hand caught her.

"Come sit here, Miss Stewart," Harlowe said, far too loudly.

"What are you doing?" she hissed at him.

He widened his wicked blue eyes—as if anyone could think him innocent. "Why, I'm about to partake of some very fine roast beef and cheese."

"You're drawing attention to us," she snapped as she reluctantly yielded to the tug of his hand. She sat on a large purple pillow, tucking her feet under her skirts.

Tess, who had been circling the mound of pillows and fabric, collapsed with a groan next to her.

Freya absently petted the dog's soft ears.

"The only thing that might draw attention to us is your squawking. Look around. Everyone else is busy flirting." Harlowe lounged back on a pile of multicolored silk pillows looking like some barbarian king. "Besides, I was under the impression that you hardly cared what the rest of the party thought of us."

"There is no *us*," she retorted rather lamely.

He shook his head as if saddened by the rejoinder. "I'm afraid that there you are wrong. It was made quite plain to me at breakfast that *everyone* knows I attempted to propose to you and that you swiftly turned me down."

"Gossips, the lot of them."

"Oh, quite."

Freya sighed irritably and glanced around, only to find the viscount staring at her in disapproval. "Mr. Stanhope certainly isn't flirting."

"No," Harlowe replied, handing her a glass of wine. "I'm beginning to think the man is a monk. But I have other matters to discuss with you," he continued, watching her far too intently. "I realized this morning that I never thanked you for what you did in the well house."

She looked at him in surprise. "There's no need."

"There's every need," he replied seriously. "I nearly lost my mind in there. Your voice and presence were a balm on my fevered brain. I should've been comforting you, and yet it was you who were forced to comfort me. Thank you."

She stared at him. Really it was rather hard to continue to be angry at him when he was thanking her so graciously.

The bastard.

"You're welcome," she muttered, and then confessed, "I'm glad that I was there with you."

"Truly?" He smiled doubtfully. "I was half out of my mind, you missed your supper, *and* it was cold."

"Yes," she said simply, because it was true. She *was* glad she'd been with him. Judging by his panic when the door had shut, he might not have made it through the night alone without injuring himself. Or worse. The thought made her restive. She didn't want Harlowe hurt by anyone save herself.

And she was no longer sure *she* really wanted to hurt him.

"You're a remarkable woman," he said now softly. "Had I the choice of all the people in the world, I would've chosen you to go through that ordeal with me."

She looked away, feeling her cheeks warm, and sipped her wine—which *was* very good, she had to admit.

"I hope you've had no ill effects from that night?" He snapped his fingers at one of the footmen and gestured for a plate of food.

"No." She glanced at him feeling almost shy—*not* a usual emotion for her at all. "And you? How are you?"

He flashed a smile at her, making him look ridiculously boyish. "I've fully recovered. Thank you for asking." The footman brought him two filled plates, one of which Harlowe immediately handed to her. "That was not the only reason I wanted to talk to you."

"Oh?" Tess raised her head to take an interested sniff at the nearby food.

"Have you seen Mr. Plimpton?"

"No." She knitted her brows at the luscious strawberries on her plate. "Not since yesterday morning, I think."

He nodded. "Plimpton's gone."

"What?" She stared at him. "Are you sure?"

"He wasn't at supper last night, and this morning when I went to confront him, he would not answer. I had Lovejoy open his room," Harlowe said. "He wasn't there and most of his things were missing, including the letters." His mouth twisted. "*If* he ever had them here at all. The only thing I can think is that he panicked after locking us in the well house and ran."

Freya paused. She'd been so sure that the Dunkelder—whoever he was—had been behind locking them in the well house. The witch's mark had seemed to confirm it. But now she realized that all during that long night she'd never discussed the matter with Harlowe. "How do you know it was Mr. Plimpton?"

He raised his eyebrows. "He sent the note. He fled. Who else could it be?"

"I don't know," she said slowly, not even sure why she was arguing the matter with him. But if the Dunkelder *hadn't* locked them in, then he must still not be aware of her identity. The problem was, she couldn't tell Harlowe *why* she might suspect someone other than Mr. Plimpton. "You said you weren't entirely sure the note was from Mr. Plimpton. Why would Mr. Plimpton go to the trouble of locking us in the well house when he wanted your money?"

He eyed her thoughtfully. "Do you have another candidate?"

She hesitated for a fraction of a second. "No."

He took a sip of his wine, watching her, before carefully setting the wineglass down. "I hope that you would tell me if you had any information about this business."

Freya busied herself tearing her bread into increasingly smaller pieces. Absently she fed one to Tess. The bizarre thing was, she *wanted* to tell him. It was as if, having finally confided in Messalina after five years of hiding, she'd uncorked a bottle. All her secrets and lies were pouring out, and she couldn't put them back in any more than she could grasp wine with her fingers.

Harlowe's warm hand covered her own, stilling her restless fingers. "Tell me."

She looked up and saw his cerulean eyes. He was watching her, his face intent, focused only on her, and she had a sudden overwhelming urge to tell him.

To let him in.

But she couldn't.

"There's nothing to tell," she whispered, and that lie— one of a thousand she'd told—was like a needle driven into her own skin.

CHAPTER ELEVEN

*When Rowan opened her eyes again she stood
somewhere else. There beside them was the wood and
grotto, but all color had been stolen from the world.
Everything was etched in shades of gray.
Rowan turned and saw that Ash's purple eyes still
held color.
His lips quirked. "Your hair is like a beacon,
Princess." He grew solemn then. "Remember:
neither eat or drink anything in this place. Not unless
you wish to stay forever." ...*
—From *The Grey Court Changeling*

Christopher watched as Freya's face closed. She was hiding
something from him. It was obvious.

And why shouldn't she?

While he might feel after a night together in the well
house—a night in which he revealed the worst parts of
himself—that he was somehow closer to her, bound in friendship, if nothing else, she obviously had no such sentiments.

He exhaled slowly, facing the fact that he felt more for
her than she did for him.

To her he was still the man who had destroyed her family.
There was no reason for her to trust him.

Now or ever.

Plimpton had disappeared, and with the blackmailer gone,

there was no excuse for Christopher to stay at the house party. If he considered the matter dispassionately, he should leave.

And yet he didn't wish to leave—or to give her up.

He wanted to stay for her.

"Can you explain something to me?" he said slowly to Freya. "I understand you don't wish to marry me. But do you truly plan to remain a companion for the rest of your life?"

"I like the work I do for the Hollands," she said, avoiding the question altogether. Her brows drew together. "You won't tell them who I am?"

"No," he replied at once. "There's no reason for me to tell them anything."

She nodded, picking at her bread again, crumbling it into inedible bits. "Thank you. It's just that if they knew I'd lose the situation."

"Would you?" He glanced to where Lady Holland was talking with Lady Lovejoy. She struck him as a lady of good humor. "Are you sure? Lady Holland seems rather fond of you."

She looked up in alarm. "Please don't tell her, Kester."

Kester. The boyhood name brought him up short. "You're using my nickname to sway me," he said slowly, watching her. "You imply intimacy with me while withholding yourself."

She blinked. Had she not noticed that she'd used his nickname? "I...*Harlowe.* Will you promise me that you won't tell anyone my secret?"

Perhaps he shouldn't have pointed it out. He rather liked it when she called him Kester.

But she was glaring at him now, so he held up his hand. "Never fear. I won't talk." He watched as her shoulders lowered and wondered if she truly feared being dismissed so much. "Is that why you hide your hair? As a sort of disguise?"

She put her hand to her cap and then hastily lowered it. "It's more so that I don't draw attention to myself. The chaperone shouldn't deflect from the girls she guides."

Men would no doubt be drawn to her fiery locks—her fiery *temper*—if she let herself be seen as who she was. From what he knew of society, she would have very little trouble finding a suitable husband, despite her family's lowered expectations.

Which made it all the more odd that she was hiding her identity. "You don't intend to marry yourself?"

She looked startled. "I didn't say that."

"Yet you're in hiding." He cocked his head, eyeing the dust-colored riding habit she wore today. "It would take an incredibly perceptive gentleman to notice you as you are."

Her eyes suddenly rose, pinning him. "You didn't seem to have any trouble."

"Obviously I'm incredibly perceptive," he said dryly. "Do you *want* to marry?"

"Perhaps. I haven't really thought about it."

She was frowning down at the cheese on her plate as if it had offended her terribly. It wasn't an expression he would associate with a woman happy at the thought of marriage. "No? Then it's simply me you don't wish to wed."

She glanced up as if startled. "I . . . No, that's not it at all. You don't understand."

"Then help me," he said softly.

She picked up a strawberry and bit into it, the fresh red juices staining her lips. "When a girl is growing up, she's told that she will marry. It's simply what everyone expects. What they *assume*. To remain unmarried is considered odd." She stared at him as if trying to find the right words. As if she had something very important to tell him. "But what if it *wasn't* expected? What if women could decide to bind themselves to a man or not and still live a happy, free life?"

"But ladies do have such a choice," he said, puzzled. "It's not as if every woman is forced to marry as soon as she turns eighteen. Many women never marry."

She was already shaking her head. "Quite a few women *are* forced to marry—by their fathers or other male relatives or by their circumstances. And once married they give up all free choice."

"Aren't gentlemen under the same strictures? After all, *I* was forced by my father to marry."

"Yes, but once married you retained your autonomy." She leaned toward him, her plate of food forgotten in her passion for her argument, her green-gold eyes sparkling. "A woman is legally subservient to her husband. He controls her money and her person. If he wishes to take their children away from her, he can. If he wishes to deprive her of money, he can."

He took a sip of his wine, conscious that everything seemed sharper, more real around him. "Some gentlemen might do that," he said. "Despicable gentlemen. But wouldn't you agree they are in the minority? The majority of gentlemen care for their wives. They provide their wives with everything they are capable of: food and clothing, shelter and children."

"But as an *inferior*. Like a child. Once a woman marries, even to the most liberal of husbands, she must needs give over her own determination. She's no longer whole in and of herself. She is *halved* in order to become part of her husband."

"Not necessarily," he argued. "Shouldn't a husband and wife, in the best of marriages, combine to make a greater whole?"

She sat back, staring at him. Her breasts rose and fell rapidly beneath her gauzy fichu; her gold-flecked eyes were lit with fervor. "Perhaps. In an ideal world. In an ideal marriage. Perhaps a man and woman could bond together and be better than themselves separate. But I don't think that this *is* an ideal world, and I, certainly, am not an ideal woman. I think were I to marry, the pieces of me would be picked apart, bit by bit, until nothing remained of me alone."

"What a very cynical view," he said gently. "And so you'll go through life alone and celibate? Never having either lover or children?"

"I don't know," she said. "I would like children."

"I think you'll need a gentleman for that at least," he replied, his voice expressionless.

She scoffed and threw the top of her strawberry aside. "I am aware. I know something about the world and gentlemen. I *have* lived in London for five years."

What that had to do with knowing gentlemen, he wasn't sure.

"Yes?" He felt his lips twitch at her solemn assurance that she was a woman of the world. "Have you…erm… conversed with many London gentlemen, then?"

Her eyes narrowed as if she wasn't sure exactly what he was implying.

He wasn't sure himself—he just knew he was enjoying talking with her enormously. He hadn't simply conversed with a woman in a long, long time. Sophy and he had had very little in common, certainly not enough for a lengthy discussion.

It was nice, sitting here in the sunshine, talking with a passionate woman. Thinking of ways of countering her arguments. Remembering the heat of her mouth.

If they were alone…

But they weren't. He sat up straight at the thought, glancing around, but no one was paying them any attention. In fact, most of the attention seemed to be on an argument between Lord Rookewoode and Viscount Stanhope.

He turned back to Freya.

To find her eyeing him with a small scowl on her face. The look sent a spike of arousal through him. Odd that her prickliness should be so beguiling to him.

"I've talked to gentlemen before," she said.

"Have you?" he asked, interested—and a little jealous. Had other men discovered the fire underneath her dusty exterior? "*Intimate* intercourse?"

"I..." Her eyes narrowed, and he could practically *see* her brain trying to work out what that meant, exactly. "I don't know if *intimate* is the right word."

"No?" He frowned as if in thought. "Familiar? Personal? Cozy?"

She stared suspiciously. "Cozy intercourse?"

"Yes." He smiled guilelessly at her. "Have you had frequent cozy intercourse with gentlemen?"

"I..." She lifted her chin, looking both defiant and vulnerable. "No. Not *frequent*, but I have had, erm... intercourse?" Her voice was doubtful on the last word.

He really ought to take pity on her, but then again, she wasn't such a weak woman that pity was called for. She was a warrior. That being the case, it would be an insult to give up any ground gained.

"With many gentlemen?" he asked innocently, and tore off a bite of bread, watching her as he chewed.

She was frowning again, her plush lips pulled down rather adorably. "Nooo, not many."

"I'm glad," he said softly. "I'm honored to be one of the few you've shared your intercourse with."

* * *

Freya stared at Harlowe, feeling her cheeks warm. Was he...*flirting* with her?

Surely not.

Not after she'd argued with him. After she'd pricked him with her sword.

After she'd told him she'd never forgive him.

After she'd declined his proposal.

But then there were those kisses. Unless he made a habit of kissing everyone he argued with—and her mind boggled at the thought—he'd been...interested in her.

Perhaps he was interested in that sort of thing only now that she'd rebuffed the idea of marriage—kissing and what came after. Certainly she'd heard enough warnings as a girl about men and what they wanted.

She'd given such warnings herself—to Regina and Arabella—but now she paused. If he were really interested only in *that*, surely he could find someone who didn't slap him when she was angered.

What, then, was he after?

"You..." She cleared her throat, trying to find the right question. "You wish to *talk* with me?"

"Amongst other things." He smiled, his teeth flashing white in a face too tanned for a gentleman. "I'm interested in intercourse with you, haven't I said? Intercourse implies more than simple discussion."

"What then?" Freya found herself leaning toward him as if lured by his words.

He shrugged, never taking his gaze from hers. "The exchange of ideas. Building a foundation of mutual thought and consideration. Acknowledging that we two are equals in mind and spirit so that when we argue we are on level ground. I enjoyed our discussion about women and marriage even if I don't agree with everything you said. I'd like to continue such debates."

She stared. She'd never met a man who considered a woman his mental equal. She'd never even *heard* of such a thing. What a strange creature Harlowe was.

And how utterly seductive his proposition was. She'd been used to speaking her mind when she'd lived with Aunt Hilda and the other Wise Women. One of the hardest things about her work in London was hiding what she truly thought.

To engage as equals with a man who *respected* her mind.

The thought sent a shock through her, and she felt warmth pool low in her belly.

She said carefully, cautiously, "What sort of ideas?"

His eyes had more than a hint of triumph, as if she'd somehow conceded something, but before she could think about that too much he spoke. "Whatever you might want to discuss. Anything and everything. History? Politics? Philosophy? Religion?"

Her lips parted. Such a grand world he threw so carelessly at her feet. *Anything and everything.* Had he any idea what he offered her?

But this was too good. *Too* effortless. She looked at him suspiciously. "What if I disagree with something you hold dear?"

He shrugged and picked up an apple. "Then I shall tell you why I think you wrong and listen to your reply."

He bit into the apple, crunching loudly.

Slowly she smiled at him, feeling almost giddy.

A corner of his mouth curled up and he offered her the other side of his apple. "Bite?"

She placed her hands around both the apple and his fingers and bit into the juicy fruit.

When she looked up, his blue eyes were glittering at her.

She slowly chewed and swallowed the bite of apple. "Do you read?"

He tilted his head, a smile playing about his mouth. "Of course."

"I mean, what sort of books do you like?"

"History, mostly," he mused. "English books were rather rare in India. Those of us who had them traded them back and forth. So although I'd brought Herodotus and Tacitus and several histories of England and Scotland, I also read what other men—and women—liked."

"Such as?" She took a sip of her wine, the sweet bite sparkling on her tongue.

"Oh, the usual. *Robinson Crusoe*, *Don Quixote*, one or two of Shakespeare's plays, *The Compleat Angler*—the last rather wasted in Calcutta. But there were other books as well." He glanced slyly up at her from under his ridiculously black eyelashes. "There was a battered copy of *Moll Flanders* that went the rounds and an even more disreputable *Fanny Hill*."

Freya imagined Harlowe reading such scandalous literature. She'd never seen *Moll Flanders*—though she'd heard of it—but there was a copy of *Fanny Hill* hidden in the Holland library. She'd found it one rainy afternoon when the girls were away on an overnight trip with their mother and father.

Found it and read it . . . and now the memory made her bite her lip.

When she glanced up she found Harlowe watching her, his eyes amused. "You know them."

She nodded. "I've heard of both books."

"Have you?" He relaxed back on his elbow, the movement bringing him closer. The arm he was propped on nearly touched her knee. "But you haven't read either?"

She smiled and reached for a strawberry. "I've read *Fanny Hill.*"

She watched him as she bit into the strawberry, sweet juice filling her mouth.

"Have you." He watched her mouth as he took another bite of his apple. "Did it have illustrations?"

Her brows rose. *Illustrations?* There could be only one type of illustration for that book. "No."

"Pity." He finished the apple and threw the core into the brush before turning back to her. "The copy I read did, but I'm afraid the book had been vandalized. There was only one plate left."

"Yes?" she prompted, feeling a low heat in her belly. An urge to stretch and thrust out her breasts. To let her barriers fall. She was discussing *fucking* with Kester.

"Yes," he replied, his voice dropping as if he sensed a little of what she felt. "The plate depicted the first time Fanny lay with Charles."

She contemplated what a *picture* of that act would look like...and then she laughed.

Many men might feel that she laughed at them and take offense, but not Harlowe.

He smiled as if in reaction to her laughter. "You find that humorous?"

"No, not the picture, exactly," she replied. "It's just that when I read Fanny's description of Charles I thought he was too soft for my tastes."

"Indeed?" His voice was deeper.

"Yes." She leaned closer to him and whispered, "I thought that Mr. H—, her second lover, was much more appealing, even if he did betray her with the maid. He was big and *manly.*"

Harlowe opened his mouth to reply, but movement caught

her eye behind him. The party was beginning to leave, the footmen packing up.

She'd lost track of both time and where she was.

How was that possible? When she was on a mission she was always careful to keep her mind focused and aware of her goal.

She'd never been so careless before.

"You look worried," Harlowe said softly.

She glanced at him and saw sympathy in his expression.

Oh, he was *dangerous*—both to her and to her mission.

"I shouldn't have spent the picnic talking to you exclusively," she muttered, irritated with herself.

He rose as well. She could see his buckskin breeches out of the corner of her eye.

"I wanted to talk to you. I couldn't care less what the rest of the party thinks," he said with all the arrogance of a gentleman whose place in society had never been doubted.

Who was a *duke*.

"Yes, well," she murmured, "I'd rather not draw attention to myself."

There was a short silence, and she wondered if she'd offended him.

She looked up to meet warm blue eyes. A corner of his mouth twitched. "I understand. You're hiding your name. Your past."

His eyebrows drew together in a small frown as if he wanted to say more...and she wanted to hear what he said. Desperately. Wanted to *continue* this dangerous discourse.

Freya swallowed. She'd already revealed quite enough to Harlowe today.

"If you'll excuse me," she muttered.

And all but fled.

* * *

"I just don't understand," Lady Holland said incredulously that night after supper, "how you could decline a *duke*."

Freya sighed. It was not the first time her employer had expressed this opinion—and she had the feeling it wouldn't be the last.

They both sat in Lady Holland's room. Selby, Lady Holland's maid, was brushing out her mistress's hair in preparation for bed. Lady Holland sat in front of a mirrored vanity, the items from her traveling toilet spread before her.

She met Freya's eyes in the mirror and must have seen rebellion there. "Truly, Miss Stewart, I don't understand why you are protesting his offer. He's the *Duke* of Harlowe. Had he proposed to either of my girls I would've been most pleased."

Freya smiled a little wearily. "Even if he were marrying one of your daughters purely for her dowry, my lady?"

Lady Holland frowned. "But he's not marrying you for your dowry. Unless I'm very much mistaken, you don't *have* a dowry. I don't understand your objection."

Freya sighed and walked to the window, looking out even though she couldn't see anything through the dark glass.

Explaining why she didn't want to marry a duke was harder still when she longed for Harlowe right this minute. She'd thought of all manner of subjects that she wanted to discuss with him after ignominiously running from him this afternoon. She wanted to know his opinion on Dante, how he felt about kippers for breakfast, whether he was a Whig or a Tory, and if he'd ever considered breeding Tess and if so would he mind letting her have a puppy. Really, she could spend the rest of her life simply *talking* to the man.

Except of course that she enjoyed his kisses very much as well.

Not that the last should take precedence over other attributes, but it was certainly something to take into *consideration*.

For a moment she *considered* how masterful his mouth had been on hers two nights before.

Then she brought her thoughts back under control.

She had no wish to marry *any* man. To do so would be to put far too much trust in him—not only her heart, but her independence would be in his hands.

No. She was simply too suspicious and cynical a creature to rely upon *words* and *feelings* to determine her future.

Even if Harlowe could make her *feel* quite a lot.

Freya turned back to Lady Holland. "You're quite correct, my lady. I *don't* have a dowry. It may seem entirely foolish to you to decline His Grace's proposal. He's rich, titled, and powerful. Against that I'm merely a poor nobody in the world's eyes. A mouse beside a lion." She inhaled, marshaling her argument, and looked at Lady Holland. "But you see, to *me* I'm not just a nobody. I am myself and I am important. In *my eyes*, I am a lioness beside a lion. And as such I am free to accept or reject a gentleman for any reason, including the fact that he has proposed purely for society's sake."

Lady Holland stared at her for what felt like a very long time.

Then she sighed, let her shoulders slump, and said to Selby, "Oh Lord, get the brandy."

Freya suppressed a smile. It wasn't as if she wanted to best Lady Holland in argument. She was rather fond of her employer, not least because Lady Holland always traveled with a bottle of brandy in her toilet kit.

Someone knocked at the door.

Lady Holland nodded. "See who it is before we bring out the brandy. We might shock an impressionable maid."

But when Selby opened the door, it was to reveal Messalina and Lucretia with, hovering behind them, Lady Lovejoy.

Lady Holland raised her brows. "Yes?"

Messalina took a step into the room, looking determined. Lucretia and Lady Lovejoy followed and Selby closed the bedroom door. Messalina turned to Lady Holland. "Have you forced Freya into accepting the duke?"

"Freya?"

Messalina blinked. "Erm...Miss Stewart."

Lady Holland raised an eyebrow, shooting Freya an inquiring glance. "I thought your Christian name was Aethelreda?"

"Freya is a nickname."

"For Aethelreda?" Lady Holland asked, both eyebrows now elevated.

"Yes," Freya replied with dignity.

"Hm." Lady Holland turned back to Messalina. "Am I to understand that you and your sister came to make sure I hadn't browbeaten...erm...*Freya* until she agreed to marry the duke?"

Messalina lifted her chin. "Yes."

"Well, you may rest easy," Lady Holland replied wearily. "I've failed." She glanced at Lady Lovejoy. "And you, my lady?"

Lady Lovejoy arched a brow. "Well, it *is* my house. I was curious."

"Quite understandable under the circumstances." Lady Holland sighed. Again. "Would anyone care for brandy?"

Five minutes later everyone in the room had a small

splash of brandy in a glass, including Selby, because, as Lady Holland said, "You might as well join us."

It was Lady Lovejoy who broke the silence, looking at Freya. "Don't you like the duke, Miss Stewart?"

"Oh, I *do*," Freya said. She was sitting on a settee by the fire and her usual rigid posture had...relaxed a bit. "I really, *really* do. That's not the problem."

"I should *hope* not," Messalina muttered, glaring into her glass.

"Well, it's not," Freya replied. "It's just the *principle* of the thing, I think."

That statement met with silence, broken only by a "Hmm" from Lucretia.

Lady Lovejoy lowered her brandy glass. "I do see your point, really. If you were a bright young thing, just entering society, it would be one thing." Her eyes slid to Lucretia, who was staring rather dreamily into her glass. "One feels that the young should be protected, as it were, against the scourge of gossip. But once one reaches a certain age"—her gaze skipped to Messalina—"ought not one be considered an individual?"

"Yes," said Freya, rather astonished that Lady Lovejoy had turned out to be such a freethinking lady. "A *person*."

"A woman," Messalina said with a nod.

"Free," Lucretia murmured.

"Exactly." Lady Lovejoy leaned back on a settee opposite Freya's, her arm stretched along the back, her ankles crossed in front of her. "Rather like a man, if one wants to make that point. Just as a man comes into his majority and is made independent and capable of making his own decisions, so should a woman."

"Hear, hear," Lady Holland said, raising her brandy glass rather mockingly. "But that isn't the crux of the matter, is it?

Freya *can* make her own decisions. She can decide to refuse marriage to a titled, rich, strikingly handsome—"

"*In*-deed," murmured Lucretia.

"—gentleman whom she self-admittedly likes, but if she does so there will be many in society who punish her, no matter how noble her reasons."

"Christopher doesn't really have a choice, either," Lucretia said.

Everyone looked at her.

She shrugged. "Well, he doesn't—not if he's at all honorable."

"True," Lady Lovejoy said judiciously. "But now that he has offered, I think most would agree that whatever duty to do the honorable thing is over. The matter certainly won't affect his ability to marry later. In contrast, Freya might never be able to marry."

"Perhaps I don't wish to marry," Freya retorted, getting into the spirit of the debate.

"Don't you?" Lucretia asked with interest.

Now everyone was looking at her.

"I don't know," she said slowly. She glanced around at the other ladies. "I don't know."

CHAPTER TWELVE

Rowan followed Ash through the gray wood. No birds sang. No wind blew. All was still, as if the world had never lived.
Rowan looked up to see if the sun was gray as well, but though the gray sky was clear of any clouds, she could see no sun.
A single drop of dew fell from the trees above and landed on her lips.
Absently Rowan licked it away....
—From *The Grey Court Changeling*

It was just after midnight when Christopher was woken by Tess's low growling.

He lifted his head, listening in the darkness, and heard footsteps in the hall outside his door. His room was at the corner of the hallway and there was only one room beyond the turn.

Plimpton's.

Surely the man wouldn't be such an idiot as to return.

But then again, he *had* left half his possessions behind. To a man in financial straits a suit and a pair of boots might be worth the risk.

Christopher pulled on his shirt, breeches, stockings, and shoes, and then quietly opened the door to his room. If he craned his neck he could just see around the corner.

There was a light beneath Plimpton's door.

Tess followed Christopher as he stalked into the hall, rage making his shoulders bunch. Plimpton had been the one to contact him with his outrageous demands. Plimpton had insisted on meeting him at this house party. Plimpton had locked Christopher *and Freya* in a ghastly, dark, cramped little well house.

And then Plimpton had run away.

The man acted like a nervous virgin with Christopher in the role of pursuing satyr.

Except the woman he'd actually pursued hadn't bothered to run. She'd simply stood her ground and turned him down flat.

But then Freya was by any measure the more courageous of the two.

He reached Plimpton's room and knocked at the door.

There was a rustle from within and then silence.

"Plimpton," Christopher growled, his mouth close to the door. "Let me in or I'll kick this bloody door down."

He heard fumbling on the other side, and then the door opened a crack.

Plimpton's handsome face, looking rather *less* handsome than usual due to a sheen of sweat over the surface, peered out. "Harlowe. The thing is, I really can't give you the letters without the money. You see—"

Christopher set his palm against the door and shoved it open.

Plimpton apparently hadn't been expecting that. He stumbled back into the room.

Christopher kicked the door closed behind him. "You locked me and Miss Stewart in the damned well house."

Plimpton's eyes went wide. "I don't—"

"Whatever do you have against Miss Stewart?"

"That was an accident."

"You blindfolded her and then *padlocked the door*." Christopher advanced on the man, rage creating a red mist before his eyes. "She might've died in there."

"Wait. Wait. *Wait*." Plimpton was backing up, but he'd hit the wall.

"Where are the letters?"

"I don't—"

"I've had enough of your sniveling excuses. Did you bring the letters or not?"

"O-of course," Plimpton stuttered.

"*All* of the letters?"

Plimpton's features twisted with distress. "I-I can't—"

Christopher growled.

"Yes!" Plimpton mopped his brow with a handkerchief. "Good Lord, this is why I thought to lock you in that well house in the first place. You're *violent*. I fled yesterday because I was sure you were going to kill me. It was only because I'd run out of funds at the local inn that I returned. All I want is the money you have. You needn't be so *beastly*."

"You seduced Sophy," Christopher snarled. "And now that she's dead you're using her memory and good name to blackmail me. If anyone is *beastly*, it's you."

"Unfair!" cried Plimpton. "It's just that I'm in need of a bit of ready blunt. I'm overextended, I've got tradesmen pounding at my door, demanding I pay my bills and refusing to extend my credit. *You* can easily afford to pay me. I doubt you'll even notice the money's gone from your ducal coffers," he finished rather resentfully.

"Not notice ten thousand *pounds*?" Christopher shouted. "I'd have to be Midas himself to not notice that."

"You owe me," Plimpton retorted, taking another tack.

"You all but abandoned poor dear Sophy. She used to cry on my shoulder, she was so lonely and miserable. I was her friend—her only friend—in Calcutta. She loved me."

For a moment Christopher closed his eyes with pure, inarticulate fury.

When he opened them again, Plimpton was watching him with a self-righteous frown on his face.

"I *owe* you nothing at all." Christopher inhaled and said very, very softly, "Yes, Sophy no doubt thought she loved you. After all"—he gestured to the man—"You're pretty enough, you dress stylishly, if cheaply, and you have a sort of surface charm. So she loved you. And when the nawab's army came, you ran away and left her to her fate like the bloody coward you are."

Plimpton was looking outraged. Which might explain the unwary reply he made. "Her *fate* was that you killed her in that Black Hole."

Christopher gave up all pretense of civility and punched him in the face.

* * *

"James the footman's found a scullery maid let go just last week," Messalina murmured in Freya's ear. The other ladies were still debating marriage and a woman's position in society while Freya had taken a seat a little apart by the fire.

Freya turned to stare at Messalina, only inches from her face. "So soon?" And she hadn't explicitly told James to search for other servants dismissed from the Randolph household. The footman showed a nice ability to think for himself.

Messalina nodded. "The girl is in hiding at her uncle's

cottage. He says he can bring her here so we can question her."

"When?" There was only a week left of the house party. After that everyone would go back to London—and Freya would be forced to retreat to Dornoch by order of the Hags.

Unless she found new information—*real* information—against Randolph so that she could make a plea to delay her return.

Messalina shrugged. "We asked James to bring the scullery maid at once, but he says she's scared out of her mind. It may take some time for him to persuade her."

Freya was still working through that information when she heard the scream.

She blinked and glanced at her glass of brandy—her second glass. But then she looked up and realized everyone else had heard the scream as well.

"Good Lord," Lady Lovejoy exclaimed. "Whatever is it?"

She rose as Lady Holland struggled into a wrapper with Selby's aid and the other ladies jumped up as well.

"I suppose we ought to go see who it is," Messalina said, frowning.

"Yes, indeed," Lucretia exclaimed. She was already at the door.

They spilled into the hall, where they found Lord Lovejoy and the Earl of Rookewoode running toward the part of the house where most of the gentlemen's rooms were.

Lord Lovejoy stopped when he saw them. "I'm sure it's all right, ladies. If you'll simply return to your rooms the earl and I shall see what the matter is. Jane, perhaps you can send for er...tea."

Naturally his wife ignored him, as did the rest of the ladies. The entire group tromped down the hallway and were encouraged when a shout and a flurry of barking came, pinpointing the area of distress.

It turned out to be Mr. Plimpton's room.

"Good Lord, is that Mr. Plimpton? When did he return?" Lady Holland murmured.

Freya stood on tiptoe, trying to see over the heads of the other guests as Lord Lovejoy flung open Mr. Plimpton's door.

"Damnation," Lord Lovejoy exclaimed. "What is the meaning of this?"

Freya caught a glimpse of Harlowe, standing in the center of the room, looking particularly grim as he pummeled Mr. Plimpton. Tess was to the side, well out of the way of the struggle, but barking frantically at the two men. "Oh no!"

She pushed through the people in front of her and edged by Lord Lovejoy, who was blocking the doorway.

What she saw when the view was clear was not good. Mr. Plimpton hung limp from Harlowe's left fist, which was wrapped around his neckcloth.

Tess abruptly stopped barking.

"Where the hell are they?" Harlowe roared.

"Th-there," Plimpton hissed through a swollen mouth.

He was waving his hand in the direction of a rather battered portable desk.

Freya crossed to the flat box and opened it. There were blank paper, pens, a stoppered bottle of ink, and, shoved in a narrow drawer, a bundle of letters.

She turned with the letters clutched in her hand. "I have them, Harlowe. Let him go."

Harlowe swung toward her and opened his hand, not even looking when Mr. Plimpton slumped to his knees. The blackmailer was bleeding from a cut on his eyebrow and a split lip.

"Whatever is the meaning of this?" Lord Lovejoy demanded.

"Plimpton locked both Miss Stewart and myself in the well house. He confessed to me." Harlowe spared a glance at the cowering man and his eyes narrowed dangerously. "I believe he had a fit of madness."

"Well, I suppose then that it's only what he deserves," Lady Holland said, looking disapprovingly at Mr. Plimpton.

Harlowe straightened to his full towering height. His mahogany hair was down around his shoulders, he was flushed, and he wore a ferocious scowl on his face.

He was absolutely breathtaking.

Mr. Plimpton glanced up and stupidly opened his mouth.

"*Madness*," Harlowe emphasized. "Because of course were he *sane* I would have to bring a charge of attempted murder against him."

Mr. Plimpton went pale and snapped shut his mouth.

"I think, under the circumstances," Lord Lovejoy said coldly, addressing Mr. Plimpton, "that you should gather your things and remove yourself from my house. I shall send several footmen to assist you." He turned to Harlowe. "Is that agreeable to you, Your Grace?"

Harlowe nodded. "Yes, thank you."

Lord Lovejoy looked at his guests, still crowded at the door to the room. "Now, I believe this matter is settled and we can all retire for the night."

He held out his arm for Lady Lovejoy, who took it and said, "Well done, my dear."

Lord Lovejoy turned a rather endearing shade of pink.

The gathering reluctantly left the room, tramping down the hallway.

Freya lingered, still holding the bundle of letters.

Harlowe took Freya's hand and pulled her after him as

he strode from the room, Tess trotting at their heels. "Come with me."

* * *

Christopher's knuckles hurt and he still felt the disorientating dregs of anger.

But Freya's fingers were warm and solid in his palm, and for some reason that brought a measure of calm to him. For a moment he thought about what it would be like to have her always beside him, gold-green eyes flashing, telling him the blunt truth, leaning toward him as she argued a point, the scent of honeysuckle in her hair.

Making him smile.

Would this warmth, this calm be with him always if she was beside him? Could she fill the emptiness inside him when the darkness closed in?

He shook his head. She'd made it more than plain that she didn't want that.

Didn't want *him*.

Still. Right here, right *now*, she followed him.

He turned the corner of the corridor and slammed into his room. Tess, who had been following loyally, went to her place by the fireplace and lay down with a great sigh.

The moment he closed the door, Freya pulled from Christopher's grasp. She walked to the fireplace and turned, eyeing him. "Was it entirely necessary to beat Mr. Plimpton?"

He sighed, running his hand over his hair. Beating that ass, Plimpton, had been very satisfying, but had it been necessary?

He looked at Freya. "Yes. He refused to give up the letters until I beat him."

Her brows drew together. "But why are the letters so important to you? I mean"—she held up a hand to forestall his interruption—"I know the letters reveal that Sophy took Mr. Plimpton as a lover, but she's *dead*, Christopher." She shook her head. "Is it worth it to avoid a small scandal? To assuage your male pride?"

He laughed then. "*My* pride has nothing to do with it, I assure you."

"Then what?" she demanded, her brows drawn together over stormy eyes. "Did you love her so much?"

He closed his eyes and inhaled. This was what he'd wanted to avoid, but if anyone was owed the truth it was Freya.

He looked at her. "Open the letters."

"I..." She glanced from the letters in her hands to him, uncharacteristically hesitant. "Are you sure?"

"I am. I think it the only way to adequately explain."

She nodded and sat on one of the stuffed chairs before the windows and carefully pulled loose the bit of string holding Sophy's letters together.

She opened the top letter and read as he poured himself a glass of brandy from the decanter on his washstand.

He watched her as he took a healthy swallow of the liquor.

Her brows slowly drew together as she read, and her lips parted as if she were about to say something.

But then she went to the next letter.

And the next.

When she finally looked up he'd finished his glass of brandy and was sitting beside her.

"They're all..." She turned back to the letters in her hands. "How old was Sophy?

He smiled. Wearily. Sadly. "A year older than I."

"But she…" Freya shook her head. "Her writing is like a child's. The things she says in this letter are childlike as well. Was she…?"

"Yes," he said, answering her unspoken question. It was almost a relief to do so aloud. "Sophy was very childlike. I didn't know her before we married. As I said, I'd only met her twice. We were in company and she hardly spoke. I thought she was shy." He shook his head, remembering. "She had a sweet smile."

"But when you found out…"

He watched her, a corner of his mouth curling unhappily at her horrified expression. "I didn't realize at first. There were signs, but I was caught up in the scandal, worried and afraid of what was happening in my life. I was selfish."

"How did you find out?" she whispered.

"When we were finally alone on our wedding night she cried and pulled away from me. She refused to sleep in the same bed as I." His mouth twisted as he remembered his shock. His bewilderment. "My father told me that most gently bred ladies knew nothing of the marriage bed. But that wasn't the point, of course. Sophy wasn't merely ignorant— she was *simple*. When I realized the truth, I knew I couldn't bed her. It would've been fundamentally wrong."

He got up to pour himself another glass of brandy.

"I'm so sorry, Kester," she said, setting down the letters and rising to come to him. She laid her palm against his cheek, searching his eyes. "It was terribly unfair for your father to marry you to a woman who had a child's sensibility. He should not have done it."

"My father probably told himself that it was only what I deserved. He'd never been particularly affectionate with me, but when I was caught up in the scandal—when I ruined his name—he all but washed his hands of me." He smiled wretchedly. "The point of the marriage was to put a patch on the scandal and get me out of the way. In that he succeeded. I doubt my father ever considered whether or not the marriage could be a happy one."

She bit her lip. "How did Mr. Plimpton become involved?"

"That bastard." Christopher felt his upper lip lift. The hatred he felt for Plimpton was hard to control. "He wormed his way into Sophy's affections. He gave her flowers and cheap trinkets. By the time he told her that he was in need of money, she thought herself in love with him."

"Oh no." Freya's eyes widened. "He seduced her?"

He grimaced. "I don't think he actually bedded her—thank God. But he made her think he loved her and that she was in love with him. She gave him all her jewelry and then all her pin money. When I noticed some of my possessions missing—a watch fob, a hand-colored illustrated book of birds, a jeweled snuffbox—I finally asked her. She wept and told me that Plimpton needed the items because he would starve otherwise. I told the servants that he was no longer welcome in the house. Naturally, with his source of money dried up, he left—and broke her heart." How wretched he'd felt then, with poor Sophy sobbing until she made herself sick. He looked at Freya. "I'd chased away the only thing that delighted her."

"If you hadn't he would've taken everything you and Sophy had," she said gravely.

He shook his head. "Plimpton made sure to save the letters Sophy had written him. I think even in India he meant to blackmail me. He waited, though. It wasn't until after Sophy died, after I became a duke and returned to England, that he made his demands. Money or he'd smear Sophy's name." He brushed her cheek with one finger. "You have to understand. I couldn't let him do that to Sophy's memory. I wasn't a good husband, and at the last I failed to save her, but this—*this*—I could do for her."

"I don't think you were a bad husband," Freya said. "I think you did the best you could with a marriage you never wanted."

Then she stood on tiptoe and kissed him.

CHAPTER THIRTEEN

*At last they came to a large clearing where crystals
towered in jagged pillars and fairies, people, and
other beings danced.
Among them Rowan saw Marigold.
Rowan started for the girl, but Ash laid a hand on
her arm. "Wait, sweeting."
He nodded to the center of the clearing.
There sitting on a crystal throne was a fairy
wearing a crown of finger bones. He was cold and
silver and still, and he was so beautiful he made
Rowan's heart hurt....*
—From *The Grey Court Changeling*

Freya pressed her lips to Harlowe, tasting the brandy on her
tongue and his. He'd looked so sad. So tired. And she'd
wanted only to give him some solace.

But her lips parted helplessly as he snatched the cap from
her head and threaded his fingers through her hair, tumbling
it to her shoulders.

Her heart was thumping, her breasts pressed to his hard
chest, and excitement rose in her throat.

Perhaps she'd known, deep down, that this would happen
if she touched him again. Despite her hesitation. Despite her
philosophical doubts.

She wanted him with an instinctive pull that had nothing to do with higher thought.

The heat of his body, the prickle of his stubble against her face, the strength of his hands.

The sly, growing knowledge that she affected him just as much as he affected her.

She tore her mouth from his. "Show me."

His eyes had gone dark, color high on his cheekbones, his mouth wet from their kiss.

She reached for the top of his shirt with one hand and began to undo it.

He stood frozen, like some classical statue in modern dress. She wanted to see what lay underneath.

She held his eyes and pulled open the first button, the fabric making a small rustling sound that was loud in the silent room.

He watched her without any movement to prevent her.

Her breath was coming much too fast. She raised both hands and slipped the second button free.

It felt as if she'd somehow leaped a great distance. As if she'd crossed a border into a strange, new country.

A country she wanted to explore.

The next button came undone and then the next, her fingers working faster and faster.

He groaned under his breath but still he didn't move, merely letting her do as she willed.

And that—his tacit permission to play with him, to explore him—was more exciting than anything she'd ever felt.

The shirt buttoned to midchest and she was very careful to undo each button. Gradually the shirt parted, revealing his strong neck, the dip between his collarbones, and then whorls of hair.

His body was so different, so *fascinating*. She wanted to

discover all the ways he was different from her. Wanted to map and trace and taste.

Freya breathed out, feeling her heart beat so hard she worried he could hear it. Fanny Hill's lover had had body hair, and when she'd read that, curled in a window seat in a deserted library, she'd had to press her legs together.

She'd grown wet at the thought of a man naked.

Of a man's body, so strange and different.

And now...

Now she had one before her to do with as she wished.

She smiled a private smile and tugged his shirttails free from his breeches.

He raised his arms without prompting, and she lifted his shirt as high as she could before he pulled it off the rest of the way.

He stood before her naked to the waist.

She stared.

Breathing in and out. Simply looking.

She thought him beautiful. That wasn't the word one was supposed to use for men, but for him it was true.

Beautiful.

From the rolling muscles on his shoulders to the tiny red-brown nipples to the curling hairs that thickened at the middle of his body below his navel.

She smiled at him, looking in his eyes with delight, and his own eyes widened as if he was surprised by her approval.

His wife had rejected him physically. There had probably been other women, but such a basic blow would remain hidden under the skin, a bruise painful to the touch.

She could give him balm for that wound.

Her hand touched the left side of his chest. Over his nipple.

Where his heart might be under that smooth olive skin.

He had hairs on his chest, and she drew her fingers together, stroking, feeling the soft rasp, watching the curls spring back.

So foreign.

So wonderful.

Carefully she leaned forward and touched the tip of her tongue to the base of his throat. He was warm, living, and he tasted of man and faintly perhaps of salt.

She closed her mouth and kissed him there as her fingers worked on the falls of his breeches.

His great chest rose and fell beneath her lips. She felt as if she held a dangerous wild thing in her hands. An animal far stronger than she, who nevertheless permitted these liberties.

His falls opened and she worked more quickly at his smalls until she could push both down his legs. There *it* was, pointing at her, larger, *thicker* than she'd expected. His penis, cock, *prick*. There were so many names for it, but she remembered one from *Fanny Hill*: "battering ram," which, really, sounded quite intimidating and possibly repulsive.

She wasn't repulsed by this penis. It was ruddy and veined. Sturdy and somehow rather magnificent. She wanted to touch, but was forestalled as he stepped out of the clothes bunched around his ankles, kicking off his shoes as well.

When he bent to his stockings—his only remaining clothing—she laid a restraining hand on him.

"Let me."

He said nothing, but his lips parted, gleaming in the candlelight.

She knelt at his feet.

Strange, that. She was in the supplicant position and

indeed she played the servant, carefully rolling down his stockings.

But it was she who was fully dressed. He who was vulnerable and naked.

She wielded her power at his feet.

And when his stockings were at last pulled off, when he was fully nude, nothing to shield him from her gaze, she knelt up and took his genitals between her palms.

He hissed through his teeth.

His bollocks were heavy, the stones within rolling like eggs in a sack. She might've kissed him there, but hair covered the orbs.

Instead she placed her lips on his cock head. She'd been shocked and not a little disbelieving when she'd first read of this act in *Fanny Hill*. But the longer she thought about it—and somehow she couldn't *stop* thinking about it—the more intriguing it seemed.

She felt her legs shake as she finally tasted his prick.

Oh, it was hot, as if molten lava boiled beneath the fine silky skin instead of mere blood.

He made a sound over her, but she didn't look.

Her attention was on matters below.

His foreskin was pulled back, the purple crown nosing out, and she licked the bead of moisture there and then wrinkled her nose. It was bitter.

Not distasteful necessarily. Just...different.

Unlike anything she'd ever tasted before.

She parted her lips and kissed him again, this time prompting a rumbling groan.

At last she looked up.

He stood, his legs braced, his face flushed. Obviously aroused but not acting on it.

Permitting her the lead.

She smiled and sucked the head of his cock into her mouth, even as she kept her eyes locked with his. She could feel the wetness at her center, seeping between her thighs. It seemed terribly odd, that this act she did for him should cause her such excitement.

"Freya," he groaned, his voice so deep it sounded like gravel. He watched her with heavy-lidded eyes. "Darling, move your hand on my prick."

She did as he bade her, touching him at first gingerly and then with more sureness. His skin moved independent of the hard muscle beneath. She could feel his heat and the pulse of his blood and suddenly it was too much.

She rose and went to his bed, flinging herself onto it, rolling to her back and looking at him, standing stock-still. She grasped her skirts in her fists and raised them, pulling the fabric clear past her thighs, over her hips, until her mound was exposed.

She deliberately spread her legs. "Harlowe."

He was across the room at once, climbing onto the bed, climbing onto *her*, his face wild, his teeth bared.

He knelt over her, his legs between her widely spread thighs, and looked down at her like a lion at a fallen gazelle.

Except she was no gazelle.

She was a lioness—fierce and brave.

She took hold of his shoulders and pulled him toward her. "Now. Please, now."

He lowered his hips, his cock skidding across her thigh. He nudged between her legs, making her widen them still farther, and his penis caught at her entrance.

She looked at him, memorizing his features in this moment. Feeling wild with expectation and triumph.

He speared her.

There was a burning pain, but she made no sound, and he retreated and drove into her again.

Spreading her.

Filling her.

Marking her.

If she was the lioness, then he was surely the lion. A mate fit for her, strong and protective. He thrust into her again and again, moving into her in slow increments until he was fully seated.

She was breached, impaled, and should have felt weakened by defeat.

But this was her victory. She arched beneath him, urging him to move.

To complete the act.

He withdrew and thrust. Withdrew and thrust. She tried to mirror his movement, and for an awkward moment they merely clashed, bumping against one another.

But then they caught, rising in rhythm together.

She flung back her head, gasping at the sensation.

At the *wonder*.

Her heart was swelling, a strange affliction tied to what this man was doing to her.

She might be a lioness, but she knew now she wouldn't leave this battle unscathed.

Her legs shook and her palms slid over his shoulders, slick with sweat, striving, striving for a summit, a common goal.

She groaned as his body drove her to feel things she'd never felt before. To doubt she could live through this.

"That's it, darling," he whispered, his voice strained. "Nearly there. Nearly there."

But she wasn't sure. Nearly where? Was this something she wanted?

And then she reached it, an impossible peak, and she shrieked, barely noticing when he covered her mouth with his.

She fell. Sparking, bursting, filled to overflowing with pleasure.

With feeling.

For this man.

For Harlowe.

She opened wide her eyes and watched him fall, too.

* * *

Christopher woke the next morning to the scent of honeysuckle.

His nose was buried in a tumble of red waves.

Carefully he sat up to lean over Freya and study her face.

She lay on her side, one hand curled beneath her chin, her plump lips slightly parted and her eyes closed. Asleep she looked sweet and young. A docile maiden waiting for a prince to wake her with a kiss.

Christopher snorted under his breath. Freya was no docile maiden, and he was certainly no prince.

Still, when he bent and brushed a kiss against her cheek it was soft and almost reverent.

She murmured, her nose scrunching.

He smiled and kissed her again, a trail of small touches over her brow and down to the tip of her nose.

She blinked, and then he was looking into gold-flecked green eyes.

Something within him turned over. What he wouldn't give to wake every morning thus, to Freya's sleepy moan, the light in her eyes that he wanted to believe was for him and only him.

"Good morning," she husked.

"Good morning to you as well, my lady," he returned.

"What time is it?"

He glanced at the clock beside the bed. "Almost seven," he said regretfully. "My valet will be here in half an hour, and although I trust him..."

He trailed away because she was already moving, tumbling from the bed. She'd fallen asleep still clothed, so all she had to do was shake down her skirts and look for her shoes.

He wanted her to stay. Wanted this time together to go on, perhaps forever.

But even as he was thinking that, it was over.

She darted to the door, and for a moment he thought she would simply leave without further word to him. But then she turned, looking at him, her eyes curiously vulnerable. "I...Thank you for last night."

She opened the door and left.

Christopher flopped back on the bed as Tess decided to join him. He ruffled her ears as he thought. Freya's parting words were a rather formal dismissal save for the fact that she'd blushed as she said them. She was such a guarded woman, as if her heart were walled in by thorny vines. A man wishing to brave those thorns was sure to be bloodied in the endeavor.

Almost any other woman would be easier to woo.

And yet he didn't want any other woman. He wanted her, *Freya*. If he could not persuade her to his side, he had the feeling there would be no other opportunity in his life for companionship.

For love.

It was Freya or no one.

He lay abed a moment longer with Tess before he rose

and drew on a banyan. Christopher paused when he saw Sophy's letters lying forgotten on the table by the bed.

Freya had drawn his attention away from them, first with her sympathy and then with her seduction. When she'd touched him *nothing*, not even the end of the world, would have distracted him from her.

But even in the midst of that sensual exploration, he'd known that she hadn't been experienced. Or at least not very experienced—and the difference hardly mattered in any case.

And having once made love to her? He couldn't imagine never doing so again. His chest physically hurt at the thought. He had to somehow persuade her that he could wed her without taking her freedom from her.

But first there were other matters.

Christopher stirred the embers in the fireplace, tossing coal on them until flames flared up. Then he plucked Sophy's letters from the table and fed them, one by one, into the fire, watching as they blazed and crumbled to ashes. Perhaps he should feel something—a sense of justice, of a duty fulfilled.

But destroying the letters brought no satisfaction.

Sophy was still dead.

* * *

"This is the most exciting house party I've ever attended," Lucretia said later that morning, buttering a piece of scone. She popped it into her mouth and chewed, looking around the breakfast table cheerily.

Lucretia was the only one so bubbly this morning, Messalina thought sourly. She had a sore head, possibly from overimbibing brandy the night before. Lady Holland was a bit pale and very quiet. Mr. Plimpton, of course, was absent from the table, having been almost literally thrown from the house, and the remaining party members were not talkative.

There was one exception—or rather two. Arabella Holland was sitting beside Lord Rookewoode, her face alight with obvious joy as they idly made morning conversation.

Messalina had to suppress a wince. To wear one's emotions so openly on one's sleeve seemed to beg fate to bring one crashing to the ground. She sipped her tea, hoping her cynicism was without merit.

"I wonder if Mr. Plimpton has found a way to return to London?" Lucretia said, still abominably cheerful. "He did look in a state last night after the duke was done. Why do you think His Grace took such a dislike to him?"

"I think it's better we don't ask," Messalina said darkly.

Viscount Stanhope cleared his throat portentously. "My man informed me that Mr. Plimpton was seen riding in a wagon leaving the nearby town this morning."

The table turned their attention to this unlikely source of gossip.

"Then he's gone?" Mr. Aloysius Lovejoy asked, brows raised.

"It would appear so," Lord Stanhope replied. "I myself wonder what would make Mr. Plimpton lock the duke and Miss Stewart in the well house in the first place. Perhaps he had knowledge of the duke the rest of us do not?"

"Or perhaps he's a conniving little worm," Lady Lovejoy said sweetly.

The viscount blushed, and Freya walked into the breakfast room, drawing everyone's attention.

"Good morning," Lucretia said brightly as at the same time Regina Holland said, "Oh, Miss Stewart, there you are."

Freya blinked at the sudden assault of voices.

She said, "Good morning," and took the empty seat beside Messalina.

Everyone was carefully not looking in her direction— everyone but Lucretia, who was munching on her second scone and staring at Freya interestedly.

"Tea?" Messalina asked because the pot was in front of her.

"Yes, please." Freya widened her eyes in question.

Messalina shook her head slightly and murmured so only she could hear, "Jane told me James the footman is bringing the scullery maid to meet us this morning."

Freya's expression was politely inquiring. "When?"

"As soon as he comes back—probably directly after breakfast."

Freya gave a small nod and attended to her tea as the table conversation turned to more benign matters.

A few minutes later a footman entered the room and bent to whisper in Jane's ear.

Jane nodded and glanced at Messalina. "I wonder if you'd like to see those new fashion dolls my modiste sent from London?"

"Yes, of course," Messalina said, rising.

She sent a significant glance at Freya before following Jane from the breakfast room.

They crossed the hallway and went into a small sitting room, where they found James standing next to a thin girl. The footman was dressed in a common worker's clothes, a soft hat pulled over his face. Beside him the scullery maid was a tiny little thing, all raw bones and reddened knuckles. She couldn't be more than fourteen or fifteen.

The door opened behind them and Freya slipped into the room. "Have I missed anything?"

"No." Messalina shook her head. "We haven't started yet."

Freya glanced at Jane. "With your permission, my lady?"

Jane nodded. "Please."

Freya squared her shoulders and turned to the footman. "James, is it?"

"Yes, ma'am."

"Who have you here?"

James came to attention at Freya's calmly authoritative tone. "This is Lucy Cartwright, who used to be a scullery maid at Randolph House."

Lucy, who was wrapped in a gray knit shawl, looked as if she wanted to bolt from the room.

"Now, Lucy," James said with paternal sternness, "these ladies wish to ask you some questions. All you need to do is answer them."

Lucy nodded timidly as the three ladies took seats around her.

Freya smiled at the girl. "Have you worked for Lord Randolph long, Lucy?"

The girl lifted one shoulder. "A year, miss."

"Then you no doubt knew Lady Randolph."

"Yes."

"What was the relationship between Lady Randolph and Lord Randolph like?"

Lucy's wide eyes darted to James. "Relationship? They was lord and lady, miss."

"Yes," Freya said patiently, "but how did Lord Randolph treat Lady Randolph? Was he a loving husband?"

Lucy knit her brows before her expression cleared. "He's a shouter, if'n that's what you mean."

"Indeed it is," Freya replied. "Did he often shout at Lady Randolph?"

"All the time, ma'am, and in awful nasty terms, too. My

lady was right sad about it. Her lady's maid used to tell the kitchen that Lady Randolph wept in her rooms."

Freya raised her brows a little, as if this news were only of little interest, and asked casually, "Did he ever hit her?"

Lucy stared. "Oh no, miss. Lord Randolph isn't one to raise his hand."

Messalina felt her shoulders slump in disappointment.

But then Lucy continued, "He didn't even hit Lady Randolph when she tried to run away."

Messalina exchanged an excited look with Jane. *This* was real information.

Freya cleared her throat. "Can you tell us about that, Lucy?"

"Well..." Lucy scrunched up her face. "Mind, I wasn't there when it happened, 'cause it were at night. But Bob the stable boy told me that Her Ladyship was found in the stables in just her chemise and cloak. Hastings, the head groom, would've turned a blind eye, but His Lordship was there as well. He took Lady Randolph's arm and dragged her through the rain and back into the house. Bob said he could hear the shouting even from without. Awful bad, it was."

"And after that?" Freya asked.

Lucy shrugged. "Nothing, miss. I never saw her after."

"Blast," Messalina muttered. She'd felt so confident when they heard about Lucy that finally she would learn something about Eleanor's final days.

"What about when they called the doctors?" Freya persisted.

"There wasn't any doctors called," Lucy said, sounding puzzled. "They just put her in the cellar."

For a moment Messalina missed the implication.

Then she sat upright. "Lady Randolph was put in the cellar?"

"Yes, miss?"

"Is that where she sickened?" Freya asked softly. "In the cellar?"

"Sickened, miss?" Lucy asked.

"The illness she died from," Freya clarified.

Lucy's brow cleared. "Oh, Lord love you, miss. Lady Randolph isn't *dead*."

Beside Messalina, Jane stifled an exclamation.

Messalina maintained her calm with difficulty.

Freya was leaning a little forward now. "You're saying Lady Randolph is alive and imprisoned in Randolph House's cellars?"

Lucy glanced at James as if verifying that aristocrats were this dim. "Yes?"

"Oh my God," Jane said, apparently unable to hold back her emotion anymore.

Messalina was about to ask Lucy to explain exactly where the cellars were when the door to the room opened and Lucretia entered.

Messalina turned. "What is it?"

Lucretia glanced at the servants and then her. "Lord Randolph has returned to Randolph House."

CHAPTER FOURTEEN

*Ash led Rowan to the Fairy King and urged her to
kneel with him.
"My liege," Ash said, head bowed.
The Fairy King slowly turned. "Why have you
brought a mortal to my court, Brother?"
"This woman has a boon to ask of you."
The Fairy King stared at Rowan with silver eyes.
"Speak, mortal."
Rowan trembled with fear, but she lifted her chin. "I
want Marigold back."
The dancers stopped dancing....*
—From *The Grey Court Changeling*

That afternoon Freya strolled the small enclosed garden at
the back of Lovejoy House, trying to think of a plan to
save Lady Randolph. If she could get Eleanor out, then they
might be able to use Lord Randolph's abominable treat-
ment of his innocent wife as leverage against the Witch Act.
Even in an English society biased against women, a husband
telling everyone his wife was dead but secretly imprisoning
her was beyond the pale.

As she understood it from James, whom she'd ordered to
watch Randolph House, the problem in freeing Lady Randolph was that the cellar had only one entrance, which was
well guarded. Lord Randolph had already declared his wife

dead, complete with funeral and headstone. If he was alerted in any way that there was to be a rescue attempt, he might simply murder Lady Randolph to cover up his crimes.

If Lady Randolph had a living male relative of any power whatsoever, they might call upon him to take up her cause, but Eleanor did not.

Freya trailed her fingers over a pale-pink rose, peering into the curled heart of the flower. Lady Randolph was well and truly at her husband's mercy. He could imprison her, he could kill her and cover up the crime, and he could use her dowry to do it.

The whole thing was terrible, wrong, and *infuriating*.

The only way that Freya could see to foil Lord Randolph was to produce Lady Randolph herself for society and prove that she was alive and entirely sane.

But to do that they first had to liberate her.

Freya sighed. Lady Randolph's horrific use by her husband rather gave a woman pause when it came to dealing with the male sex. Yet she'd freely lain with Harlowe just the night before.

She bent to inhale the heady perfume of the rose. Should she feel guilty for sharing herself with Harlowe?

For taking a lover?

Yes, most definitely, according to all she'd been taught growing up by governesses and vicars. A lady should preserve her virginity, even if she meant never to marry.

But her heritage was with the Wise Women. Her mother and grandmother and great-grandmother and on beyond time had been Wise Women. Any woman brought into the family by marriage was taught their ways by the de Moray women. All daughters were initiated when they came of age.

The Wise Women saw sex and marriage from a slightly different point of view. Most Wise Women were married and had children, but there were some who lived in Dornoch who remained unwed and took lovers. Some had children without a husband. Some had no need of men at all. And some took other women as lovers.

No one way of being a woman was considered better than another. If she decided to return to Dornoch to live she would be welcomed, *particularly* if she was carrying a child.

Every child was considered a gift by the Wise Women.

The crunch of boots on gravel made her turn.

Harlowe walked toward her with purposeful steps, the sun making his hair glint bronze. He wore black today and he looked both stern and heart-stoppingly handsome. Tess trotted behind him, pausing now and again to sniff a flower beside the path.

"Good afternoon," she said.

He walked right up to her and curled his big hand around the back of her head, holding her as he bent to kiss her.

The kiss caught her by surprise, sudden and intense. She moaned beneath his lips, opening her mouth for more, greedy for his taste.

He let her go, looking quite satisfied with himself. "Are you ready to go riding?"

She nodded as Tess came up to her for a welcoming pat. Freya had received a note from him just after luncheon, proposing a ride, and she already wore her habit.

He held out his arm and she took it as they walked to the stables.

This was strange. For five years she'd lived as a paid chaperone. Her status had been just above the servants', and she'd grown used to sitting in the background while the Hollands rode or danced or were courted by gentlemen.

Was she being courted?

She glanced from beneath her eyelashes at Harlowe. He

had been her childhood dream so many years ago, and for a moment she felt a sense of vertigo. She remembered him as a youth, tall, bony, handsome but unformed.

And now: still tall, but broader, fully matured, a shadow of cynicism in his dark eyes. The two images wavered and merged, for he was the same being, a man she'd known all her life.

With a fifteen-year gap.

She flexed her fingers on his arm, feeling the muscle beneath the cloth. He was real. He was here.

Her life had been turned upside down that night fifteen years ago. The de Moray family hadn't realized it at first, but they'd all of them lost their standing, their friends, their place in the world, and things had remained that way for Freya.

Now in an odd way her life had been turned upside down again. A gentleman of her own rank was walking with her.

This, once upon a time, had been what was expected of her life.

Freya wasn't sure how she felt about it. She'd lived so many years alone and independent. Perhaps it was too late to revert to what the rest of the world considered normal.

They came to the stable yard, where two horses were waiting already saddled. The horse she was to ride, she couldn't help noticing, was a better mount than the one she'd ridden to the picnic. He was a bay gelding, shaking his head as she settled herself in the sidesaddle.

She looked at Harlowe, and at her nod, he turned his horse's head and rode out of the yard with her by his side.

He chose the opposite way from that strange little wood, following the path they'd traversed to the picnic. Tess loped ahead of them, sometimes stopping to investigate the hedges that grew beside the road.

The sky was a wide, deep blue, with clouds making dashed white brushstrokes on the horizon. It was a beautiful day.

After a minute or so Freya asked, "I suppose you heard that Mr. Plimpton has quit the area?"

His upper lip curled. "Yes, and good riddance."

"That does seem to be the general consensus."

He snorted but didn't reply.

For several minutes they rode in silence.

Freya kept thinking about Lady Randolph's dilemma. She wished she could ask Harlowe's opinion.

That thought brought her up short. She didn't usually seek anyone's advice. She might work with the Crow or Messalina, but she made her own decisions, debated her next move only with herself.

Suddenly that seemed rather lonely.

Harlowe glanced at her almost as if he'd heard her thoughts. "All right?"

She took a breath. "Yes."

"Good," he said gravely. "I wouldn't want you to endure a jaunt about the countryside simply for my exemplary company."

Freya bit her lip, fighting down a smile.

"Come." Harlowe turned off the main road and onto a path, urging his mare up a hill.

Freya followed, leaning forward slightly in the saddle.

Tess burst from the bushes beside them, running past the horses, tongue hanging from the side of her mouth in dog joy.

Freya's gelding shied in a quick step to the side. She swayed, catching hold of the brace handle on the far side of her saddle, her heart leaping.

"Steady?" Harlowe asked, his gaze sharp.

She inhaled and nodded. "Yes."

They reached the summit of the hill. Harlowe halted his horse and dismounted, looping the reins over a scraggly bush. He came to Freya's side as she was unhooking her upper leg from the pommel. She slid down into his arms, feeling his heat against her chest, and caught her breath, looking up at him.

She'd let this man into her body the night before. Felt him move against her, his big shoulders sliding beneath her palms, his legs between hers.

She still ached inside, there between her legs. Not badly. Just enough to remind her every now and again.

He stepped back and tethered her horse as well before taking her hand and drawing her to turn around.

Freya caught her breath. There beneath them, the country-side spread out in green rolling hills. She could see fields bordered by hedges and walls, the road trundling on, and brown cow dots grazing in a field. She could see a tiny needlepoint church steeple in the distance, and, closer, two men walking along a path, long rakes over their shoulders.

She could see the world.

"It goes on forever, doesn't it?" she said.

She felt him look at her. "Perhaps. It's England, green and growing. One of my ducal estates is just beyond that hill." He pointed to a spot somewhere to their right. "I haven't had a chance to visit it yet."

She glanced at him. "Do you have many estates and manors?"

"A ludicrous amount." His mouth twisted. "When I think of my father plotting my marriage to Sophy and bemoaning the fact that he had to pay for it with a few acres, it seems rather ironic."

"But he had no idea you would inherit the dukedom," she

pointed out. "You said your line was quite removed from the succession."

"No, you're right," he said, still looking out over the rolling hills.

She hesitated, then asked, "When did your father die? I'm afraid I don't remember."

Harlowe shook his head. "There's no reason you should. My father passed away four years ago. While I was in India. He died alone—Mother had succumbed to a fever a year after I left England. He never remarried, and as far as I can tell was never close to another lady."

"He must've loved her dearly," Freya said softly.

"No," he said with calm finality. "I don't think my father ever loved anyone but himself."

She swallowed. "I'm so sorry, Kester."

"Thank you." He shook his head slightly. "But it no longer matters. He doesn't have any power over my life anymore."

Didn't he? Freya wondered. Wasn't a person always affected by their parents, even if they were long dead? It seemed to her that a parent's influence—for good or bad—was a permanent thing. Something impossible to escape. She'd been molded by her mother and father's love and by Aunt Hilda's stern affection.

Wouldn't Harlowe have been just as affected by a *lack* of love?

But she didn't say that. Instead she asked, "What about your mother? Were you close to her?"

His mouth quirked. "I believe so. The first year I lived in India she sent me four letters. The only letter my father sent me was the one informing me of her death."

She reached out and touched his hand.

He threaded his fingers with hers, his eyes on the hills

below. "I had no voice in my marriage. I accepted Sophy as my wife because I had no choice. I was eighteen and without power. But now I am a man and a duke. I don't want a girl who is afraid of me, or one who will agree with everything I say and do." He turned to her and took her other hand as well. "I want a lady who will be my partner. A woman who knows her own mind. Someone like *you*, Freya. Someone to bring me comfort at night."

She squeezed his hand, but she said cautiously, "I don't know if I'm the woman you want."

He inhaled, his brows drawing together as if he were bracing himself for battle. "Why?"

She looked away from his too-intense cerulean eyes. "I'm not the girl you knew before..." She took a breath. "Before that night."

A trace of impatience flared in his face. "I didn't know you as a child, not really. You were my friend's younger sister. A boy nearly a man doesn't pay attention to girls so young."

"But you think you know me now?" She cocked her head. "You only met me again days ago. You know nothing of my life over the last fifteen years. You know very little about my life now. There may be things you won't like about me."

"Such as?" he challenged.

She looked him in the eye. It was time she told him. "Do you know who the Wise Women are?"

* * *

"Wise Women?" Christopher eyed Freya curiously. What a strange question. He couldn't see how it related to this discussion. But he respected Freya and her opinions. He thought and then said, "I seem to remember my nurse when I was quite small talking about witches and calling them Wise Women."

Freya snorted in a very unladylike way. "Wise Women are *not* witches. Only very superstitious or fanatical people think that. The Wise Women are a sort of sect that began before the Romans in this country. Before records were written down, because we *had* no written language."

He stared at her. "How do you know about them, then?"

"Because I'm a Wise Woman," Freya said. She said it as if it was something important. Portentous.

"What does that mean, exactly?" he asked slowly.

She sighed, turning to look out over the land below. "Many things. A Wise Woman vows to help other Wise Women and women in general. She learns our history and, if she wishes, she can learn other esoteric matters." She glanced at him. "The uses of certain herbs and how to grow them. The secrets of childbirth and how women's bodies work. We have a large library, books written by our foremothers with all the knowledge and history of our order. Once, centuries ago, there were many thousands of Wise Women. During that time a Wise Woman could live her life in a village or town and not do anything particularly different from other women besides meeting with other Wise Women. But then came the witch hunters."

"Your sect has actually been hunted as witches?" Christopher frowned. He didn't like this. Superstitious people could be very dangerous.

"Yes," she said grimly. "Wise Women were hunted as witches beginning in the fourteen hundreds. Thousands were tortured and burned. We retreated to Scotland, but then the witch hunts flared in Scotland in the last century." She looked at him, her eyes fiery. "A worse sort of witch hunter arose—the Dunkelders. They're fanatical and relentless.

They know about the Wise Women and they systematically hunt us."

He took her arms, drawing her close, because what she was telling him was arousing all his protective instincts. Why would she *seek out* destruction?

"You remember I told you about my aunt Hilda?" she said softly.

He nodded, almost wishing he couldn't hear more.

"The burns on her face and the damage to her lungs that eventually killed her were from a Dunkelder attack. The Dunkelders came when she was a young woman and burned the cottage that she and her friend were living in. Aunt Hilda tried to save the other woman. She wasn't able to, but in the process her lungs were burned as well as her face."

"Freya," he said, keeping his voice even with effort. "That witch mark on the well house—are you being hunted by a Dunkelder?"

She hesitated. "I've been warned that there's a Dunkelder in the house party, but besides the witch mark, I've seen no sign of him," she said simply, as if it were the most normal thing in the world that she might be being stalked by a crazed fanatic who wanted to *burn* her. "But it's important that you keep all of this secret."

"Of course I'll keep it secret," he said impatiently. "But you need to leave Lovejoy House. Come with me. I can keep you safe in—"

"No."

He stared into her eyes and saw that she was *disappointed* by his reaction. *What the hell?*

Christopher took a deep breath. Then another, reminding himself that Freya liked to make decisions for herself. "Why not?"

"Because I have a position in the Wise Women," she said matter-of-factly. "I'm the Macha. That means, well…*spy*, I suppose, is the easiest explanation. I gather information for the Wise Women. There are so few of us left now. Our leaders and most of the Wise Women have retreated to a town in the far north of Scotland. So you see why I'm needed to warn them of dangers that might come from the wider world. I don't know if you're aware of it, but there's such a danger in Parliament. An act permitting the torture and trial of witches again. I can't let such an act pass."

"How will you stop it?" he asked, trying to keep his voice level. Was she insane, as he'd first thought her? Thinking she could stop a *Parliamentary act* from being passed?

"The man leading the push to pass the act is Lord Elliot Randolph, the Lovejoys' neighbor. He's imprisoned his wife. If I can free her, I can use what he did to her to keep him from backing the act."

He stared at her, this ferocious, brave, *mad* woman. "Freya…"

She raised her brows. "Yes?"

He shook his head, seizing on the simplest objection. "I thought Lady Randolph died last year."

"We have information that she's still alive."

"Even if she is, what makes you think that he's done something so terrible?" he asked gently. "Perhaps Lady Randolph has gone off her head and he's confined her for her own good."

"In the *cellar*?" she asked sharply.

He winced. "Very well. I agree that what you say seems most likely—"

"Thank you," she replied, her voice dripping sarcasm.

He sighed, leaning his brow against hers. She'd been so tender last night, but this was the other side to his Freya:

a warrior who went into battle without fear. "Must you put yourself in danger? Must you do this alone?"

"I have allies," she said softly, placing her hand against his cheek. "And as for danger, yes, I'm afraid so. This is my mission within the Wise Women."

Christopher thought he might hate the Wise Women. "Very well. You are a Wise Woman. You will not avoid danger, even if I ask it. I accept this about you. In return, will you accept that I want you as my wife? Not to imprison, not to halve, but to walk by my side? To hold and cherish?"

She'd rejected him before, and Christopher wasn't so vain that he thought she would agree to marry him so soon afterward...although he had made love to her in the meantime. No, this battle was better fought as a long game.

She shook her head. "There's the matter of my family as well. Not only Ran, but Lachlan, Caitriona, and Elspeth. Even if I could reconcile myself to our past, I have no hope that they—"

"We don't have to deal with that right now," he interrupted. "The past, your family, Ran, and everything else are things to think about later. At this moment all I need to know is this: Are you willing to *try*?"

She was staring at him with a suspicious expression now and he waited, a little amused despite the alarming information she'd given him.

Despite the specter of their past.

Then abruptly she nodded, oddly proud. "I've warned you, Kester. If you find at the end of this that I am not the woman you thought me, if you are disappointed—"

He kissed her, stopping the warnings. She was warm in his arms, her lips hot as they moved beneath his mouth. She was still protesting even as she kissed him back.

This woman. This aggravating, argumentative woman. He

wanted her—that he already knew—but as he bit her bottom lip gently he realized something he hadn't foreseen. He might need her. In body. In mind. In spirit.

He lifted his head, watching her dazed eyes clear.

Hoping he wasn't as bemused.

Wanting was one thing.

Needing was quite another.

He turned and pulled her back to her horse. "Let's return. It'll be time to dress for supper soon."

He whistled for Tess, who had been curled in a ball beneath a tree. She stood and stretched and then shook before trotting to them.

Christopher could feel Freya's gaze on him as he cupped his hands to give her a step.

She placed her hand on his shoulder and her boot in his palms, as trusting as a babe, and despite his newly discovered worry over her role as a Wise Woman, he felt a flush of pride.

He'd win her and then he'd keep her safe always.

Because she'd be his.

They descended the hill, Christopher taking the lead, until they came to the country road again. There he pulled back so Freya could come abreast.

He turned to her to ask—

A rabbit started from its hiding place beneath a hedge, running directly in front of Freya's mount.

The gelding bolted.

* * *

Freya remembered being eight and listening outside a room while her mother and a group of ladies discussed in hushed voices the death of a neighbor.

The neighbor had been dragged to death by her horse.

The gelding rocked and bumped beneath her, and she clung desperately on.

If she fell she might die outright.

Or her habit might catch on the stirrup and she, too, might be dragged to death.

The gelding swerved, and she desperately threw her weight against the far side of the saddle so she wouldn't slip. She couldn't pull him to a stop. He was out of control.

She was going to die if she couldn't think of a way to save herself.

Her heart was battering her rib cage, her breath caught in her throat, and she saw a turn in the road up ahead.

She pulled with all her might on the reins, ignoring what the bit must be doing to the horse's mouth. She needed to stop the horse before the turn.

And if she couldn't, she'd have to leap off.

Better to have *some* control over her fall than to be thrown from the horse.

"Jump to my horse!"

She looked to her left and saw Harlowe riding beside her, his face grim and determined.

He caught her eye and shouted, "I'll catch you."

Impossible. She'd fall between the horses and be trampled. She shook her head fiercely. "The only way is to jump free of the saddle to the ground."

"*Freya.* Goddamn it, *trust* me."

She glanced to the side again.

Harlowe was bent over his horse's neck, his face grim. "Kick your boot from the stirrup!"

"I'll fall!" she screamed back.

"No." He turned his head, and for a second in that awful race to death she saw his set face, his determined eyes staring at her. "I'll catch you. *Believe me.*"

She kicked her foot free.

The gelding lurched, shying away from Harlowe's black.

She jumped—

And he caught her.

One arm wrapped hard about her waist. Her body dangling to the side of his horse.

The gelding swerved away.

She gasped, trying to draw breath.

He couldn't hold her so. She was a dead weight and his other hand was busy controlling the horse.

He grunted and with one arm lifted her bodily over the saddle in front of him.

She clutched at him, grasping his forearms in terror, mindful not to get in the way of the reins.

He slowed the horse to a trot, his thighs clenching beneath her.

She bumped against Harlowe's chest for a few seconds before the horse blessedly began walking. She spied Tess loping along beside them, a cautious distance between her and the horse.

Harlowe's arm was still around her waist, a band of iron, making her stays dig into her flesh.

But holding her safe.

So safe.

She closed her eyes and drew in a calming breath.

"Are you all right?" he asked, his voice hoarse.

"Yes." She nodded. "Yes, thank you."

He laughed breathlessly. "You're most welcome. Were you really going to jump to the ground?"

She twisted a little to see his face. His expression was odd—as if she'd performed some unexpected feat. "Yes. What would you have done if you'd been on a spooked horse?"

"Held on with my knees until I could bring him under control."

She arched an eyebrow. "And if you happened to have both knees to one side of the horse because you were riding sidesaddle and therefore were about to fall?"

He looked at her, his brows pulled together as he answered. "I'd jump."

"Quite."

"I bow to your greater logic," he drawled above her. "Come up here." He heaved and settled her more securely before him. "Can you throw your leg over the horse?"

"I'd have to pull up my skirts," she said practically. Her skirts were bunched beneath her. "I don't know if I'd remain decent—"

"Fuck that," he muttered, rather shocking her. "I don't want you falling again."

She'd rather not fall, either, and upon consideration decided that expediency was the better part of modesty.

With a bit of very awkward wriggling she freed her left leg and got it over the horse's withers.

Harlowe pulled her against his chest and turned the horse's head in the direction of Lovejoy House.

Freya was still catching her breath. She shivered.

"Are you well?" he asked above her, his deep voice calm. "You're not injured?"

"I'm perfectly fine," she replied, trying to steady her voice.

"Hm." She felt the brush of his lips on her ear. "I'll feel better when we're back at Lovejoy House."

"Yes."

Twenty minutes later they rode into the stable yard.

A groom came running out to catch the horse's bridle. "Your Grace! I'm that glad to see you. The gelding came trotting back with foam on his withers. We were just about to send out a search party."

Harlowe nodded. "Thank you, but we are unharmed."

"By God's grace," the man exclaimed.

Harlowe dismounted. He turned and held up his arms for Freya.

She managed to move her leg back over the horse's neck and then slid into his arms.

He pulled her close. "Come."

As he led her into the house, Tess trotting behind, Freya couldn't help but think how safe she'd felt in Harlowe's arms. She'd never had quite that feeling with another person before—the sensation that he would keep her from harm at any expense.

That feeling of safety, of *care*, was seductive. Perhaps too seductive. She was vulnerable to this—the attentiveness of another person. *Harlowe's* attentiveness.

She must be sure that any decision she made she made with a clear head, unbiased by her own weaknesses.

CHAPTER FIFTEEN

Ash did not move, but Rowan felt his fingers tighten
on her arm as if in warning.
The Fairy King smiled, and his mouth was filled with
sharp teeth. "Very well. You may take sweet Marigold
back to the mortal realm if you can tell which of my
court is she. If you cannot, you and she will stay with
me forever. Do you agree?"
"Yes."
Rowan turned to the courtiers...and saw that every
one looked like Marigold....
—From *The Grey Court Changeling*

Late that night Christopher stood by his window in breeches, shirt, and banyan as Gardiner moved about, straightening things.

"Will that be all, Your Grace?" Gardiner murmured.

Christopher turned away from the window and nodded. "Get to your own room, Gardiner. It's late."

"Yes, Your Grace." His valet bowed and closed the door behind him.

Christopher blew out the candles in the room. He went to the dark window and waited, staring out at the night.

Nothing moved.

At last the china clock on the mantel chimed the half hour after midnight.

Christopher turned and looked at Tess, lying by the fire. "Stay." She thumped her tail once on the marble tile, but didn't bother raising her head.

He strode to the door and listened before he quietly let himself out.

The hallways were empty.

After their perilous ride Freya had spent the remainder of the day with the ladies of the party. He'd seen her only at dinner, and then, of course, she'd sat at the far end of the table.

With the knowledge that some fanatical madman might be hunting her, Christopher wasn't going to leave her safety to chance. Freya herself would no doubt deny that she needed protection from him—and perhaps she didn't. She'd certainly been planning to save herself from a runaway horse that afternoon.

But even if she was a capable warrior, he'd still go to her. The need to protect her was a primitive force within him.

He turned into a small passage, less well lit than the one his own rooms were in, and tapped softly at the last door.

Freya peeked through the crack in the door and then opened it wide, letting him in.

She was wearing only her chemise.

His vow to himself to guard her without touching her fled.

Her breasts were unbound, round and full, the indentation of her waist a curve to incite a man to violence.

To ruin.

He stared at her, his higher reasoning having conceded rule of his brain to his prick. He wanted to touch. To hold.

To devour.

She was a goddess.

She stood still, watching him, her eyes mysterious and knowing.

"Take that off," he said gruffly.

She reached down and pulled up the skirt, skimming shapely calves, dimpled knees, smooth thighs. Her bush was gloriously red orange, the curls hiding the slit underneath. Her belly was creamy white, the indentation of her belly button one of the most erotic things he'd ever seen.

He felt sweat break out on his forehead.

The chemise was lifted higher, revealing round, beautiful breasts with the palest pink nipples.

She took off the chemise and threw it aside.

Freya stood before him proudly, like a Rembrandt nude come to life. Pink and white and red orange. And her flaming hair fell about her shoulders, wild and curling and free.

Like *her*.

Like Freya.

He walked to her and drew her into his arms, running his hands across her silky skin before he bent to set his mouth against hers.

She sighed as she came to him and her sweet breasts were crushed against his chest. Her lips parted for him, and he licked into her mouth until she suckled his tongue.

His prick was pounding his heartbeat against the falls of his breeches, each pulse building on the last until his entire being pulsed for her.

Body, soul, and cock.

Christopher picked her up and with two strides had her on the bed. He stepped back and stripped quickly and efficiently. When at last he was nude he looked up and saw her watching him.

He stilled, letting her gaze her fill, feeling the lust building in him as he reined himself in.

She broke the spell by holding out her hand.

* * *

There was something freeing in baring herself to a man.

In baring herself to *Harlowe*.

Freya watched as he stalked to the bed, his heavy cock swaying as he moved. It was swollen and erect, standing up almost in threat.

But she was not frightened.

On the contrary. Her thighs were slippery with her liquid and her nipples ached to be touched.

He crawled up over her, his shoulder muscles bunched, his gaze intense, and bent to take one nipple into his mouth.

She arched, shocked by the sudden action, shocked by the pull of his lips.

Shocked by the lust that overcame her.

She reached up, trying to pull him down on top of her, but he was braced and would not move.

He let go of her nipple and licked it, then pulled back and blew.

She moaned, the sound loud in the room. She couldn't believe that she was panting and gasping—simply because he'd touched one very small part of her body.

"I dreamed of these," he said, his voice low.

She stared at him, feeling transfixed by his look of desire. She'd hardly undressed the night before. He hadn't seen her breasts.

His mouth twitched. "Your breasts, your lush, beautiful breasts. You hide them all the time behind those damned fichus—not even an inch of skin below your neck shows. That fichu leaves me to imagine."

He traced a finger under her breast, delicate, arousing. Her nipple came to a point and he trailed his finger around the center, not quite touching.

"I thought of white skin," he said, watching that nipple.

"I thought of soft flesh. I thought of how your breasts would feel in my hands." His gaze met hers and she inhaled at the intensity of his sky blue eyes. "But I didn't have enough imagination. Come here."

He rolled over, pulling her up and into his lap as he sat back against the carved headboard of the bed. She lay across him, her legs to one side of him, her head at his shoulder as he cradled her.

She was suddenly self-conscious. She'd thought he would immediately make love to her.

"Let me discover you," he murmured, and she could feel herself tighten with desire.

He gathered her breasts into his hands and bent his head, licking, sucking, *feasting* on her nipples. He tugged at first one, then the other with his lips, and then pulled one into his mouth, sucking strongly.

Her legs moved restlessly, as if something foreign were taking over her body. She could feel his penis, hot like a brand against her bottom, and she wanted him now. She was *ready*. She didn't understand why he delayed.

Was he *trying* to torture her?

He urged her to face him fully, making her straddle his lap, and then it was much better. His cock rose against his stomach and she spread herself—her *fanny*—over him and rubbed against him. That little bud, that bit at the top of her sex, was swollen and aching, and she sought relief from him, but her movements only made her ache more.

And as she moved on him he pulled at her nipples, both at the same time, pinching and squeezing with his fingers. Sending a pulse of need to her center.

Oh.

She rose up on her knees. Placed her hands against his chest and rubbed harder.

His penis slipped to the side and she whimpered at the loss.

"Here, darling," he said, his voice rough. "Just..."

She felt his hand between her legs, the backs of his fingers brushing against her wet folds, and then something thicker.

He'd placed the head of his cock at her entrance.

He met her eyes. "Push yourself down on me."

She nodded because words were beyond her. If she didn't quench this thirst soon she might lose her mind.

She canted her hips, feeling that broad head invade her.

Oh, so beautiful!

Her head fell back as she lifted a little—not too much, she didn't want to lose him—and then screwed herself down on his cock once more. Forcing the length, the breadth, the *heat* of him up into her.

Scratching her itch.

His fingers had gone lax as he was suddenly seated, and she looked at him with a whimper. "Please. *Please* touch me."

His nostrils flared. "Like this?" His voice was both rough and so very tender as he pinched her nipples—*hard.*

She arched at the pleasure mixed with pain. "*Again.*"

He smiled dangerously and squeezed her nipples.

She leaned forward on a moan.

"Hush," he growled.

He caught the back of her head, bringing her mouth down to his even as he shoved up into her.

She whimpered, the sound muffled by his tongue thrusting into her mouth. She was on top, but he was the one ramming into her.

Again.

And again.

She shook atop him, feeling the pleasure spread like a pool of heat through her pelvis. He grabbed her bottom with both hands, holding her firmly down as he *ground* up into her.

A scream built in her throat, helpless and agonizing as the first waves hit her.

He tore his mouth from hers and shoved his thumb between her lips. "Bite if you have to."

And she did, tasting salt and man, shuddering atop his cock as he battered her with his pleasure.

She could feel his gaze on her face, watching as she revealed herself, layer by layer, until he saw her intimate, vulnerable center.

She would've hidden herself if she'd been able.

She couldn't.

He stilled suddenly and she dragged open her eyes to see his own vulnerability.

His eyes were narrowed, his lips parted, and he looked as if he were dying for her.

She arched beneath him, receiving the hot spill of his semen.

* * *

Christopher woke early the next morning. The room was lit only by the remains of the fire, but he knew at once that he wasn't alone.

Freya breathed softly beside him, her arm flung over his chest as if she meant to claim him in her sleep.

A pity she didn't feel so possessive while awake.

She lay on her side, plump breasts pressed together, creating an intriguing valley, and peeking out of that valley was Ran's ring, strung upon a thin silver chain. He stared at it, this symbol of everything he'd done wrong as a youth.

Everything he'd lost: honor and England and family.

He had England back. His honor wasn't something that he thought he'd ever completely regain. And family?

Could he find family again?

He looked at Freya's sleeping face and wished he could cut open his chest and reveal his heart, because he hadn't the words to tell her what she meant to him.

He sighed and touched the silver chain, letting it run between his fingers to catch the ring. The merlin silhouette was enigmatic. Strange. He'd worn this ring for fifteen years, but he wasn't sure he'd ever truly examined it.

It had been a reminder of his greatest shame.

Now he saw that the black stone, worn and abraded over centuries, reflected no light, making it all but impossible to read the motto beneath. He already knew what it said, though. *Parvus sed ferox*: "Small but fierce."

He let the ring drop and she stirred, her face scrunching.

"Good morning," he said.

She blinked, looking like a little girl. A confused little girl.

He smiled.

She recovered quickly, of course, her expression clearing with almost frightening speed. She was very like her family's symbol: swift, deadly, always alert.

Small but fierce.

"You're still here," she said coolly.

He arched an eyebrow. "Yes, darling, but never fear. I'll leave before the servants begin their rounds."

A line appeared between her brows. Perhaps he should feel sorry for her—she'd just woken, no matter how alert she looked—and take pity on her. Withdraw while she was soft and vulnerable. But on the whole he thought that taking advantage of any weakness a good idea when it came to Freya.

She had so few.

He brushed a finger down her cheek, marveling at the softness of her skin, but she pulled back.

His hand fell to the bed. "You wear armor all the time, did you know that?"

She gave him an odd, almost vulnerable glance, and then her expression smoothed again. "I don't know what you mean."

"Don't you?" He sat up, resting his arms on his knees, and didn't miss that she averted her face from his nudity. "I feel sometimes that I fight a battle for your regard—a battle I'm losing."

"Perhaps you are," she said softly.

He felt a place in his chest close, and despite the pain said very, very gently, "Perhaps I am."

She shook her head, looking away. "What would you have me do? I cannot change myself." She glanced at him. "You wouldn't change yourself for me."

He inhaled. "How do you know?"

She merely stared at him.

He sighed and got out of bed. "You haven't asked me. Perhaps you don't have the desire to."

He picked up his smalls from the floor and donned them as he listened to her silence.

Finally he glanced at her. She sat in bed, her arms folded defensively across her breasts, wearing a mutinous little frown. He didn't want to leave her on such a sour note. He should kiss her, tell her how beautiful she was, and walk out the door before they could argue.

But that wouldn't get him any closer to her. "Freya. Have you ever loved? Ever taken a lover?"

She looked at him from the corner of her eye. "Only you. You know that."

"No." He pulled on his shirt. "Why should I know that?"

"I thought gentlemen could tell." A becoming pink blush was rising in her cheeks.

His fierce little merlin was embarrassed.

He almost climbed right back in the bed.

Instead he said, "No. I could tell you were perhaps inexperienced, but not that you were a virgin. And here's a piece of information about me, which I'll tell you without you asking. I've never had a lover before you."

She frowned. "But—"

He held out a hand to forestall her. "A bed partner, yes. One or two. But not a *lover*. I think there's a difference, don't you?"

She stared at him mutely.

He closed the door very gently as he left.

CHAPTER SIXTEEN

Ash bent and whispered in Rowan's ear, "Hold your love for Marigold in your hands and you will find her."
Rowan frowned. But she didn't love Marigold. She didn't even like her.
Rowan stood and walked slowly around the circle of identical girls, peering into each face, trying to remember all the years she'd spent with Marigold by her side.
The girls all looked the same, and Rowan feared she would spend all eternity in the Grey Lands....
—From The Grey Court Changeling

Later that morning Messalina lounged on a bench in the garden, an arm flung over her eyes, desperately trying to think how they could save Eleanor. The gentlemen of the house party had ridden off to shoot grouse or pheasant or possibly peacocks. The remaining ladies were mostly in the front of the house, playing some sort of lawn game, but Messalina was too worried about Eleanor for frivolous amusements.

"What if," Lucretia said rather thickly from beside her, "we set the house on fire?"

Messalina raised her arm just enough to peek under it at her sister. Lucretia had somehow found a half dozen lemon curd tartlets and was devouring them with the greed of a three-year-old. "How would roasting Eleanor alive help her?"

Lucretia shrugged. "I was thinking we could get in the house while everyone else ran out."

"At which point *we* would roast with Eleanor."

Lucretia's smooth brow wrinkled. "Do you think so?"

"*Yes*," Messalina said with more force than was absolutely necessary, but then she was quite at her wit's end. "She's in the cellar. We'd all be trapped." She frowned severely at her sister. "And while we're on the subject, when did you become so ruthless?"

Lucretia licked the lemon curd from a tart and grinned like a demon. "I'm a Greycourt, remember?"

"Point." Messalina let her arm fall back over her eyes. "I think first we need to draw Lord Randolph away. Servants are always more easily swayed without a clear master."

"Machiavellian," Lucretia murmured approvingly.

"I'm a Greycourt as well."

"So you are," her sister said, and then sighed gustily. "I've eaten the last tart."

"I don't understand why you aren't the shape of a balloon."

"I should be, shouldn't I?" Lucretia sounded far too pleased with herself. "But now I'm thirsty. I think I'll go in and find some tea."

"Mmm." Messalina didn't bother looking up. She simply lay and listened to her sister's retreating footsteps.

They needed to get Eleanor out of that wretched cellar as soon as was humanly possible. Lord knew what state she must be in after a year locked up. Lord Randolph really was the devil.

Messalina jumped up from the bench. She needed to consult with Freya—surely she was more experienced with freeing imprisoned ladies than Messalina was.

She took one of the paths along the outer edge of the garden, admiring the roses in full bloom as she passed.

She turned the corner and halted. Ahead, at the side of the path, was a bench, and on the bench sat a man. He was dressed neatly all in black. He had sleepy black eyes above sharp cheekbones, and despite a thin white scar under his left eye he would've been handsome had it not been for his eyebrows. They came to a sharp point above his eyes, making him look decidedly satanic.

"What are you doing here, Mr. Hawthorne?" Messalina asked sharply.

He rose gracefully, his full, wicked mouth curved at each corner.

As if he were laughing at her.

Still, Gideon Hawthorne's voice was grave when he answered, "Whyever shouldn't I be here, Miss Greycourt?"

His accent was perfect, as if he'd been raised in wealth and privilege, though she suspected he hadn't.

"You're spying on me." She fought to keep the fear from her voice.

"Perhaps."

"You can tell my uncle that I resent this constant surveillance by his *creature*," she spit.

His face went blank for a split second before resuming its previously calm expression. He tilted his head to the side, looking like a curious rook. "He only wishes to keep you safe."

"We both know that's a *lie*," she said forcefully. "My uncle cares for no one but himself. *Go away.*"

Messalina didn't wait for his rejoinder. She turned and walked rapidly toward the house. She could feel her heart beating—too quickly, too lightly, and she couldn't quite catch her breath.

Damn Gideon Hawthorne and her uncle.

She made the terrace, and it was a battle not to turn.

To see if he was behind her like some horrid childhood monster.

She opened the door to the house and went in, shutting it firmly. Then she sank into a chair, her head in her hand.

Had he followed them here? *Why?*

"Messalina?"

She jerked upright.

Freya stood in front of her, looking concerned.

Messalina cleared her throat. "Yes?"

Freya eyed her intently. "Are you all right?"

"Yes, of course." Messalina rose and busily smoothed down her skirts. "Actually, I'm glad to see you. I wanted to talk to you about Eleanor." Her eyes widened. "But aren't you supposed to be playing lawn games?"

Freya smiled. "Lady Holland sent me in for her shawl."

"Then I'll accompany you upstairs," Messalina decided.

They turned toward the stairs.

"Where is Lucretia?" Freya asked.

"She's probably returned to her bed," Messalina replied. "My sister is the laziest thing you've ever seen."

Freya's lips twitched in that manner she'd had ever since they were eleven. "Even lazier than Quintus?"

Messalina snorted in a quite unfortunate way. "Do you remember when we sneaked into his room and tickled his nose with a feather?" They'd been very bored that summer, and Quintus with his high rages had always been too tempting.

Freya grinned. "I remember he jumped up roaring and chased us through the house. I was never so scared."

"You were giggling the entire time!"

"I was." Freya looked down, her smile dying as they mounted the stairs. "How is he? Quintus?"

"He's well." She glanced up at Freya and then away. Quintus had spent a year in outbursts of nearly homicidal rage after Aurelia's death and then become very quiet. Truly she had no idea how he was—she could no longer tell. She said awkwardly, "It was hard for him—for all of us—when Aurelia died."

"I'm sorry," Freya said, taking her arm and bumping her shoulder companionably. "It must've been awful."

Messalina felt tears start in her eyes. "Thank you."

Freya nodded. She turned to the remaining stairs. "I've been thinking."

Messalina blotted her eyes with a handkerchief. "Yes?"

"Do you think Jane could invite Lord Randolph to supper tomorrow night?" Freya asked slowly.

"As far as I know they're on amicable terms," Messalina replied, suddenly alert.

"Good," Freya said grimly. "Then I propose you and I rescue Eleanor tomorrow night."

* * *

Freya headed for the sitting room before supper that night. The thought of seeing Harlowe again after the gentlemen had been away all day made something spark in her chest. She'd *missed* him.

She caught herself on the thought. When had she begun noticing Harlowe's absences?

More, when had she begun to *rely* on his presence to lift her mood? Surely this wasn't healthy or good, this sort of feverish joy? She couldn't make a clear decision about marriage to Harlowe with this warm feeling zinging through her veins.

It was almost as if she'd drunk too much brandy, and

she certainly would not make an important decision if she'd done *that*.

And then she realized that she had started seriously thinking of marriage to Harlowe. *Despite* the fear of losing herself and her autonomy.

Despite her family and the Wise Women.

Perhaps she was drunk on lust.

By the time Freya halted at the door to the sitting room, she was quite peeved with herself.

She scanned the room and went to sit by Lady Holland. "My lady."

"There you are, Miss Stewart," her employer said rather absently.

Freya followed Lady Holland's gaze to Arabella, sitting next to Lord Rookewoode, their heads close together. Arabella was giggling while the earl looked at her through his eyelashes, amusement plain on his face.

Her brows rose. "That seems to be going well."

"Hm," Lady Holland hummed noncommittally.

Freya darted a quick glance at her. "No?"

"What?" The older lady glanced at her, and her eyes seemed to clear of her internal thoughts. "Oh, don't mind me. One should not make plans for one's children," she said somewhat obscurely. "They never turn out as one thinks they should."

Freya was still wondering about that comment when a figure in the corner caught her eye.

Lord Stanhope was staring at her quite malevolently.

Freya looked away. "Where is Regina?"

Lady Holland sighed. "Abed. I fear she's pining for Mr. Trentworth." Her gaze drifted back to Arabella, who was laughing softly over something the earl had said.

Freya studied her employer for a moment and then said,

against her better judgment, "You are her mother, my lady. If you truly disapprove of the earl, couldn't you simply forbid that she see him?"

Lady Holland laughed wryly. "On what grounds? That he's too rich, too well born, too handsome, and too likable?" She shook her head, sobering. "No, that would only make him more appealing to her, I think. And to tell her the truth of the matter—that I think he's not well matched to her—would break her heart. I'll not do such a thing to my Arabella."

Freya knit her brows and said slowly, "You've mentioned nothing unacceptable about Lord Rookewoode. In fact you list only his good traits. Forgive me, but I don't see why this would be a bad match."

"Don't you?" Lady Holland smiled a little sadly. "Perhaps I'm seeing future sorrow where there will be none, but tell me: Do you think the earl loves my daughter?"

Freya blinked. In all her many years witnessing English society and matchmaking, she'd never heard the word *love*.

She turned to watch the couple. Lord Rookewoode really was very elegant, wearing the latest style, lace at his wrists and throat. His smile was quick and a little cynical. One had the feeling that he was almost *too* charming. But he looked at Arabella with a gentle expression, leaning closer to hear what she said to him.

"He obviously values her opinion," Freya replied. "Look how he listens to her. I'm not sure if one can diagnose love from afar, but he's quite obviously fond of her."

Lady Holland nodded. "He's fond of her, but I think my Arabella loves him."

"Isn't that to be desired?" Freya asked, puzzled. "If Arabella loves Lord Rookewoode, then she should be very happy to marry him."

"Ah, but marriage isn't only one day—or even one week,"
Lady Holland said. "It's years and years of living with the
same person, discovering their habits and possibly being disappointed by their more human foibles. If one doesn't have
deep and abiding love to see one through marriage, I think
there's the danger of eventually feeling contempt for one's
spouse."

"Surely not."

Lady Holland turned to her with a sad smile. "You're a
romantic, Miss Stewart. I assure you that I've seen many a
marriage falter in later years, the partners becoming more and
more cruel to each other. Or worse, ignoring one another."

"But," Freya objected, "you've said you think Arabella in
love with the earl."

"Yes, and I said I think the earl is *fond* of Arabella." She
looked at Freya. "Fondness isn't love."

Lady Holland thought a marriage between her daughter
and Lord Rookewoode would inevitably deteriorate—
because he didn't love Arabella. Freya frowned at the couple. But Lady Holland might be wrong. Perhaps Lord
Rookewoode would discover Arabella's wit and kindness.
Perhaps his affection would turn to love *during* a marriage.
That would be a wonderful fairy tale.

Freya didn't believe in fairy tales.

Arabella was such a sensitive woman. She seemed to experience everything—joy, grief, rage—more deeply. If Lady
Holland was right, this had the makings of something awful.

Beside her, Lady Holland inhaled sharply.

Freya looked up, expecting her eyes to be on Arabella.

But it was Viscount Stanhope who stalked toward them,
an oddly triumphant expression on his face.

He stopped right in front of Freya and said with clear satisfaction, "Witch."

* * *

Christopher paused in the doorway to the sitting room, startled by the accusation Stanhope had spit at Freya.

Witch.

Dear God. Stanhope must be the Dunkelder—the man who wanted to *burn* his Freya.

Christopher glanced at Freya. She'd gone entirely blank.

Damn the man. How dare he accuse her of bloody *witchcraft*?

"What are you babbling about, Stanhope?" he demanded, stalking across the sitting room.

Stanhope was staring steadily at Freya, his eyes wide, a rather eerie smile on his face. "I'm talking about witches, Your Grace. Those who traffic with the devil. Who engage in foul rites in order to gain power over their fellow females—or males. Witches must be questioned, tried, and *burned*." He licked his lips. "*This* witch needs to be burned."

"Nonsense," Christopher growled.

"Is it?" Stanhope's large brown eyes were suddenly sardonic when he looked at Christopher. "But then a man beguiled hardly makes the best judge."

Lady Holland sighed as if their argument was a tedious waste of her time. "What makes you think that my companion is a"—her lip curled ever so slightly—"witch?"

"I have knowledge of her past," Stanhope cried, so loud that Lady Holland recoiled from him. "She is from a family that is well known for witchcraft. Her own aunt was declared a witch and escaped burning only by the vilest sorcery. *Look at her hair.*" He darted forward and snatched the cap from Freya's head, revealing her red hair. "They all have hair of such a vile color in that family."

"What madness!" Lady Holland's face was ruddy and

she sounded outraged. "Do you mean to tell me that you're charging my companion with witchcraft because her hair is *red*?"

Freya had gone white as a bone. She stood from her chair and faced Stanhope, her expression calm. "I'm not a witch."

"Of course you're not a witch," Lady Holland exclaimed under her breath. "Silliest thing I've ever heard."

"I think you need to apologize to the lady," Christopher said, looking around the room. Most of the guests were curious, or startled, or eager for spectacle, but Lord Lovejoy was eyeing Freya with something close to alarm. Christopher raised his voice. "No person of sense believes in witches or witchcraft. You're either drunk, Stanhope, or you've overheated your brain in the sun this afternoon."

The viscount's lips were thin and bloodless. "By taking her part you reveal yourself as an ally to the devil. Beware, Your Grace. Wealth and rank will not defend you against the angels and their just revenge. You, too, will feel the fires of hell burning your flesh."

"Oh, for God's sake." Christopher took a step toward the other man, looming over him. "Leave the room, Stanhope, before I make you."

Stanhope sneered, but his eyes had widened in what looked like alarm. He turned and hurried from the sitting room.

"What a terrible man," Lady Lovejoy exclaimed.

"Yes, but why would he think Miss Stewart a witch?" Lord Lovejoy asked, staring at Freya with a hint of suspicion.

Christopher scowled and opened his mouth, but Lord Rookewoode beat him to it.

"Because he's obviously insane," the earl drawled. "Imagine believing in witches in this day and age."

Lord Lovejoy frowned. "But what of the new Witch Act?

There are those in Parliament who obviously find witches quite concerning."

The earl sighed heavily. "*Despite* my esteemed colleagues in the Lords, we live in an age of reason. Only the most unsophisticated would fall prey to primitive superstitions."

Rookewoode caught Christopher's eye and nodded subtly.

Christopher felt a sudden wash of gratitude toward the man. He nodded back in thanks.

"I for one hope that act never passes," Lady Lovejoy said quietly. She looked at her husband. "Far too many were harmed in the witch hunts of the past."

Lord Lovejoy looked uncertain.

"Well," Aloysius Lovejoy said brightly. "I'm famished. Time for supper, what?"

"And that is why I love you, dear Aloysius," Rookewoode drawled. "Nothing comes between you and your stomach."

Christopher felt his shoulders relax fractionally. Stanhope was a definite threat to Freya—who knew what a fanatic might do?—but at least the remainder of the party didn't seem to side with the man.

He bowed to Lady Holland. "Might I escort your companion into the dining room, my lady?"

"Please," Lady Holland responded.

Christopher crossed to Freya and held out his arm, watching her closely. Her face was pale and her mouth thinned and tense, but she was beginning to regain some color.

She gave him a tiny smile and laid her hand on his arm.

The small gesture shouldn't have made his entire body warm, but it did.

He escorted her into the dining room and damned all propriety by seating Freya at his right side. He wasn't letting her out of his sight until he figured out what to do with Stanhope.

Supper was roasted grouse—the game the gentlemen had shot earlier in the day—and was very good, which seemed to go a long way toward relaxing the company after the altercation in the sitting room.

Christopher sipped his wine before he said to Freya, keeping his voice low, "Stanhope is the witch hunter you told me about."

There wasn't much doubt in his mind, but he still felt alarm when she inclined her head.

"Will he try to hurt you?"

"That *is* what Dunkelders do," she said with far too much serenity. She must've sensed his outrage, for she went on, "You needn't worry about me. I've run across Dunkelders before."

"Have you," he growled, feeling violent.

She drew her brows together, glancing at him warily. "Yes, I have. And I'm quite capable of dealing with Lord Stanhope."

"Why should you deal with him alone?" For some reason he felt a pang of hurt. "Did it ever even occur to you to ask my help in the matter?"

"Frankly, no." She took a sip of wine.

Did he mean nothing to her?

Christopher inhaled, trying to keep his expression neutral. "Will you at least let me help you if you find yourself in need?"

She hesitated.

He knew her answer plain enough. "*Why?*"

"Why what?" she asked, beginning to sound irritated.

"Why can't you ask me for help?" he said, trying to keep his voice down. They were at the dinner table, surrounded by the other guests, but he couldn't find the patience to postpone this discussion.

"I don't need your—"

"*Damn you,*" he hissed. "Don't you tell me you don't need me."

She turned and met his gaze. Her calm expression was belied by the flags of color in her cheeks and the warning narrowing of her eyes. "Why does it bother you so? Why *should* I need you?"

"Because," he said, struggling with himself, trying to find another way to put it and in the end simply giving up and laying it bare between them. "Because I need you. Because if you don't need me then all that has happened between us is for naught. Because *need* is the most fundamental part of love—without it there isn't anything."

She blinked, seeming to waver at the word *love*.

Then she lifted her chin. "I cannot help it if I don't need your help."

"No, no, you can't." Strange he could still speak with his chest caving in, here in this bloody public setting. He made himself drain all emotion from his voice. "It must've been hard, all these years, living away from your family, relying only on yourself. In any case, my offer remains. If you need me, I will come to you."

He turned to his left and listened without comprehension as Lady Holland prattled on about fashion.

He felt as if he'd lost something important because he knew.

Freya would never ask for his help.

CHAPTER SEVENTEEN

Rowan came to the last girl in the circle and felt
despair, for she looked like all the others.
But this girl, unlike the ones before her, met Rowan's
eyes and smiled.
Rowan's heart swelled and she knew.
She placed her hand on the girl's shoulder and
turned to the Fairy King. "This is she. This is my
friend, Marigold."...
—From *The Grey Court Changeling*

"Are you forbidding me from seeing him?"

The words stopped Freya outside Lady Holland's rooms that night.

They were spoken in Arabella's low contralto.

Freya looked behind her. The hallway was empty. Most of the guests were already abed. She was awake only because she was returning Lady Holland's shawl, which had somehow ended up in Freya's room.

"Bella," Lady Holland said, sounding pained.

Freya started to turn away—this was obviously not a conversation for a witness.

The door opened and Arabella hurried from the bedroom, nearly running into Freya.

Freya opened her mouth, but Arabella gave her one tearful glance before disappearing down the hall.

"You might as well come in," Lady Holland said wearily.

Freya turned and saw her standing in the doorway.

Lady Holland gave a rueful smile. "Never attempt to dissuade a young girl from what she considers love."

She turned back into her bedroom.

Freya cleared her throat as she entered and shut the door behind her. "The earl?"

Lady Holland nodded, pouring the last of her brandy into two glasses. "He's asked leave to propose to her."

Freya took the proffered glass and slowly sat. "*What?* But they've known each other less than a fortnight."

"So have you and the duke." Lady Holland gave her a sardonic look over the rim of her glass.

Freya felt a pang as she remembered the argument with Harlowe at supper. At the time she'd been furious at the suggestion that she might need his help. After all, she'd been Macha for five years, and in all that time she'd never, ever needed the help of a man.

Then again, she'd never had a lover during that time, either. She'd always assumed that an offer of help from a man could come only with concessions on her part. That in the very act of accepting help she'd lose her autonomy.

But what Harlowe offered was without ties or caveats.

Like a gift.

She sighed softly. "I don't think the duke likes me very much at the moment."

"Nonsense," Lady Holland said. "I saw his face when Lord Stanhope made that ridiculous accusation. His Grace is worried about you. That's the *opposite* of not liking you, in case you were wondering. What is more, you give away something of your feelings when you look at the duke. You are not unmoved by the man, I think."

Freya felt herself blushing unwillingly.

"You're a good match," Lady Holland said softly.

"Because he's a duke?" Freya asked cynically.

"A duke is nothing to scoff at." The older woman smiled gently at her. "Money, land, and a title are things only spurned by those who already have them. But even if he had none of those, I'd still advocate a union between the two of you."

"Why?" Freya asked unwillingly.

"Because you are equals in intellect, wit, and emotion, and that's quite uncommon." Lady Holland shook her head, strolling to glance at her toiletry items on the dressing table. "Arabella doesn't have that with Lord Rookewoode, certainly."

Freya offered hesitantly, "They seem equally suited in temperament and mind."

"But not emotion." Lady Holland glanced up at her. "That man doesn't love my Bella."

Freya frowned. "But he must be at least taken with her. Why else would he offer for her if he doesn't love her? He's titled and presumably wealthy."

"Oh, he's quite rich—his mother was an heiress and the dowry she brought to the marriage is legendary." She stared into her glass. "Frankly, I'm not entirely sure why he means to offer for Arabella—and that makes me nervous."

Freya nodded. "Will you give the earl your permission?"

"Yes." Lady Holland threw back the rest of her brandy.

Freya stared.

Her employer saw her look. "I have no choice. If I decline Lord Rookewoode it won't stop Bella from loving him."

"It would keep them apart," Freya pointed out. "And eventually Lord Rookewoode would marry someone else. Perhaps Arabella would forget him."

Lady Holland nodded. "Perhaps. But I don't think so.

She's not a girl who imagines herself in love every second month. She wants him—*loves* him—and I can't hurt her." She sighed. "I can only hope that he will come to love her."

Freya sipped her brandy, wishing there was something she could say. She couldn't help but think that it would be better for Arabella if her mother didn't love her so.

A more indifferent mother might simply say no to the earl. Then again, a more indifferent mother would probably be so thrilled by the prospect of an earl for a son-in-law that she'd never think about her daughter's feelings.

"I'm sorry," Freya said.

"As am I," Lady Holland replied. "Now tell me. What were you arguing about with the duke at supper?"

Freya pressed her lips together. "He says that I should need him. I told him that I didn't need him and he seemed quite put out."

Actually more than put out. She remembered the hurt on Harlowe's face—and shied away from the memory. She'd never meant to hurt him.

"I don't see how I can blame him," Lady Holland replied.

"Don't you?" Freya looked at her. "Why should I have to rely on anyone? Why must I *need* him in order for him to be happy?"

"How would you feel if he didn't need you?" Lady Holland asked.

Freya scoffed. "I wouldn't care."

"Even if he found he needed another woman?"

"Does *need* mean something else I don't understand?" Freya asked suspiciously. "I wouldn't be happy if he found another woman, but frankly, I'm not sure I want to give up my independence."

"Don't be a fool." Lady Holland narrowed her eyes.

"That man respects your intellect. Do you know how few men do? The majority of English gentlemen regard their wives as little more intelligent than their hounds."

"And that's so very important?" Freya asked.

"To most ladies? Perhaps not. To you? *Yes*." Lady Holland pinned her with a stern look. "The Duke of Harlowe *listens* to you, Miss Stewart. While most ladies might not care very much what their husband thinks of their intellects, you, my dear, will find it very important indeed. You'll need to search far and wide and for many years before you find a gentleman like the duke again. Don't be a fool. Seize him while you can."

* * *

Late that night Christopher strode down the hallway with Tess trotting by his side. He wasn't at all sure of the reception he would get when he reached Freya's bedroom, but he was going to do his damnedest to stay and protect her.

Even if she didn't think she needed him.

Stanhope had been summarily escorted from the house by Lovejoy's footmen after supper—a move Christopher had heartily approved of. He rather thought it was Lady Lovejoy who had persuaded her husband to throw Stanhope from the house, but Christopher didn't care as long as the man was gone.

The problem was, Would he *stay* gone?

As far as Christopher could see Stanhope was a fanatical madman. One couldn't expect rational action from him. For all they knew the viscount might try to sneak back into the house and kill Freya in her sleep.

He made her room and tapped at the door.

She opened it, wearing only that damnable chemise.

He tried—rather hard, in fact—to keep his eyes on her face, but apparently he'd lost all control when it came to her.

His gaze swept over her generous curves, and his cock, stupid thing, sprang erect as if ready to engage.

Not tonight.

He pushed past her with Tess and shut the door.

"There's no *need* for you to be here every night," she said rather tartly.

"Perhaps no *need*, but I assure you there's quite a lot of *want*." He picked up a stuffed chair that had been standing by the bed and placed it in front of the fire. Tess trotted over, circled before the fireplace, and heaved a sigh as she flopped down.

"What are you doing?" Freya asked.

He sat in the chair and glanced up at her scowling face. "I think that evident. I'm sleeping here tonight."

"But—"

What an odd expression she wore. He was almost amused. "Yes?"

"Well…" She waved one hand as if that explained the rest of her sentence.

He cocked his head, spreading his hands in the common gesture for *What?*

"Oh!" Her face was pink—and growing pinker—and now she was beginning to scowl. He was growing rather fond of her scowl. "You know very well."

"I'm afraid that I've never been very good at reading the minds of females, and yours is particularly complex," he said.

"You don't have to spend all night in that chair!" She gritted her teeth as if bracing herself. "Come to bed with me."

"No." He turned his head to gaze into the flames.

"No?" Now she sounded bewildered—and a little hurt. Which was just rich, frankly. "You've grown tired of me."

In any other circumstance, he might laugh. "Quite the opposite. I don't trust myself to sleep platonically with you in that bed."

"Oh."

He waited for argument, but none came. And then of course he had to deal with his own feelings of hurt. Why he thought she would want him enough to try to persuade him, he didn't know. Obviously she did not.

And that was just fine. He would—

She walked around him.

Naked.

She'd taken off her chemise and she stood before him, wearing only that damned chain with the signet ring on it.

For a moment he wished he could take it off her and fling it into the fire. The last thing he wanted to think about tonight was their past.

And then she climbed onto the chair, straddling him.

"Come to bed, Kester," she whispered huskily, and kissed him.

All his resolutions flew out the window. He surged up, grasping her waist, angling his head to thrust his tongue in her sweet mouth. She was a siren, a demon, his one weakness.

He'd rise for her.

He'd fall for her.

Christopher stood, lifting her with him, never breaking that soul-shattering kiss. This woman was everything to him: the hope of family, the despair of solitude. He wanted her more than he wanted the next beat of his heart.

And he was very much afraid that he was going to lose her. That he'd wake tomorrow and she'd be gone.

Tonight, though, she was in his arms.

He strode to the bed as she writhed against him like the wanton she was.

"Freya," he breathed as he came down on top of her, his hand clutched in her glorious hair. "Freya, Freya, Freya."

He sounded delirious even to his own ears.

She chuckled wickedly as she arched against him. Perhaps Stanhope and his filthy comrades had it right. Perhaps she *was* a witch, lovely and relentless, bent on ensorcelling him.

She needn't bother. He was already bespelled, his heart, head, hands, and cock tied to her and her will.

He would die for her.

If only she would let him.

He palmed her breast, all sweet softness, and pinched her nipple gently. His prick strained the buttons on his falls, and if he didn't act soon he'd spill in his breeches like a stripling youth.

She moaned beneath him, her thighs parted wide, her calves hooked over his legs.

He pushed his hand between them and tore his falls open, uncaring at the sound of ripping fabric. His cock throbbed with pent fury and he trailed his fingers down her soft belly, rejoicing when he reached her curls and found them soaked with her desire.

He lifted his hips even as she whimpered in protest and tried to pull his shoulders back down.

His cock slid against her thigh, the touch almost enough to undo him, then prodded at her opening.

So wet.

So hot.

He nudged against her, flexed his hips, and thrust hard.

Sliding, sliding in.

He flung back his head, his eyes squeezed shut, gritting his teeth. She squeezed him in living silk, almost agonizingly good.

He breathed out, controlling himself, waiting a beat until he was certain he could move without spilling.

But she, wicked creature that she was, bit his lip and ground against him, almost unmanning him at once.

He growled and opened his eyes. "Lie still."

Her gold-green eyes glowed like something devilish. "No." She undulated against him.

He pulled almost all the way from her and shoved his length back into her. Roughly. Without grace or finesse.

She tilted back her head and sighed blissfully.

Damn her.

He bent his head and licked her arched neck as he began thrusting. He wasn't going to last long, but while he did he meant to fuck her into the damned mattress.

His sweet vixen.

But his crisis caught him unawares only moments later, making him convulse above her. *In* her. Spilling his seed and making him shake.

She moaned beneath him as his limbs turned to wet paper, but he knew she'd not come. He pulled himself from her and, while she was still grasping for him, slid down her body.

He kissed her quim openmouthed, tasting himself and glad of it.

She was his, his, *his*.

He wrapped his hands about her legs, holding her open for him, and inhaled her musk, heady and wild. She was so tender here, trembling and wet. He licked and mouthed at her, enjoying the sound of her breath growing raspy. When he suckled her bud, her thighs clenched against his ears as she went rigid, gasping and shaking.

He was *glad*. Near vicious with his victory.

He'd given her this, this moment of blissful agony. If nothing else in the entire bloody world he could give her this.

But even as he dragged his exhausted body up her, he knew:

It wasn't enough to keep her.

* * *

"Messalina."

The voice was whispered, which tied in nicely with the dream Messalina was having. A dark woods, a man who could not be trusted, and a monster somewhere behind her. She turned, her heart beating in her throat. Sleepy black eyes smiled at her, alluring and terrifying.

"Messalina, *please*."

That, on the other hand, didn't fit at all. She'd never known him to plead.

She opened her eyes, which wasn't a help, as the room was nearly pitch black. Only the embers on the hearth sent up a faint glow.

"Jane?" Her voice emerged a bass croak, and she cleared her throat before speaking again. "What time is it?"

"I don't know. Almost dawn, I think?"

Messalina blinked and sat up slowly. "What's happened? Why are you here?"

"James the footman woke me," Jane said worriedly. "He says there's something happening at Randolph House. The lights are on and the grooms are moving about. Oh, Messalina, he thinks they may be moving Eleanor."

Messalina was up in a flash, pulling on stays and a simple dress that hooked in the front. "Are you sure?"

"No, of course not." Jane's words were sharp, but her voice was worried. "Oh, why couldn't Lord Randolph wait until after tonight? He accepted our invitation to supper. Everything was planned."

"Perhaps that's why he couldn't wait," Messalina said. "Perhaps he suspected something."

Jane stared. "I don't see how."

Messalina shook her head, trying to clear it so that she could *think*. *Why* Lord Randolph was acting now hardly mattered. What mattered was that if he moved Eleanor, she'd disappear again.

They couldn't allow that.

"We need to find out what he's doing," she decided.

"How will we do that?" Jane asked anxiously.

"I don't know," Messalina replied, pulling on sturdy boots. "I'm going to ask Freya."

Five minutes later they were tiptoeing down the corridor to Freya's room. Messalina scratched at the door and then wondered if she could risk waking others by knocking.

She didn't have to because the door was pulled open.

Freya looked out.

"Lord Randolph is up to something," Messalina said, and explained the situation as concisely as she could.

"Wait here," Freya said, and then closed her bedroom door.

Messalina raised her eyebrows, interested that the other woman wouldn't let them into her room.

A minute later Freya opened the door fully dressed and slipped out. She gestured for Messalina and Jane to follow her and talked as she strode to the stairs. "Now then. Messalina and I will go to Lord Randolph's house with James. If he is indeed moving Eleanor, we'll send James back to you, Jane, and then you'll send reinforcements—

specifically the duke. He knows about Eleanor and Lord Randolph. If this is all simply a false alarm, we'll return with no harm done."

Messalina looked at Jane.

Who nodded. "Yes, very well. That sounds as if it will work."

Freya's eyes suddenly widened. "And...erm...if you do need to find the duke, Jane, you might want to look first in my bedchamber."

Messalina's eyebrows shot up.

Jane cleared her throat. "Naturally."

Messalina and Freya gathered James, who was waiting downstairs, still clutching a lit lantern, and set out.

The night was cool and dark, the moon hiding behind clouds. The woods were unpleasantly silent, save for the eerie hoot of an owl.

An evil omen, or so Messalina's nurse had always told her.

Their little party was silent as it tramped through the woods, as if afraid of waking something in the night.

It wasn't until they were nearly free of the looming trees that Freya said to James, "Douse the lantern."

He slid a panel closed and the light winked out.

They stood a moment adjusting their eyes as best they could to the gloom.

Down below there were several lights flickering at the windows of Randolph House, and Messalina could hear faint voices, carrying on the night breeze.

"Let's go," Freya whispered, and they crept forward.

Her eyes strained to make out any movement at the house or stables. Had they come too late? Had Eleanor been moved?

Or worse, murdered?

They were nearly at the stables when light flared.

Directly behind them.

Messalina turned as James was felled by a blow to the head.

Lord Randolph grinned in the flickering light. "Miss Greycourt. How unexpected."

CHAPTER EIGHTEEN

Well, the Fairy King was not best pleased.
"Brother," he hissed, "take the girl, Marigold, and
leave my realm."
Ash's purple eyes darkened. "And Rowan?"
"That one stays here."
"You said I could go!" Rowan cried.
The Fairy King stared at Ash as he replied, "Ah, but
you tasted the dew in the Grey Lands. You are mine."
"It was only a drop," Rowan whispered.
The Fairy King smiled his sharp-toothed smile. "A
drop is all it takes." ...
—From *The Grey Court Changeling*

Christopher woke in the early hours of the morning to an empty bed. For a moment he lay in the darkness, winding his way between sleep and wakefulness. He patted the bed beside him. Rolled over and felt until he reached the bed's edge.

Nothing.

He sighed and nearly fell back into that black pool of sleep, but then his mind sent a jolt, startling him awake with the knowledge that something was very wrong.

Freya wasn't there.

He sat upright.

The sheets next to him were cold.

Tess lay before the fireplace, curled into a ball and sleeping.

The fire itself was but glowing embers, which meant it must be close to dawn.

Freya wasn't in the room.

Christopher swore and climbed from the bed, his brain seizing with horror. How the hell had she left without him waking?

He still wore his shirt and breeches, and it was the work of a moment to don waistcoat and coat. If she was merely down in the kitchens looking for a nighttime snack, he was going to take her pretty neck between his hands and strangle her.

After kissing her in relief.

He was stepping into his shoes when there came a scratch on the door.

He crossed to it and flung it open.

Outside stood Lady Lovejoy, dressed and white faced.

No.

He knew this was not good, not good at all, even before she opened her mouth.

She looked at him, her eyes wide and frightened, and said, "Miss Stewart and Miss Greycourt went to Randolph House an hour ago with my footman and they haven't returned."

* * *

Lord Randolph was a huge man. He had a red, pockmarked face, an overhanging brow, and a lumpy potato of a nose. His shoulders sloped from a neck so thick it almost looked deformed. His chest and belly strained at his waistcoat and his thighs were like tree trunks. He'd intimidate most in a ballroom.

In a dim cellar, with his temper out of control, he was simply terrifying.

Freya watched Lord Randolph pace and tried to control her own fear. She needed to keep alert for any sign of an opening. A way to get them all away from here.

She was aware that the likelihood of their escaping was near nil, but to give up was to die without a fight.

She wasn't about to do that.

For a moment she saw Harlowe's disapproving face. He would hate this if he could see it. Would want to rescue her and sweep all danger away because that was what he thought he was put on earth to do: always be the savior.

He was going to blame himself if Lord Randolph killed her.

That. That hurt the most.

She was brought back to the present by His Lordship's bringing his ham-like fist down on an empty wine rack, breaking the thing with a terrific crack.

"Interfering females," he shouted, kicking the pieces of the wine rack. "Stanhope told me stories about witches in the area, but at first I thought the man overly cautious."

"Sorry to disappoint," Messalina muttered with more bravado than intelligence.

Randolph whirled on her. "What were you doing, witch? Were you going to set a curse on my lands? Hold some unholy ceremony?"

Freya didn't like that all his attention was on Messalina. "We're not witches, I assure you."

Randolph sneered. "Indeed you are. Stanhope told me about you, Lady Freya. Your damnable name is well known to the Dunkelders, and I shall take great satisfaction in making sure you confess and repent of your sins before you die. I only wish you hadn't fouled my home with your presence. This, too, is my *wife*'s fault, I suppose."

He turned to glare at poor Eleanor, who gave a muffled sob.

Freya, Messalina, and Eleanor were lying on the damp floor of the Randolph House wine cellar. James was nowhere in sight, and Freya could only hope the footman was still alive. Judging from the ancient groined brick ceiling, the cellar was older than the house that now stood above it. The bricks themselves were crumbling, and the low, squat ceiling seemed to loom much too close.

Freya shuddered.

She had the awful feeling that the ceiling and all the tons of soil and house above it could come crashing down on her at any moment.

And there was nothing she could do about it. She was tied securely, her arms pulled behind her back at an awkward angle. Messalina and Eleanor were similarly bound. Eleanor's face looked awful in the flickering candlelight, pale and shining like something that hadn't seen the sunlight in weeks.

Because she hadn't. Lord Randolph had kept Eleanor in this awful, cramped place for a *year*. It was a wonder she was still sane.

Freya glanced at the man restlessly roaming the small cellar and wondered what would happen when he stopped ranting.

Nothing good.

"Why did you lock Eleanor up, my lord?" Freya called, hoping to distract him or keep him talking or really just anything.

It was torture being held helpless with the knowledge that this man was most likely going to kill all three of them when he stopped talking.

Freya hadn't expected Lord Randolph to actually answer

her, but he whirled at her question. "She's mad, can't you see? Kept arguing with me, saying she wanted to leave me. Leave? She's *married* to me. A woman can't leave her husband. I only put her here to save her from humiliating both herself and me." He glared at Eleanor as if it were her fault he'd had to imprison her. "I should've just killed her, but I was too kindhearted to do so."

Beside her, Messalina cleared her throat. "I think it time you let us go, my lord. After all, my uncle will inquire about me should I not return."

"*Be quiet*," Lord Randolph snapped at her without turning his attention away from Eleanor. "Whyever did I marry you? You've caused me nothing but trouble since our wedding day."

Eleanor closed her eyes wearily. She'd said very little since they'd found her, and Freya had the awful feeling she might've been punished for *speaking* in the past.

"Let us go," Freya said calmly. "We'll take Eleanor far away. No one will ever know she's alive. She'll never bother you again."

Lord Randolph stared at her. He leaned down and suddenly slapped her hard across the face.

Freya's head whipped back, hitting the wall behind her.

"I don't believe you, *witch*," Lord Randolph said through the ringing in her ears. "And I'll not let you befoul my wife any more than you already have." He turned and left.

Taking with him their only light.

Messalina was swearing with a shocking versatility and Eleanor was softly sobbing.

On the whole this did not look good, and Freya had a brief vision of Harlowe as he had appeared last night in her bedroom. Calm. Caring. Certain.

Of her.

If something did happen to her, if Lord Randolph carried out his threats and killed her and the others, Harlowe would mourn for her.

She knew it in her bones, and with the acknowledgment something came loose in her breast. Her last barrier—pride, stubbornness, or simple cynicism—fell and she knew. She loved Harlowe. Truly and forever.

She wanted—*desperately*—to live to see him again.

They needed to get away before Lord Randolph got back.

"Can you move your hands?" she asked Messalina. She kept her voice soft in case Lord Randolph hadn't gone far.

From what she remembered when Lord Randolph's footmen had dragged them in here, the cellar seemed to be a long corridor with rooms or bays on either side. They were in the last bay, at the end of the corridor. Here the footmen had bound them—though not without a fight—and tied their hands to iron rings in the wall.

Eleanor had already been chained to the wall when they arrived. By the sores around her ankles, she'd been held this way for quite some time.

"No," Messalina said grimly. "The rope is too tight. I don't think I can feel my fingers."

Freya frowned at that but still turned to Lady Randolph. "Can you reach Messalina, Eleanor?"

"No." Her breathing was loud in the blackness. "I can't. I'm so sorry."

"It's not your fault," Messalina muttered fiercely. "None of this is your fault."

Eleanor's only reply was renewed weeping.

"Perhaps if we pull on the iron rings," Freya said, trying to keep all their spirits up against overwhelming odds.

She yanked at the iron ring she was tied to. It gave a screech, but didn't move. It felt as if her bonds were tighter now.

She rested her head on the nasty, cold wall.

Eleanor sounded as if she might've fallen asleep, though it was hard to tell if she was snoring or simply breathing heavily.

"I think my mother might've known about the Wise Woman," Messalina whispered suddenly.

Freya blinked in the darkness. "Why do you think that?"

She carefully twisted her wrists, trying to get an idea of how the ropes were tied. She thought she might feel a slight give in the rope.

"I don't know. Well, that's not true," Messalina corrected herself. "After *that* night, Lucretia and I were sent away. The very next morning, in fact. We went to live with a distant cousin of Mother's."

Freya frowned. "That doesn't sound particularly suspicious." If she could just get her thumb under one of the loops...

"No," Messalina agreed. "But it was the person Mama chose to escort us. She was a tall, almost gaunt woman I'd never seen before or since. She barely spoke to us for the entire journey, but I do remember that she had the oddest name. Crow."

Freya felt a thrill go through her. Like Macha, the name Crow was handed down to each new woman in the position. Messalina and Lucretia had been guarded on their journey to safety by the Wise Women's Crow at the time.

"Did your mother say anything about the Wise Women?" she asked.

"Nothing," Messalina said, and Freya couldn't quite make out what she heard in her voice. "She died very shortly after we left. Perhaps a day or two. She was ill, remember?"

"Yes." Freya swallowed. She did remember now—how had she forgotten? Mrs. Greycourt had spent most of her time in a chair or in bed, her face thin and sallow, her hands shaking. But she'd smiled—a sweet, wide smile—whenever she'd seen Freya. "I think you're right: the Wise Women helped your family."

Messalina sighed in the darkness. "How do you become a Wise Woman?"

Freya relaxed for a moment, trying to ease the strain on her shoulders. "Mothers who want to bring their girls into the Wise Women usually do so a year after they first bleed. That's when the girls learn the secrets of the Wise Women. You were probably too young still to be initiated."

"Then how did you become a Wise Woman?" Messalina asked. "Your mother..."

Freya's mother had died in childbirth with Elspeth. "I was too young when Mama died. But my aunt Hilda took care of us girls after the tragedy. She was the one who taught me and my sisters about the Wise Women." She sighed, remembering that indomitable woman—all the indomitable women who had come before them. "I'm sorry about your mother. I didn't know when exactly she died. We didn't attend the funeral, of course, and there was no one to bring the news. I would've liked to..."

What? Help mourn the woman who had been so kind to her when her own mother had died? Given her sympathies to the family that had destroyed hers?

It was all so mixed up—so *awful*—and she was weary of the whole mess.

"I know." Messalina's soft words interrupted her thoughts. "I would've liked to have been with you when your father died. I would've liked to have been with you through *all* of it. I wish we'd remained friends. I wish…"

"We never really had a choice, did we?" Freya murmured. "It was all taken away from us."

"But we have a choice now," Messalina whispered, and even in the dark Freya could hear her smile. "I'm glad we found each other again and made up. I'm glad I'm your friend, Freya."

Freya opened her mouth to reply, but the sound of approaching footsteps stopped her.

Lord Randolph loomed into view with his footmen. "I think it's time to end this, don't you?"

* * *

Christopher cocked his pistol and placed the barrel against the back of Lord Stanhope's head. "Where are the women?"

They stood in the Randolph House kitchen, which was eerily deserted. Christopher had two brawny Lovejoy footmen at his back—good men who had helped him get inside the house. There they'd run into luck: the viscount lurking by himself in the kitchen.

"You're too late," Stanhope said.

Christopher sneered and knocked the barrel of the pistol against Stanhope's skull. "Tell me."

The viscount darted a malicious glance at him. "They're in the cellar."

Christopher stared at him. Stanhope had given the information entirely too easily.

Christopher turned to the footmen. "Search the rest of the house."

"Yes, Your Grace," the elder of the two said, and they ran from the kitchen.

He looked back at the viscount. "Show me."

Stanhope shrugged and led him to a low doorway on the far side of the kitchen. Beyond the doorway the cellar was black.

"We'll need a candle," Stanhope said.

Christopher felt sweat start at his lower back. God, he hated this. Hated that Freya was down there in the dark. Hated the thought of descending into that black pit.

But if Freya was down there, he would go down.

For her.

"Then light a candle," Christopher growled.

He watched as the viscount picked up a single candlestick and lit it from the fire, then looked at him inquiringly.

Christopher impatiently motioned to the cellar stairs.

Stanhope grimaced and went down the spiral stairs with Christopher following close behind.

"She's a witch, you know," Stanhope said, his voice echoing. "It goes back centuries in her family."

"Shut up."

Stanhope's laughter floated up to him from farther down the stairs. The viscount had turned beyond the central pillar, and his light was a mere flicker on the walls.

Christopher felt the sweat slide down the small of his back. He should've brought his own candle. He rounded the pillar and almost ran into Stanhope, standing at the bottom of the stairs, his face lit from below by his candle.

He looked like every child's nightmare bogeyman. "They fuck the devil, you know. Witches do."

"You're insane." Christopher had had enough. The stale air was pressing against him, making him think he couldn't catch his breath. "Where is Miss Stewart?"

But Stanhope wouldn't be moved from his subject. "They hold midnight masses and sacrifice newborn babes." His eyes glittered. "They *drink* the blood of the innocents."

Christopher raised his eyebrows. "You've seen this yourself, have you?"

He looked past the viscount's shoulder. The cellar appeared to be a long room with smaller rooms off it.

The end disappeared into darkness.

He glanced back at Stanhope. The man had bright spots of color on his cheeks, as if he were feverish. "Where is Lady Randolph?"

Stanhope blinked. "Lady Randolph? Do you want to see Lady Randolph?"

"Yes," Christopher said.

Stanhope pivoted without a word and marched into the darkness.

Christopher followed him warily.

At the end of the corridor the viscount disappeared into one of the rooms.

Christopher stopped.

"Are you coming?" Stanhope asked, and his words echoed in the empty cellar.

"What do you have in there?" Christopher growled.

"Come and see."

Christopher smiled grimly. "Oddly enough, I don't trust you."

"*You* don't trust *me*?" Stanhope barked a laugh. "*You* consort with witches."

"Miss Stewart isn't a witch," Christopher said. The ceiling was so damned low. He could touch it without extending his arm fully above his head. The thought made his breath come faster. "There's no reason for me to come in there. If you're only playing games—"

There was a thump and a muffled scream.

Christopher rounded the corner.

To find Lord Randolph aiming a dueling pistol at him.

Christopher instinctively ducked.

But Randolph didn't shoot. "You coward. You should've seen your face just now."

"Where is Miss Stewart?" Christopher asked. Messalina and Lady Randolph were tied up at Randolph's feet, both gagged.

Stanhope stood in the corner, looking wary.

Messalina looked like she wanted to kill someone—most probably Randolph.

Christopher dragged his gaze away from them. He needed to keep his attention on Randolph and his pistol. "If you shoot me, I'll shoot you."

That seemed to amuse Randolph. "Oh no. Stanhope has told me all about your fondness for the witch. You deserve to see each other before you both die. In fact I've a mind to kill the witch in front of you before I shoot you."

Christopher stiffened, but kept his face expressionless. He needed Randolph to show him where he'd hidden Freya.

"That way." Randolph waved his pistol toward the doorway behind Christopher.

"Which way?" Christopher asked, turning so that he could keep his pistol on Randolph as he backed to the corridor.

"To the right," Randolph said.

Christopher raised his eyebrows. The passage to his right led to the dead end of the corridor. He obeyed, though, conscious all the time as he sidled sideways down the corridor that there was a pistol pointing at him. He kept his own pistol leveled on Randolph as he moved.

But it wasn't entirely a dead end. As Christopher neared and the single candle Randolph held lit the way, he could see one more room, although *room* was perhaps too generous a word.

It was more like a cubbyhole.

Bloody hell. He could feel sweat on his brow as they neared, the beginning of the awful panic beating its wings in his chest.

The flickering candlelight reflected on a face close to the ground.

Freya.

White faced, gagged, and bound.

Christ.

Christopher cleared his throat and said, "I don't see anything."

"No?" Randolph laughed derisively, striding forward. He swung his pistol away from Christopher and toward the cubbyhole and Freya. "Perhaps you'll see *this*."

Christopher shot him in the head.

The candle clattered to the floor and the cellar descended into blackness.

CHAPTER NINETEEN

The Fairy King held out his hand to Rowan.
But Ash stepped between them, kneeling gracefully
once more. "Mercy, my liege. I've grown fond of
this mortal princess. Let her pass with her friend.
Do it for my sake."
The Fairy King waved the fingers of his gray hand.
"For your sake, Brother, I will let this mortal go,
but as in all things I will need payment."
Ash looked at him. "Name it."
The Fairy King smiled. "Your eyes."
    —From The Grey Court Changeling

The blast of the gunshot deafened Freya and she jerked, hitting her head against stone. Had both men's guns gone off? Oh God! Where was Harlowe? Had Lord Randolph shot him?

Was he dead?

She wrenched at her bonds, trying to get her hands free, and rocked violently on the floor of the nook she was in.

And then she heard his voice. "Freya. *Freya.*"

Warm hands grasped her, and Harlowe's face was pressed against her own. Tears started in her eyes, running sideways down her face because she'd fallen to the side. How dare he frighten her so? How dare he make her think he'd left forever?

He was shaking, his big body trembling with panic tightly kept in check.

Damn it. She needed to talk to him. To tell him it was all right.

They were both alive.

His hands were on her now, cutting away at the cords with a penknife, and he was murmuring all the time.

"You're fine. It's all right. Don't be afraid. God, Freya, *God.*"

Her hands came loose and she tore the cloth from her mouth. She caught his face between her palms and pulled him to her, kissing him.

Tasting his life. Tasting the salt of her own tears.

"Kester," she whispered. "Kester."

She was shaking, and he caught her in his arms. "It's all right, sweetheart. It's all right."

He thought she was frightened for herself, she could tell, but that wasn't it. The entire time Lord Randolph had held them, she'd thought only of Harlowe.

She tried to tell him that, but her words were caught underneath his lips, and then he was lifting her into his strong arms.

He turned, and she saw lights coming closer from the foot of the spiral staircase.

"Your Grace!" one of the Lovejoy footmen called. "What happened?"

"Lord Randolph tried to kill Miss Stewart," Harlowe said as they went by. He never broke stride. She could see that his face was gray and drawn in the candlelight. "I shot him."

Someone swore.

Freya said frantically, "Don't forget Messalina and Lady Randolph."

Harlowe met her eyes and paused. "Miss Greycourt and Lady Randolph are in the next room. Lady Randolph will no doubt need a physician." He glanced at the footmen. "Make sure Viscount Stanhope doesn't interfere."

Freya saw the footmen hurrying to the room where Messalina and Eleanor were as Harlowe turned and carried her away.

"I can walk," she said, less loudly than perhaps she might've.

"No." He mounted the stairs seemingly without effort.

The Randolph kitchen was crowded with men.

"Your Grace," Lord Lovejoy said, looking flushed. Aloysius Lovejoy and Lord Rookewoode were behind him. "My wife told me that you were in need of help."

Harlowe nodded. "Your footmen are below and may need assistance in bringing Lady Randolph up the stairs. She has been most terribly treated by her husband."

"She's *alive*?" Lord Lovejoy's jaw dropped.

Harlowe merely nodded, setting Freya down on a chair.

"I really can walk," Freya said softly as Harlowe examined her scraped wrists. "Harlowe?"

"I thought I'd lost you," he said abruptly, head bowed over her hands. "Damn it, Freya, why the hell didn't you rouse me and tell me where you were going? Lady Lovejoy had to *wake* me to alert me to the fact that you were in trouble." He glanced up finally, and she could see that his brilliant blue eyes were haunted. "I could've slept through your *murder*."

"It's my work," she said, knowing it sounded weak. "I'm sorry."

He shook his head and then, evidently deciding that her wrists were fine, lifted her again.

"Harlowe?"

He ignored her, striding through the house and out into the yard.

The sun was just breaking over the horizon.

There were horses tied in the stable yard, and he placed her on the back of one, swinging himself up behind her.

He rode back to Lovejoy House with her in his arms, still without speaking.

Almost as if he were afraid of what he might say if he opened his mouth further.

Freya closed her eyes. Perhaps she ought to be supervising Lady Randolph's release or arguing feminine autonomy with Harlowe. But all she could bring herself to do was enjoy the slight breeze on her face, the rocking of the horse beneath them, and the warm, solid feel of Harlowe behind her.

She was *alive*.

They both were.

Harlowe insisted on continuing to carry her when they reached Lovejoy House. They swept past an astonished, sleepy butler and up the stairs to Harlowe's room.

He kicked the door shut behind them.

Tess trotted over, tail wagging, to greet them.

Harlowe placed Freya on the bed as carefully as if she'd been made of eggshell and began to undress her.

She watched him, this grave, handsome man. This man who had killed another for her.

The man she'd thought she'd never see again only hours before.

His brows were drawn together as if he worked on the most important chore in the world.

Several strands of hair had come loose from the tie at the nape of his neck. She lifted a hand and stroked a lock back over his ear.

"I thought Randolph might've already killed you," he said, his voice low. "When Stanhope led me to the cellar. I thought Stanhope might be about to show me your body before Randolph killed me."

Her hand stilled, and then she lightly touched his cheekbone. "But he didn't. I'm alive." She searched his cerulean eyes. "You came down into that horrible cellar for me. You put aside your own agony to save me."

He shook his head as if denying any bravery and pulled her bodice and stays off. He threw them rather cavalierly to the floor before removing her skirts, stockings, and shoes.

"I didn't know what I would do if Randolph had killed you," he said, standing to kick off his shoes. "I thought about letting him shoot me."

Her heart seized and she said very carefully, "I'm glad you didn't."

He stripped off coat, waistcoat, shirt, breeches, and underclothes, and then pulled her to her feet.

He lifted her chemise over her head without saying a word.

She started to speak, then saw his set face and raised her arms instead.

Then she was as nude as he.

Only at that point did he pause, his hands hovering as if he was afraid to touch her.

She looked at him and saw bleakness in his face.

That wouldn't do.

She lifted her hand and laid her palm over his left nipple.

Over the place where his heart beat most powerfully.

She could feel the beat beneath her fingers, strong and steady.

Rather like the man himself.

"Freya," he whispered, and drew her into his arms.

He was so warm. His chest pressing against her breasts, his thighs on hers. His cock bumping into her belly.

He bent his head and kissed her. Sweetly at first, his lips brushing over hers.

But that didn't last long. As if a chain had snapped, he opened his mouth hungrily over hers. She parted her lips, letting him tip her back, feeling the room whirl as he picked her up and set her on the bed again.

"Freya." He lifted his head to whisper against the corner of her jaw. To trail his lips down her neck, to mouth at her collarbone. His hands were stroking, caressing her hips, her belly, her breasts.

She gasped, trying to regain her equilibrium, but his urgency was carrying her along. Taking her without letting her think.

Overpowering her with the feelings he provoked.

She'd thought she'd lost him.

She didn't ever want to feel that again. She wanted to tell him. To explain how her heart was beating too fast and he was the only one who could keep her from flying apart.

That she didn't want anyone else but him. Forever and ever.

But the words were caught and flung away by the storm between them.

His mouth was on her nipple, sucking strongly, and she cried out, arching beneath him, spreading her legs.

She could feel his penis, hot and hard, slipping along her inner thigh.

She reached down and grasped him, putting him at the entrance to her body.

He raised his head and stared in her eyes as he pushed into her. Thrusting without pausing, without relenting, making her body part and receive him.

As if this was where he was meant to be.

As if she'd waited her whole life for him to fit his body to hers and make them one being.

She lifted her legs and wrapped them over his hips, trapping him there.

They were perfect.

Holding each other, breast to chest, belly to belly, cock to quim. Halves made into one whole. He laid his mouth against hers and kissed her as he rocked his hips into her.

It was a gentle, almost infinitesimal movement. Like the ripples that spread from a pebble thrown into water. Silent. Slight. Nearly invisible.

But there all the same.

He rippled against her and she felt it in her soul.

This was beautiful, what they did here together.

She dug her fingers into his broad shoulders, wordlessly urging him on. Silently pleading.

Everything that had ever happened in her life had led to this point. All the actions she'd taken, both good and bad, wise and foolish, she had taken them all but to arrive here, in this quiet bedroom, rocking together with *this* man.

Achieving immortality.

It was building within her, she could feel it. That greater wave, those sparks lighting here and there throughout her body. She wanted...she wanted...

Oh, her center was on that edge.

She tore her mouth from his, gasping, trying to get closer. To *squirm* until she could feel his cock rubbing that spot, that spot, *that spot*.

But he wouldn't move any faster, any deeper, and for a long moment she thought she'd go insane, standing on her tiptoes, here on the edge, her body rising and rising.

She couldn't take this.

Her eyes flew open and she saw no compassion in his blue gaze. Only determination. Only ruthless drive to bind them together forever.

Her mouth opened and she moaned as she dove, falling faster and faster, her body convulsing, her gaze locked with his.

So she saw it when he came after her, his lips curling back, the lines in his face deepening in agonizing pleasure.

She watched as they fell together and when they hit the water together she was still watching.

The ripples went on forever.

* * *

Christopher lay on his back, staring at the ceiling, the person most precious in the world to him in his arms. Strange that only weeks ago he'd not thought about Freya at all. She was a tiny piece of his past, lost and forgotten.

And then she'd exploded back into his life and stolen his heart.

His lips quirked at the thought. "I love you."

She froze beside him. "What?"

He raised himself to one elbow, gazing down at her. Fiery hair spread in tangled waves over his pillow, gold-green eyes wide and startled. Pink, plump lips parted.

He wanted to remember her face for all the years of his life and beyond.

"I love you," he repeated. "Will you marry me?"

Her brows drew together, and he read the answer in her eyes before she spoke.

"I don't know..." She bit her lip.

It should be a small sop that it appeared to hurt her even to say it.

But it wasn't. The pain spread through his chest, as lethal as a spear to the heart. He took a deep breath. "Why not? Can you tell me?"

She searched his face. "It isn't because I don't love you. Please don't think that, because I *do*. I love you with all my being, Kester."

"I know, sweetheart." He stroked her hair back from her face. "That almost makes it worse."

She nodded. "I don't want to hurt you."

He felt his lips quirk. "I know that, too." He didn't say that she was hurting him anyway, because he knew they both knew that.

She closed her eyes. "It's...it's just that before this house party I never even *thought* about marriage. I was a de Moray, I was a Wise Woman and the Macha, and that seemed enough." She opened her eyes again. "But now in the space of days *everything* I thought I knew and believed has been upended. I *think* I want to marry you, but how can I tell? I've spent every day here in close proximity to you. It's like we're in a special world. What if away from you I don't feel the same? What if when I leave here and go back to the greater world I find out that I was wrong?"

"You think you might realize you don't really love me?" he asked carefully.

"No." She touched his jaw with her fingertips. "No, never that. But that's just the point. I *know* that I love you. But I *don't* know if marriage is the right thing for me. You influence me. When I'm around you all I want to *do* is be around you. I don't know if I'm thinking straight."

Her brows drew together.

He pressed a fingertip to her lips when she would've spoken again. "No. Listen." He took a deep breath. "This is your decision and I'll not sway it, no matter how much

I want to, because I love you and this is what you need. Make no mistake: I *hate* it. I'd rather try and woo you and persuade you. Argue with you and take advantage of your love for me. But you have made it clear that you want—that you *must*—make this decision for yourself." He paused, swallowing. "That in fact, you need to have the choice to refuse me forever if that is what you think best for yourself."

Tears slid down the side of her face and into her hair as she listened to him.

Ran's ring lay in the sweet dip between her breasts. He nudged it with his finger, feeling the body heat it held from her, and looked her in the eye. "I once swore on this ring that I would never retreat again from what was right. To *me* it feels right to stay by your side and give you comfort and protection. But that isn't what you want." He smiled painfully. "It may not even be what you *need*."

"*Kester*," she whispered.

"I'm thinking of you now. I'll do as you wish. I'll give the decision to you. But I *can't* stay a day longer here, knowing that you are not mine, and be a dispassionate observer as you make your decision." He leaned over and softly kissed her. "Therefore I am foresworn. I love you, Freya, more than anything else in this world. That is why I'm leaving."

* * *

When Freya opened her eyes, it was to the late-afternoon sun coming in the window in her bedroom at Lovejoy House. Her eyes widened. She hadn't meant to sleep the day away. In fact, after leaving Harlowe's bedroom that morning, she'd asked for a bath in her room, fully intending to dress properly and help the household and Lady Holland.

Instead she'd laid down just for a moment and apparently slept all afternoon.

"How do you feel?"

The voice came from beside her bed, but disappointingly it wasn't Harlowe's.

No, he'd told her that he was leaving in order to let her make up her own mind about whether she could marry him. Her heart seemed to ache.

It was quite ridiculous to feel so sad when he'd done what she'd essentially asked him to do.

Freya turned her head and blinked at Messalina. "I feel very rested. But you had just as bad a morning as I. Why are you nursing me?"

Messalina shrugged—a strangely awkward gesture from such an elegant woman. "It's what friends do, don't they? Care for one another."

Freya smiled. "Yes, I suppose it is."

Messalina grinned back at her companionably.

Freya felt peace wash over her. This was good, sitting with Messalina. Having this tentative accord.

But she couldn't lie in bed forever. "I suppose I must get up and dress for supper."

"You can if you want, but I doubt it will be a very formal affair," Messalina replied. "Jane has set poor Eleanor up in a room here. I think the doctors are still tending to her."

"How is Lady Randolph?"

Messalina winced. "Better than I thought she would be, given how horrible this last year has been for her. Jane says she can stay as long as she wishes to recuperate. Of course she's lost Randolph House now that Lord Randolph is dead, but I don't think she'll feel that's any great tragedy."

"*I* certainly wouldn't want to enter that house again," Freya said.

"Nor I." Messalina shuddered, then looked at Freya. "How does this all affect the Wise Women?"

"I hope you don't think me ghoulish, but Lord Randolph's death is very good for us," Freya said practically. "Without him, the Witch Act loses its major backer—he was the one who wrote the act and meant to present it. It won't be presented to Parliament now."

"Then you fulfilled your mission?" Messalina asked.

"Yes." That at least was satisfying—she'd made the Wise Women a little safer.

"His death was best for Eleanor as well," Messalina said darkly.

"Does she have any funds at all now?" Freya wondered. The estate was no doubt entailed, and the Randolphs had no children. Some distant relative would probably inherit.

"Well, that's the odd thing," Messalina said. "Apparently Lord Randolph drew up a will when they were first married and he never bothered to change it. Eleanor will have a tidy income, and there's a dower house in London when she's ready to enter society again. I'm afraid that however she does it, though, there will be quite a scandal when it's revealed that she's alive."

"Yes, I suppose so." Freya winced. Poor Lady Randolph hadn't done anything to deserve the notoriety that was about to descend on her. She glanced at Messalina. "What about Lord Randolph's death?" Surely Harlowe wouldn't be brought to trial for murder—he was a duke, after all—but her own history showed quite well what gossip could do if it got out he'd killed Lord Randolph.

"Fortunately Lord Lovejoy is the local magistrate," Messalina said. "He's ruled it an accident whilst Lord Randolph was cleaning his gun."

Freya raised her eyebrows doubtfully. "And everyone who knows what really happened has agreed to this explanation?"

Messalina's mouth twisted. "Lord Randolph was *very* unpopular in the area."

"Hmm." Freya murmured. "What about Lord Stanhope?"

Messalina snorted. "Apparently he's in a great deal of debt," she said with satisfaction. "Mr. Lovejoy knew about the debt through gossip and told his father who told Christopher. Christopher had the viscount clapped in irons and sent back to London to debtor's prison. Christopher also made sure that the Randolph footmen and housekeeper were all arrested for imprisoning Lady Randolph. I don't know how he managed to do so much before he left."

Freya glanced away, feeling the prick of tears at her eyes. "Then he's gone already?"

Messalina hesitated. "Yes? He left for his country seat, I believe. In Sussex? Or perhaps it was Essex."

All Freya could do was stare at her and blink. She'd somehow thought—against all reason and despite the fact that he'd said he'd leave immediately—that she'd have another chance to talk to Harlowe before they parted ways.

To say goodbye.

CHAPTER TWENTY

*"No!" cried Rowan, horrified. "Why should you
want Ash's eyes?"
The Fairy King spread his hands. "Color is rare and
much sought after here. Why wouldn't I want such
pretty purple eyes?"
Rowan turned to Ash. "You mustn't."
Ash ignored her, speaking to his brother. "You'll free
her if I do this? You give your word?"
The Fairy King inclined his head....
—From* The Grey Court Changeling

A week later Messalina watched from her carriage window
as Lovejoy House receded into the distance. She'd said a
rather tearful goodbye to Jane and a much improved Eleanor,
and her eyes felt irritated as a result. Freya and she had
parted two days before when Freya had headed to
Scotland—much to the dismay of the Holland ladies. Freya
had promised to write Messalina, though, and had given an
address in some benighted place in Scotland.

Messalina was already composing letters to her in her
head.

"I really don't think I'll ever attend another house party
in my life," Lucretia said thoughtfully from the seat across
from her where she sat with their shared lady's maid,

Bartlett. The maid's head was nodding so both women were trying to speak in lowered tones.

Messalina shrugged. "I've been to worse."

Lucretia looked at her with interest. "*Have* you? I'd like to hear about those if they're more horrible than wife imprisoning and the death of a neighbor."

Messalina winced. "Well, not *worse*, but most definitely almost as bad."

Lucretia's expression was dubious.

"Quite uncomfortable?" Messalina tried, and then gave up and waved her hand. "Never mind. You're right. This was horrendous. At least, though, Eleanor is all right. She was already looking better when I went to say goodbye to her this morning."

"That is good," Lucretia returned soberly. "How horrible it must have been to be married to such a monster. And I'm sure she had no idea when she married him."

"I don't think so, no," Messalina said. "I'm rather glad on the whole that he's dead."

"I think *everyone* is glad he's dead," Lucretia said with bloodthirsty enthusiasm. "I only wish he'd died before he'd imprisoned Eleanor."

"Yes." Messalina shook her head. "But it's over. Let's not talk about such tragic things. What will you do when we return to London?"

"Well," Lucretia began. "I have the most urgent desire for a new gown, and the address of the dressmaker for—"

Their carriage suddenly jolted to a stop.

Bartlett started awake with an "Oh!"

Messalina just had time to glance in alarm at her sister when the door was opened.

Gideon Hawthorne was again in black. His curling, black hair was pulled severely back, emphasizing his high cheekbones and devilishly slanted eyebrows.

"What do you want?" Messalina snapped, and immediately regretted it. He'd know that her loss of control signaled fright.

He bowed gracefully. "Your uncle requests your presence, Miss Greycourt."

"You can't have her," Lucretia said, young and brave.

He still stared at Messalina, and a corner of his mouth quirked as he said softly, "Can't I?"

They all knew he could.

Her heart was beating too hard. She was terrified, but she'd be damned before she let him know.

She caught her breath and said steadily, almost dismissively, "Very well."

Her sister began to protest, but Messalina sent her a warning glance. "Darling, you'll have to continue without me. Be sure to give Quintus and Julian my love."

"Of course." Lucretia gave a subtle nod.

Good. She'd understood the message.

Bartlett, who was a sturdy woman of forty years or so, spoke up for the first time. "I'd better come with you, Miss."

Messalina nodded to her in gratitude. She'd much rather the buffer of the maid than traveling with Mr. Hawthorne alone.

She rose and made herself place her fingers in the terrible man's outstretched hand as she stepped from the carriage. "Lead on, Mr. Hawthorne."

* * *

Two weeks later Freya stood on a hill, the breeze pressing a lock of her hair against her cheek, and traced the ancient carving on a battered standing stone. The carving looked

like a stylized downward-facing crescent moon with an ar-
row broken at a right angle and piercing both points of the
moon. The stone marker had been here on this hill several miles outside Dornoch, Scotland, since the beginning
of time.

Or at least since the beginning of the Wise Women.

"Freya!"

She glanced up to see her sister Caitriona making her way
up the hill, her dark blue skirts whipping in the wind.

"Are you coming to luncheon?" Caitriona called as she
neared. "Elspeth has made something quite awful with a leg
of mutton, I think."

Freya winced. "That doesn't exactly make me eager to
come."

Caitriona stopped beside her, heaving a breath. She was
the tallest of the de Moray sisters, angular and strong like
Aunt Hilda had been. Her red hair was bound up loosely in
a haphazard knot on the top of her head. "No, but we ought
to at least taste it. She's worked all the morning at it."

Freya looked at her out of the corner of her eye. "It won't
be like the fish stew last week, will it?"

"Well, I hardly think we'll choke on the mutton bone,"
Caitriona replied practically. Somehow Elspeth had forgotten to debone the fish before making her stew. "You can see
forever up here, can't you?"

"Yes," Freya said softly. "Forever and a day."

In front of them, in the distance, was the sea with the
road to Dornoch a winding thread between. To their left was
where the Wise Women lived, in a walled medieval abbey.
From here they could see the many outbuildings, the garden, and the orchard. And behind them were ancient rolling
mountains.

This was what she'd missed in England—the Scottish

hills, her sisters, the sweet wind, and the familiar community of Wise Women. But now that she was here she found herself longing for Christopher.

Quite desperately.

As if sensing her thoughts Caitriona leaned against her. "It's been lovely having you back."

Freya sent her a quick smile. "It's been lovely to *be* back."

"But," Caitriona murmured, "I have the feeling you won't be staying with us."

Freya hadn't lasted two days before telling her sisters about Harlowe one night after rather too much wine. She shook her head. "I should stay. This is home."

"Is it?" Caitriona pushed back a trailing lock of hair. "But Christopher isn't here. And you don't have particular work to keep you here—maintaining the library like Elspeth or gardening like me."

"I could *find* work," Freya muttered. "I could make a life here. I'm a Wise Woman."

"Well of course you *could*," Caitriona replied, sounding amused. "Once a Wise Woman always a Wise Woman. Married or unmarried, with a man or not, you will always have the Wise Women. No man or man-made marriage can take that from you. But, Freya, you *love* Christopher. Go to him."

"Love isn't the problem," Freya said. She was so weary of this fight within herself. She just wanted to lay down her sword and go to *Harlowe*. "It's *marriage*."

Caitriona heaved a sigh. "I don't know why you doubt yourself. Do you truly think that you'd love a man who would abuse your faith in him?"

Freya turned to look at her sister in astonishment. "It's not as simple as that!"

"Isn't it?" Caitriona looked curious. "Why not? If you

love him and want him and he loves you back, why not simply take him? Don't be such a coward. Marry the man." She shook her head and turned to start down the hill. "In any case Elspeth's mutton leg won't be any better cold. Come have luncheon."

Freya stared after her sister, indignant. *Coward?* She was no coward.

Suddenly she felt lighter, as if her heart were flying.

Like a merlin seeking her mate.

* * *

"Will there be anything else, Your Grace?"

Christopher absently shook his head at Gardiner as he threw the afternoon post aside. There wasn't anything interesting there.

There never was.

He'd arrived back at Renshaw House, the seat of the Dukes of Harlowe, nearly a month ago. Every day he rose, dressed, and ate breakfast as one of his land stewards apprised him about his holdings. After that he might meet with his lawyers—the dukedom really had been in a wretched state when he'd inherited. In the afternoon he wrote letters with his secretaries—he had two—in his study. Sometimes he took callers. Tenant farmers with complaints, the vicar of the local church asking for funds to reroof the church, or the mayor wanting him to sponsor the grammar school.

There was always something.

It was only in the late afternoon, in the hour or so before supper, that he took time to himself. Let himself think.

Gardiner cleared his throat as if about to say something else, and Christopher glanced at him.

Somehow he'd forgotten the valet was still here. "Nothing, Gardiner. You may go."

Gardiner looked indecisive, but then he bowed and left the bedroom.

Christopher snapped his fingers at Tess, lying before the fireplace. "Come on, then."

She rose eagerly, tail wagging.

At least Tess enjoyed their evening walks.

He descended the grand staircase—marble imported from Italy—and walked to the front door.

His butler bowed, and two footmen opened the door. Obviously it would have been too much for *one* footman.

Christopher nodded to the men and mentally chided himself. Renshaw House provided needed work for over one hundred people. That was one of the responsibilities of being a duke.

One of the *many* responsibilities.

He started down the drive. The day was beautiful, the sun still summer bright despite the time of day. The grounds had been meticulously landscaped, surrounding Renshaw House with a parklike setting.

It was a lovely estate.

And he'd be happy here, even with the work and responsibilities, if only Freya...

But best not to think of that.

He was a rich man—a very, *very* rich man—and that should be enough.

It wasn't.

He stopped in the middle of the drive and threw his head back. How was it possible to continue breathing with such pain? Perhaps he should go to her. It had been a *month* with no word. He could try one more time to convince her...

No.

He blew out his breath, closing his eyes. *No*. She knew full well what he felt for her, and if that was not enough—

Tess set up a cacophony of barking.

Christopher opened his eyes to see what the problem was.

A figure was at the end of his drive, walking toward him.

Tess galloped toward her—she was wearing a dress, so definitely a *her*.

Christopher began walking.

Tess reached the woman, ran in a circle around her, barking all the while, and turned to race back to Christopher.

It couldn't be.

Tess made her next lap back to the woman. The sun had turned her into a black silhouette, but the set of her shoulders, the tilt of her head...

Christopher walked faster.

She wore a dress the color of flames and a wide-brimmed hat instead of the cap, but it was Freya. She dropped a soft bag and bent to fondle the damned dog, who was nearly dancing at her feet, and Christopher broke into a run.

She looked up and straightened, her expression uncertain, but then she smiled.

Freya, his Freya.

He caught her about the waist and swung her up and around, ignoring her shriek of surprise.

Then his mouth was on hers and it was right.

So right.

He held her in his arms and something settled in his chest. The bewildered feel of loss and loneliness evaporated.

She was here and all the world was right again.

"Christopher," she gasped, trying to pull away.

He didn't want her to. He wasn't sure he wanted to hear why she'd come.

And if she said she was leaving again, he didn't think he could bear it. He might break and fall to his knees to beg.

But he couldn't hold her and kiss her forever.

"Why are you here?" he asked. "How did you come?"

"I took the stagecoach from Edinburgh," she said. "And then I walked from your little town."

"*Walked?*" His brows snapped together. "Whyever didn't you send word? I would've sent a carriage—or come myself."

"It wasn't far, truly," she said.

"But you shouldn't have to walk it. You're my guest and I—"

"I have something for you," she blurted, interrupting him. She reached up and drew off the thin silver chain around her neck. He expected to see Ran's ancient signet ring, battered and worn, but a different ring hung from the chain now. A gold ring.

She slid the ring off the chain and held it out to him.

He took it and examined the ring. Engraved on it were a lion and a lioness, necks twined together. Christopher shook his head, glancing up. "I don't—"

She laid her fingertip against his lips, silencing his protest.

"I love you and I do trust you," she said quietly. "I think I have for some time, I just didn't realize it. There has been so much between us—between our families—that I had difficulty seeing through the conflict and hurt and history to what you are to me now." She took a breath. "To what I am to you."

"Freya," he whispered.

"I'm not done. I have something to ask you," she said, her voice a little wobbly. "I'd like... That is... Will you... No, that isn't right." She took a deep breath and looked into his eyes. "Christopher Renshaw, Duke of Harlowe, will you marry me?"

He laughed, throwing back his head. Then he picked her up and swung her around again. The dog barked. A flock of birds startled from a nearby tree.

And she shrieked once again.

But when he set her down she was grinning, so beautiful, so *alive*.

"Yes," he said. "Yes, I will marry you, Lady Freya de Moray, because I love you. Because my life is empty without you. And because when you're not by my side my world is unbearably boring."

"Oh," she said, her eyes flooding with tears. "Oh, I *do* love you, Christopher. I know I'm not the most pleasant woman at times, but I'll try to—"

He stopped her words with a kiss and then whispered against her lips, "Don't change. Don't *ever* change. I like your prickliness, your scowls, the way you argue with me so fiercely. I want a *lioness*, not a lamb."

"Oh." Her cheeks were pink. "Oh, that might be the nicest thing that anyone has ever said to me."

His mouth twisted. "Then I shall endeavor to tell such nice things every day, though I warn you: I'm not the most eloquent of men."

She shook her head, her lips twitching. "Do you really think I need pretty flattery? I don't. I need only you, just the way you are—overbearing and quick-witted and entirely besotted with your dog. Don't change, Kester. I love you as you are."

He couldn't help but kiss her, then, long and slow, and when he eventually raised his head he was pleased to see that she looked a bit dazed. "Are you going to be my wife, then, Freya de Moray, and scowl at me every morning over breakfast?"

"I shall certainly try," she replied primly, though when she bit her lip it rather gave away her grave face. "Come, give me your hand."

She took the ring and placed it on his third finger, where it fit perfectly.

He gazed at it thoughtfully. "I think we will have to have a matching ring made for you, don't you think, my love?"

"Yes," she said simply, and laid her palm in his.

And they walked back to Renshaw House, Tess beside them.

ℰPILOGUE

*The Fairy King stretched long fingers toward his
brother's face.
But Rowan grabbed his hand, flinching at the icy
cold of the Fairy King's flesh. "Take my hair
instead."
The king hesitated.
Ash blinked. "Are you sure, Princess?"
Rowan glared at him. "Do you wish to be blind?"
A small smile tilted the corner of Ash's mouth. "No, I
confess I do not."
"Well, then." Rowan took a deep breath and glared at
the Fairy King. "Will you take my flame-red hair
instead?"
The Fairy King shrugged. "Done." He reached for
Rowan's hair.
But this time it was Ash who stopped him. "A minute,
dear brother."
The Fairy King looked at him with something like
exasperation in his silver eyes. "What?"
Ash stood. "You will let Marigold go?"
"Yes."
"You will let the Princess Rowan go?"
"Yes."
"And you will let me go." Ash smiled ironically. "In*

return for Rowan's hair, you will let us go with no reservation, caveat, or trickery?"

"Yes," hissed the Fairy King, his silver eyes narrowed. "This I do swear."

Ash bowed. "Then so be it."

A wind blew through the clearing, pulling and snatching at Rowan's hair. She screwed tight her eyes.

When she opened them again the world was filled with color and she, Ash, and Marigold stood in the castle gardens.

And her head was completely bare.

Before Rowan could hide her baldness, Marigold hugged her.

"Thank you!" cried Marigold. "Oh, thank you, Princess Rowan, for rescuing me from the Grey Lands."

"Well," Rowan said, oddly touched. "It was nothing for a friend."

Marigold stepped back and looked at her in wonder. "Am I your friend?"

"Of course," Rowan said. "You are my dear friend, now and always."

"Now and always," Marigold whispered, and smiled like the sun rising for a new day. "I must see my mother and father now. If you will excuse me?"

Rowan nodded, trying not to feel self-conscious about her bald head.

Marigold walked toward the castle, and Rowan turned to see Ash watching her with a smile.

Her hands flew to her head. "Don't look at me."

But he came to her and took her hands and drew

them away from her crown. "Why not? I have eyes to
see, thanks to you."

"But…" *Rowan stared at him in wonder.* "But I'm
ugly now."

"No." *He shook his head.* "Your hair is gone, but
you're just as beautiful as you've always been."

*And Rowan might've argued the point, but Ash
covered her mouth with his and kissed her.*

When he raised his head again he said, "Will you let
me wed you, Princess? For I find that I may have kept
my eyes, but I've lost my heart to you."

"Yes," *Rowan whispered.* "Oh yes."

So they did and lived quite happily…

Ever after.

—From *The Grey Court Changeling*

Don't miss Elizabeth Hoyt's next book in
the Greycourt Series!

Turn the page for an excerpt from
When a Rogue Meets His Match

There is never a *good* time to be accosted by highwaymen. However, to be accosted whilst emptying one's bladder is a particularly *bad* time.

Messalina Greycourt froze, the last drops of her urine tinkling into the pretty china bourdaloue she held between her legs. She stood awkwardly in the carriage, both her maid, Bartlett, and her uncle's wicked factotum, Mr. Hawthorne, having stepped out to give her privacy not two minutes before.

Outside the carriage it was ominously quiet, as if the shouted order "Stand and deliver!" had stilled everyone there as well.

She swallowed as she strained to hear any sound.

Boom! The gunshot broke the silence.

Messalina let her skirts fall.

The carriage door flew open and Bartlett was pushed inside. For a second Messalina saw Mr. Hawthorne's savage face, his evil black eyes glittering as he ordered, "*Stay.*"

Then the door slammed shut on the sounds of shouts, gunfire, and whinnying horses.

Bartlett, normally a sturdy, practical woman, looked at Messalina with wide eyes.

The carriage rocked as if something large had been thrown against it.

"How many highwaymen are there?" Messalina demanded, swaying, but not spilling a drop from the bourdaloue.

"I don't know, Miss," Bartlett replied shakily. "At least half a dozen I think." Her gaze dropped to the bourdaloue and she added more prosaically, "Oh, let me take that."

The bourdaloue looked like nothing so much as a gravy boat. Oblong and with a handle at one end, it was a delicate pink, edged in gilt around the lip. Usually of course Messalina would hand the bourdaloue out of the carriage to Bartlett, who would dispose of the contents. Now her poor lady's maid was left standing, holding a china vessel full of piss inside a rocking carriage. This was all Mr. Hawthorne's fault. If the man had simply let her stop *prior* to nightfall as she had suggested, she—

The door was wrenched open again and a large, filthy man filled the frame, his fleshy lips pulled back in a leer.

Bartlett shrieked.

Messalina snatched the bourdaloue from her hand and flung it in the man's face. The china dish bounced off his forehead, dowsing him in urine, and Messalina shoved him hard.

He tumbled backward out of the carriage.

She slammed the door closed after him and looked at Bartlett.

The other woman's face was white. "That was…erm… quick thinking, Miss."

Messalina straightened, trying and failing to control the heat rising in her cheeks. "Yes, well, needs must."

Outside someone screamed and was suddenly cut off.

Messalina found herself holding her breath.

The carriage door opened and Gideon Hawthorne climbed in, looking as if he'd just stepped out for a midnight stroll. His curly black hair was pulled back into an immaculate tail, his severely black suit was without stain, and his expression composed.

"Are they gone?" Messalina demanded.

"Quite," he replied dismissively, flicking a thin knife closed and hiding it on his person. Had she seen *blood* on his blade? "Hardly any trouble at all."

There were only two servants in the carriage box. Even if Bartlett had overestimated the highwaymen, Mr. Hawthorne and his men had been badly outnumbered.

Messalina stared at the maddening man. "What..." she began and then noticed Mr. Hawthorne's proffered arm.

He held her bourdaloue.

"I think," he said, examining the vessel with unseemly interest, "that this belongs to you, Miss Greycourt."

Her mouth dropped open.

Bartlett snatched the bourdaloue from Mr. Hawthorne's hand. "*I never...*" she muttered as she hid the thing away.

Mr. Hawthorne's wide mouth twitched. He gestured gracefully to the carriage seat. "Shall we...?"

"Yes, of course," Messalina gritted out and sank to the seat.

Mr. Hawthorne knocked on the roof of the carriage, and in minutes they were on their way again.

Messalina should be grateful to be moving—as the recent events had shown, stopping on the road to London late at night was an invitation to robbery—but she was rather dreading their destination.

Nearly a week ago Mr. Hawthorne had waylaid her

own carriage in the north of England and informed her that her uncle, Augustus Greycourt, the Duke of Winde-mere, required her presence immediately. So immediately in fact that he'd sent Mr. Hawthorne to personally fetch her.

Which was how Messalina had come to spend the past week traveling with the odious Mr. Hawthorne.

Messalina examined the man from beneath her eye-lashes.

Gideon Hawthorne was slouched in his seat, somehow gracefully, apparently asleep now that the danger was over. His booted feet were crossed at the ankles and his tricorn hat was pulled down over his eyes. The carriage lantern threw glowing light on a sculpted chin and the hint of breath-takingly high cheekbones. His mouth was curled at the corners as if he was privately amused at some lewd joke. The upper lip was thin and strictly constrained to a classical Cupid's bow, but the lower lip belied the upper's repression by its obscene plushness.

He had the most depraved mouth Messalina had ever seen on a man.

Mr. Hawthorne looked like nothing so much as a rather desolate barrister.

Looks, in this case, were quite deceiving, for she knew—as did everyone else—that Mr. Hawthorne had emerged from the worst stews in London. There were rumors, in fact, that her uncle had found him earning his living by competitive knife-fighting when Mr. Hawthorne had been but sixteen. *That* gossip seemed a bit too lurid for fact, but there *was* a thin white scar bisecting his left cheek like the trail of a teardrop, so who knew?

Not that any of this mattered. Messalina had known Mr. Hawthorne for nearly fourteen years, ever since he'd come into her uncle's employment when she'd been fourteen. And she'd been aware, right from the start, that Gideon Hawthorne was *dangerous*.

Messalina shivered and looked away from her guard dog. Instead of daydreaming about Mr. Hawthorne she ought to be considering Uncle Augustus's reason for summoning her. Of course Mr. Hawthorne had refused to give her any hint of the reason, so she'd spent the past week becoming more and more anxious.

Not that she let it show.

If Uncle Augustus had decided to exile her to the Americas or present her with a new riding mare, or cut her living expenses entirely, she would meet his news as phlegmatically as possible.

The Duke of Windemere fed on fear and distress.

"Ah, now we're in London proper, Miss," Bartlett whispered and nodded toward the bright lights outside the carriage window.

Messalina glanced at Mr. Hawthorne, but he was either asleep or pretending asleep.

She turned back to the window and waited, watching as they neared her uncle's palatial town house.

Fifteen minutes later the carriage drew up outside Windemere House, the London residence of the Dukes of Windemere.

Mr. Hawthorne stirred immediately, sitting upright and looking as alert as if it had been morning, damn him.

The carriage door opened and a footman handed Messalina down. She looked up from shaking out her skirts and nearly started.

Uncle Augustus was waiting at the top of the stairs, looking like a dusty vulture in a periwig.

"Ah, sweet Messalina," he croaked, a smile afflicting his

face, "I'm so glad you could come to see your old uncle the night before your wedding."

Messalina felt a ghastly chill run down her spine. *What wedding?*

But Uncle Augustus continued, an unholy gleam in his eye. "And so gallant of your fiancé to make the trip to the north to escort you himself."

Fiancé.

Slowly Messalina turned her head.

And met Mr. Hawthorne's diabolically gleaming black eyes.

Elizabeth Hoyt is the *New York Times* bestselling author of more than twenty-three lush historical romances, including the Maiden Lane series. *Publishers Weekly* has called her writing "mesmerizing," and in 2018 she received the *RT Book Reviews* Career Achievement Award for Historical Romance. She also pens deliciously fun contemporary romances under the name Julia Harper. Elizabeth lives in Minneapolis, Minnesota, with three untrained dogs, a garden in constant need of weeding, and the long-suffering Mr. Hoyt.

The winters in Minnesota have been known to be long and cold and Elizabeth is always thrilled to receive reader mail. You can write to her at PO Box 19495, Minneapolis, MN 55419 or email her at Elizabeth@ElizabethHoyt.com.

You can learn more at:
ElizabethHoyt.com
Twitter @elizabethhoyt
Facebook.com/ElizabethHoytBooks

Advice columnist Patience Friendly's relationship with her stubborn, overbearing publisher, Dougal MacHugh, is anything but cordial. Dougal challenges Patience to take on a rival columnist in a holiday advice-a-thon, and sparks fly clear up to the mistletoe hanging from every rafter. Will Patience follow the practical guidance of her head, or the passionate advice of her heart?

For a bonus story from another author you may love, please turn the page to read *Patience for Christmas* by Grace Burrowes.

PATIENCE FOR CHRISTMAS

To those who must work when the rest of the world frolics.

CHAPTER ONE

"Professor Pennypacker is wise, kind, cheerful, and witty. Why shouldn't I loathe him?" Patience Friendly's honest question met with smirks from her dearest friends in all the world, though she'd spoken the plain, seasonally inappropriate truth.

"You don't loathe the professor," Elizabeth Windham said. "You have a genteel difference of opinion with him from time to time, such as educated people occasionally do. More tea?"

Patience paid regular visits to the four Windham sisters because they were excellent company, though their lavish tea tray figured prominently in her affections as well.

"Half a cup, and then I must be going."

Elizabeth obliged, her idea of a half portion coming nearly to the cup's brim.

"It's the first Monday of the month. Does Dreadful Dougal

demand your time, again?" Charlotte Windham asked around a mouthful of stollen.

"Mr. MacHugh is my publisher. I ought not call him that." In her thoughts, Patience called him much worse. "He might be lacking in polish, but Dougal P. MacHugh ensures my little scribblings find their way into many hands."

Dougal referred to Patience's advice columns as little scribblings, but the coin her writing earned was not so little to a spinster without means.

"Your advice to that boy who bashed his sister's dolly was lovely," Megan Windham said. Unlike her sisters, she wasn't embroidering (Elizabeth), knitting (Anwen), or devouring tea cakes (Charlotte). Megan had a quiet about her that soothed, though Patience suspected that quiet hid a lively imagination.

All four sisters shared Patience's red hair, but they were from a ducal family. If they'd gone swimming in the Serpentine, that would have become the latest rage. Their red hair made them striking, while Patience's earned her frequent admonitions from her publisher to control her temper.

"I'll take you up with me in the carriage," Anwen said. "I'm to read to the boys this afternoon, and one wants to be punctual when setting an example for children."

"You're passionate about that orphanage," Patience said. "I wish Dread—Mr. MacHugh permitted me to write about the plight of poor children in winter, instead of limiting me to an advice column."

Nothing in all of creation compared to the pleasure of a good, strong cup of black tea on a cold December day, unless it was the same cup of tea shared with friends. Without the company of these four young women, Patience would likely have been reduced to rash acts.

Marriage to the curate, for example.

As Anwen put away her knitting and Charlotte wrapped up the stollen—most of the loaf for the orphans, but two slices for Patience—snow flurries danced outside the parlor window. A brisk breeze pushed them in all directions, and the gray sky threatened a proper snowfall.

Mr. MacHugh would call it a braw, bonnie day, but he was Scottish, and his view of life paid little heed to tea cakes, cozy parlors, or mornings spent with friends. He was all business all the time, the opposite of the company Patience treasured most dearly.

"You'll come by the Wednesday before Christmas to see how we're progressing with our holiday baking, won't you?" Elizabeth asked as Patience accepted a cloak and scarf from the Windham butler. "We still use your mama's recipe for lemon cake."

A woman who lived alone didn't bother with the expense of holiday baking. "I'll see you on baking day, just as I do every year, and I'll try to get Mr. MacHugh to publish a piece on Anwen's urchins. If people won't contribute to charity at Yuletide, then we've become a hopeless species indeed."

The prospect of persuading Mr. MacHugh to do an article on Anwen's favorite orphanage was daunting, and as Patience bundled into the Windham coach, a predictable melancholy settled over her, as heavy and familiar as the woolen lap robes.

How many more years would pass in this same pattern? Writing at all hours, battling with Dougal MacHugh over the content of the columns, envying friends their holiday luxuries, and hoping the winter was mild?

The problem wasn't entirely poverty. Many families with little means found joy in one another's company and celebrated the holidays cheerfully.

The problem was Patience's life, and no advice columnist in the realm—not even her kindly, wise, dratted competitor, Professor Pennypacker—could tell her how to repair an existence that felt as bleak and barren as the winter sky.

* * *

"I have never met a female more inappropriately named than Patience Friendly," Dougal MacHugh muttered. "If I ask her to meet me on the hour, she's fifteen minutes early, and if our meeting requires an hour of her time, she's pacing my office thirty minutes on. Send her in."

"Shall I put the kettle on, Dougal?"

Harry MacHugh was a good lad, but he was a cousin—most of Dougal's employees were cousins of some sort—and thus he presumed from time to time where prudent men would not.

"She'll not take tea with me, Harry. Ours is a business relationship." A lucrative one too. But for that signal fact, Miss Friendly would doubtless have ejected Dougal from her life as briskly as she dispatched her readers' problems.

"Even business associates can share a cup in honor of the season," Harry said. "I'll just—"

"You'll just show the lady in, and then dash off a note to your mum and da. It's Monday."

"Aye, Dougal."

Oh, the martyrdom a fifteen-year-old could put into two words and a heavy sigh. Over the past year, as Harry had shot up several inches in height, his penmanship had improved, as had his vocabulary and grammar. Dougal had the boy review the ledgers too, and purposely made the occasional error to test Harry's skill with figures.

Harry clomped out of Dougal's office as the clock on

the mantel struck a quarter till the hour. Miss Patience Un-Friendly whisked through the open door a moment later.

Once a month, Dougal endured the disruption of her presence in his office. Discontent accompanied her everywhere, a discontent she channeled into repairing the lives of readers without the sense to solve their own problems—bless their troubled hearts. Even the rhythm of her footfalls—rapid, percussive, confident—spoke of a woman determined on her own ends.

And the damned female had the audacity to be lovely. She wasn't simply pretty—pretty was for daffodils and landscapes—she was...all wrong.

A woman dispensing advice as the practical, blunt Mrs. Horner ought not to have a full mouth made for kisses and smiles. She ought not to have features that bore the serene grace of a Christmas angel, and she had no business having a figure that put Dougal in mind of cozy Highland winters and a wee dram shared before bed.

He'd hoisted an occasional wee dram to Miss Friendly's beauty, and many more to her blazing intelligence and nimble pen.

"Miss Friendly, good day. Perhaps your watch is running a bit fast."

"Mr. MacHugh, greetings." She pulled off her gloves and tossed them onto the mantel. "Sooner begun is sooner done. Shall we get to work?"

She usually remarked on how much Harry was growing, and how fat the office cat—King George—had become.

"Are you in a hurry, madam? We can reschedule this meeting if you'd like, but I've a special project to discuss with you."

"No time like the present, Mr. MacHugh. Let's be about

it." She took her customary seat at Dougal's worktable, a
battered, scarred article that had been in the MacHugh
family since Robert the Bruce had been in nappies.

"Shall I build up the fire, Miss Friendly?"

"Why would you do that? Coal is dear, Mr. MacHugh, as
you well know."

From her twitchy movements and the bleak quality in
her gaze, Dougal knew something was bothering her—more
than the usual weight of the world she carried on behalf of
her readers. The daft woman took her job seriously, considering her replies to each letter as if the fate of entire
neighborhoods might rest on whether she could solve the
reader's dilemma.

Dougal added half a scoop of coal to the fire in the hearth.
"You're still wearing your cloak. I thought you might be
cold."

She shot to her feet and plucked at the buttons marching
down the front of her cape. "You're absolutely right. How
silly of me. My mind is on this month's stack of letters,
and—"

Miss Friendly fell silent, her expression disgruntled as
she fussed with the fastenings at her throat. In the clerk's office, she would have had a mirror to aid her, but Dougal had
no need to examine his own features.

"Allow me," he said, brushing her hands aside. She'd
knotted the strings more tightly rather than loosening
the bow, and Dougal took a small eternity to get her
free. In those moments, Miss Friendly stared over his
shoulder as if he were a physician taking medically necessary liberties, while Dougal tormented himself with stolen
impressions.

She smelled of damp wool, for the day had turned
snowy, but also of lemons and spice. Clove, cinnamon, he

wasn't sure what all went into her fragrance, but it put him in mind of Christmas cakes, cloved oranges, and blazing Yule logs.

The backs of his fingers brushed against her skin, which was surprisingly warm, given the inclement weather. Also soft. For a moment, her pulse beat against his knuckles, and then the strings came free.

"There ye go." His burr showed up at the worst moments, when he was angry or tense.

Or drunk.

"My thanks." Miss Friendly stepped away to draw the cloak from her own shoulders. She hung it over a hook on the back of the door and started fishing in the pockets.

Her hems were damp, and her boots were likely soaked. Dougal discreetly moved her chair closer to the fire and waited for the lady to take her seat.

"Are you looking for something?" he asked when she'd searched both pockets thoroughly.

"I've misplaced my glasses, or forgotten them. Without them—"

"Use mine," he said, plucking the spectacles from his nose. "You'll be able to see halfway to the Highlands with them."

Her gaze went from the eyeglasses in his hand—plain gold wire and a bit of curved glass—to his face, back to the glasses.

"I couldn't take your spectacles, Mr. MacHugh."

Because he'd worn them on his person? "We'll get nothing done if you can't see the letters to read them. I have a spare pair."

He retrieved the second pair from his desk and donned them, though the earpieces were a trifle snug and the magnification wasn't as great.

"So you do. Well." Miss Friendly was practical, if nothing else. She put the glasses on and took her seat. "Let's get to it. The holidays bring all manner of problems, and I'm sure I can offer some useful advice in at least a few instances."

"You'll have to do better than that," Dougal said, settling into the chair across from her.

Always across from her, for two reasons. First, so he could torment himself with the sight of her, sorting and considering, losing herself in her work; and second, so no accidental brush of hands, arms, or shoulders occurred.

"I do not care for your tone, Mr. MacHugh," she said, taking off the spectacles and polishing them on her sleeve. "I always do my best for my readers. If you imply something to the contrary, we shall have words."

"I'm a-tremble with dread, Miss Friendly," he said, passing her a wrinkled handkerchief. He loved having words with her. She hurled arguments like thunderbolts, didn't give an inch, and was very often right—and proud of it.

"What is this?" she asked, peering at the embroidery in the corner. "Is this a unicorn?"

"Wreathed in thistles. My cousins Edana and Rhona MacHugh do them for me. Winters are long in Perthshire, and Edana and Rhona like to stay busy."

Eddie and Ronnie had a small business, about which their brothers probably knew nothing. They and the ladies of their Perthshire neighborhood embroidered various Scottish themes on handkerchiefs, gloves, bonnet ribbons and so forth, and shipped them to Dougal. He distributed the merchandise to London shops and fetched much higher prices for the goods than the women could have earned in Scotland.

"It's quite pretty," Miss Friendly said, passing the handkerchief back. "More of a lady's article than a gentleman's though, don't you think?"

"Perhaps, but it reminds me of home and family, and fashion is hardly foremost in my mind."

"One could surmise as much." She gave him a perusal that said his plain attire was not among the problems she was motivated to solve, then picked up the first letter in the stack.

This was Dougal's favorite part of the meeting, when he could simply watch Patience at work. She read each letter, word for word, considered each person's problems and woes as if they were her own, then listed and discarded various possible solutions to the challenge at hand. By the time she left, she'd have a month's worth of worries put at ease, a month's worth of difficulties made manageable for some poor souls she'd never meet.

"We'll have to work quickly today," Dougal said before she'd reached the end of the first letter.

"Because of the weather?"

The snow was coming down in earnest now, though it could easily let up in the next five minutes.

"Because I've got wind of a scheme Pennypacker's publisher has devised to take advantage of the holidays. You said it yourself: The holidays bring problems, and old Pennypacker isn't about to leave his readers without solutions."

"It's unchristian of me, but I dislike that man."

"No, you do not." Dougal hoped she did not or the poor professor was doomed to a very bad end.

"The professor takes issue with my advice at least once a month, and directs people into the most inane situations. Why he's become so popular is beyond me, though I'll grant you, the man can write."

Ever fair, that was Miss Friendly. "He can make you a good deal of coin too." Dougal rose to retrieve a ledger from the blotter on his desk. "These are your circulation figures from last November and from this November."

She studied the numbers, which Dougal had checked three times. "We're doing better. We're doing appreciably better."

That news ought to have earned Dougal a smile at least, but the lady looked puzzled. "I'm not doing anything differently," she said. "Mrs. Horner's Corner dispenses kindly, commonsense advice and responds to reader pleas for assistance with domestic problems. What's changed?"

Exactly the question a shrewd woman should ask. Dougal passed her another sheaf of figures.

"Take a look at August and then September. The numbers begin to climb, and the trend continues into October and then last month. The increase isn't great between any two months, but the direction is encouraging."

The rims of Dougal's spectacles glinted in the firelight as Miss Friendly ran a slender, ink-stained finger down a column of figures. The picture she made was intelligent, studious, and damnably adorable.

"That man, that dreadful awful man," she murmured, setting the papers aside. "Pennypacker began writing his column in August. You think the readers are comparing my advice to his?"

"I'm nearly certain of it," Dougal said. "All too often, Pennypacker deals with at least one situation that's remarkably similar to the situations you address, and his advice is often contrary to yours. In the next column, you'll elaborate on your previous suggestions, annihilate his maunderings, and further explicate your own wisdom. He returns similar fire, and in a few weeks, we have a bare-knuckle match over the proper method for quieting a querulous child at Sunday services."

"Gracious, I'm a pugilist in the arena of domestic common sense."

Now she smiled. Now she beamed at the flames dancing in the hearth as if Dougal had handed her the Freedom of the City and a pair of fur-lined boots.

"Pugilists have to defend their titles, Miss Friendly, and if we let this opportunity slip by us, the crown will go to Pennypacker."

She glowered over the spectacles. "He's a posing, prosy, pontificating *man*, Mr. MacHugh. Why on earth his opinions of household management should signify, I do not know. The professor has likely never rocked a baby to sleep or kneaded a loaf of bread, if he's even a professor."

Had the prim Miss Friendly ever tended a baby? Did she long for an infant of her own, or even a family complete with adoring husband? Self-preservation suggested Dougal ask that question at another time.

"You might think gender alone disqualifies Pennypacker from having anything useful to say," Dougal replied, removing his spare glasses before they gave him a headache. "But his publisher intends to let him natter on for twelve consecutive days as we lead up to Christmas. Yuletide special editions they're calling them, the publisher's holiday gift to the masses, though the gift won't be free."

Miss Friendly drew off the spectacles and covered her face with her hands. The gesture was weary, but when she dropped her hands, sat back, and squared her shoulders, the light of battle shone in her blue eyes.

"Twelve consecutive days? That means answering dozens of letters."

"Sundays off, I'm assuming, but yes. At least three dozen

letters answered in less than two weeks. I know it's a challenge when your friends will be expecting you to socialize and exchange calls."

Her shoulders slumped. "They will. It's baking season. Drat."

When Dougal had opened his publishing house three years ago, he'd faced enormous odds. London had a thriving, highly competitive publishing industry with each house specializing in certain products—herbals, sermons, animal husbandry, memoirs, and so forth. A readership took time to develop, and Dougal's inheritance was all he'd had to sink into his business.

He'd teetered on the brink of ruin until Patience Friendly had shown up in his office, full of ideas, pen at the ready.

Mrs. Horner's Corner had rescued an entire publishing house—women were avid readers, it turned out—and when Dougal had moved her column to the top of the front page, the entire business had found solid footing. He was on his way to becoming the domestic advice publisher, and Patience Friendly was his flagship author.

Dougal could not afford—literally—to either coddle her or earn her disfavor. "I know the timing is poor," he said. "I'm sure you don't want to spend your holidays ignoring friends and family—but this is an opportunity. If we don't step into the ring with the professor now, we'll lose ground when we could take ownership of it. You have the better advice, and the ladies who buy my paper know it."

"My readers are very astute," she said, worrying a nail. Her readers, not the customers, not *the* readers. *Hers*, just as Dougal had referred to the paper as *his*. "And yet, they depend on me. Do you know, my laundress discusses my column with my housekeeper, and they both say that at the baker's, the ladies talk of little else."

Yes, Dougal knew, because he frequented taverns, coffee shops, booksellers, churchyards, street corners, all in an effort to aim his business where the public's interest was most likely to travel.

Dougal kept his peace. Twelve special broadsheet editions in fourteen days was an enormous undertaking, but he was determined that his business thrive, and that Miss Patience Friendly thrive too.

He owed this woman.

And he always paid his debts.

* * *

Heavenly choruses, a dozen columns in two weeks!

The part of Patience that loved to be of use, to write, to feel a sense of having made a contribution leaped at the prospect. The part of her who'd had enough of Professor Pontifical was ready to answer every letter in Mr. Mac-Hugh's stack.

But other parts of her…

Across the table, Dougal MacHugh waited. He was deucedly good at waiting, arguing, persisting—at anything necessary to further his business interests. Patience admitted to grudging admiration for his tenacity, because at one time MacHugh's determination to build a business had been all that stood between her and a life in service, or worse, dependence on a spouse.

She didn't *like* his tenacity. Didn't like much of anything about him, though he had a rather impressive nose.

He'd taken off his spare glasses, and thus good looks entirely wasted on a Scottish publisher were more evident. Untidy dark hair gave him a tousled look that made Patience want to put him to rights.

He'd probably bite off her hand if she attempted to straighten his hair.

His eyes were a lovely emerald color, fringed with unfairly thick lashes, and his mouth—Patience had no business noticing a man's mouth. Anybody would notice Mr. MacHugh's broad shoulders and his height. He was a fine specimen, which mattered not at all, and a finer businessman.

That mattered a great deal.

"You think we can do this, Mr. MacHugh? Put out twelve special editions in two weeks?"

His regard was steady. Patience liked to think of it as a man-to-man gaze, because not even her dear friends regarded her as directly.

"I think *you* can do this, Miss Friendly."

Did Mr. MacHugh but know it, his confidence in her was worth more than all of the pence and quid he paid her—and he did pay her, to the penny and on time.

"My compensation will have to reflect the effort involved."

"Madam, if this goes well, your compensation will result in a very fine Christmas for some years to come."

Patience longed to pick up the next letter and lose herself in the worries and quandaries of her readers, but she'd yet to agree to take on Mr. MacHugh's project.

"What do you mean, a very fine Christmas for some years to come?"

He came around to her side of the table, bringing pencil and paper with him. He moved with an economy of motion that Patience associated with cats and wolves, not that she'd ever seen a wolf.

Mr. MacHugh took the chair beside her. "Look at the numbers, Miss Friendly."

Who would have thought a publisher would smell of apples and pine? That scent distracted Patience as Mr. MacHugh explained about the printer's pricing scheme, the potential market for broadsheets in London, the publishing houses that had recently closed, and the magnitude of the opportunity awaiting Mrs. Horner's Corner.

"So the professor has chosen an excellent time to cast a wider net," Mr. MacHugh concluded. "I'd suspect him of being a Scotsman, his maneuver is so exquisitely timed."

Patience picked up the page, half covered with numbers and tallies. Impressive tallies. "Not all keen minds are Scottish, sir."

Patience wasn't feeling very keen. Her earnings had crept up, true, but she'd used the monthly windfall to pay off debts and set aside a bit for leaner times. What would it be like to know she had enough when those lean times came around?

For they inevitably did.

"You hesitate to spoil your holiday season with too big an assignment." Mr. MacHugh stuck his pencil behind his ear. "I can't blame you for that, it being *baking season* and all."

He lowered his lashes in a manner intended to make Patience shriek, his tone implying that crumpets would of course hold a woman's attention more readily than coin.

"Without a steady income, Mr. MacHugh, there can be no crumpets. My concern is that the work you put before me must meet the standard I've set over the past two years. Perhaps the professor can churn out his drivel at a great rate, but my efforts are more thoughtful."

"Your efforts are very thoughtful."

Mr. MacHugh knew how to deliver a compliment that was part contradiction, part goad. Rather than toss his own spectacles at him—they were fine eyeglasses—Patience got up to pace.

"Christmas falls on a Saturday this year," she said. "If we're to publish twelve editions, the last on Christmas Eve, that means—"

"The first edition should come out this Saturday, December eleventh. The twelfth and the nineteenth being the Sabbath, that means—"

"This Saturday! That means we go to the printer's four days from now."

"Aye. Glad to see your command of the calendar is the equal of your ability with words. Can you do it?"

Could she give up the baking, the buying last-minute tokens for Elizabeth, Charlotte, Megan, and Anwen? Hustle past the glee clubs singing in the holidays on London's street corners when she longed to linger and bask in the music? Give up sitting quietly at church just to hear the choir rehearse the holiday services?

Upon reflection, yes, she could. Putting aside holiday folderol for two weeks to secure a nest egg was the practical choice.

"You hesitate," Mr. MacHugh said, tossing his pencil onto the table. "This is a once-in-a-lifetime opportunity to build Mrs. Horner's Corner into an institution, and you hesitate. What are you afraid of, Miss Friendly?"

Of all Dougal MacHugh's objectionable qualities, his perceptivity ranked at the top of the list. Were he not also unflinchingly, inconveniently, relentlessly honest, Patience could not have endured his acuity.

When her writing was weak, he told her. When the solution she proposed was poorly thought out, he told her. When she was repeating herself, preaching, making light of a problem, or otherwise missing the mark, he told her.

And worst of all, when he was wrong—a maddeningly infrequent occurrence—he admitted it.

Patience took her seat beside him, where the fire threw out the most warmth. "What if I can't do this?"

"Failure is always a possibility, but we minimize it with planning and hard work."

"You haven't left me any time to plan."

"Opportunity looks like inconvenience to the indolent."

She wanted to stick her tongue out at him. "Must you be so Scottish?"

"I am Scottish."

"You needn't make it sound as if that's the most wonderful status a man could boast of. Back to the matter at hand, please. If I attempt this twelve-edition madness and fail, it's worse than if I'd let the professor bore everybody for two weeks straight. The readers will say I've exceeded my limits and overtaxed my dim female brain."

"Your brain, while admittedly female, is anything but dim. Think like a general. What do you need for your campaign to succeed?"

Generals were not female . . . except *some of them were*. Patience had learned from the same tutors hired to instruct her brother—Papa had seen no reason to also pay governesses—and throughout history, some generals had been female.

There were female deities, female saints, and female monarchs. All the best tribulations in mythology had been female too. The Medusa, the sirens, the furies.

"I'll need help," she said. "I'll need immediate editorial reviews, somebody to run errands for me, and *crumpets*. Lots and lots of crumpets."

She'd surprised him. How Patience loved that she'd surprised the canny, competent, *Scottish* Mr. MacHugh.

"There's a bakery on the corner for your crumpets. Detwiler will be happy to edit material as you complete it, and I will be your personal errand boy. Shall we begin?"

Gracious warbling cherubim. Patience knew the bakery well—she walked past it every time she dropped off her columns. Mr. Detwiler was as fast as he was competent, but as for that other item...

Apparently, Mr. MacHugh could surprise her too.

"We begin now, and your first assignment as my errand boy is to fetch me a batch of crumpets."

CHAPTER TWO

Dougal set a package of warm crumpets on the worktable. "I had a thought."

"You had a thought." Miss Friendly lifted the parcel to her nose and inhaled without even untying the bow. "Does that unprecedented development require a broadsheet alerting the masses to your good fortune? Perhaps we might refer to it as a seasonal miracle."

"You're quite on your mettle, Miss Friendly." Surrounded by letters, with the cat napping on the mantel behind her, she looked a little less wan, a bit less weary than she had when she'd arrived for the monthly meeting more than an hour ago.

"You brought me warm cinnamon crumpets." She tossed the string toward the hearth, though it caught on the screen. "How could I not be inspired?"

"I'm inspired too," Dougal said, unwrapping his scarf and hanging it over the hook on the back of the door. "The professor is printing twelve special editions, and that means he'll have to start on Saturday if he wants to get them all out before Christmas."

"Why Mr. MacHugh, you've learned the days of the week by heart. Perhaps Harry has been tutoring you. Such a dear boy, though somebody needs to let down the hems on his trousers."

Dougal shook his greatcoat then hung it over his scarf. "The professor's twelve days begin on Saturday. Ours ought to begin Friday."

She'd lifted a crumpet halfway to her mouth, and it remained there, poised before her. "*Friday?* Have you misplaced what few wits you claim, Mr. MacHugh? That means we have to have the first column to the printer on Thursday morning."

"Which means if you have it written by tomorrow evening, we can edit it Wednesday, and beat the professor at his game."

She took a dainty nibble of her sweet as cinnamon perfumed the office. The cat woke, stretched, and nearly fell off the mantel before re-situating himself more comfortably.

"You want me to write a column of insightful, kind, articulate advice." She took another bite of crumpet. "We haven't even chosen all of the letters yet, Mr. MacHugh. I can't conjure solutions without time to think them up."

"We'll argue them up." Dougal took the chair beside her, because the day was bitter and his backside craved the warmth of the fire.

"We're good at that," she said, nudging the crumpets toward him. "Take more than your share, and you'll get no columns from me."

Dougal used his penknife to slice one of the four crumpets in half, took a bite, then gestured with the remaining portion.

"Are these the letters you're considering?"

"Yes. Don't get crumbs on them."

He picked up the first one and scanned it. "The old *my sister is making eyes at my husband.* Husband's holiday token ought to be a month of slumber on the sofa, or a stern warning from sister's husband—and his brothers."

"Don't be such a man."

"I am a man."

"Don't be such a crude man. We don't know if husband is making eyes back at the sister. If he is, there's a problem. If he's not, then the sister is simply making a fool of herself. We don't know if the sister is married, which also matters. The issue, though, is loneliness."

The issue was lust.

Dougal spoke around a mouthful of crumpet. "How do you figure that?"

"If the sister were content with her lot, she'd not be trying to attract the attention of her brother-in-law, which efforts are doomed to misery, no matter where they lead."

"True enough." Though Dougal had yet to have an entirely miserable time sharing a bed—as best he recalled those few and distant occasions—and a shared bed was the logical conclusion to this domestic drama.

"If the wife were secure in husband's affections," Miss Friendly went on, "she would not be troubled by her sister's behavior."

"Some women are born troubled."

Sharing that eternal verity with Miss Friendly earned Dougal the same look George gave him when the cat had been put out first thing on a snowy day.

She paused before starting on a second crumpet. "If the husband were entirely secure in his wife's affections, he wouldn't strike the sister as a man who could be tempted."

"Some men like to be tempted. They aren't interested in the sin itself, they just like to know they could be naughty if they wanted to."

She frowned at her half crumpet. "Like some women keep men dangling after them. There are names for women like that, but when a man is flirtatious, we call him a gallant."

The last of her crumpet met its fate, and an unhappy silence grew.

"Whoever he was," Dougal said, pushing to his feet, "he was an idiot, and you're better off without him. I need some tea."

He left the office not to see to the teapot—the clerks always had one going on the parlor stove in cold weather—but to put distance between himself, Miss Friendly, and thoughts of shared beds. Dougal had no business *speculating* where Patience Friendly was concerned, but he'd long ago given up lecturing his imagination on that score.

As he brought a tea tray back into his office, it struck him that for Miss Friendly, being closeted alone with a man under the age of eighty must be an unusual occurrence. If she'd had a flirtatious swain in tow at some point—a gallant— she wasn't the daughter of a merchant, schoolteacher, or yeoman.

"Will you answer the letter about the flirting sister?" he asked.

"I can use the letter as a point of departure regarding holiday loneliness and remind the readers that problems admit of solutions when we're in possession of all the relevant facts. Shall you eat that last half crumpet?"

Dougal set the tray down and regarded the sweet. The part he'd eaten had been delicious. Perfectly baked, between cake and pudding in the center, sweet, spicy, delightful.

"No."

Miss Friendly reached for it, and Dougal grabbed her wrist. "You've had three, madam."

"It shouldn't go to waste."

Someday, Dougal wanted her to look at him the way she regarded that last half crumpet.

"It won't. Harry!" he called. "Come clear up this mess, please."

Harry trotted into the office, wrapped the paper around the last half crumpet, and swept the table free of crumbs.

"Anything else, Dougal?"

Before non-family, Harry was supposed to call his employer Mr. MacHugh. "Aye. Send 'round to the chophouse for two plates at half four. The usual portions, and tell the lads they can go home an hour early if the snow keeps up. Fill up the coal buckets before you go and sweep off the steps."

"Right, Dougal."

The instant Harry had gone, Miss Friendly was on her feet, hands at her hips. "I can't believe you just threw away a perfectly good half of a delicious..." Her eyes narrowed. "You saved it for the boy."

"Nothing edible goes to waste when Harry's on the premises. Now, about this letter?"

She flounced back to her seat, and then the real arguments began.

* * *

Patience had never spent most of a day at her publisher's office. The insights gained were fascinating. The pace of the work never let up, with clerks coming and going, errand boys and printer's assistants adding to the traffic, and packages coming in by the hour.

The bustle was distracting at first, but then it became a sort of music, like a string quartet playing in the background at a Venetian breakfast. Several hours of choosing and discarding letters with Mr. MacHugh also revealed that clerks did not always use refined language, and most of Mr. MacHugh's staff spoke with thick Highland burrs.

As for MacHugh himself, he was the biggest revelation of all. He was gruff, demanding, tireless, and devoted to his staff.

"You sent your clerks home early," Patience said, getting up to fetch a cushion from the sofa. "Will you dock their pay?"

"Of course not. They're paid little enough as it is, and they'd work late if I asked it of them. We should finish up here. We've chosen enough letters to last you the first six days, and it's dark out."

Patience tossed the cushion onto her chair, then resumed her seat. To blazes with decorum when her backside ached.

"The food was surprisingly good," she said, surveying the remains of their meal. The chophouse had sent around a hot sandwich, ham and cheese, the cheddar almost melting but not quite, a perfect dash of mustard turning good food into a feast.

At home, dinner would have been soup made from the leftovers of the Sunday joint, but mostly broth, potatoes, and carrots.

"We're faithful customers at the chophouse," Mr. Mac-Hugh said, moving the empty plates to the desk. "Shall we be on our way?"

"You needn't walk me home, Mr. MacHugh."

He leaned back against the desk, arms folded across his chest. At some point, he'd taken off his coat, and Patience had taken off her boots.

A far cry from the propriety with which she'd been raised, but propriety did not keep the coal bins full.

"Miss Friendly, I conceded to you on the matter of the child who'd pinched horehound candy from the sweet shop. I capitulated regarding the mother-in-law's awful bread pudding. I compromised regarding the best way to scent tapers without spending a fortune, but I will not allow a woman in my employ to walk alone on the streets of London at night."

The snow had stopped, but slippery footing was not the worst that could befall a solitary woman on London's streets, especially at night. Poor women took their chances, while wealthy women never went anywhere unescorted.

Patience would never be wealthy again. "Can't you send Harry with me?"

"Can't you accept my company for the distance of a few streets? You've spent the better part of a day with me, and we didn't come to blows."

"A near thing, and only because I disapprove of violence."

"You disapprove of me," he said, pushing away from the desk. "Get your boots on, and I'll see to it you're home safe in a half hour. I'll send Harry around to fetch the first column from you tomorrow afternoon."

He passed her the boots, which needed new heels, but kept her feet reasonably dry over short distances. The temptation to argue was strong, also unwise. Patience put her boots on, then wrapped herself in her cloak and scarf and let Mr. MacHugh accompany her to the front stoop.

Down near the corner, some elderly soul shuffled along, bent against the bitter breeze, but the thoroughfare was otherwise deserted.

"Let's be off," Mr. MacHugh said. "A bit of fresh air is all well and good, but I don't fancy a lung fever when the work is piling up." He tucked Patience's hand around his arm and set off at a surprisingly considerate pace, given the difference in their heights.

Fatigue descended as they walked along, and in the privacy of her thoughts, Patience was grateful for Mr. Mac-Hugh's presence. The streets were unsafe for a woman traveling by herself at this hour.

And they were lonely.

After all the bickering, discussing, arguing, and debating, the silence of the December night was profound. The new snow muffled even church bells, and the smell—coal smoke on a frigid breeze—was desolate.

They had turned onto Patience's street when she broke the silence.

"I don't disapprove of you."

Mr. MacHugh made a disparaging noise between a snort and a huff.

"I don't," Patience went on. "I might not...That is to say, I don't know what to *do* with you. I was not raised to be in anybody's employment. I don't care for it, but I don't care to rely on charity either."

"You'd rather be idle?"

His curiosity was genuine, not a taunt aimed at a class of society for which Mr. MacHugh had little respect. At least he hadn't asked if she'd rather be married.

"I'd rather be the employer, if you must know. I cannot abide somebody telling me what to do, presuming to know what's best for me, or how I ought to go on."

"Especially not a man?"

"Not anybody."

Patience braced herself for a lecture on the way of the world, the dictates of the Almighty, nature's laws, and other masculine flights of self-importance. If men were so infernally smart, competent, and ideally suited to ordering creation, then why was most of the Continent constantly at war, and why hadn't men been chosen to endure the agony of childbirth?

"I don't care for being told what to do myself," Mr. MacHugh said. "There are sheep and there are shepherds. I'm not a sheep, and I'm not convinced gender matters the way the preacher claims it does, but that's just a former schoolteacher's point of view."

They'd reached Patience's doorstep, the only one on her side of the street with a lamp lit.

"You were a schoolteacher, Mr. MacHugh?"

"Aye, and still would be, except my grandfather left me some means. In the schoolroom, I saw what a difference knowledge could make to a receptive mind. I must admit small boys are not always ideal students, while little girls on the whole struck me as cleverer than the boys, more eager for knowledge. I had hoped that as a publisher, I might be able to do more to make knowledge available to receptive minds."

Mr. MacHugh's high-crowned hat gave him extra height in addition to what nature had bestowed, and yet, a hint of the small boy remained in his gaze as he studied the lamp post.

"Have you given up so easily on that dream of sharing knowledge, Mr. MacHugh? Your publishing house is not quite three years old."

He took off his hat and dusted a few snowflakes from the brim. "I'd planned to be the publisher who brought enlightenment to the masses, you see. Science, languages, tales of faraway lands, all for a reasonable price. No Gothic novels, scandal sheets, or fashionable nonsense for me. It hasn't worked out that way."

Half the elderly women who dwelled across the street were probably peering out their parlor windows, horrified that Patience was having discourse with a man on her very doorstep.

Warmth blossomed in her heart nonetheless, because Dougal MacHugh was not quite the pinchpenny taskmaster she'd thought him to be. He had dreams, he'd known disappointment. He'd not been above instructing little girls or noticing their intelligence.

"If this project goes well," Patience said, "you'll have some latitude, some room to put a bit of knowledge before the masses and see if they like it. That will be my holiday wish for you, Mr. MacHugh, that your dream can come closer to reality."

He tapped his hat back onto his head. "Give the professor a sound drubbing, Miss Friendly. That's all I ask. I'll bid you good evening."

Patience made her way up the steps, while, like a suitor, Mr. MacHugh waited for her to safely enter her home. She closed the door behind her and, before she undid her cloak and scarf, peered out the window.

Mr. MacHugh was already in motion, his stride confident, his dark cloak flapping against his boots. He hadn't scoffed at Patience's dreams, and he had dreams of his own. Watching him make his solitary way down the street, Patience considered she might have something else in common with Mr. Dougal MacHugh.

Perhaps he was lonely too.

* * *

"You canna tell the woman to leave her husband," Dougal shouted. "You'll put me oot t' business, ye daft woman. I'll have preachers six deep on m' doorstep citing Scripture, and a bunch of harpies quoting that Wollstonecraft woman in response."

For the space of a day, Dougal had pondered his walk through the snowy evening with Patience Friendly. From his perspective, their dealings had subtly shifted as a result of that walk, the shared meal, and the long afternoon spent shaping the details of their holiday project.

He'd given her a piece of his past, something none of his competitors knew. The schoolteacher from Perthshire aspired to commercial success, and Patience Friendly had not mocked his ambition.

Now, he aspired to turn her over his knee.

"The poor woman's husband is gambling and drinking away coin needed to feed her child," Miss Friendly retorted, marching across the office. "If she stays with him, she and the child will die, or worse."

"Such drama over a man enjoying a wee dram or two. What could be worse than death?"

She aimed a glower at him, magnificent in its ferocity. Up close, her eyes were storm gray rather than their customary blue, though she still bore the fragrance of lemons and spices.

"Must I spell it out for you, Mr. MacHugh? You've lived three years in London. Are you still in ignorance of the Magdalene houses and foundling homes?"

"Don't insult me, Patience Friendly."

"Don't ignore a woman whose child's life is imperiled, Mr. MacHugh. I say my reply to the letter stands. If a man is fonder of his pint than he is of his own child, he's a menace to the child. A father's first obligation is to protect his young."

"Find me Scripture to back up that position, and I'll let you quote it, but that's as far as I'll go."

"You arrogant varlet." Miss Friendly's voice cracked like a tree trunk sundered by gale-force winds. "Scripture is *written by men, interpreted by men, translated by men, and preached by men.* What would a man know of a lady's plight in this situation? The mother—a countrywoman from your benighted Scotland—didn't write to the all-knowing professor, she wrote to *me.*"

The staff was accustomed to Dougal raising his voice, and heated arguments among the clerks were not unusual. Dougal wasn't above dressing down a printer who failed to deliver on time, and some of the other authors—the male authors—could be colorful in their choice of words.

To have provoked Miss Patience Friendly to shouting felt like both an accomplishment and a disgrace. A violation of some natural order that stood above even Scripture.

"She's right," Harry said, sauntering through the open door with a bag of crumpets. "'Let the women keep silent in the church,' for example. Why wouldn't God want to hear from half his children? Doesn't make any sense to me, and yer auld mum would agree, Dougal."

"There you have it," Miss Friendly snapped, snatching the bag of crumpets from Harry. "From the mouths of babes, or in this case, strapping youths coming into the full glory of their intellectual powers." She tore open the bag and passed Harry a crumpet.

Harry accepted the sweet, bowed, and smirked his way out the door.

"We'll set the letter aside for now," Dougal said. "Plenty of others remain, and we needn't tackle that one first."

Miss Friendly held her crumpet as if she were considering pitching it at him. "We can set the letter aside for now, but the misery of poor children ought to be a suitable topic for the holiday season. You will not convince me otherwise."

For them, this was a compromise. A show of diplomacy was in order. "Convince you to change your mind once you've formed an opinion? Daft I might be, but I've no desire to end my days prematurely. Enjoy your crumpets."

Dougal tried for a dignified exit, but Miss Friendly tore off a bite of cinnamon heaven and popped it into her mouth as he passed her.

"You don't care for a crumpet, Mr. MacHugh? They're very tasty."

"I'll have a half."

The rest of the afternoon went the same way, bickering and sweets, then the occasional philosophical argument, followed by a heated difference of opinion over the placement of a comma.

All quite invigorating, and yet the disagreement over the gin widow's letter left a sour taste in Dougal's mouth.

"Has Miss Friendly driven you from your own office?" Harry asked as the clerks began packing up. "I can still make a run to the chophouse if you're going to demand more work from her."

Dougal eyed the closed door to his office, which sported his name—Dougal P. MacHugh, Publisher—in shiny brass letters. An hour ago, that door had opened enough for a disgruntled King George to be shoved into the clerk's room, but Miss Friendly hadn't emerged or demanded more crumpets.

"She's working," Dougal said. "You lot go get the greenery, and mind you, don't overspend. We've a budget in this office."

"We've a budget even for a frolic," Harry retorted. "Is it any wonder the Scotsman has a dour, miserly reputation?"

"Hear, hear," old Detwiler chorused from his desk.

"Traitor." Dougal pushed a few coins into Harry's hand.

"Stand the lads to a pint when you're finished outside. Detwiler must buy his own, though."

The office emptied, save for Dougal, King George, and the literary force of nature who'd taken over Dougal's office.

Miss Friendly had said she wanted to be the employer, an unusual ambition for a woman her age. Widows could own entire networks of coaching inns, breweries, and all manner of establishments, but a single woman of Miss Friendly's age—a spinster—could dream of managing only her own household.

"Rrrlf."

George stropped himself against Dougal's boot. Dougal considered shoving the cat back through the door, a sort of reconnaissance maneuver, but decided on safety in numbers instead. He picked up George, did not knock on his own door, and entered the office.

He faced a writer's version of a battlefield. A dictionary lay open on the table. The remains of a bag of crumpets sat beside it. Foolscap had been crumpled and tossed toward the hearth, and more sheets covered with scrawling penmanship were scattered over the table.

Miss Friendly sat at Dougal's desk, her arms crossed on the blotter, her cheek pillowed on her forearm. Dougal set the cat on the mantel and crept closer, for his most popular author was apparently fast asleep.

"Miss Friendly?"

Her breathing continued in the slow, mesmerizing rhythm of exhausted sleep. A quill pen lay beneath her right hand. At rest, her features were more elegant, more delicate than when animated with her endless opinions.

Dougal slid the quill from beneath her grasp, and still she remained asleep. George paced back and forth on the mantel, as if waiting for a laggard minion to build up the fire.

Instead, Dougal lit a candle from a spill and took the candle to the desk. Better light didn't change what he'd observed when he'd first approached his sleeping beauty.

Miss Friendly was tired—her eyes were shadowed with fatigue, and her sleep was sound. She had also been upset, apparently, for in her left hand she clutched a lace-edged handkerchief, and her cheeks were stained with tears.

* * *

Patience dozed in that half-dreaming state where sounds from the waking world had no significance and thoughts drifted freely.

At least she hadn't cried in front of Dougal MacHugh. He wasn't exactly dreadful anymore, but he was disappointing, which was worse. On Monday, he'd acknowledged that even a young female might have a nimble mind. Today, he'd gone right back to parroting hidebound attitudes merely because they'd keep his business from offending the good clergy of London.

Let the women keep silent in the church, indeed.

"Miss Friendly."

Patience wasn't feeling very friendly. Other snippets of Scripture floated past, none of them useful when a child's belly was empty. The cat rustled about the office, and Patience had the odd thought that she liked having George underfoot.

"Madam, wake up. The lads will say I worked you to exhaustion."

That growling burr was familiar, and not.

Somebody gently shook Patience's shoulder. "Woman, ye

canna be sleeping in my very office. We'll stop at the bakery and get some tarts, for I'm certain you've eaten every crumpet in Bloomsbury."

The word *crumpet* had Patience opening her eyes. "I adore a fresh lemon tart."

Dougal MacHugh knelt beside the desk, his emerald eyes full of concern—for her?

"I'll buy ye a dozen. Why were ye cryin', Patience?"

Patience. He avoided using her given name, but she liked the way he said it.

"How did you know I was crying?" For she had been, and dissembling would simply make her look foolish. More foolish. She sat back, knowing her sleeve had left a crease on her cheek, and her hair needed tidying.

She'd taken a break to read the morning paper and seen an engagement announced. Not just any engagement, but the one that ten years ago should have been hers.

A callused male thumb stroked her cheek. "I see the evidence of your tears. If somebody needs a beating, I'll gladly do the honors." In his way, Dougal MacHugh claimed a certain rough charm.

"He's a viscount now. He'd see you put out of business and laugh about it with his friends."

Mr. MacHugh brushed an errant lock of hair back from Patience's brow. "I liked teaching little children their letters, sums, and history. I'd like teaching a viscount his manners more. I take it your papa wasn't in a position to hold the bastard accountable."

Bastard was such a vulgar, *appropriate* word. "Papa was the reason the viscount went on his way, even though the engagement had been all but announced."

This was ancient, entirely irrelevant history. The Windhams knew all the details and had stood by Patience through it all, though the rest of her acquaintances had dropped her flat. Used goods. A jilt. A jade. Patience was no stranger to vulgar words, though she had denied herself use of them regarding the viscount.

"Was there a disagreement, lass?"

Small children had likely confessed all of their troubles to Dougal MacHugh when he put questions to them so gently.

"There was a predictable melodrama," Patience said, "though I was the only one not given the script. Papa, like many younger sons, lived beyond his means. He had a falling out with his older brother, and the debts began to pile up. Papa realized that he couldn't afford more than one Season for me, but for that one Season, he spared no expense."

Mr. MacHugh turned and perched with his back to the desk drawers. "And when the viscount realized you were not an heiress, not even in possession of good settlements or on good terms with the head of your family, away he went. He broke his word, and he broke your heart."

"Well put." The first mattered more than the second, in hindsight.

"Your uncle was no help?"

"My uncle was determined to teach my father a lesson, my father was intent on the same exercise where the baron was concerned, the title has since gone to a cousin I've never met. I think Scottish families must be different."

"Scottish families are poorer, for the most part. We can't afford such meanness to one another."

Meanness, another appropriate word. "The viscount proposed to me. Not down on bended knee, but sitting in the pergola. He proposed, and I accepted. I know now why a young man is left alone to propose to his lady."

"Because men can't bear to have witnesses when they're rejected?"

"That too, but also so they don't have witnesses when their proposal is accepted. He later claimed I'd misconstrued his words, I'd read into friendship a regard that hadn't been tendered."

Mr. MacHugh rose straight to his full height. "Patience Friendly, if ever a woman had a fine command of the language, and the many subtleties thereof, you are that woman. You misconstrued nothing, and the viscount was never your friend."

He tugged Patience to her feet, and because she'd been sitting so long—surely that was the reason—she wobbled and clutched at the nearest stable object.

Her arms found their way around Mr. MacHugh's waist, and—later was time enough to wonder why—his enfolded her.

"Nobody has ever said that to me." She gave him her weight, and he obliged with a genuine embrace. "My parents questioned me endlessly. What had he said? Was I sure? Could I have misheard him? What words did he use? It's as if they wanted him to be right and me to be a witless ninny."

"You were right, they were wrong. You are not a witless ninny. Your parents' first responsibility is to protect their young—I have this on the best authority—and they failed you."

A queer feeling came over Patience, part sadness, because her parents had failed her spectacularly, but also part relief. No witnesses could verify the harm done to her by a faithless young man, and thus doubt had assailed her, even from within.

Had she misheard? *Was* she exaggerating? *Did* she misconstrue words intended to convey only general esteem?

"Papa said I must have misunderstood. I didn't misunderstand the viscount's hands under my skirts. Only a fiancé or a cad takes such liberties."

She buried her face against Mr. MacHugh's shoulder, appalled at her own honesty, and even more appalled at how ignorant she'd been ten years ago.

"Losing our innocence is painful, but it's how we find out what sort of person we are."

The desk and the chair prevented Patience from stepping back, and yet, she wanted to see Mr. MacHugh's eyes, wanted to assure herself he brought no judgment of her to this discussion.

Because if he did not judge her, perhaps she might cease judging herself. She'd accused herself of ignorance, while Mr. MacHugh pronounced her guilty only of trusting the wrong man.

She scooted onto the desk, and Mr. MacHugh remained where he was—close enough to hug, his hands at his sides.

"You could have gone into a decline," he said. "Thrown yourself on your uncle's charity, embroiled the viscount and your family in worse scandal than a simple reversal of fortune. You didn't. You soldiered on. You are still soldiering on, and God pity the fool who thinks to take advantage of you ever again."

Dougal MacHugh's approval made Patience want to cry all over again, also to smile. To beam, to laugh, to hug him again.

How odd.

"I could not allow my brother to suffer as a result of my situation. Mama pawned her jewels to buy him a commission and found work tutoring bankers' daughters in elocution, deportment, and French. She wrote pamphlets on the same subjects, and then I took up that occupation when she died."

Please don't ask about Papa. She could see the question in Mr. MacHugh's eyes, could feel it bearing down on her.

"And your father. Did he drink, Patience?"

"Sometimes. Mama said he expired of shame. We moved in with her mother, and that's the only reason I have a roof over my head. Grandmama left everything she had to me. You mustn't think my circumstances are pathetic."

Precarious, yes. Never pathetic. Not as long as Patience had friends and meaningful, paying work.

"I think you are resourceful, resilient, and brilliant at what you do, but it's time I got you home, Miss Friendly."

Patience didn't want to leave, and she didn't want to be *Miss Friendly*. She wanted to sort through the remaining letters, eat more of the hot, delicious food from the chophouse, and argue with Dougal until full darkness had fallen.

Except it already had. "Is my first column ready for the printer?"

"We'll send it over bright and early tomorrow. Three letters, all answered with your signature good sense. Come Friday, the professor will have an apoplexy."

"Good," Patience said, scooting off the desk. "He's certainly given me a few bad moments. The man is insufferable. Thinks he knows everything, and what he lacks in pragmatism he makes up for in long-windedness."

She was wrapped in her cloak and at the front door when it occurred to her that something about the office had changed. The scent was different, for one thing. Beneath the coal smoke, ink, and paper smell lay the fragrance of pine.

"You decorate for the holidays? Doesn't that cost a bit of coin, Mr. MacHugh?" The windows were swagged with pine roping, a wreath of pine and holly graced each of the double doors, and cloved oranges hung from the unlit wall sconces.

"The clerks enjoy decorating, the patrons like it, and my competitors do it, so I make a few gestures. It's in the budget, though I'll have a word with Harry tomorrow regarding fiscal restraint."

He pointed a gloved hand upward, to a sheaf of greenery dangling by a red ribbon from the chandelier.

Every spinster's worst holiday nightmare hung overhead— mistletoe, and plenty of it.

"Come along," Patience said, wrapping her arm through Mr. MacHugh's. "Tomorrow will be another demanding day, and we've tarried long enough."

She nearly shoved Mr. MacHugh through the door, and then engaged him in a discourse on the writings of Mrs. Wollstonecraft. Patience wasn't familiar with the author's philosophies, but if they had earned Mr. MacHugh's notice, she'd remedy that oversight posthaste.

CHAPTER THREE

The previous evening, Dougal had prosed on for the duration of three quiet snowy streets, regaling Patience with the writings of a woman either ahead of her time or bent on destroying the social order, depending on the critic's perspective. All the while, Dougal had been rearranging his emotional budget where Patience Friendly was concerned.

She was, indeed, a lady fallen on hard times. Very hard times, very much a lady, and her contrariness was a result of betrayed trust rather than arrogance. No wonder she argued every comma, demanded a say in which letters she answered, and had thrown herself into this project.

On Thursday morning, the office was tidy and neat—unlike Dougal's thoughts—thanks to Harry's efforts, though Dougal had enjoyed seeing the battlefield where Patience had thrashed her next deadline into submission.

"Shall I buy more crumpets?" Harry asked, shuffling

through the door. "I can take them with me when I fetch Miss Friendly's column for tomorrow."

"I'll fetch her column," Dougal said. "You can take down the mistletoe, my lad. This is a respectable establishment."

"I'm not tall enough to take it down—yet. Mind you don't be pinchin' the lady's sweets, Dougal. I'd hate to have to peach on you to Cousin Hamish."

Cousin Hamish was head of the Perthshire branch of the family, a former colonel who owned two breweries and considerable acreage. His brother, Cousin Colin, owned a distillery, while their sisters, Rhona and Edana, had yet to settle on a single enterprise. In England, the ladies might be discouraged from commercial ventures. In Scotland…

Family supported one another. Hamish had been the one to talk Dougal into trying his hand at publishing, for example.

"Cousin Hamish is hundreds of miles to the north," Dougal said, "and he likes it up in Perthshire. Be gone with ye, and don't be telling tales that reflect on a good woman's name."

Harry folded himself into one of the chairs facing Dougal's desk. "Are you thinking of offering for her?"

"Are *you*, Harold Bruce Sylvester MacHugh?"

Harry's ears turned red, but his grin was pure MacHugh. "I haven't sown my wild oats yet, or she'd succumb to my legendary charm in a thrice, and you'd have no one to write Mrs. Horner's Corner. Speaking of writing, what's that you're working on?"

Dougal picked up the page and poured the sand from it back into the tray. "None of your business, but it's almost ready for the printer. Fetch Miss Friendly's completed column from Detwiler, give it a final read, and you can take this with you when you make the morning run to the printer."

"I don't fancy running anywhere today, Dougal," Harry said, rising and holding his hands out toward the hearth. "That sky is getting ready to snow from now until Christmas. Mr. Detwiler's sacroiliac is acting twinge-ish, and you know what that means."

"It means when we need him most, Detwiler will take a day off, claiming his back has laid him low. It's winter, Harry. The sky looks like a winter sky. See to Miss Friendly's column, please."

Harry left off petting King George and went about his assignment. He was indeed growing out of his trousers—again—and would need new boots before too long as well.

Dougal read over the page he'd written, looking for mistakes or even a comma out of place. In his dreams, he'd give this piece to Patience to tear apart, edit, and refine, but that way lay a war Dougal wasn't prepared to fight.

Not yet, possibly not ever.

* * *

"That scoundrel!" Miss Friendly cried, boots thumping on the office floorboards as she stalked about like King George in a taking. "That dastardly, underhanded, pestilential, infernal—oh, I wish I were more proficient with foul language."

"Scurrilous dog?" Mr. MacHugh offered. "Varlet?"

"Too trite, but certainly in the right direction. How did he know, Mr. MacHugh? How did the professor know we were starting a day early?"

Patience stood at the front window, one floor above a familiar scene. On the nearest corner, Jake, the newsboy with the loudest voice, hawked the MacHugh and Sons broadsheets to the Friday morning crowd.

"Mrs. Horner solves all your holiday woes! Family squabbles, lack of funds, stains on the tablecloth—no problem for our Mrs. Horner! Disaster avoided, and a happy Christmas from MacHugh and Sons!"

On the opposite corner, a slightly older boy offered the competing product. "Professor Pennypacker packs all the advice you'll need into one column. Why listen to a nattering old woman when the learned professor has all the answers?"

This had been going on for half the morning, with each newsboy obligingly falling silent when his opponent held forth. A strolling fiddler played holiday tunes on the third corner, and a meat-pie vendor occupied the fourth.

"I have my sources in the offices of the other publishers," Mr. MacHugh said. "I'm sure Pennypacker's newsboy occasionally chats with my lads over a pint. I've Harry keeping an eye out, but where's the harm in some friendly competition?"

Mr. MacHugh stood behind Patience at the window, close enough to remind her that they'd embraced, even held each other, for a few moments. The sky hadn't fallen, King George hadn't abdicated his place on the mantel, but Patience's opinion of Mr. MacHugh had shifted—a bit.

He wasn't ambitious for his own sake. He employed a dozen relations and had sunk his last groat into his business. That took courage, daring, and determination, all of which were admirable qualities.

In a man.

Necessary qualities in a woman without means.

"Is Jake the best choice?" Patience asked. "He's smaller than Pennypacker's boy. Younger. The cold might be harder on him."

"Because his family is from Jamaica? Jake was born in

London—he knows our winters—and he's good at what he does. I thought we might move him to Oxford Street when he sells out this lot."

"Oxford Street?" Patience turned from the window. "The great houses of Mayfair don't need Mrs. Horner's advice."

Mr. MacHugh perched against his desk and folded his arms. That gesture usually signaled an opinion cast in granite. It also accentuated the breadth of his shoulders.

"Think about it, Miss Friendly. The great houses of Mayfair sit in Mayfair, but the day help, the merchants, the clerks, shopgirls, and not-so-great all come and go between Mayfair and the rest of London. Oxford Street sees much of that traffic, and the professor's not distributing his wares there."

A week ago, Patience might have spent half an hour arguing: Jake would waste at least thirty minutes getting to Oxford Street, but he could sell a few copies along the way. Pennypacker's boy might simply follow Jake and stand him to one of those pints Mr. MacHugh had mentioned. The entire lot of papers might end up in the ditch if young Jake took a tumble on the snowy streets.

Courage, daring, and determination were not the exclusive province of a man in business.

"Oxford Street," Patience said. "A different block every day, so Pennypacker has to chase us. One of the other boys can bring Jake a fresh lot on the hour, so Jake doesn't have to waste time coming and going from here every time he runs out. If it's a war Pennypacker wants, it's a war he shall get."

"We'll have Harry take Jake's place out front, and send Jake out the back."

"Oh, that is diabolical, Mr. MacHugh. I take back everything I ever said about you—well, some things. The parts about being—"

He took off his glasses and polished them on his sleeve. "Time for crumpets?"

Patience was tired of crumpets. The treat that had loomed beyond her means had lost its appeal in a few short days.

"Lemon tarts. This calls for lemon tarts, and then I must apply myself to the next set of letters."

"Harry!" Mr. MacHugh called. "To the bakery, and tell Jake to come in when he's sold the last of his stack. Lemon tarts for Miss Friendly today."

"And a lemon tart for Jake if he sells out in fifteen minutes!" Patience called.

A cheer went up from the clerks, along with promises to take newsboy duty for the next week, for the next year, if *fresh tarts* were part of the compensation.

Patience not only understood the ribaldry, she delighted in it. "What are you smiling at, Mr. MacHugh?"

His smile transformed him, from a sober and somewhat ruthless man of commerce, to a buccaneer of business, a pirate prince of the publishing world. A quantity of alliterative excesses occurred to Patience, but they all came down to the fact that when Mr. MacHugh smiled at her, he was as attractive as a plate of fresh lemon tarts.

Delicious, complicated, spicy, tart, with just the right amount of sweetness too.

"I'm smiling at a general forging of a path to victory. Pennypacker is no match for you, Patience Friendly, and I think his good fortune has turned against him."

"What do you mean?"

"You're selling more copies because he came out a day early, just as you did."

The newsboys called back and forth to each other, exchanging taunts and jibes. "So is Pennypacker."

"He won't be on Oxford Street." The smile came again,

along with a lifted eyebrow that promised doom to the presuming professor.

Patience smiled back and got to work on the next column.

* * *

Patience Friendly was gorgeous when she smiled. Full of mischief, plans, and energy. When she smiled, she sparkled like moonlight on snow. To see her illuminated with joy was like imbibing a fine dram on a cold night. Every particle of Dougal's soul was warmed and cheered by the sight, just as he delighted to watch her hurling thunderbolts of advice in active voice.

Friday had been lemon tart day. Today she'd had Dougal send for stollen and divided the loaf among all of the clerks, then disappeared back into Dougal's office.

"So you've put out two editions now." Detwiler tossed half a scoop of coal into the parlor stove, then straightened on an old man's sigh. "How's your plan working, lad?"

"You're wasting coal, Aloysius Detwiler. The lads have left for the day." Dougal remained perched on Harry's stool, for it was closest to the fire. Only Detwiler, as the senior editor, merited his own desk.

"But Mrs. Horner remains in your corner, scribbling away." Detwiler moved about the room, tidying up. Good editors were born to tidy and fuss, and Detwiler was the best. Fortunately, he was married to a MacHugh and had some notion of family loyalty.

"Time I walked the lady home, then," Dougal said. "She'll be pleased with today's sales."

The clerks came in an hour later on Saturday morning and left at midafternoon, though there had been plenty of time for Jake and Harry to sell out their supplies of broadsheets.

"Miss Friendly wasn't pleased that the professor followed us to Oxford Street." Detwiler went around the room, putting all the quill pens at the same angle in their standishes. "She'll be furious to learn she's been working for the professor himself."

"You promised you'd not breathe a word."

"The door is closed, and as much time as you spend in there with Miss Friendly, I'll not find you any more alone than you are now. You're playing a dangerous game, Dougal. What's to stop Mrs. Horner from going into business for herself? Ladies write entire books when the need for coin is great enough."

"Patience hasn't the coin to compete with me." Not to mention, she was female, of marriageable age, unwed, and without male relations who might mitigate those unfair realities.

"You should tell her, Dougal."

He should. A woman who'd been played false regarding her entire future would not take kindly to being manipulated, even in the interests of securing greater income.

"I'll tell her when we've put out the remaining editions. She works wonderfully under pressure and has an instinct for battle. She should have been a barrister."

Detwiler settled onto the cushion in his chair and withdrew a pipe and nail from a pocket. "That, my boy, will be twelve editions too late. For Christmas, you will reveal to Miss Friendly that she's been lied to, played for a fool, taken advantage of, and exploited without mercy. All to put coin in your pocket."

"Yours too, and hers." Especially hers. "I've increased the print runs for next week, we're doing so well."

The nail scratched across the bowl of the pipe. "If you say so, professor."

"She might never find out."

Scratch, scratch, scratch... The world of London newsprint journalism was about the size of a Highland village, and twice as prone to gossip.

She'd find out. "Take yourself off, Aloysius, and my regards to Cousin Avery."

Detwiler tapped his pipe against his palm and tossed the ash into the bin beside the stove. "You and Harry joining us for Christmas dinner this year?"

For the past three years, Dougal had been the bachelor relation taken in over the holidays as a kindness on the part of his relatives. Where would Patience spend Christmas? With whom? As far as Dougal could tell, she hadn't even a cat to share her household.

"I'm sure Harry will devour half your goose, but I've other plans, thanks very much."

"More for Harry, then. See you Monday." Detwiler pushed to his feet, got his coat and scarf, and shuffled out into the gray afternoon. London winters weren't as dark as their Perthshire counterparts, but an overcast December day was still a glum undertaking.

When a man had a guilty conscience.

"Has Harry left for the day?" Miss Friendly stood in the doorway to Dougal's office, his glasses perched on her nose, a folded broadsheet in her hand.

"Aye, but we can stop at the bakery when I walk you home."

Her brows twitched down. "I'm in the middle of a reply, but did you see the professor's column for today, Mr. MacHugh?"

He'd written it. "What transgression has the old boy committed now?"

Patience stomped across the clerk's office. "You have re-marked that he and I often deal with similar situations, and a general discourse follows regarding who had the better advice."

A general donnybrook followed, of the literary sort, and the readers loved it. "I've wondered if people don't write to you both, just to see whose advice is superior."

She paused at Harry's table and nudged his pen around in a circle. "You think the readers are playing us off each other? Making up situations to pit the professor against me?"

"I hope they are. That tells me the readers are invested in your column, like a sweepstakes, or a cricket match they've bet money on."

She clambered onto Harry's stool. "My advice column isn't a sporting match, Mr. MacHugh. I care about my read-ers. I genuinely want to help them with life's more vexing challenges. I'm not writing to entertain, I'm writing to educate, to commiserate."

Why did she have to turn up philosophical now? "You're writing to earn coin, Patience." Dougal stalked into his office and busied himself banking the fire, but a familiar tattoo of feminine boot heels followed him through the door.

"I earn coin for helping people sort out their difficulties," Patience said, a strident note creeping into her voice. "I'm not a dancing bear, writing farce for the masses. A woman who'd poach on her own sister's marital preserves is not a joke, Mr. MacHugh."

Dougal straightened and found himself face-to-face with King George lounging on the mantel. The cat's expression was superior, even smug. *Tell her, laddie. Tell her now.*

"I should put George out," Dougal said, scratching the idiot cat's head.

"*Mr. MacHugh.* You posit that my advice is not even

addressed to real problems. You will please assure me that the letters I diligently sort through and consider each week are received from the post?"

"They are."

"Since when has petting that beast become such a fascinating undertaking that you can't face me as we have this discussion?"

Dougal turned. "The letters you respond to are received from the post, Miss Friendly. I can assure you of that. I suspect some might be fabricated."

That much truth filled her with consternation. If Dougal had told her the bakery had closed up shop, or he was canceling her column, her expression could not have been more perplexed.

"How do you deduce such a thing?"

Because Dougal saw every word of every letter, not only the redactions and paraphrases printed in the broadsheets. "You dealt with a sister making calf's eyes, and he addresses a brother engaged in the same sort of flirtation."

"Exactly!" Patience said, brandishing the broadsheet. "Do you know what his advice was?"

Yes, Dougal knew. "Tell me."

"To ignore the whole situation! To do nothing, to pretend obvious displays aren't taking place, and a marriage at risk for serious damage is fine, fine, just fine. The professor counsels dignity and forbearance."

Dougal took the broadsheet from Patience and laid it on his desk. "While you said without a command of all the facts, devising a course of action was difficult. Sound advice." Which Dougal had not thought to offer.

"Boring advice," she retorted. "I should have told that good woman to accost some handsome man under the mistletoe while her husband looks on. The professor would never have come up with such a bold approach to the situation as that, and the readers would have been impressed with the novelty of a woman taking action."

Dougal had gone all day without arguing, but that... that... *pronouncement* required a response.

"The professor would never have been so daft. Kissing some callow swain to provoke jealousy is the stuff of the very farce you seek to avoid."

She pushed her glasses up her nose, marched up to him, and jabbed at his chest with one finger. "A passing indulgence in a venerable holiday tradition, in which you yourself apparently see no harm, is not a farce."

"I told Harry to take that damned stuff down."

She smiled, looking very much like King George when Dougal had spilled the cream pot all over the desk blotter.

"Language, Mr. MacHugh."

Dougal might have yet salvaged a respectable argument from the moment, but Patience smoothed ink-stained fingers over his neckcloth, turning victory into a rout.

"Profanity is the crutch of the linguistically uninspired," she went on, quoting from one of Mrs. Horner's most popular articles.

Dougal was inspired—to sheer foolishness. "You think a kiss under the mistletoe is a harmless holiday tradition?" He took Patience by the wrist and led her from the office. "A mere gesture, of no significance? A quaint tradition, nothing more?"

"A venerable tradition, but quaint, yes. Mr. MacHugh? What are you—Mr. MacHugh?"

Dougal led her to the front door, to a spot beneath the offending greenery hanging from its red ribbon.

He yanked both shades down, gave her the space of two heartbeats to register a protest—which he would have heeded, had any been forthcoming—and then he kissed her.

* * *

The heavenly choruses that had appeared to the shepherds in Bethlehem might have inspired the same upwelling of joy Patience experienced under the mistletoe with Mr. MacHugh.

She'd braced herself for an admonitory lecture of a kiss, having every intention of lecturing Mr. MacHugh right back. Instead of that figurative lump of coal, Mr. MacHugh's kiss was full of sweetness, tenderness, and delicacy.

He offered her a cinnamon biscuit of a kiss—he even tasted of cinnamon—offer being the operative verb. His attentions were beguilingly gentle and his palms cupping Patience's cheeks warm and cherishing.

"I don't know how—" She didn't know how to kiss, where to put her hands, *what to do*, and her ignorance was a terrible burden.

Mr. MacHugh solved those dilemmas by putting Patience's hands at his neck and stepping closer.

"There's no wrong way to kiss, Patience. A kiss doesn't have to be constructed with consistent tenses and agreement of gender, number and case. Kissing is for moments beyond words."

Mr. MacHugh gave her a treasure trove of such moments when he stroked the backs of his fingers against her cheek, when he cradled her head against his palm, when he traced his tongue over the seam of her lips.

She retaliated—reciprocated, rather—and his lips parted.

Oh, gracious. Oh, Happy Christmas, Happy New Year. Where to put a comma—a most excellent premise for a discussion—had nothing, *nothing* on the complexities of how to turn a kiss into a conversation.

Patience shifted and accidently trod on Mr. MacHugh's toes. She stepped back, horrified to have put an end to such a rare delight, and found Mr. MacHugh beaming down at her in the dim foyer. He held out his hand, an invitation, and the festivities recommenced next to the unlit sconce.

Mr. MacHugh braced his back against the wall, and Patience bundled in for another round of affection, exploration, and—heavenly choruses in the happiest of keys—arousal.

This was what it felt like to be intimately interested in a man, to desire *him*, not the secure future his proposal offered, not the protection of his name, or the dream of children to love, but *him*.

Patience smoothed her hand over broad shoulders and a muscular back, then sank her fingers into thick, dark hair. Mr. MacHugh's flavor was spicy, sweet holiday treat, his textures were varied—silky hair, whiskery cheeks, lean angles, soft lips, hard...

Patience had inspired Mr. MacHugh to arousal as well, to the heat in the blood, the catch in the breath, that signaled two adults susceptible to passion for each other.

The joy of that, the startling, gleeful satisfaction of it, had Patience leaning against him, all her attention centered where his arousal pressed unapologetically against her belly.

"Tell me, Patience. D'ye still think advising a kiss beneath the mistletoe is in keeping with Mrs. Horner's signature common sense?"

She wiggled, and he sighed. The cloved orange bobbed against her elbow, and Patience could not recall a time when she'd been so utterly, completely, unexpectedly happy—or glad to be wrong.

* * *

Dougal could not recall a time when he'd been so utterly, completely, inexcusably dunderheaded—though happily dunderheaded.

He'd stolen a kiss, and Patience Friendly had stolen his every good intention, not that the lady was accountable for his actions. She was untutored in the art of kissing, but a damned fast learner. Her kisses were as eager as they were inexpert.

And God above, the passion in her. As dedicated as she was to her writing, as exacting and demanding as she was about the written word, her kisses were ten times more…*more*.

"I have an idea," she said, her hand trailing over Dougal's chest.

Perhaps this idea would involve the sofa in his office, in which case Dougal would have to pitch himself out the window into the nearest snowdrift.

"I've always admired your nimble mind, Patience." And her ink-stained hands, which Dougal wanted to kiss. Her curves were delightful too, as was her vocabulary and her ability to reduce a complex problem to its simplest form.

"I'll write holiday couplets for Jake to sing when selling the broadsheets."

Dougal made himself focus on assembling her words into a sentence he could comprehend, for the weight of her against him was perdition personified.

"Holiday couplets?"

"Yes! The clerks can help with them." She whirled away, back into the clerk's office. "You know, 'God rest ye merry, gentlemen, here's a broadsheet you can read / Mrs. Horner has a clever solution to your every single need.'"

"That sounds naughty." Memorable, though. Very memorable.

She stopped short and patted Dougal's cheek. "You've been disporting under the mistletoe, Mr. MacHugh. Try to focus on the issue at hand."

As he trailed Patience into his office, all Dougal could focus on was the twitch of her skirts. "Couplets aren't a bad idea, but a whole chorus would be better."

"One aimed mostly at the women." She ensconced herself behind Dougal's desk. "Let the professor sing to the men. I also think we should collect up the holiday columns and publish them as a pamphlet, Mrs. Horner's Help for the Holidays. Has a nice ring to it. Let the printer know now, so ours will be ready to go days ahead of the professor's feeble reprise. Toss in a bonus column on difficulties surrounding celebration of the new year."

One kiss, and the woman was on fire.

One kiss, and Dougal had made a delicate situation impossible. "Patience, we're alone here."

She extracted a penknife from one of the desk drawers. "I know, else I shouldn't have kissed you." She pared a fresh point on his best quill pen, her movements economical and practiced.

"*You* kissed *me*, did you?"

The penknife paused. "I thought I did a passably good job, for being out of practice." A hint of vulnerability infused her words. She put the knife away and took a fresh sheet of foolscap.

Dougal banked the fire, though George's tail dangled about his head all the while. "If that's your idea of a passably good kiss, then heaven defend the man who's on the receiving end of your polished efforts. I'm walking you home, Patience. Now."

She brushed the quill across her mouth, and Dougal had to look away.

"I believe your nerves are overset, Mr. MacHugh. Perhaps it's best if we do take some air. Based on your discourse regarding Mrs. Wollstonecraft, I've arrived at a few insights regarding the dictates of propriety."

Yes. Frigid, fresh air. Just the thing. "Mrs. Woll—? Oh, her."

"Does George go out?"

"I'll come by on my way to services tomorrow and put him out for a bit. He guards the castle at night, or that's the theory. Mice can do a lot of damage to paper and glue. Your cloak, madam."

How could she do this? Maintain an animated focus on literary affairs while Dougal wanted to toss Mrs. Horner's Corner, the professor, and the entire yuletide problem into the nearest bowl of Christmas punch.

So he could resume kissing Patience.

She prattled on for the length of three London streets about how the rules of propriety were a subtle scheme to protect not the young lady, but the fortune that accompanied her hand in marriage. Women of lesser station received much less protection, but their relative poverty also gave them more freedom.

This theory was just outlandish—and logical—enough that Dougal could pay some attention to it. Not as much attention as he gave to the way Patience spoke with her hands when impassioned by a topic, or to the memory of those hands smoothing down his back.

Next time, she might venture a bit farther south.

God help me. There must be no *next times*.

"You're not inclined to argue with me?" she demanded as they turned onto her street.

"I'll consider your theories as we take our day of rest tomorrow." Dougal would spend that day furiously drafting the professor's last few columns, with apologies to the good

Presbyterian pastor in Perthshire, who'd be horrified at such industry on the Sabbath. "Why has nobody lit a single lamp yet on your entire street?" London homeowners were subject to regulations requiring porch lights.

"We're thrifty in this neighborhood," Miss Friendly said as they approached her doorstep. Her building was fashioned so the first floor overhung the doorstep, creating an alcove protected from the elements and, at this gloomy hour, from the view of prying neighbors.

Dougal wrestled with the realization that he could kiss her again.

"I'll wish you a peaceful Sunday," Patience said, "and look forward to an industrious and lucrative two weeks."

Industrious and lucrative. Dougal MacHugh, proprietor of MacHugh and Sons, Publishers, should have applauded those sentiments. They were exactly what he'd envisioned when he'd concocted this ludicrous twelve days of competing broadsheets.

Patience offered her hand, and Dougal bowed over it. "A peaceful Sabbath to you too. Miss Friendly."

Before he could tug her closer, gaze longingly into her eyes, or otherwise make an ass of himself, she ducked through the door and left him alone in the freezing air. Dougal took himself back in the direction of the office, the wind stinging his cheeks and his toes going numb.

Which did nothing—not one thing—to get his mind off the question that had plagued him the whole way to Patience's doorstep.

If one kiss sent the woman off into flights of cleverness—God rest ye merry, gentlemen, indeed—then Dougal marveled to think what a bout of passionate lovemaking might do for her creativity.

CHAPTER FOUR

The yuletide season was bringing Patience all manner of insights, about herself, about life, about Mr. MacHugh. She occasionally slipped and referred to him as Dougal in her thoughts, because Mr. MacHugh might be a penny-pinching, ambitious merchant, but only Dougal could acquit himself so impressively beneath the mistletoe.

Only Dougal escorted her home, giving her companionship as she left the hum and bustle of the office for the near silence of her home. Only Dougal lent her his copy of Mrs. Wollstonecraft and told her to keep it.

Wednesday morning, though, he was very much Mr. MacHugh.

"If the professor has followed us to Oxford Street, then we should remove to Piccadilly," Patience said. "He'll take up at least part of a day finding Jake, and in that time we'll sell to throngs of holiday shoppers the professor will miss entirely."

Dougal—Mr. MacHugh, rather—plucked away the pencil Patience had tucked behind her ear and tossed it among the foolscap, pen trimmings, sand, and crumbs on the table.

"Madam, you do not understand. What sells so many copies is the very competition between you and Pennypacker. You and he are putting on a prize fight for the literate. Piccadilly is that much farther from Bloomsbury for Jake to travel, and next you'll be telling us we should sell in Haymarket."

Mr. MacHugh looked tired, as if even the effort to explain—his term for denigrating Patience's logic—wearied him.

"We should do both," Patience said. "Sell in Haymarket and Piccadilly. They're crowded locations, and we'll be a novelty. We should do a special edition, one that's out the previous evening, and give away a few copies so that by morning—"

Mr. MacHugh rose, pinching the bridge of his nose in a gesture reminiscent of a longsuffering governess Patience recalled from nearly a quarter century past.

"Need I remind you, Miss Friendly, we are doing twelve special editions, and to compensate the printer for an evening run would be costly, if he could do it at all with virtually no notice. You'd have Jake shivering in the dark, wasting his health, your time, and my money, all to prove to some gold-plated pompous ass of a professor that you can sell more copies of a broadsheet than he can."

Patience liked that Mr. MacHugh would raise his voice when a point mattered to him. That was one of the revelations this holiday project had brought.

"Mr. MacHugh—Dougal—sit down, please. The professor and I often disagree about how a problem ought to be solved, but he's not pompous. He's erudite, compared to me. Far better read than I am, as is obvious from the literature he quotes. I'm better at Scripture, but that's because my mother inclined toward the Dissenters."

Mr. MacHugh didn't sit so much as he collapsed into his chair. "You defend Pennypacker now?"

Patience fished among the detritus on the table for her pencil. "The professor, as you've pointed out, has made me a significant sum of money, and you as well. I doubt he's a gold-plated anything. I know how hard we're working to get these columns. He has to be putting in comparable effort. Shall we order from the chophouse?"

"I don't want to order from the blasted chophouse."

Something was troubling Mr. MacHugh, which made no sense. He was never happier than when the business thrived and he could pit his wits against his competitors. The clerks and newsboys were in a fine humor of late, and the printer had sent around a basket of holiday fruit. Even King George seemed less cranky.

"You are worried this whole scheme will collapse," Patience said, thinking out loud. "You anticipate that because all is unfolding exactly according to your plan—you've increased the print run twice already—disaster will soon strike. This is the thinking of a jilted debutante, sir, and I'll thank you to put it behind you."

He ran his hand through his hair, then sat back in one of the poses Patience found most fetching. His ankle crossed over his knee, one arm hooked over the back of the chair. A gentleman would never sit thus before a lady, and a dandy's breeches would have been too tight to even attempt such a position.

"I'm a jilted debutante? Madam, were you up too late reading that drivel from Mrs. Wollstonecraft?"

Patience had devoured the entire treatise in a single sitting on Monday night.

"You can't bait me that easily, Mr. MacHugh. I'm speaking from experience. When I realized the viscount had been in love with my settlements, not me, I saw betrayal everywhere. If the coal man made a mistake on his bill, if the pastor failed to greet me personally on the church steps, I was certain they intended thievery and insult."

He sat forward and organized the loose papers into a stack, then swept the crumbs and trimmings into his palm. "How do you know the coal man wasn't trying to cheat you, or the pastor trying to cut his association with you?"

"The coal man had never cheated us previously, not in years of service. The pastor was a busy man. They hadn't changed, I had. You planned on modest success, you didn't plan on this scheme making you the talk of the town."

The orts and leavings from the table went into the dustbin. "I'm not a problem to be solved, Patience. What will you do about the lady who's overspent her holiday shopping budget?"

"Why won't you let me answer the woman whose husband is drinking away the rent money?"

He lifted the cat off the mantel and resettled in his chair. "I'm working on that one. Give me some time. You can't suborn petit treason and expect this publishing house to stand."

A week ago, Patience would have argued this issue too, but since then, she'd seen the publishing house from the inside. Most of the staff was young, just starting out, and if the business failed, they'd face a long, expensive journey home to Scotland. Some of them wouldn't have the means to make that journey.

Jake was the oldest of six, with another on the way. His

father was a groom at a coaching house, his mother took in mending.

Harry aspired to become a man of business.

Mr. Detwiler was old and slow and couldn't work the long hours the youngsters could, but he knew everything about London publishing and the English language.

"I'll give you a week to decide how I can help that woman, but she deserves an answer," Patience said, petting the cat. King George's purr was the small thunder of feline contentment, though more than she wanted to pet the cat, Patience wanted to touch Dougal.

Running a business was a burdensome ambition. What she'd realized in the past week was that she enjoyed seeing how Dougal met that burden. Instead of penning her columns in solitude on Tuesday and Thursday afternoons, the twelve-edition project meant she was at the publishing house daily, ruminating on columns by night and monitoring sales with an enthusiasm she hadn't previously.

Having a job could give the day purpose. Having people who shared that job meant forming bonds of a sort. Trade, in other words, could be exciting.

How the other debutantes who'd come out with Patience ten years ago would have swooned at such a notion.

"What are you planning now?" Mr. MacHugh asked. "You're absorbed with some thought."

"Do you know how boring it is to be wealthy?"

The cat extricated himself from Mr. MacHugh's arms and strolled across the table.

"I have no firsthand experience with the condition. My cousins are quite well-to-do, and they don't strike me as bored."

"They aren't pretty little debutantes whose signature accomplishments are parlor French, a sonata or two, and embroidery. How did I stand it, Dougal?"

Mrs. Wollstonecraft bore some of the blame for Patience's changed perspective, but so did the realization that Mrs. Horner mattered, she made a difference, not only to Patience's financial situation, but to others.

Did a waltzing debutante know what it was to *matter* in any regard except as breeding stock for some titled nincompoop? What could she look forward to, other than a remote sort of maternal involvement in the lives of children raised by nurses, governesses, and tutors?

"I'm guessing you dealt with your boredom by reading a great deal," Mr. MacHugh said. "I certainly did."

The cat flopped down among the papers, his front half covering the page of the dictionary beginning with *evince*. A companionable moment sprang up as Patience stroked George's furry head.

"I read my papa's entire library, several times over, and then we sold the bound books. Will you kiss me again, Mr. MacHugh?"

Patience hadn't intended to ask such a question—a proper lady wouldn't. But a woman who made her living with words, and presumed to solve problems for others, needn't be such a ninnyhammer.

"That kiss was by way of argument, Miss Friendly. Not well done of me."

"I thought it was very well done of you."

Mr. MacHugh was on his feet and shrugging into his greatcoat. "Back to the profligate holiday shopper with you, madam. I'm for the chophouse."

Patience scooped the cat into her arms. "Coward." What a delight to be so honest in her discourse with another, much less with a man whom she'd kissed. But how lowering too, that she couldn't tempt him to kiss her again.

"Not a coward, but a gentleman," Mr. MacHugh countered, "in my bumbling fashion. A gentleman making a tactical retreat. I don't regret kissing you, Patience, but you might one day soon regret kissing me. Shall I stop by the bakery?"

"No more sweets for me. I'll feast on the knowledge that we're outselling even your most optimistic projections. I'll also counsel the holiday shopper to forgive herself for yielding to generous impulses where friends and family are concerned."

Mr. MacHugh took his leave, though he forgot to don his scarf—a cheerful, bold green and blue plaid.

Patience put George on the mantel and tried to focus on crafting her reply to the shopper who'd disrespected the budget set by her husband. The reply was slow to come and required much revision, for Patience was preoccupied with a question.

Why on earth would she ever, ever regret sharing a wondrous kiss under the mistletoe with Dougal P. MacHugh?

* * *

"You sent Harry along home with your lady?" Detwiler asked, settling on the side of the table nearest the hearth. "Was that wise, Dougal? The boy's growing, true, but he's not much protection against thieves or pickpockets."

"There's still plenty of light," Dougal countered, except in his soul, night was falling. Patience wanted more kisses—a fine notion, but for the fact that Dougal wasn't the man she thought him to be. He was Professor Pennypacker, a braying, useless old nodcock who spouted platitudes and quotes and generally sounded like the retired schoolteacher he was.

"Dougal"—Detwiler glanced at the closed office door—"you have to tell her."

"I can't tell her now. She's enjoying herself too much."
As the week had progressed, Patience had thrown herself
into her work with an energy that put the youthful clerks
to shame. The entire office was more cheerful, more productive, and *better*. The lads competed to come up with
the cleverest holiday rhymes, Detwiler arrived on time most
mornings, and even George was friendlier.

Patience blossomed more gloriously with every hour she
spent at MacHugh and Sons, while Dougal watched the
earnings increase along with his sense of guilt.

"Did you notice Jake has started smiling?" Dougal murmured, propping his feet on a corner of the desk. "The boy
has a beautiful smile." And a smiling newsboy sold more
copies, earned more coin, and had more reason to smile.

Patience had done that, with her rhymes, her roving
newsboys, her clever wit on the page.

"Any boy enjoying a steady diet of holiday sweets has
cause to smile," Detwiler said, "while you have become
positively glum."

"I'm Scottish. I'm allowed to be glum."

"You're a Scotsman whose coin is multiplying," Detwiler
replied, shifting in his chair. "You enjoy good health, and
in Patience Friendly, you've found a gold mine. What's
more, she has a gold mine in you. Very few other publishers
would have seen her potential, Dougal, much less given her
a chance to shine like this. All over London, people are quoting Mrs. Horner and saving their broadsheets to pass on to
their friends and neighbors."

"They're quoting old Pennypacker too. That was the plan.
She'll hate me if I tell her now, Aloysius." Dougal nearly
hated himself.

"What's the worst that could happen? You have a rousing
spat, and then she sees what a fine scheme you've concocted.

She'll settle her feathers and come up with more ways to increase the readership. That woman respects coin of the realm. I suspect there's some Scots in her, a generation or three back."

Dougal rose, because he could not stand to be in his office another moment. A subterfuge was in progress on his premises, and every day that went by, the dishonesty he perpetrated bothered him more.

"Patience respects me," he said, getting into his coat. "I'd like to keep it that way."

"Where are you off to? I thought you wanted to discuss this letter from the gin widow?" Detwiler brandished a thin, much-folded piece of a paper.

Dougal studied the direction on the letter, jammed his hat on his head, and grabbed his scarf. "Before it starts to damned snow again, I'm going for a walk."

"Away with you, then, and George and I will manage the lads in your absence."

"Fire the professor, why don't you? He's a pontificating old bore who's served his purpose."

Detwiler snorted, and Dougal went on his way. The clerks were enjoying a heated argument about which of the nearby taverns had the best recipe for rum buns, and the printer's lad was helping himself to an apple from the basket in the window. From the street below, an impromptu glee club had borrowed some of Mrs. Horner's lyrics for a bit of holiday Handel, and brilliant afternoon sunshine poured in the windows.

All was merry and bright, and Dougal had never dreaded the yuletide season more.

* * *

"How do you endure this?" Patience muttered. "Detwiler claims to be ill, the dratted cat has shredded two days' worth of work, it's pouring ice outside, and nobody will buy anything until the weather improves."

"The lads go from pub to tavern to coaching inn, and they'll sell a fair amount, despite the weather," Mr. MacHugh said. "I can buy you some crumpets, if that will help."

The cat, who'd spent an evening scratching three of Patience's columns to bits, was draped like so much holiday greenery on the mantel.

"Throwing George out the window might help."

Mr. MacHugh went to the window and raised the sash. Bitter, coal-smoke air wafted in, though the cold at least revived Patience's flagging energy.

"Stop being literal, sir."

He lowered the sash. "I am a publisher. Of course I'll be literal. George would simply land on the roof of the awning, scramble down the trellis, and come in the back way. He's a Scottish cat and not as decorative as you might think."

George's owner was very decorative. Since kissing Mr. MacHugh more than a week ago, Patience had done little else but notice how thick his lashes were, how lovely his burr, and how the muscles of his forearms flexed when he sat at his desk and wrote. Before the clerks and the trades, he always had his coat on and his neckcloth neatly tied, but in the privacy of his office, he could be less proper.

He was kind to Detwiler, strict but fair with the boys, and scrupulously honest with the printers, authors, and merchants upon whom a publishing house depended.

"I thought a publisher was an idler," Patience said. "A man who sat about all day, smoking noisome cigars and joining gentleman's clubs."

One corner of Mr. MacHugh's mouth quirked up. "Like a debutante tatting lace? Virtually indolent, but for some light reading?"

"I imagined you could engage in political discourse, which a debutante would never do. Be glad you weren't consigned to studying fashion plates by the hour, or memorizing Debrett's."

What bleak years those had been, what meaningless, empty years. This past week had given Patience the words to describe those years. For nearly a decade, she'd thought the problem had been her failure to secure a husband. The problem was that finding a husband was all young ladies from good families were allowed to do.

"Temperature's dropping," Mr. MacHugh said. "We should get you home, Miss Friendly."

The sky had been delivering a combination of rain, ice, sleet, and snow all day. Ice clicked against the window, though sunset was still a good two hours off.

"If I go home, I'll be behind. The professor will have the street corners to himself come Thursday, and I cannot possibly allow him to have the last word."

Christmas fell on Saturday, and Patience had already decided to spend the entire day in bed, swilling tea, and not eating crumpets, or tarts, or stollen. With fresh, free sweets available in quantity, Patience had lost her taste for them. She still sent the boys out for parcels from the bakery, but her consumption was more for form's sake than out of any craving.

She did fancy another kiss with Mr. MacHugh though.

"So let the professor have Thursday," Mr. MacHugh said, "and you can put out your final column on Christmas Eve. It's not the Sabbath, and people will be on the streets visiting back and forth and calling on family."

Patience rose because her back ached. Her eyes ached, and her head ached, but she had three columns to replace before she'd quit the premises.

Her conscience ached too, truth be told.

"I like that—having the last word," she said. "I'll recreate my three columns and then I'll go. If you need me after today, send Harry 'round to fetch me. You never did let me offer that gin widow any advice."

And Dougal MacHugh would not have lost track of the letter. He was relentless about details, and that letter was not a detail.

"I'm off to fetch a cab for Detwiler," he said. "If that old man walks home in this mess, Cousin Avery will report me to the authorities for disrespecting my elders."

Mr. MacHugh departed, and the silence in his wake was bewildering. He no longer argued with Patience, didn't contradict her, didn't instruct her on the finer points of managing a competitive enterprise. She caught him watching her, peering at her over his glasses, leaning against the doorway of the office when she looked up from her writing.

By the time he came back—soaked to the skin—Patience was busily rewriting one of the columns George had destroyed. Mr. MacHugh shook out his greatcoat, droplets of melting snow dotting the floorboards.

One of them hit her on the cheek. She swiped it away and got back to work.

"Patience, the weather is truly foul. Let me get you a cab."

"I have one more column to go. The rain will let up, and then you won't need to call me a cab."

"It's not raining now. It's snowing like it means business."

"Ah! I need another word for business."

A great sigh gusted from across the room. "Commerce, enterprise, trade, mercantile endeavor."

Patience considered the walking thesaurus grousing at her from across the room. "I like that last one, mercantile endeavor. I have a question, though, about your own mercantile endeavor. Why name it MacHugh and Sons? You're not a fundamentally dishonest person, but you are in want of progeny."

He shook his scarf out next. Some of the shower hit the cat on the mantel. George woke up, glowered at his owner, then went back to napping.

"MacHugh and Sons is poetic license," Mr. MacHugh said. "If I make a go of this place, then I'll be free to marry, and the sons might well follow. One wants to sound successful while one is trying to be successful."

Patience sprinkled sand on the page she'd completed. "Just as I'm Mrs. Horner, a staid, respectable matron with years of domestic experience. Do you suppose Pennypacker is a professor?"

Every time she brought up the professor, Mr. MacHugh's eyes went bleak. "He knows his books. He's no match for you when it comes to domestic issues. I'm for some tea. Would you like a cup?"

She rose and came around the desk. "You haven't been getting enough rest. Is that why you're so surly lately?"

"I'm no' surly."

Mr. MacHugh's hair had a tendency to curl when damp, and it was a touch longish at the back. Patience liked it longish. She liked *him*, and she did not like that he was troubled when, for the most part, all was going well. Rather than kiss him, she slid her arms about his waist and leaned close.

"Patience, you mustn't..."

"This is a hug. H-u-g. Detwiler says we don't know

where the word comes from, but Shakespeare used it, so it has to be good old English. You mustn't worry, Dougal. Your plan is going brilliantly, and all will be well. Do you miss Scotland?"

Patience had missed *this*, the feel of him close and solid in her arms, the rhythm of his heart beneath her ear, the fragrance of his heathery soap blending with the ink-and-starch scent of a publisher at his trade.

"I'll miss you, lass." His arms came around her on that cryptic admission, and for a long moment, Patience remained in his embrace. To be held like this was fortifying, a boon most couples probably took for granted after the first few weeks of courting.

And yet, holding Dougal was frustrating too. He made no move to kiss her and no move to leave her embrace.

Was he humoring her? On that horrifying thought, Patience drew back. "Fetch your tea, and I'll finish up these last paragraphs. I won't know what to do with myself, now that—what day is this?"

Now he smiled. An indulgent, understanding smile. "Tuesday, December 21, in the year of our Lord, eighteen hundred and—"

"I forgot *baking* day. I've made nothing to contribute to baking day and I can't arrive empty-handed. The Windham ladies will be wroth with me."

"Heaven forbid you lost track of baking day. Shall I send Harry off with a note conveying your apologies?"

Beyond the window, a proper snow squall was in progress. "Not in this weather. I'll send an apology tomorrow."

He kissed her forehead. "Don't fret. At the pace you've been working, it's not unusual to become absorbed in the task. The instant you're finished with your last column, I'm walking you home."

And then he was gone, yelling for Harry to shovel the walkway and steps, lest the lord mayor of London fall on his bum and on their very doorstep.

"I like working here," Patience informed the cat. "I like working here all too well, and Mr. MacHugh kissed me. Not much of a kiss, but something. How am I supposed to concentrate after that?"

George yawned, stretched, flicked his tail a few times, and commenced washing his paws.

CHAPTER FIVE

If one thing held Patience Friendly back as an author, it was self-doubt. She quibbled over words, commas, responses, and revisions. Some of that dithering was the writer's delight in every detail of her craft, but much of it was what happened when nobody appreciated a natural talent, obvious though that talent might be.

"Have I ever thanked you for how much you encourage Harry and the other lads?" Dougal asked as Detwiler bundled into a coat.

"I'm the editor," Detwiler said. "My job is to correct, improve, and admire. The boys are loyal to MacHugh's, and they are a bright lot."

Unlike the publisher. The words hung in the air as Detwiler went about putting the quill pens in order.

"Be off with you, Aloysius. The cab is waiting at the door." Dougal slid into the seat behind Detwiler's desk, opened a drawer, and withdrew the professor's final two columns.

At the top of the first page, the overspending housewife—a newlywed in this version of the letter—silently reproached him.

"You tell that poor woman to throw herself on her husband's mercy," Detwiler said, tossing a scarf around his neck. "But when it comes to confessing your own transgressions, you're not half so forthcoming, *professor*."

"You have the correcting part off by heart, old man. The cab driver's horse is standing out in this weather while you sermonize at me."

"I do admire you, Dougal, and I fancy Miss Friendly does too. Start there—with all that mutual admiration—and the transgressing takes on a different perspective. If a housewife can admit she's bought a few too many holiday tokens for her loved ones, can't you admit that your ambitions for a talented author got away from you?"

Dougal's ambitions for Patience hadn't merely got away from him. They'd gone completely to Bedlam.

"That's the problem," Dougal said, staring at the words marching across the page. Schoolteacher words, very articulate, but lacking the warmth Patience brought to her advice. "Patience will think all I admire is her writing ability. She'll think I've engaged her affections merely to use her talent for my own ends."

Detwiler jammed a newsboy's cap on his head. "You are thinking too hard, being too much the academic fellow and not enough the callow swain. There's a flask in the bottom drawer. May it bring you the comfort and joy my common sense cannot."

A gust of cold air wafted in as Detwiler shuffled through the door.

Somewhere in Detwiler's haranguing, Dougal sensed a kernel of wisdom.

A schoolteacher learned the value of judiciously praising ability and honest effort. He also saw the nearly irreparable harm done when both were ignored for too long. How was a woman to have confidence in her abilities when for her entire upbringing she was trained not to bring notice to herself?

Dougal hurt for Patience and promised himself he'd remedy the harm done to her self-confidence, assuming she spoke to him, wrote for his publications, and gave him the time of day once she learned that the entire Christmas project had been based on a lie.

He read over his columns one last time and put them back in the drawer, then put his feet up on the corner of the desk and indulged in a pastime from his youth: reading the dictionary. For each letter, he read the entry for the first word his gaze landed on.

Admire. Patience was a gifted author, and she had a keen instinct for the publishing business. Dougal admired that about her.

Besotted. Dougal was, in fact, besotted with her energy, her intellect, her kisses, and her determination. She'd made the best of a trying situation, when she might have thrown herself on the charity of distant family, or accepted the proposal of any doddering opportunist who came along.

That thought gave him a very bad moment, indeed.

Callow. Patience would have no interest in the attentions of a naïve, unfledged boy. She deserved a man who'd stand toe-to-toe with her, give as good as he got, and yet, grasp that fostering her confidence would be a delicate undertaking.

Dougal had made it past o-is-for-obligation and onto

p-is-for-passion, when a signal truth beamed up at him from the pages of the lexicon.

He owed Patience Friendly for giving him the foundation upon which he could grow his business.

He also loved her.

The realization put something fundamentally right with him, because love was the word that encompassed all he felt for Patience. Affection, desire, respect, protectiveness, friendship, all tied up with a bow defined as *love*.

And with that realization, he grasped as well how to unravel the problem he'd created with the fictional Professor Pennypacker.

For Christmas, Dougal would offer Patience all that had been tendered to her previously—a future, a husband, a lover, security, a family of her own. At some point, years and several babies hence, Dougal would find a casual, merry moment over breakfast and mention that he might have penned a column or two as Professor Pennypacker.

Patience would be surprised and amused, and tell him she'd speculated as much—might he please pass the teapot?—and they'd share a laugh as they recalled how well the whole plan had worked.

Dougal continued to leaf through the dictionary, pleased with the reply he'd fashioned to the conundrum of his situation with Patience. He didn't read any more words, he simply enjoyed the feel of the lexicon in his hands, the sound of each page turning.

Marriage. Good old, traditional, happily-ever-after marriage. The notion, worthy of the learned Pennypacker himself, left Dougal feeling so rosy and replete, he started humming Christmas carols.

* * *

A rough, warm sensation against Patience's wrist woke her.

"George."

The cat paused in his licking, squinted, then resumed taking liberties with Patience's person. In the darkness, the beast's eyes glowed like nacre, giving him a predatory beauty he lacked when lounging above the hearth.

The fire had burned down to little more than coals, and outside, all was darkness.

"Oh dear. I suppose I must thank you. The columns are complete." Very good columns they were too. Patience put them in Dougal's top drawer, King George having proven himself a menace to paper, if not to mice.

The next challenge was extricating herself from Dougal's chair. Her back protested, her feet were cold, and her eyes gritty. She detected neither light nor sound from beyond the office door. Dougal would never have left her alone on the premises, and yet, business hours had apparently ended.

Patience lit a carrying candle and went to the clerk's office. The air was noticeably cooler, and because the heat source was a parlor stove, the room was without illumination other than her candle. Dougal sat at Detwiler's desk, his feet propped on one corner, a book open in his lap. His arms were folded, and his chin rested on his chest.

"Oh, you poor dear." Patience took a moment to memorize the sight of him, the ambitious publisher asleep amid the trappings of his empire. His weapons were the quill pens and foolscap neatly stacked on each clerk's high table, his mission to relieve ignorance and boredom at a reasonable price.

She gently lifted the book from his lap—a dictionary, of course—and then unhooked his spectacles from his ears.

As a younger woman, she would have pitied the lady whose lot was to be courted by a man in trade. A merchant or professional was all very well for those born to that strata, her papa had claimed, but better families could look higher.

"What higher purpose is there," she murmured, "than to enlighten and enliven the lives of those who do the actual work in this life?"

Dougal's eyes opened. "Is that a quote?"

Patience handed him his spectacles. "We can make it the MacHugh and Sons business motto." His gaze was tired—this project had demanded quite a bit from him too—but even weary, he was attractive.

He sat up and rubbed his eyes, then put his glasses back on. "Patience, why didn't you wake me? It's dark out."

"I fell asleep too. George woke me, probably to tend his personal fire. Are we alone here, Dougal?"

He rose and stretched, hands braced on his lower back. "But for George, I suppose we are." He flipped open a pocket watch, the gold case gleaming by the light of the single candle. "God in heaven, Patience, it's nearly nine o'clock."

Patience rummaged around in her emotions for dismay, alarm, some vestige of the young lady's fear of ruin, and found only anticipation. Ruin lay ten years in her past, but to be alone with Dougal at such an hour inspired all manner of fancies.

He was at the window, scowling down at the street. "There's two feet of snow on the ground and more coming down. It will take ages to get you home in this mess."

"Dougal, don't be daft. Nobody has shoveled the walkways at this hour, and the only people abroad are those preying on the unwary. I wouldn't let you walk me home tonight for all the crumpets in London."

"You've grown bored with crumpets," he said, letting the curtain drop. "This is not a good situation, Patience. If anybody learns that we've been alone for this long, under these conditions, your good name is compromised beyond recall, and so is mine."

"Your safety matters more to me than my good name, Dougal, and so does my own welfare."

She expected him to argue, and looked forward to it, in fact. Lately Dougal had passed up every opportunity for confrontation, and she'd missed his logic and his unshakable confidence in his own perspective. He was a worthy opponent and thus a worthy ally.

"Your safety matters to me more than my own," he countered. "I haven't seen a storm like this since coming to London. After this much snow, the temperature can plunge drastically. The Thames will likely be frozen by morning, or very nearly."

While Patience's heart was melting. Tired, worried, and rumpled, Dougal was ten times the man the viscount had ever aspired to be. Happy Christmas, Happy New Year, happy rest of her life.

"You're often the last one here at night, aren't you, Dougal?"

"Aye. I own the place. If it fails, I own that too. Are you hungry?"

Starving. "A bit, also chilly. I should keep a shawl here."

He looked at her, a direct, considering gaze, the first in many days. "I can get you warm. Let me see to the fire in the office, and we'll assess our situation over a pot of tea."

"For a cup of strong, hot tea, I would write you an entire column at no charge, Mr. MacHugh."

"You've grown light-headed with fatigue," he said, moving into his office. "Don't jest about giving your work away, Patience. When your labor is your sole means of earning coin, then nobody should expect you to part with it in the absence of compensation."

"Are you sure you were a schoolteacher, Dougal? You sound like a preacher."

He stopped before the hearth. "You are very calm for a woman who's in the process of being compromised. This situation is serious, Patience."

Patience went up on her toes and kissed him. Not a buss to the cheek, but not a declaration of unending passion either. He had a point: Her words were valuable.

So were her affections.

"When the viscount tossed me aside, my name went into the ditch along with my prospects. I don't know if he saw to that, or if polite society—notice nobody refers to them as compassionate, kind, or tolerant society—did me that favor. My true friends stood by me, Dougal, and they won't quibble because I had the sense to stay out of a dangerous storm."

"The lads won't breathe a word," Dougal said, tucking a lock of Patience's hair behind her ear. "Detwiler's discretion is absolute. I only wish…"

In all of Patience's dealings with Dougal MacHugh, she'd never heard him use the verb *wish*. "What do you wish, Dougal? My last columns are complete. Your project has earned MacHugh's the notice of half of London, and the new year promises success to us both. I wish you'd thought to pit me against Pennypacker like this two years ago."

He took her hand and led her to the sofa. "The time wasn't right. You were still finding your balance, and there wasn't a Pennypacker to pit you against."

They sat side by side, and Dougal kept her hand in both of his. The moment might have been awkward—last week's kiss was but a memory, and Dougal had been anything but amorous since—and yet, Patience was at peace.

Hard work had won her a measure of security, and though her feelings might not be requited, she'd found a man she could esteem greatly. Dougal was capable of desiring her, for all he seemed reticent to take any further liberties, and that reassured the part of her rejected so long ago.

The problem wasn't her—the problem had never been her.

"Patience, I account myself an articulate man, but some words elude capture when I need them most. You know I respect you."

What was this? "You argue with me." Nobody else did. Nobody else took her opinions seriously enough to differ with her.

"Arguing with you is a certain sign of my esteem. I think you enjoyed our kiss under the mistletoe."

"I can barely recall our kiss under the mistletoe, Mr. MacHugh, and you've shown no inclination to refresh my memory."

He kissed her knuckles. "I'm glad you're making me work for this. The prize is worth every effort."

"I'm not a prize. I'm a talented writer who has a lot to offer her readers, and—" Patience heard the battle cry in her words, heard how easily she'd taken up the cudgels, even in the absence of any threat. "Dougal, what are you trying to say?"

"I'm bungling this. I'd planned to wait, to see how the finances for the year closed, to have more to offer you, so I could take the next steps when it was prudent to do so, but circumstances have changed, and—"

He slid off the sofa, down to one knee. "Patience Friendly, will you do me the great honor of becoming my wife?"

Gracious heavens. Perhaps fatigue had made him light-headed. "Dougal, get up. You'll get cat hair on your trousers."

He resumed his place beside her, keeping her hand in his all the while. "Is that a yes?"

Douglas was proposing—proposing *marriage* to her. As
the wind howled outside, and the fire danced in the chimney
drafts, Patience savored the moment, and the clasp of Dougal's hand. This was how a proposal ought to be offered,
clearly, calmly, *sincerely*. Bless Dougal forever, because
he'd thrown into high relief the disrespect done Patience by
her titled former suitor.

She wanted to say yes, to Dougal, to a future that included love and meaningful work both, to a busy life far
from what she'd been raised to expect. The thought that
stopped her from giving him the response he sought was: *If
I marry, I lose my house.*

Her grandmama's legacy, all that had preserved Patience
from a dreadful marriage or a life of drudgery. If Patience
married, that house became her husband's. If she married,
she gave up even the right to spend her own wages. If
she married...if she became Mrs. Horner in truth, then she
ceased to be Patience Friendly in any meaningful sense.

"I've surprised you," Dougal said.

Ambushed her, more like. She should have known that
his brooding looks and odd distance were symptoms of a
scheme afoot.

"I care for you, Dougal P. MacHugh. So much. I hope
that's not a surprise, but I don't even know where you live.
I've never met your family, and two weeks ago..."

"Come," he said, rising and bringing Patience to her
feet. "I can show you where I live, and we can talk about
the rest."

He grabbed the candle and led her to a door that Patience
had assumed was a closet. A stairwell rose up into darkness,
the air frigid.

"It's not much," he said, "but it's mine and quite conve-
nient."

A merchant family often lived above or behind the shop. Why shouldn't Dougal do likewise? His apartment was at the top of the stairs, his sitting room cozy, much like the one Patience had inherited. A velvet sofa sat before a brick hearth. A dry sink held china and glassware—also a pair of decanters.

"I didn't realize you had quarters up here."

"This apartment is part of the reason I bought the place," Dougal said, kneeling before the cold hearth. "Starting a business calls for long hours, and the less time spent gadding about the streets, the more time spent on productive labor."

The distinguishing feature of the room was the number of books. Shelves along one wall included classics, novels, atlases, histories, poetry, and herbals.

"You do love to read," Patience said as Dougal coaxed a fire to life. "You speak French?"

"I was a schoolteacher. Once you have the Latin, you've a toehold on French, Italian, Spanish, Portuguese, and Greek. I like the look of you here, Patience, among my books and treasures."

No longer Miss Friendly. "Show me the rest."

He dusted his hands, replaced the fireplace screen, and bowed her through the door into the second room.

A sanctum sanctorum. In the corner stood a very large bed—neatly made, a blue and white patchwork quilt over the whole. More books graced another set of shelves, and a large desk occupied the corner nearest the windows. The table beside the bed held three books, one of them open, and on the desk the standish, stack of foolscap, and blotter sat in the same arrangement as on the desk one floor below.

A faded carpet of cabbage roses covered the floor, and a pair of large, worn slippers were positioned by the bed.

Those slippers would be exquisitely comfortable.

Patience peered behind the privacy screen and confirmed that Dougal was a tidy man, even in his private quarters. His wardrobe was similarly arranged, everything in order.

He wouldn't expect her to pick up after him, and he'd set that example for their children.

That mattered, but still, Patience could not find the words to tell Dougal she'd marry him. She'd said yes once before—clearly, unequivocally—and hadn't ended up married.

Perhaps instead of words, deeds might do.

She crossed the room and stood before Dougal. "I care for you a very great deal, Dougal P. MacHugh, publisher. I esteem you greatly, and circumstances have conspired to give me an opportunity to esteem you intimately as well. Take me to bed, Dougal."

His brows rose, suggesting she'd surprised him, and then he raised her hands and kissed them, one after the other.

"Are ye sure, lass?"

"I'm sure," Patience said, stepping into his embrace. Mrs. Horner and the professor would be scandalized, the Windham sisters might not understand, and Patience wasn't entirely sure of her own motives, but she knew exactly where she wanted to spend the night, and with whom.

* * *

The part of Dougal that reveled in words worried that Patience hadn't explicitly said yes to his proposal. Perhaps he should have asked permission to court her, which was how the Quality went about an engagement, except he wasn't a true gentleman, in the strict definition of the term.

And yet, Patience was kissing him as if he were the crown prince of her every dream.

Dougal kissed her back, because she *was* the crown princess of his every dream, also the queen of his mercantile ambitions and the empress of his good fortune.

Patience shivered, and Dougal recalled that his bedroom was damned near freezing. "Come with me," he said, leading her into the front room. "Swing the kettle over the fire, and I'll get a blaze going in the bedroom. There's bread, cheese, and apples in the window box. I'll be but a moment."

He needed that moment to regain his self-possession, then gave up the exercise for hopeless when all he could think of was Patience warming up the bed with him. He turned down the covers, traded boots for slippers, made sure the fire was off to a good start, then prepared to persuade a lady to accept his proposal.

Patience sat on the sofa, staring into the fire. "There's much I don't know about you," she said. "How old are you?"

Dougal took the place beside her. "I'll be thirty-two on St. David's Day. What else do you want to know?"

"You don't care how old I am?"

"You've reached the age of consent. A few years one way or the other aren't relevant. I would like to know what day you were born."

She drew her feet up under her skirts. "The viscount valued my youth."

Him again. "The viscount was a shallow, greedy, arrogant young fool. Cuddle up, Patience."

The dubious glance she shot him confirmed that in addition to many other failings, the viscount hadn't bothered to share simple affection with the woman he'd proposed to. Dougal hefted Patience into his lap and drew his grandmother's quilt around her.

"Like so," he said. "Cozy and friendly. Ask me more questions."

"When will you take me to bed?"

"Your enthusiasm for this venture warms my heart, Patience. May I remind you, you haven't eaten since noon. If we're to put that bed to its best use, you'll need your strength."

She straightened enough to peer at him. "You'll need yours too."

"I live in that hope." Dougal also hoped he'd be able to restrain his passion enough to please his lady, and he further hoped the snow didn't let up for a few days, because recovering from his good fortune might take that long.

"Tell me about your family, Dougal."

Over tea, cheese toast, and sliced apples, he obliged as Patience pulled pins from her hair. MacHugh the saddlemaker was his cousin, as was MacHugh the stationer. MacHugh the fishmonger wasn't related as far as they could tell, but the trail was promising, three generations back on the Irish side.

Cousins Hamish, Rhona, Colin, and Edana might visit London in the spring, though Hamish had no use for city life. Dougal's younger sister Bridget was walking out with the blacksmith's son.

"So many people," Patience said around a yawn. "Do you suppose the bedroom has warmed up?"

"Aye. I do admire your ability to focus on a topic, Miss Friendly."

She was back in Dougal's lap, a warm, lovely weight of female cuddled in his arms. She'd put away a good quantity of food, while the wind had rattled the windows and spindrifts of snow had whirled from the rooftop.

"I like this," she said. "I like that you're affectionate. I suspect I am too."

Please, may it be so. "Let's find out, shall we?"

Dougal rose with Patience in his arms and carried her to

the bed. For all that she'd asked after his relations, his education, his favorite books, and whether he knew how to ride a horse, she still hadn't officially, entirely, unequivocally accepted his proposal.

He settled her on the bed and closed the door, the better to keep in the heat. "Do you need help with your hooks and stays and whatnot?"

"Hooks, yes, but I favor jumps," she said, pushing off the bed and giving him her back. "I have experience, you know. The viscount saw to that."

She swept her braid away from her nape and stood before Dougal, her back to him, a tender, private part of her exposed for the most mundane reasons.

"You must not tell me the viscount's name," Dougal said, starting on the three thousand hooks marching down the center of her back. "Not ever."

"You can't call him out. He's a titled gentleman, and he'd decline to meet you, owing to the differences in your stations. That tickles."

"I'm not about to give some useless prat of a title a chance to injure me," Dougal said, "but between the MacHughs, the MacQuistons—my mother was a MacQuiston—the MacDuffs, and the MacPhersons, all of whom I claim as relations, the viscount's every debt, inane blunder, stupid wager, or expensive mistress would soon become common knowledge if you tell me his name. My competitors would pay dearly to publish that sort of tattle."

Patience peered at Dougal over her shoulder. "You don't publish tattlers. Why not?"

"It's not my calling. How do you ever get dressed in the morning?"

"My housekeeper assists me, and not all my dresses are this impractical."

Her chemise was a surprisingly frothy, frilly affair peeking up over her jumps. Dougal was not a connoisseur of lady's underlinen, but he wanted to see Patience some fine day wearing only that chemise and a smile.

Though stockings might be a nice touch too. White silk with red garters.

"All done," he said, wrapping his arms around her waist. "I haven't a sheath, Patience. Do you know what that means?"

He felt the heat of a blush rise over her skin. "It means the apothecary on the corner is a gossip, among other things. Can't you...wait?"

Dougal kissed her nape. "Withdraw, you mean?"

"Is that the term for when you don't spend?"

Her blush would have scorched the entire West End. "*Coitus interruptus* gets the notion across as well. The idea is to prevent conception. I'll withdraw."

He paused between kisses in case she had any other comments, questions, or pithy observations to offer, but the lady had gone quiet. Dougal acquainted his lips with the soft skin below her ear and the pulse beating beneath that.

The simple act of kissing her neck had him aroused. He slid a hand down over her derriere and gave her a gentle shove in the direction of the privacy screen.

"Use my tooth powder, and I'll heat you some wash water."

Patience moved off to the privacy screen on a soft rustle of fabric, her braid swinging gently above her fundament.

Dougal went into the front room, opened a window, and breathed in a half-dozen lungfuls of frigid air. He was considering whether arctic air wafting over his open falls might aid his flagging self-restraint when *God Rest Ye Merry, Gentlemen* floated from the bedroom on a soft hum.

He warmed an ewer of water from the steaming kettle on the pot swing, sent up a prayer for fortitude, then brought Patience her wash water.

"Will you undress, Dougal?" she called from behind the screen.

He passed her his nightshirt over the top of the screen. "In a moment." *Will you become my wife?*

Tonight, he would become her lover. For now, that was Christmas gift enough. By morning, he had every intention of becoming her fiancé.

Though for that to happen, she'd have to say yes to his proposal, wouldn't she?

CHAPTER SIX

Late on a bitter winter evening, Patience delighted in her own personal springtime. The soft breeze of Dougal's breath at her nape had been her only warning that a man could kiss a lady in places every bit as interesting as her mouth. The sensations that followed had been sweet, surprising, lovely, and so...

Words failed. Patience suspected they'd fail frequently when it came to Dougal P. MacHugh's lovemaking. His nightshirt bore the scents of heather and lavender, his blue and white quilt put her in mind of the sky on a fine May morning.

He came around the privacy screen, his manly wares on display from the waist up.

Gracious, everlasting angels. "What was the point of combing your hair, Dougal?" She would delight in mussing it up for him.

"To be presentable for my lady. My nightshirt has never

looked so fetching. I haven't a warmer to run over the sheets."

Patience had cuddled in Dougal's lap for the better part of an hour, and nothing—nothing at all—compared to the snug, cozy intimacy of his embrace.

"I suspect a warmer won't be necessary."

"I wish I had one, though," he said, starting on the buttons of his falls. "Seemed like an extravagance for a bachelor. For you, I want only warm sheets, fresh sachets, and a steaming pot of chocolate in the morning."

He might have been reciting the legend of Beowulf for all Patience could heed his words. The tone, though—the intimate, casual tone—did odd things to her insides. The placket of his falls draped open, and he stepped out of his remaining clothing all at once.

He folded his breeches over the privacy screen, giving Patience a good view of his backside.

"I've seen statues," she said. "The Elgin Marbles, for example."

Dougal, as naked as God made him, banked the fire. "Are you a connoisseur of ancient sculpture, then?"

Patience's breath had developed a hitch to go with the peculiar leaping about of her heart. "I have a lively sense of curiosity, which I suspect you are generously obliging."

The viscount certainly hadn't. He'd fussed about under her skirts, told her to close her eyes, and then commenced slobbering, poking, and muttering mangled French allusions to flowers and honeybees.

"I am a great believer in the power of knowledge," Dougal said, hanging the cast-iron poker on the hearth stand and facing Patience. "I also favor deliberation over a heedless rush."

Patience had lost the ability to fix her gaze where a lady should. She'd apparently acquired the eyes of a lover, because every inch of Dougal fascinated her. His arms, his knees, the distribution of hair over his chest, and...elsewhere.

"That ancient sculptor would have needed a deal more clay if you'd been his model."

Dougal scratched his chest and yawned, looking magnificently male and oh so gloriously comfortable with it. "I beg your pardon?"

"If you were one of those Greek fellows, in the museum. The sculptor would need...perhaps the Greeks were a diminutive lot. I'm babbling. Are you giving me time to change my mind?"

Had Patience been cold earlier? The sight of Dougal in his natural glory pooled heat low in her belly.

He stepped closer. "You can change your mind, Patience. If you ask me to share that bed with you and not touch you the whole night through, I'll do it. Don't adhere to an earlier decision out of stubbornness, pride, or some notion that Mrs. Wollstonecraft would approve. Become intimate with me solely because you want to."

Dougal's regard was the least lover-like expression Patience had ever seen on a man. He was serious, almost somber.

"You could share a bed with me, having proposed marriage to me, and simply roll over and drop off to sleep?" She didn't like that idea at all. Her fists were clenched with the effort to not touch him, to not lean in and taste him, not feel him body to body.

"I'd be daft by morning," he said, threading a hand beneath Patience's braid. "You might find me lying in the snow stark naked on the roof of the awning, only George to guard my carcass, but if you tell me to keep my hands to myself, I will."

"I'd rather you made the effort to warm up the bed with me."

He swept Patience up against his chest and deposited her on the bed, then came down over her.

"Do you have any questions, Patience?"

She loved Dougal for that. For making one last gesture as the man who believed in knowledge, the lover who was determined her role would not be passive.

"When can I take off this nightshirt?"

He shifted to the mattress beside her and pulled the covers up over them. "When the sheets aren't as cold as the rooftop, I'll be more than happy to assist you with that nightshirt."

"You are so warm." Warm like sunshine on daffodils, like a soft breeze on green fields.

To see Dougal behind his desk, polishing his spectacles, working at his ledgers, or reading the broadsheets put out by his competitors, Patience would not have suspected him of warmth.

But when he left the last of his crumpet for Harry, petted the lazy old cat, or strutted about his quarters in the altogether for Patience's benefit, she saw a generosity of spirit that kindled both tenderness and desire.

"I'm having my cousins knit you some proper stockings," Dougal said, working an arm beneath Patience's neck. "Your feet are...they wake a man up."

"Sorry."

He cuddled her close. "I wouldn't change a thing about you, Patience. If you've cold feet, I'll warm those up too."

Too? Well, yes too. Dougal rolled to his side and recommenced the kissing at a lazy, daundering pace. At first Patience tried to hurry him, to urge him on. She went so far as to put his hand on her breast—surely that was part of it?—but Dougal made no move to...*move*.

"I think the sheets are quite comfortable now," Patience said as Dougal traced her eyebrows with his nose.

"I think you are in much too big a hurry. We haven't a deadline here, my love. If, for example, you wanted to touch me—my chest, say—you have as much time to do that as you like."

My love. What a delightful pair of words. "Touch... your...chest."

The sheets were toasty by the time Patience realized that Dougal had presented himself as an assortment of sweets. She could select the curious textures of his chest—springy hair, odd little nipples, solid muscle, and a steady heartbeat—or she might prefer the satisfaction of sinking her fingers into the silky abundance of his hair and clutching tightly, the better to delight in his kisses.

Or those kisses might be her choice—soft, tender, passionate, playful. Dougal's kisses were like spices wafting from a busy kitchen. Tantalizing, heady, exotic.

So much he offered her, and so generously.

This is how lovemaking is supposed to be. In the midst of this abundance, Patience felt both anger and sorrow for the young woman who'd been willing to settle for a mere prancing title.

"They lie to us," she whispered. "The parents, governesses, and dancing masters. They lie, Dougal. And thus we lie to ourselves, until the truth is so obscured, a young woman dares not recognize it."

Dougal shifted over her. "My feelings for you are honest, Patience. I love you. All that I am, all that I have will be yours forevermore."

She kissed him, for having listened to her, for the very deliberation that had so frustrated her earlier.

"If you don't get me out of this blasted nightshirt, Dougal, I will—"

He sat back, a rearing lion of a healthy male. "Sit up, then, lass."

Patience wiggled to her elbows, and there was an awkward moment when her breasts were first bared to her lover. The awkward moment didn't last, because she was too busy studying the part of Dougal that would now require *far* more clay than those puny Greeks in the museum had.

"Touch me," Dougal said. "I adore your curious mind."

They touched each other. Patience learned the contours and textures of the aroused male, and Dougal obliged her with all manner of caresses and kisses to her breasts. She also learned that lovemaking could happen in a variety of positions—Dougal claimed most of his knowledge was theoretical, which diplomatic untruth she allowed him.

No man who brought a lady this much pleasure was working entirely from theory.

And Patience was through with testing theories anyway.

"Enough talk," she panted, for Dougal's attentions to her breasts left her breathless. "Enough Latin, cant, and anatomy. Are you laughing at me?"

"I'm delighting," Dougal replied, bracing himself on his arms above her. "It's no' the same thing a'tall."

His burr grew thicker, along with other parts of him. Patience positively reveled in that knowledge.

"Make love with me, Dougal. There's a deadline now. A tight, pressing deadline."

"Never that," he said, hitching closer. "This is the easy

part, Patience. We take all the time we please, maybe even have a wee discussion as we go."

"This is not an editorial meeting, Dougal, in the name of all that is—oh, that's lo-ve-ly."

A woman who made her living with words did not speak in syllables, but as Dougal joined with Patience, she lost even that ability. Sighs were all she had left, along with soft moans, kisses, and all manner of caresses.

The sensation as Dougal joined with her was one of fullness, of intimacy so overwhelming and right, Patience gave up trying to label it and surrendered to the glory of being an adult female at her pleasures. Dougal's stubborn unwillingness to hurry became a determination to cherish, and how Patience treasured him for that.

"Patience, stop thinking. Feel the rhythm, *be with me.*"

Dougal punctuated his words with a particular emphasis to his thrusts, and celestial choirs could not have distracted Patience from the resulting sensation. She met him the next time, went seeking that same exclamation point of arousal, and found it.

Again, and again, and again, until she was the one creating the rhythm, and all she knew was that to find where it led, she must be closer to Dougal.

Pleasure coalesced where they joined, a bright, astounding, precious sunburst. Dougal didn't leave her hovering in view of the beautiful vista either. He stayed with her, knowing somehow exactly how to make the joy last, how to be both the breeze that held her aloft and the connection that let her fly free.

A sense of vindication gilded Patience's repletion when the soaring moments settled gently back to reality. She'd guessed that lovemaking should have been much more than she'd been allowed to know. The viscount had betrayed her in many ways, but the self-doubt he'd created was at last allowed to die.

He'd been like those statues in the museum. Not enough clay, no real life, no individual features, so thoroughly had privilege and arrogance worn away his humanity.

This lovemaking with Dougal was real.

This was love.

Dougal slowly withdrew, and as Patience held him close, he spent where it would cause no risk of a child. He was being responsible, and yet, a part of Patience resented his self-possession. She wanted the limitless passion for him too. Wanted to be the tether that kept him safe while he soared, whether his passion was conjugal, commercial, or—she suspected he was a fine writer himself—creative.

And she could be that for him. She absolutely could be.

He lifted away from her some moments later. "I've made a wee mess."

"I like it," Patience said. "It's a lover's mess. It's what consideration and keeping your word feel like and smell like." Not exactly a fragrance, but to Patience, it was the scent of knowledge.

"God, you are ferocious." Dougal kissed her nose and retrieved a handkerchief from the nightstand. The tidying up was the work of a moment, and then he subsided to the mattress and pulled Patience into his arms.

"Are ye warm enough?"

"I'm warm enough." At long last, she was warm enough. "Tomorrow, we'll talk about a wedding date, Dougal, and perhaps a wedding journey north in spring."

He kissed her temple. "I'd like that. I'd love that, in fact."

Patience couldn't keep her eyes open, so she wrapped her arms around her beloved and surrendered to dreams in which neither Mrs. Horner nor Professor What's His Name figured *at all*.

* * *

"Patience is missing baking day," Megan Windham said, pacing before the hearth, a newspaper rolled up in her hand. "We've had not even a note from her. She has shared baking day with us every year for the past dozen at least. We always finish with her lemon cake, so it's warm for her journey home."

"We have done holiday baking with Patience since before my come out," Elizabeth said from a stool beside the music room's great harp. "Which means the tradition goes back to antiquity. Perhaps yesterday's foul weather dissuaded her."

Elizabeth made more and more references to her age, and Megan had no idea what to do about it. Based on the look Charlotte and Anwen exchanged, they didn't either.

"Patience knows she could have bided with us overnight," Megan countered. "She's stayed here before when the weather turned disagreeable."

"The weather is glorious now," Charlotte observed from the window. "Blindingly so. Perfect weather for a snowball fight."

Sun on heaps of freshly fallen snow made the morning brilliant, and yet, Megan was worried. "Patience lives alone, or the next thing to it. What if she's fallen ill? She could have sent us a note."

"She has a housekeeper," Charlotte said, moving away from the window. "Patience enjoys great good health, most of the time."

She'd had a nasty lung fever the previous spring.

"We should take her some lemon cake," Anwen said,

knitting needles clicking away. "That's not hovering, not assuming the worst. We're being neighborly if we bring her some lemon cake."

Megan considered that suggestion, though as far back as she could recall, Patience had visited them—they did not venture into her neighborhood to visit her.

"Do we have her direction?" Somewhere in Bloomsbury, as best Megan could recall. Not far from Mr. MacHugh's offices.

"It's off Holborn, near the museum. I recall visiting her grandmother there, years ago."

A guilty silence greeted Elizabeth's admission, but Patience hadn't been eager to entertain callers. Whether she was self-conscious about a humble dwelling, or too pressed for coin to offer a proper tea tray, the message had come across clearly: *Receive me, don't visit me.*

"Patience has been working very hard at a time of year when most of us have less to do," Megan said, stashing the rolled up broadsheet into the coal bucket. "Mr. MacHugh ought to be ashamed of himself."

"I think Patience likes her work," Elizabeth murmured, fingers drifting across the harp strings. "I daresay she likes Mr. MacHugh too—admires his pragmatism, his grasp of mercantile matters. Those broadsheets are selling like hot rum buns."

Elizabeth was closest to Patience in age, and possibly in perspective. "You think Patience *likes* Mr. MacHugh?" Megan asked.

"Lemon cake," Charlotte said. "This definitely calls for a neighborly delivery of lemon cake."

Anwen's knitting needles slowed. "Bloomsbury is halfway across London, and the snow will make traffic difficult."

Could Patience be smitten with her Scottish publisher?

"It's not like her to miss a baking day," Megan observed. "We should bring her a loaf of stollen too, in case she might want to share with her friends at MacHugh and Sons."

All three of Megan's sisters smiled at once.

"That's very seasonal of you, Megan," Elizabeth said, rising. "We'll wait until after lunch, so the streets have a chance to clear, and then we'll pay a holiday call on our good friend."

"And maybe buy a few broadsheets on the way," Charlotte added. "See what argument Patience and the professor have got into now. Hard to imagine they have anything left to dispute, the way they've gone at each other this past week."

* * *

Patience remained in bed for long, lovely moments after Dougal had risen. He was off to the chophouse to fetch breakfast or possibly lunch, while Patience was trying to find the energy to move.

When, if ever, had she been this relaxed before? This well rested? This happy? The professor's last special edition would come out today, and she wished him nothing but success with his sales.

Dougal had made love with her again before he'd left the bed, and while he'd been careful, he'd also been playful.

"I am ticklish about the ribs," Patience announced to the room at large. "So is Mr. MacHugh."

One of the many revelations of the past two weeks.

Patience shoved the covers aside, pushed her feet into Dougal's slippers, and finished the cup of tea he'd brought her before he'd left. Dressing was an awkward under-taking, but Patience did the best she could with her hooks—she'd managed without help on many previous occasions—and made her way downstairs to the office. From the street below came the regular scraping of merchants clearing their walkways. Sunshine poured through every window.

"Good morning," Patience said to George, who occupied his usual spot on the mantel. "I am in love."

George squinted at her.

"Try to contain your jealousy, cat. You know all manner of details about my beloved that I do not—yet. You know what hour he comes down every morning, when he goes up to bed, how many meals he's eaten at his desk, and what his favorite poem is."

So much she and Dougal had yet to learn about each other, but how lovely to look forward to learning it.

The bell on the front door jingled, and Patience's heart leaped. She patted old George despite his lack of enthusiasm for the day—he was not in love, poor beast—and went into the clerk's room.

"Harry, good day."

"Morning to you, Miss Friendly," Harry said, stomping his boots. "Amazing how quickly the merchants will shovel out when there's custom to be had, isn't it?"

"Did you have far to come?" *And will you tell all the other clerks that you found me here alone?*

"Not far at all. I live down the street, share a room with Wilkens. Dougal offered to let me bide with him, but a man needs a bit of privacy sometimes—and to get away from this place."

That man being young Harry, apparently. "Mr. MacHugh should be back shortly. He went to the chophouse."

"And himself didn't even start the stove," Harry groused, hanging his cap, coat, and scarf on a hook. "My auntie would box Dougal's ears for leaving a lady to freeze, but Dougal is ever one to keep his mind on business. That's a great lot of snow out there, isn't it? Did you have any trouble making your way here?"

"It was slow going at first," Patience said, opening the stove and finding only a few coals still burning. "Will the others be in soon?"

She wanted to have the place to herself and Dougal, but she also wanted the professor to know that MacHugh and Sons wouldn't let a little thing like a snowstorm stop them from publishing their broadsheets.

"Poor old professor," she muttered, pushing the coals to the back of the stove with the poker. Whatever else might be true of Pennypacker, he hadn't had as lovely a night as Patience had. "Where are the spills, Harry? This fire will take a little help to get going."

"I put them in Detwiler's desk," Harry said from Dougal's office. "George gets up to mischief when he's left here by himself for too long."

Harry came to the doorway of the office, George cradled in his arms.

"That cat shredded some of my columns, Harry MacHugh, and I rewrote them so I'd have the last word with the professor. We all have to do things we'd rather not."

"Hear that, cat?" Harry said, scratching George under the chin. "You're on dangerous ground. Any more bad behavior, and old Dougal P. MacHugh, publisher, will banish you to the tavern next door."

The cat was no more impressed with that threat than he was with anything else. Patience left off hunting for the spills.

"Harry, what does the P in Mr. MacHugh's name stand for?"

"P is for Pennypacker," Harry said, moving off toward

the front door. "My auntie's people are Pennypackers. Have a farm south of Dunkeld. Shakespeare passed through there once upon a time, so they say. C'mon, George. The Bard got all his ideas for The Scottish Play while he was in the area, so my auntie claims."

Patience subsided into Mr. Detwiler's chair, struck by the coincidence of her nemesis having the same name as her prospective mother-in-law. The publishing community was close-knit—all of the publishers belonged to the same clubs, and they regularly met for meals, for example. One of Dougal's competitors could easily have learned of his mother's antecedents and chosen the name to plague him when devising a *nom de plume* for the professor.

"Such teasing is a bit juvenile," she muttered, opening the last of Detwiler's drawers. A neat stack of paper sat inside the drawer with a layer of spills peeking from beneath it. "Hidden from bored tomcats."

Patience put the papers on the desk and set about encouraging the fire in the parlor stove back to life. It took kindling, fresh coal, and a trip to Dougal's office to light the taper, but she managed.

Ten years ago, she would not have known how to light a decent fire, even with all the tools right at hand.

She tidied up the stack of papers she'd taken from Detwiler's drawer and saw Dougal's handwriting. He had beautiful penmanship, such as she would have expected from a former schoolteacher. No blotting, crossing out, inserting, or revising. She might have been looking at a final copy of one of her own...

The piece was signed: *Professor D. Pennypacker.*

Patience was still sitting at Detwiler's desk several minutes later when Dougal bustled through the door, bringing a gust of cold air with him and the scents of bacon, toast, and coffee.

"You're up and about. I'm almost sorry—no, I am sorry. Good of you to get the stove—Patience?"

She didn't want to look at him. Didn't want to see the truth in his eyes.

"I found these," she said, brandishing the pages. "The signature is Pennypacker's, but the name is your mother's, and the penmanship is yours. *Dougal, how could you?*"

He set his parcels on Detwiler's desk and hung up his coat and scarf, while Patience wrestled with the screaming need to pitch his infernal pages into the parlor stove.

"You're angry," he said when his coat was hung just so on a hook next to Harry's. "I can explain."

He wasn't starting with an apology, or with a denial, the two strategies that might have allowed Patience to hold on to her temper.

"You have lied to me, manipulated me, played me for a fool, and probably laughed at me all the way up those stairs, Dougal MacHugh. You are Professor Pennypacker, am I right?"

The doorbell jingled again, and Harry came in, stomping loudly.

"*Am I right, Dougal?* Did you lie to me?"

"I dissembled," Dougal said, "but if you'll listen, I can provide some perspective, and perhaps then you'll see—"

Patience marched up to him and struck him across the chest with his papers. "I'll *see* that I misheard you, I was mistaken, I misinterpreted, I misconstrued, though I have it from the most self-assured authority that my command of English is superb. You never once told me that you were Pennypacker, and this whole exercise has been a farce at the expense of my dignity."

Harry's gaze slewed from Patience to Dougal.

"Harry, get out," Dougal said. "This is a private discussion."

"Wait for me, Harry," Patience said, tossing Dougal's columns at him and retrieving her cloak and scarf from the next room. "I'm leaving, and I doubt I'll be back. I cannot abide a liar, Mr. MacHugh, much less a man who lies for his own self-interest."

She nearly ran out the door, leaving Dougal standing alone, his lovely penmanship scattered at his feet. Harry—bless the boy—snatched up the parcels of food and came after her. The streets were a mess, with only narrow paths shoveled clear, but few people were abroad to hamper her progress.

"Harry, you needn't accompany me. In my present mood, nobody will accost me and live to tell of his folly."

"If I don't accompany you, what do you think my chances of surviving Dougal's temper are, miss?"

"Dougal cannot blame you for a mess of his own creation. He lied, Harry. I know he's your cousin, but he was not honest with me. This whole exercise, day after day of writing and revising, his lectures about how competition would pique the readers' interest, all that blather about increasing the print runs—I doubt he increased them, he just wanted me to think...I feel like an idiot."

Patience felt like a naïve, gullible, gormless dupe, her future in tatters—again.

"You're not an idiot," Harry said, nearly losing his balance on a slippery spot. "But I'm seeing you home, and I thought we might fortify ourselves with a bite of warm toast along the way."

"Touch that toast, Harry MacHugh, and you'll return to Perthshire in a pine box."

He passed her one of the parcels. "Yes, miss."

Patience tolerated his escort as far as her own street, then took the second parcel from him and sent him on his way. Only when Harry had disappeared around the corner did she let herself begin to cry.

CHAPTER SEVEN

Patience's sitting room bore a faint odor of bacon, despite the day being more than half gone. Other than that, her surroundings were reassuringly genteel. Megan and her sisters had arranged themselves about their hostess—Charlotte and Elizabeth flanking her on the sofa, Megan and Anwen opposite on chairs a trifle underendowed with padding.

"We were concerned," Megan said, though, in fact, she was relieved. She'd pictured Patience living in a garret, cobwebs for curtains, mice her only company. The town house was in good repair, not a speck of dust to be seen. The rugs were worn, not tattered; the furniture comfortable, rather than elegant.

Patience was managing, in other words.

The lemon cake, alas, had met its fate.

"I'm sorry for causing you worry," Patience said. "I became absorbed in the writing, and the cat shredded my columns, and one doesn't…"

"A cat?" Charlotte prompted, peering about.

"King George. Dougal—Mr. MacHugh—brought him all the way from Scotland. Said George was his first employee. Mice like to nibble the glue in book bindings, though what good is a mouser who likes to nibble paper rather than mice? George also has a taste for cheese."

Anwen put the last slice of lemon cake on a plate and passed it to Patience. "You've been taking meals at the publisher's establishment?"

Patience set the plate down without taking a bite—*of her favorite lemon cake*?

"Mr. MacHugh was more than happy to keep me fed while I undertook my little scribblings. He escorted me home at the end of the day. He sent Jake out to the main thoroughfares rather than the nearest corner. He let the lads come up with holiday rhymes."

Even Elizabeth looked concerned at this recitation. "Holiday rhymes, Patience?"

"You know." She took a breath. "Deck the halls with tales of folly, fa-la-la-la-la, la-la-la-la. Mrs. Horner will make it all jolly, fa-la-la-la-la...How I despise that man."

Elizabeth slipped an arm around Patience's shoulders and sent her sisters a bewildered look.

Megan was afflicted with poor eyesight, but her hearing was quite good, and Patience did not sound like a woman overcome with loathing for her publisher. She sounded hurt and lost.

"Patience," Megan said, "what's wrong? We're your friends, and we want to help. I thought you respected Mr. MacHugh and despised that professor fellow."

"They are the same man!" Patience said, bolting to her feet. "Dougal MacHugh was writing the professor's columns, purposely creating a competition with me, regularly taking the opposite view of matters to stir up interest among the readers."

Charlotte took a surreptitious bite of the lemon cake. "Did it work?"

"Yes, it worked," Patience cried. "If I can believe Dougal, the print runs more than doubled, Mrs. Horner is the talk of the pubs, and Jake nearly sells out before he's reached the end of the street."

"But," Megan said, "your trust in Mr. MacHugh is shaken because he concocted this scheme without letting you in on it. Badly done of him."

"That's the worst part," Patience said, turning a pot of anemic violets in the window. "He didn't bring me into it, but he did bring himself into my affections."

Well, thank the angels and celestial ministers of grace.

"One suspected you esteemed your publisher," Elizabeth said, twiddling the fringe of a pillow that might once have been pink. "If you return his sentiments, where's the problem?"

Truly, spinsterhood had got Elizabeth in its foul clutches. "The *problem*," Megan said, "is that if he lied about the professor's columns, is he also lying about his regard for Patience? Patience has little cause to trust the constancy of the courting male."

Patience flopped to the sofa and shoved the remaining half slice of lemon cake closer to Charlotte's knee. "I don't think Dougal would play me false, but then, I thought I was engaged once before. Do you know what the worst, worst part is?"

"Tell us," Anwen said.

"I love to write. I love being Mrs. Horner. In her shoes, I feel as if all the vicissitudes I've endured, the reversals of fortune, even the dratted engagement to his lordship, have some use. Others can benefit from my experiences, and I want that. I don't have what I was raised to think is indispensable—a fellow to order me about, provide me children, and require my fealty in exchange for a place in his household."

Great heavens. "Is that what marriage is supposed to be?" Megan asked. Neither she nor any of her sisters had attracted the affections of a suitable *parti* in their early Seasons. Uncle Percy was a duke, though, and the Windham family well-fixed. Megan and her sisters could afford to be choosy, though perhaps Patience had a point.

"Marriage can be unsatisfying," Patience said. "My mother was helpless to interfere when Papa went out and bought a phaeton we didn't need. Were it not for my grandmama's thrift and generosity, my fate would have been sorry indeed."

In that light, a woman's fealty might not be to the man she married, so much as to the coin he provided. How un-lovely.

"Aren't you forgetting something?" Megan asked.

"I forgot my common sense," Patience said, sitting very straight. "Mr. MacHugh has ambitions for his establishment, and my columns figure in those ambitions prominently. I shouldn't blame him for making the most of the talent he had at his disposal."

"You'd never heard of Dougal MacHugh three years ago," Megan said. "How did you manage?"

"I wrote pamphlets on deportment, tutored young ladies in their French and pianoforte, walked Mrs. Hutching's pug on rainy days, and practiced economies."

"You didn't need Mr. MacHugh," Megan concluded. "You still don't. Mrs. Horner can write for one of Mac-Hugh's competitors, she can put out her own broadsheets, she can write a book, or do all three. You have managed,

Patience—you, not your settlements, your husband, a kindly uncle, or some dashing swain. You. You have a home, a profession, and a bright future thanks to your own hard work."

"She's right," Elizabeth said. "In some regards—I will deny it beyond this room—I envy you."

"You envy *me*?" Patience said. "I reuse my tea leaves. I forego a fire in my bedroom most nights. I tune my own pianoforte rather than pay somebody or allow a man into my home for the purpose."

"*Your* tea leaves," Charlotte said around the last mouthful of lemon cake. "*Your* bedroom, *your* pianoforte, *your* home. And you manage all of this with the coin you earn with your wits and wisdom. No wonder Mr. MacHugh is enthralled with you."

Now there was a lovely word: enthralled.

"He wasn't honest with me," Patience insisted. "And he proposed marriage to me."

"How dare he?" Anwen murmured—with a straight face.

Charlotte hit her with a pillow. "One shouldn't make light of a man offering marriage."

"Was the marriage proposal honest?" Megan asked, because that mattered.

"I'll never know, will I?" Patience replied. "Was he offering marriage to secure Mrs. Horner's ability to earn coin, or offering himself, in good times and bad? Dougal is very shrewd."

Heaven help the man if his suit rested on shrewdness. "We are at your disposal, Patience, if you need assistance in any regard." Megan rose, and her sisters did likewise. Anwen looked preoccupied, Charlotte disgruntled—Charlotte was frequently disgruntled—while Elizabeth's gaze as she peered around the cozy parlor was wistful.

"We'll visit again next week," Megan said. "Perhaps Mrs. Horner will have some advice for you by then that will resolve the situation with Mr. MacHugh."

"Perhaps," Patience allowed, seeing her guests to the front door. No butler, no porter, no footman—no *man*—mediated between Patience and those who called upon her.

What must that be like? The entire street of widows and spinsters likely operated the same way, and Megan guessed they looked out for each other. They gossiped too, but mostly, they looked out for each other.

Patience was handing around scarves and holding cloaks when a knock sounded on the door.

"I have no company for years, and now I'm Piccadilly Circus North," she said, opening the door.

A young woman stood on the stoop, a baby in her arms, a valise by her side. "I've come to call on Mrs. Horner. Is she home?"

"I'm home," Patience said. "Please do come in. My guests were about to depart."

"Patience?" Elizabeth murmured, but what harm could a woman and an infant do?

"Thank you very much for the call, my friends," Patience said, kissing four cheeks in turn. "You've given me much to think about, and I'll look forward to seeing you again next week."

A farewell, rather than a dismissal. Megan got Charlotte by the arm and steered her sister out to the street. The Windham coach waited at the corner, though none of Megan's sisters moved in its direction.

"I think we should pay a call on a certain publisher," Elizabeth said.

"See for ourselves," Charlotte added. "If he's a dunderhead, we'll know it."

"Even if he's not a dunderhead," Anwen said. "He's probably feeling like one."

"We're only three streets away," Megan said. "Come, ladies. I've never paid a call on a publisher before."

* * *

The lads had straggled in as the morning wore on. Even Detwiler had made it in before noon, but nothing about Dougal's day had gone right. He'd had to fetch George down from the top of the awning, Jake had slipped and cut his knee on a patch of ice, and the bakeshop had remained closed.

"For Mrs. Horner to take the day off was brilliant," Harry crowed, swinging into Dougal's office uninvited. "Every other broadsheet I had has already sold out, and folk are clamoring for her final column tomorrow. They're more interested in our advice than in Father Christmas's visit."

Harry had been a font of nervous cheer since assuring Dougal that Patience had arrived safely to her home and that she'd taken breakfast with her.

"I'm not angry with you, Harry," Dougal said. "I was dishonest, and that's ungentlemanly. Sooner or later, Patience would have learned my middle name." At the altar perhaps. What a drama would have ensued then.

Harry took the seat opposite Dougal's desk. "Why did you lie to her, Dougal?"

George hopped up on the desk and spread himself out on the blotter. The cat's expression was more critical than curious. *Yes, why lie to the woman you want to spend the rest of your life with?*

"I have no excuses. I made an expedient decision last summer in the best interests of the business—and its employees—and then didn't rectify the situation. I don't blame Patience—"

"Excuse me, Mr. MacHugh," Detwiler said from the doorway.

"Yes?"

"You've callers, sir. Ladies."

What else could go wrong on this blasted day? "Send them in, Detwiler. Harry, see if the bakeshop is open yet. We could use some crumpets."

Detwiler ushered in the single greatest concentration of female beauty the offices of MacHugh and Sons had ever seen. Four red-headed females assembled in Dougal's office, four fine young ladies. They weren't individually stunning, but each woman was attractive, and everything, from her bonnet ribbons to her gloves, to the trim on the collar of her velvet cloak, murmured of good taste and excellent breeding.

"Dougal P. MacHugh, ladies," he said, bowing and coming around his desk. "Won't you have a seat? I've sent the boy for sweets, and I'm always—"

"Don't bother attempting to charm us, *Professor Penny-packer*," said one of the ladies. She wore blue spectacles and the plainest cloak of the four. When she'd taken a seat, the others did likewise.

Dougal remained on his feet, for these lovely creatures were ladies. They weren't Patience, though, and Dougal wanted to pitch the lot of them into the snow and go find *his* lady. If he'd made Patience cry...

"May I ask who has the pleasure of reproaching me?"

The women exchanged a look, then George leaped into the lap of the one wearing the spectacles.

"What a delightful creature," she said as George's purr reverberated across the office. "We are just come from a call on Miss Patience Friendly, sir, and as her friends, we must express concern regarding your dealings with her. Because no one is on hand to see to the civilities, I will introduce myself. I'm Megan Windham, and these are my sisters, Elizabeth, Charlotté, and Anwen."

Dougal bowed to each in turn, while in the back of his mind an ominous bell tolled. A publisher knew London Society, though he rarely mingled among its titled members. Windham was the family name associated with the Moreland dukedom, and these people were Patience's friends.

Her very unhappy friends.

"Ladies, what may I do for you?"

"Do have a seat," said Miss Charlotte Windham. "We're intent on a thorough scold."

"I deserve a thorough scold."

"You do," Miss Elizabeth Windham said. "If not a birching and pillorying. Have you any idea the extent to which Patience's trust was abused by her former fiancé?"

Dougal could dissemble again, could puff up with male pride and mutter about not discussing Patience behind her back. Fat lot of good such a course had done him before.

"I am aware of that history, and believe that in my way, I may have exceeded even the viscount's perfidy."

The smallest sister, the one with the unusual name, peered at him. "Whatever will you do about it? For matters in their present posture will not serve, Mr. MacHugh."

The lady's family was immensely powerful, and her observation might quietly threaten the ruin of Dougal's business. More to the point, however, these women would be *disappointed* in him, and that, added to Patience's disappointment, was unbearable.

A panting, red-faced Harry appeared in the door, holding up a parcel as if it were a trophy.

"Would you ladies care for some crumpets?" Dougal asked, rising and taking the parcel from Harry.

"No, thank you," said Miss Megan Windham. "We have come here for answers, Mr. MacHugh. You have wronged our friend, and we will hold you accountable."

Dougal stashed the parcel in a drawer. "Ladies, you needn't hold me accountable. I hold myself accountable."

"Pretty words," Elizabeth Windham snapped. "What will you *do*, Mr. MacHugh?"

"I'm a publisher. I publish words."

George left Miss Megan's lap and took up residence two sisters down the row, on Miss Elizabeth's lap.

"They had better be the right words," Miss Megan said.

An idea came to Dougal as he surveyed these gorgeous, fierce women. They were what Patience should have become—secure in the knowledge of wealth and station. Before these women—before all of London—Dougal could assure Patience of his regard, and his remorse, and perhaps that would be enough.

"I'd thought I'd start with, 'I'm sorry,'" he said, "and repeat it thousands of times. Ten thousand times, at least." The printer would have a fit, but he'd find the means to fill the order.

Miss Megan flicked a cat hair from her sleeve. "That's rather a lot of apologizing. Quantity of sentiment alone is merely melodrama. What *qualities* will these words convey?"

* * *

Patience had sent the mother and baby on their way, the loaf of stollen with them. The woman had refused coin, saying she had enough, thanks to Patience.

Christmas Eve arrived after a sleepless night—not quite sleepless, because Patience had dreamed of Dougal returning to Scotland, George silently reproaching Patience all the way up the Great North Road.

Christmas Eve dawned, a bright, drippy, un-merry business, though Patience's housekeeper filled the kitchen with more chatter than a flock of newsboys discussing the next special edition.

"The coal man showed me his copy of the professor's column," Mrs. Dingleterry said. "I read it twice to be sure, then ran right out and bought us our copy. You must be very pleased, Miss Patience."

The professor's last column had come out yesterday.

Patience was not pleased. She wanted bacon, toast, and coffee, hot from the chophouse. She wanted to hear Wilkens and Harry arguing about what the words to a Robert Burns poem implied about young women who sang down by the burnie-o, and she wanted... she wanted badly to see Dougal.

Which was ridiculous. Dougal had wronged her. Period. The end. Stop the press.

Patience left off staring at the teapot. "What did you say about the professor's column?"

"There it is, right there," Mrs. Dingleterry said, setting a broadsheet down by Patience's elbow. "He wishes Mrs. Horner a fine holiday and thanks her for all of her wisdom. Poor man's in love, and all of London will be waiting on the reply from our Mrs. Horner, though her column today is just more of her usual good sense. I'd give anything if his letter were real, Miss Patience. Believe me, I would. I know how hard you work and how much your readers mean to you."

Patience pulled the paper closer, her teapot forgotten.

To my dear readers,

I wish you all a Happy Christmas, but confess that my own holiday cannot aspire to joy, or even to contentment. I have wronged somebody whom I esteem greatly, and thus my yuletide is beclouded by remorse.

Mrs. Horner's words are no stranger to this page, and yet, as you well know, I quote that good lady only to take issue with her advice. Her place in your regard was firmly established, and then, several months past, I decided to insinuate myself into the conversation you and she enjoyed. I advised, I commented, and were that the limit of my presumption, I might wait upon Mrs. Horner's generous forgiveness for my poor manners.

I undertook to criticize, though, and to argue with a lady, and not because I genuinely disagree with her sound wisdom. In many cases, I was guilty of playing devil's advocate, because I knew discord would earn your notice, and I coveted that notice and the coin it would earn me.

I envied Mrs. Horner your loyalty and saw a way to turn her diligent efforts to my advantage. I am ashamed of the course I set and can take only the smallest comfort in the knowledge that Mrs. Horner's wise words may have seen greater circulation as a result of my ploy.

Renown and its attendant benefits, however, can never replace trust or respect, and I respect Mrs. Horner so very much. I humbly apologize to her for my conduct and hope she will receive my words in the wise and compassionate spirit for which we all esteem her so greatly.

Mrs. Horner, if you look with any favor at all upon the author of these words, please accept my thanks for all of your efforts and my sincere wishes that you should prosper in the New Year in all that you undertake. With humblest apologies, I remain faithfully,

Your most sincere admirer,
Prof. D. Pennypacker

"That wretch!" Patience shot to her feet. "That fiend. He'll sell twenty thousand copies of this. Callow swains will study it as a perfect apology, and the readers will deluge him with letters. Where is my cloak?"

"In the front hall, miss. The same as always. Are you well?"

"I am…I am…I am about to provide the professor a holiday greeting he will never forget."

"But you haven't had anything to eat!"

"I'll get something at the chophouse. Why don't we ever decorate for the holidays, Mrs. Dingleterry?"

"Because you say it's a silly, sentimental expense?"

"And you listen to me?"

"The professor says you're wise and kind and all that other. Shall I buy some greenery, miss?"

Patience fished in a pocket and produced some coins. "Yes, and invite all the other ladies over to help you decorate. You might bake some lemon cake too, because the scent is divine."

And if Patience could not find a way to make peace with Dougal, she'd need at least a consolatory slice or two— or three—of lemon cake. And hearty servings of stollen, crumpets, and tarts too.

CHAPTER EIGHT

"We've sold out?" Dougal asked.

"The professor and Mrs. Horner have both sold out," Detwiler said, settling into the chair across from Dougal's desk. "The printer is doing an extra run as we speak, and the name of Dougal P. MacHugh is on the lips of every publisher in London. They're all saying you're brilliant, and next Christmas, they will conduct an epistolary courtship by broadsheet."

"Let them," Dougal said, taking off his glasses. "This time next year, I might well be teaching school again in Upper Achtermachtaltiebuie."

"Is there an Upper Achtermachtaltiebuie?"

"Go home, Detwiler. I'll see you Monday, no earlier than noon."

Detwiler pushed to his feet. "I'm sorry, lad. You tried your best. Hell hath no fury like a spinster—"

Dougal rose and leaned over the desk. "Patience Friendly is *not* a spinster."

Detwiler braced his hands on the desk. "Spinster, the proper legal definition for a woman as yet unmarried. *Old maid.* A woman past the usual marriageable age, rarely applied to men in the same situation but sometimes used to designate the occupation of one who spins."

Dougal leaned nearer. "Patience Friendly is a *writer*, a *brilliant* literary talent with a *genius* for the publishing business. She is an *excellent* editor and a woman of *unshakable* integrity, whom I am *proud* to have associated with this establishment. She is also *my fiancée* until she tells me otherwise."

"You needn't shout," said a familiar female voice. "Though your sentiments do you credit."

Patience stood in the doorway, but not a version of Patience whom Dougal had seen before. Even holding George in her arms, this woman outshone the Windham sisters for self-possession, and though her ensemble was several years out of date, the quality and style were unmistakable.

"Detwiler," Dougal said. "*Happy Christmas.*"

"Oh, right. Happy Christmas to all." Detwiler took his time shuffling out the door, and when he paused to pet the cat, Dougal nearly howled.

Patience kissed the old buzzard's cheek, sashayed into the office, and deposited George on the mantel.

"Mr. MacHugh, we have business to discuss."

Dougal did not want to discuss business, but if Patience had asked him to recite *Tam O'Shanter* backward, he would have given it a go. He was so damned relieved to see her on her mettle, ready to give as good as she got, while he was damned if he had the first inkling—

Inspiration struck. "I have crumpets."

She wrinkled her nose. "Speaking as a brilliant literary talent, I'm not interested in your *crumpets*, sir. Shall we be seated?"

Dougal came around the desk and gestured to the table, then held Patience's chair for her. He'd missed the scent of her, the rustle of her skirts, the energy she brought to the office—and that was before she'd metamorphosed from Mrs. Horner into this, this force of nature.

"You smell like lemons and spices," he said, taking his own seat.

"This is a business discussion, Mr. MacHugh. Has the professor sold out?"

"Aye. In record time. Mrs. Horner right behind him."

"Mrs. Horner has a reply for him." She passed over a sheet of foolscap. "She'll beat his record."

My dear Professor Pennypacker,

While I appreciate the gracious sentiments contained in your epistle, I must take issue with two of your assumptions, for they will otherwise trouble my holiday exceedingly.

Firstly, you assume that I cannot appreciate a point of view differing from my own, which foolishness I attribute to an excess of delicate gentlemanly sensibilities. A woman who holds the public's trust takes upon herself a great responsibility. Knowing that you will step forth with well-considered criticism from time to time eases the burden of that responsibility for me.

Nobody is right all the time. Nobody goes through life without an occasional error. What a dull world we'd have if we permitted each other no room for foibles, thoughtful discourse, or respectful dissension.

Secondly, you assume that our readers cannot enjoy offerings from more than one writer, as if their appetite for succinct wisdom was limited, rather than expanded, by our mutual efforts. The good citizens who enjoy my column should be encouraged to find others they like as well. When do we ever have too much wisdom, too many insights?

So I must thank you, Professor, for your contribution to an enjoyable and enlightening exchange. My holiday wish is that we shall have many more differences of opinion and that you shall offer the benefit of your thinking whether it agrees with my own or respectfully conflicts with it.

My wish for the readers is that they will take comfort and pleasure in the knowledge that not one, but two, articulate and compassionate authors are available to address their difficulties and concerns.

I look forward to the day when our swords figuratively cross again, Professor. Until that day, I remain, with all best wishes, your good friend,

Mrs. Horner

Dougal read the letter twice, finding not a single comma he could bear to move. "Mrs. Horner and the professor are *good friends* now?"

Patience tugged off her gloves and took the sheet back. "Very is such a weak word, but good friends struck the balance between dignified and warm, don't you think?"

Dougal took the letter back and set it carefully aside. "Patience, I want to be much more than your good friend. I am exceedingly sorry I lied to you. It won't happen again."

"You were being my publisher," she said. "You fed me

crumpets to inspire my productivity, and you fed me a challenge when my readership was ready for one. Had I known the professor was a creature of your imagination, my responses might not have been so vigorous."

Well, yes, and yet, a lie was a lie. "Are you making excuses for me?"

She rose and went to the window, and even her posture struck Dougal as more regal. "I understand what you did, Dougal. I might wish you'd brought me in on the scheme, but I suspect you initially lacked confidence in it. The professor was an experiment, a lark, a private risk. I tried selling my watercolors once upon a time—I signed them Placido Amadeus. When few people bought them, the failure belonged to a fictitious Italian man, not Patience Friendly."

"Exactly," Dougal said, getting to his feet. "What if the professor's words garnered ridicule? What if you demolished him in a single column? What if he took a position that revealed his ignorance of all matters parental and domestic? Where would his publisher be?"

Patience turned to face him. "I wrote to the professor."

"I beg your—" Her words weren't difficult to decipher, and yet, Dougal's mind stumbled over them. "*You* wrote to Pennypacker?"

"I wrote to you," she said, striding away from the window. "If I wasn't confident of my response to a reader, if I wanted to test my judgment, or offer the reader a choice of approaches, then I'd put a comparable situation before the professor."

"The philandering brother-in-law was you? I thought the readers were pitting us against each other."

"I changed my handwriting, my tone, my everything, lest my letter sound too much like Mrs. Horner to a man who'd read every word she'd written. I meant what I wrote in my letter, you see. To bear sole responsibility for guiding a reader through a difficulty is a heavy burden. The professor was the only person I could turn to, and he never failed to share the load."

"You wrote to the professor..." Dougal caught her hand as she marched past him. "You fanned the flames of controversy *on purpose*. You considered Pennypacker your colleague. You, you—"

"I mispresented myself. I lied. I'm sorry, Dougal. I'm—"

He caught her up in his arms. "You're a genius! You're brilliant. You're the most clever, insightful, delightful—" Dougal kissed Patience on the mouth, and a few other places, and then set her back on her feet, but kept his arms around her. "You beat me at my own game, Patience."

She sighed, then slipped free. "No, Dougal. I've thought about this. Mrs. Harmon Dandy came to see me."

"Who? Oh, her." The gin widow. "She didn't learn your direction from me."

"She followed me home earlier this week. She wanted to leave a note for me here at the office, but then saw Harry walking me home and suspected that I am Mrs. Horner. You did a fine thing for her, Dougal, but you might have told me."

Dougal had the nagging sense that his brilliant, ingenious, though not always entirely honest, author was maneuvering toward a conclusion.

"I sent her to my cousins in Perthshire, Patience. They have a large household and won't mind making accommodations for a new mother who's an accomplished seamstress." Thank goodness for wealthy relations who weren't above the occasional charitable act.

"You probably saved that baby's life, if not the mother's too. I'm endlessly grateful, but we must learn to trust each other, Dougal. We must be partners pulling in the same direction. We each have strengths and abilities, but we're stronger together. You can't write as Mrs. Horner does, and I can't browbeat the printer into doing a special run on Christmas Eve."

"He refused you?"

Patience nodded. "He said the professor had used up the entire crew's store of holiday generosity and for no amount of money would they stay late on Christmas Eve. You would have talked him 'round, wheedled, negotiated. You're a fine publisher, Dougal, and I'm a literary genius, but we cannot succeed without being in each other's confidence."

"I will make a fine husband as well, Patience, if this trust you speak of can go both ways. I think Harry should read law, but he'll never listen to that suggestion from me. He might if you brought it up."

Her brows knit, her expression suggesting Mrs. Horner was on the job, figuring the best way to pass along advice so it might be heeded.

Dougal ran his finger down the center of her forehead. Mrs. Horner hadn't solved the greater problem Dougal had created, but Patience had. He would always love her for that, for giving a promising piece of work one more polishing, for making it the best it could be, despite all the effort involved.

Patience trapped his finger in her own. "Did you mention crumpets earlier, Dougal?"

What did crumpets have to do with—? "Fresh from the bakeshop. Shall we share them, Patience?"

"The lads have all gone home?"

"And Detwiler. I heard him lock up on the way out." Thus earning a Christmas bonus.

"Are we to be partners, sir? MacHugh and MacHugh?"

Oh, that sounded lovely. Dougal stuck out his hand.

"Partners, MacHugh and MacHugh. Might I suggest we take the crumpets upstairs to further discuss our plans for the new year?"

Patience took Dougal's hand in both of hers. "We might have to add another MacHugh to the name of the business, Dougal. Would that fit with your plans?"

Dougal snatched the parcel of crumpets from the drawer and tossed them to her. "We can add as many junior MacHughs to the name of the business as you like, Patience, but how about we enjoy our crumpets first?"

"Upstairs," she said. "At a meeting of the senior editorial board. I quite like that idea."

Dougal liked it too, enough to carry his senior editorial director up the stairs and forget all about the crumpets until at least an hour later. The meeting continued, intermittently, well into Boxing Day. They took a break to admire Mrs. Horner's response to the professor when it sold out in minutes early that afternoon. By then, the bakeshop had run out of crumpets.

And stollen.

And tarts.

The senior editorial board never ran out of agenda items, though, and both members thereof had a very, very fine Christmas—every year.

ABOUT THE AUTHOR

Grace Burrowes grew up in central Pennsylvania and is the sixth out of seven children. She discovered romance novels in junior high (back when there was such a thing) and has been reading them voraciously ever since. Grace has a bachelor's degree in political science, a bachelor of music in music history (both from the Pennsylvania State University), a master's degree in conflict transformation from Eastern Mennonite University, and a juris doctor from the National Law Center at George Washington University.

Grace is a *New York Times* and *USA Today* bestselling author who writes Georgian, Regency, Scottish Victorian, and contemporary romances in both novella and novel lengths. She's a member of Romance Writers of America and Novelist, Inc., and enjoys giving workshops and speaking at writers' conferences.

You can learn more at:
GraceBurrowes.com
Twitter @GraceBurrowes
Facebook.com/Grace.Burrowes

Looking for more historical romance? Forever brings the heat with these sexy rogues.

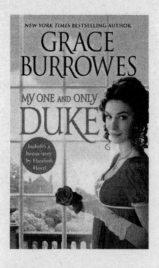

MY ONE AND ONLY DUKE
By Grace Burrowes

When London banker Quinn Wentworth is saved from execution by the news he's the long-lost heir to a dukedom, there's just one problem: He's promised to marry Jane Winston, the widowed, pregnant daughter of a prison preacher.

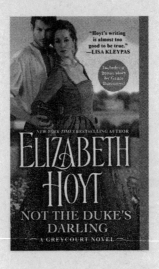

NOT THE DUKE'S DARLING
By Elizabeth Hoyt

When the Duke of Harlowe, the man who destroyed her brother, appears at the country house party Freya de Moray is attending, she does what any devoted sister would do: She starts planning her revenge.

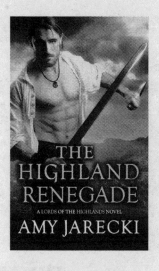

THE HIGHLAND RENEGADE
By Amy Jarecki

Famed for his fierceness, Laird Robert Grant is above all a loyal Highland clan chief. But when redcoats capture his rival's daughter, he sets aside their feud and races to her rescue. Aye, Janet Cameron is beautiful, cunning, and so very tempting, but a Cameron lass is the last woman he should ever desire.

Follow @ForeverRomance and join the conversation using #ReadForever.

HIGHLANDER EVER AFTER
By Paula Quinn

As the clan chief's son, Adam MacGregor is duty-bound to marry a royal heir. Yet when he meets his bride—a beautiful but haughty lass who thinks he's nothing more than a common savage—he realizes she's more than he bargained for.

LAST NIGHT WITH THE EARL
By Kelly Bowen

War hero Eli Dawes was presumed dead—and would have happily stayed that way. All he wants is to hide away in his country home, but when he tries to sneak into his old bedroom in the middle of the night, he's shocked to find the beautiful Rose Hayward already there.

Visit
Facebook.com/ForeverRomance

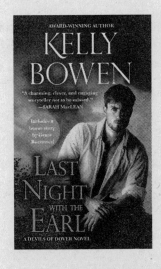